SONG
OF THE
Storyteller

A FIVE DIRECTIONS PRESS BOOK

SONG
OF THE
Storyteller

A NOVEL

C. P. LESLEY

SONGS OF STEPPE & FOREST 5

ISBN-13: 978-1947044333

Published in the United States of America.

A Five Directions Press book

Cover images: Konstantin Makovsky, *The Boyarinya* (1885); Konstantin Makovsky, *The Tsar Chooses a Bride* (1886), both public domain via Wikimedia Commons

Book and cover design by Five Directions Press

Five Directions Press logo designed by Colleen Kelley

FIVE DIRECTIONS PRESS

Soon as the evening shades prevail,
The moon takes up the wondrous tale,
And nightly to the listening earth
Repeats the story of her birth.

—John Addison

Cast of Characters

(in alphabetical order by first name)

Unless noted otherwise, all characters listed below are my invention. Even historical figures should be considered fictional, since in most cases little information about them has survived. I have also changed the first names of certain historical characters to avoid confusion with their fictional counterparts. In these cases, their actual names are noted in the entries.

Alexei Bulatovich: High-ranking Tatar, descended from Genghis Khan, in service to the Russian grand prince; Maria's husband and the father of Timur, Alexander, and Dosya. As the son of a khan, he bears the title *tsarevich.*

Princess Anastasia Petrovna Shuiskaya: Historical figure; first cousin of Tsar Ivan IV; widow of Prince Vasily Vasilyevich Shuisky.

Anfim Fadeyev: State secretary of the Treasury, specialist in foreign affairs; Solomonida's second husband; father of Lara, Tolya, and Seryozha; Anna's stepfather.

Princess Anna Glinskaya: The real-life mother of Elena Glinskaya and therefore Ivan the Terrible's maternal grandmother (d. ca. 1553). It is assumed that she and other female members of the royal family played an important role in Ivan's first bride show.

Anna Semyonovna Kolycheva: Solomonida's daughter by her first marriage; Lyuba's best friend.

Avdotya Gundorova: Bridal candidate from Vyazma, based on an actual candidate in Ivan the Terrible's first bride show.

Princess Bronislava Blednaya: Mother and sponsor of Fetinya Blednaya; affiliate of the Shuisky clan.

Bulat Khan: Father of Alexei, Ogodai, and Nasan; Timur's grandfather.

Daniil Nikolaevich Kolychev: Alexei's brother-in-law; Nasan's husband; Timur's uncle; Anna's cousin.

Darya Petrovna Sheremeteva: Solomonida's sister; Anna's aunt; Nikita's wife.

Dina Ignatyeva: Bridal candidate from Kolomna; older sister of Melita.

Dunya Morozova: Bridal candidate from Moscow; Katya's niece by her first marriage; Grunya's cousin.

Ekaterina Ivanovna Vorontsova: Known as Katya; Igor's wife; aunt to Grunya and Dunya by virtue of her first marriage.

Grand Princess Elena Glinskaya: Historical figure; mother of Ivan IV the Terrible. Elena died unexpectedly in April 1538.

Elizaveta Vadimovna Vorontsova: Known as Liza; Katya's and Yuri's aunt; sponsor of Grunya and Dunya.

Lord Felix Ossolinski: Diplomat and magnate in service to King Sigismund the Old of Poland-Lithuania; Juliana's husband; adoptive father of Klara.

Princess Fetinya Blednaya: Bridal candidate from an affiliate Shuisky clan; Bronislava's daughter.

Fevronia Ignatyeva: Aunt and sponsor of Dina and Melita.

Firuza Khatun: Alexei's sister-in-law; Ogodai's wife and co-ruler of his horde; Timur's aunt.

Prince Fyodor Ivanovich Ovchinin: Historical figure; son of *Prince Ivan Fyodorovich Telepnev,* a descendant of the Cheliadnin line. Father and son have different surnames because family names varied with each generation in sixteenth-century Russia.

Fyodor Mikhailovich Koshkin: Maria's and Lyuba's father, a high-ranking but incurably ambitious Russian nobleman; divorced husband of Juliana. He has five other adult children—Mikhail, Varvara, Foma, Timofei, and David.

Gavriil Timofeevich Vorontsov: Yuri's father; Katya's uncle; a powerful figure in the Russian court.

Grunya Morozova: Bridal candidate from Moscow; Katya's niece by her first marriage; Dunya's cousin.

Grusha: Shaman of the horde where Timur spent the years between twelve and fourteen.

Guzel: Timur's mother via a premarital relationship with Alexei.

Igor Grigorevich Bezzubtsev: Cousin of Darya, Solomonida, and Anna; Katya's husband.

Ivan IV (1530–1584): Russia's first tsar; succeeded his father, Grand Prince Vasily III of Moscow, in November 1533; a historical figure better known by his sobriquet, "Ivan the Terrible." During his reign, he married seven times and is believed to have held bride shows before every selection. The event covered here was his first.

Ivan Ivanovich Poroshin: Historical figure; descendant of the Cheliadnin line through his mother, who was Telepnev's sister; cousin of Fyodor Ovchinin.

Lady Juliana Ossolinska: Divorced wife of Fyodor Koshkin; former mistress of Alexei, now married to Lord Felix Ossolinski; adoptive mother of Klara.

Lara Anfimova: Anfim's daughter; Anna's stepsister. Lara is short for Larisa.

Lyubov Fyodorovna Koshkina: Known as Lyuba; Maria's sister; Fyodor Koshkin's youngest child; heroine of *Song of the Storyteller*.

Maria Fyodorovna Koshkina: Wife of Alexei Bulatovich; eldest daughter of Fyodor Koshkin; friend of Solomonida and Darya; sponsor of her sister Lyuba and Anna; Timur's stepmother. Her marriage to Alexei gives her the title of *tsarevna* (khan's daughter). They have two children, Alexander and Dosya.

Melita Ignatyeva: Bridal candidate from Kolomna; youngest sister of Dina.

Princess Nadezhda Shuiskaya: Widow of Ilya Shuisky; mother of his two sons, the elder of whom is Pavel; sponsor of Princess Ustinya Paletskaya.

Nasan Khanim: Alexei's sister; Daniil's wife; Timur's aunt.

Nikita Andreevich Monastyrev: Alexei's adjutant; Darya's husband; Anna's uncle.

Ogodai Khan: Alexei's and Nasan's brother; Firuza's husband; uncle who fostered Timur for two years.

Ografena Gerasimova: Mother and sponsor of Zoya.

Orina Gundorova: Stepmother and sponsor of Avdotya.

Prince Pavel Ilich Shuisky: Scion of Russia's most powerful clan; Nadezhda's elder son; potential suitor for Anna's hand in marriage.

Shah-Ali Khan (1505–1567): Historical figure appointed at various times as khan of Kazan and of Kasimov, but in this and my preceding series fictional half-brother of Bulat and, by extension, uncle of Alexei, Nasan, and Ogodai and great-uncle of Timur.

Semyon Pavlovich Kolychev: Solomonida's deceased first husband; Anna's father.

Serafima Khabarova: Bridal candidate from a boyar affiliate of the Belsky princes.

Solomonida Petrovna Sheremeteva: Widow of Semyon Kolychev; Darya's older sister; Anfim's wife; mother of Anna and Seryozha; Lara's and Tolya's stepmother.

Princess Sophia Belskaya: Sponsor of Serafima Khabarova.

Sumbeka Khatun: Bulat Khan's chief wife; Alexei's stepmother; mother of Ogodai and Nasan; Timur's grandmother.

Tasya Yureva: Bridal candidate based on the historical figure Anastasia Romanovna Yureva.

Theodosia Koshkina: Lyuba's aunt.

Timur Alexeevich Bulatov: Alexei's eldest son by a premarital relationship with Guzel; hero of *Song of the Storyteller*.

Tolya Anfimov: Anfim's son; Anna's stepbrother. Tolya is short for Anatoly.

Princess Ustinya Paletskaya: Bridal candidate based on the historical figure Uliana Paletskaya, who may have participated in the event described here.

Vera Yureva: Mother of Tasya Yureva; based on Uliana, the widow of Roman Yurevich Zakharin, whose great-grandson Mikhail became the first Romanov tsar in 1613.

Yuri Gavriilovich Vorontsov: Son of Gavriil; Anna's contracted husband, in exile at the Ferapontovo Monastery during this novel.

Zoya Gerasimova: Bridal candidate from Uglich.

Prologue

For the heritage we cherish as our past lays the stepping stones for our future. With a certain reluctance, I set my quill in the inkwell and regard these, the final words of my family saga. After years spent among heroes conquering great obstacles and setting off on long and winding journeys toward love and understanding, I hate to see the tales reach their close. I will miss the constant companionship of relatives near and distant, some alive only in my thoughts.

With my great work finished, how will I fill my days? Should I listen to those who urge me to focus on my grandchildren? The antics of the rich and powerful should not concern a woman, such self-appointed advisers tell me. Leave history to the monks. But the monks do not record the things that to me make life meaningful: ambitions and desires, alliances and enmities, the interplay of personalities. And the Russian lands again find themselves in a perilous state—defeated by the western powers, their lands and population ravaged by the Terrible Tsar, who leaves only a royal simpleton to inherit his throne. Perhaps the lessons of the past still serve a purpose in the present.

I stare at the pile of paper, the quill sticking out of the inkwell. Despite having reached the advanced age of fifty-one, I have strength and energy to spare. I'm not ready to wrap myself in quilts and settle by the fireside. I might as well declare myself a living corpse, a relic of times gone by.

Yet the histories recorded in my saga shimmer like the image of a distant shore, sweeping me back to the days of young womanhood, before I knew the form my life would take.

And just like that, the solution to my dilemma presents itself. There *is* a story I have not told, one that means more to me than even the deeds of my family: the tale of Tsar Ivan's first bride show and my part in it.

The winds of memory send a shiver down my spine, defying the summer heat of this palace so close to the Caspian Sea. Can I bear to revisit that part of my past, threatened by vicious rivalries that at times obscured all hope that love and virtue might prevail? Am I prepared to reveal that younger self—even to those close to me, never mind the generations yet to come?

Yet the writer in me is drawn to the conflict and the tension, the ancient battle between the princess and the dragon. And the bride show, shrouded in secrecy, provokes endless speculation. My children and grandchildren will enjoy finding out how it worked.

Best of all, it would mean that my saga is *not* done, as I feared. I still have tales left to share.

Reassured, I lift the quill from its well, check the point, and rejoice at finding it still sharp. Because I am a storyteller, and I cannot resist the magic of the written word.

Chapter 1

Moscow, December 1546

"The prince arrived, as princes do, when least expected"

I have always loved stories. Since the day dear Father Job
introduced me to the art of making meaningful marks on a
piece of paper, the power of those scribbled words has enthralled
me. In childhood, I decided to record the adventures of my family,
renowned in both Russia and the lands beyond, but I never
believed *I* might have a story worth telling. Who could imagine
Lyuba, lover of books, as a contender for the hand of Russia's first
tsar? My father yearned to see me in that position, it was true, but
I had long dismissed his plans as foolish ambition. At best, I would
be one among a horde of girls, most of them more eager than I to
join our sovereign in the Dance of Isaiah, the central moment of
an Orthodox Christian wedding.

In fact, on that long-ago morning—the fourteenth of December, a Tuesday—my immediate goal was to resist the demands of
my older sister, Maria, that I help Tanya, our housekeeper, supervise the maids as they tackled the weekly wash. We were ensconced in the room where Maria loved to sew (and tormented me
with exercises in needlework that led only to tangled threads,
malformed stitches, and bouts of bad temper), and we sat on one
of the heated, padded benches that edged each of the four tiled

walls. Brilliant light flooded the room from above, colored insets in the glass casting jewel-like shadows on the richly patterned carpets that lined the floor. Nevertheless, so close to the shortest day chilly drafts slipped like bandits past the edges of the panes. I appreciated the warmth beneath me.

I gazed at my sister, wondering how best to deflect her. Despite her obsession with household chores, I loved Maria as I loved few other people. Fourteen years my senior, she had overseen my upbringing since I was six. But try as I might, I couldn't convince her to share my fascination with books. For her, an embroidery needle marked civilization's highest achievement. And in her hands it did.

"But Lyuba," she protested. "You must learn to order your household. You turned sixteen in September, and whether or not Papa succeeds in having you summoned to the grand prince's bride show, he will certainly arrange a match for you within the year."

I bit my tongue. Both possibilities made me want to grab my falcon and my pony and flee for the steppe. I hated the idea of marriage to Grand Prince Ivan—who, despite any allure generated by his power and wealth, was at heart suspicious, dictatorial, and given to fits of uncontrolled rage. An alliance with a stranger selected by Papa to advance his own interests at court could not be much better. As for the bride show, I had at best a fuzzy idea what that might be like, since the last one had taken place four years before my birth. The only thing I knew for sure was that no one would ask whether I wanted to attend—or listen if I told them I didn't.

Although it would make a great story: maidens dressed in elaborate silks and velvets bowing to the ruler, then strolling past him as he decided which one he would pick. I envisioned haughty boyars huddled in corners speculating while their wives prodded each girl forward, pulling her away as she reached the far side of the hall without receiving the wedding ring and kerchief that signaled Ivan's acceptance. In my version of the tale, there would be backbiting and subtle shoving, nasty tricks to undermine potential brides. And suppose the bridegroom turned out to be like the wicked sultan Scheherazade lulled with her yarns? How dreadful to survive a bride show only to find oneself married to a monster!

"Well? Are you going to do as I ask?" My sister's tart voice hauled me back from my daydream.

I tucked a stray strand into my braid, as if only concern for my own untidiness could have delayed my response. "I know how the washing should be done. But I promised Tolya another story if he studied well for Father Job, and I have yet to start on it."

This excuse had the virtue of truth. Tolya—the seven-year-old stepbrother of my best friend, Anna—fancied himself an epic knight, and I *had* promised him a book of fairy tales if he applied himself to his lessons. Complete one more, and I could hand the current set over and start anew.

At first, I thought my ploy wouldn't work. Maria knew I enjoyed writing far more than watching maids dunk dirty linen into soapy water. She narrowed her brown eyes—so different from my gray-green, a shade or two darker than a cat's, although our hair was the same rich auburn—and I braced myself for a refusal. After a brief pause, though, she surprised me with a curt nod. "Go, then," she said.

Eager to put sloshy thoughts of laundry behind me, I wasted no time in leaving the women's sitting room for the study belonging to my brother-in-law Alexei. As I walked down the stairs, I reveled in the prospect of several hours to wander in the land of story, undistracted by friends or family. Alexei seldom bothered me while I wrote, but in any case I'd heard him storming around the house an hour ago, grumbling about some urgent meeting at the Kremlin. As a rule, Alexei liked to put as much distance as possible between himself and the court's messy and cut-throat politics, but even he had to respond to a direct summons. So he'd mounted his horse and ridden off, with his aide—Nikita Andree-vich, Anna's uncle—in attendance a short time ago. Since Niki, a gifted artist, was the only other person allowed to work in Alexei's sanctum, I felt certain I'd have it to myself.

Running my fingers down the banister as I descended from the women's quarters on the third floor to the study on the second, I put myself in writing mood by imagining what I would do first when I reached my destination. I could spend time trimming my quill and cherishing the roughness of fresh paper, the oddly com-pelling acridity of new-mixed ink. I might stroll the room, inhal-ing the aromas of leather and parchment, imagining how my tale of knight and dragon should unfold. Or should I sit down and start writing with no preparation? Sometimes my best ideas came to me without warning, as if sparked into life by my pen.

In the end, though, none of that happened. When I walked through the door, I stopped short, feet riveted to the floor, and stared. A tall, dark-haired stranger wearing a robe of rich crimson velvet stood near the window, paging his way through a stack that I recognized as my unfinished book of tales.

I reacted on instinct. "Stop! Who are you, and how dare you rifle through my papers?"

He swung toward me, and I felt my jaw drop. He was *very* good-looking, as handsome as Alexei—and that was saying some-thing, because at almost forty Alexei still turned female heads whenever he entered a room. But this man was twenty, at most, and he took my breath away. He had a lithe, muscular body, eyes as black as his hair, a trim mustache, and no more than a shadow of beard on his chin. He exuded the air of someone born to com-mand. I gazed at him open-mouthed as an absurd thought flashed through my head.

Why can't Papa find me a husband like this? I would like that so much better than wedding the grand prince!

At that moment, I recognized him. Timur Alexeevich Bulatov, Alexei's son but not Maria's. He had inherited that handsome face from his father.

He looked me up and down. "Goose, is that you?" He sounded as though he couldn't believe his own words.

I reacted from instinct. "Don't call me Goose!"

He burst out laughing. "And Goose it must be, because that's what you always say. I can't believe you didn't know who I was. And here I thought of us as inseparable."

"So did I." I laughed with him, remembering. "Goose" was his pet name for me when we were young. He came to live with us when he was nine, the week his father married my sister. I was three years younger, but we soon became the closest of friends. I'd adored him and squabbled with him, and when he returned to the steppe to train for his future role as khan, I'd mourned him for months as if he were dead, but after so long apart, the lost period of shared daily lessons and games glimmered like the memory of a distant land.

I held out a hand in welcome. "It's good to see you, Timur. It's been ages since we visited you in Kasimov."

Watching him set my unfinished stack of papers aside and cross the room, I experienced a strange urge to throw myself into his arms. He pulled me into a hug as soon as he got close enough, kissing my cheeks—right, then left, then right again. The brush of his lips brought an unexpected heat to my face. "I confess, I didn't recognize you right away either. For a moment, I thought you must be a distant relation of Maria's. What a beauty you've become." He jerked his head toward the pile of papers on the table. "And an accomplished one, if you're responsible for that book. Although that shouldn't surprise me. You always did love to write."

7

Accomplished? You like my stories?

My heart glowed with pride. "Timur," I said again, returning the kisses and the hug. "You stayed away far too long. Does your father know you're here?"

"I don't think so. I hoped to catch *Ata*"—although he answered in Russian, he used the Tatar word for "father," and the sound of it, once so much a part of everyday life and now so seldom heard, threw me back in time—"before he left the house, but Tanya says I missed him. I hope I don't give him a heart attack when he walks in and finds me."

"What brings you here?" Gently I freed myself, ignoring the inner voice that urged me to stay right where I was. I'd never recover my sanity if I continued to cling to him. "Last I heard, you were in Kasimov with your great-uncle Shah-Ali Khan."

"Yes, I'm stationed there." Like me, he took a step back. Could that be reluctance I saw on his face? If so, he conquered the emotion in a flash.

"There's a council session at the Kremlin," he explained. "Must be something big, because we received a message for Shah-Ali to present himself promptly and no excuses, thank you. I came along as Uncle's adjutant, but I'm not invited to the meeting itself, so I rode straight here. I sat down to write *Ata* a note, then realized he wouldn't get it before the meeting ends. I was setting off to look for the rest of you when I stumbled over that manuscript of yours and became engrossed in it."

Engrossed in it. Better and better.

"Then come and say hello to Maria." I gestured toward the door. My palm tingled as he took my hand, and I did my best to ignore the sensation. *What's happening to me?*

Even then, I knew the answer to that question, but I didn't want to admit that any man, even my dear Timur, could affect me so strongly. "She's in the women's sitting room," I said, striving to hide my discomfort, "and I'm sure she'll be as delighted as I am to welcome you."

Tolya's story would have to wait. Oddly, despite my eagerness to start work on it, I didn't regret that one bit.

"Look who I found in Alexei's study." I pushed open the door of Maria's sewing room and released Timur's hand. When my sister stared at him blankly, as I too must have done, I added, "It's Timur."

My sister jumped to her feet. The garment she'd been stitching—an exquisitely embroidered robe for Dosya, my six-year-old niece—tumbled unnoticed to the floor as Maria ran forward. "Oh, of course it is. Timur, how you've grown! Your father will be delighted to see you, and so am I."

He embraced her, kissing her cheeks as he had done with me earlier. I went to pick up the abandoned gown, battling a flash of jealousy and thoroughly annoyed with myself. Maria was my *sister*, not to mention Timur's stepmother; naturally he would greet her with affection. Jealousy had no place here.

And was quite unlike me, to boot. My friends fluttered and gossiped about boys, spying on them through upstairs windows and whispering speculations about which ones their fathers might pick for their husbands and what marriage to them would be like. I joined in from time to time, rather than be taken for a snob, but my heart wasn't in it. To me the boys seemed interchangeable: fresh-faced and full of themselves, preoccupied with battles and weaponry, convinced that their long and illustrious genealogies made them superior to everyone else on earth—especially women. That my father, for as long as I could remember, had emphasized his intention of finding me a husband who would benefit himself strengthened my belief that comparing one man to another was a pointless exercise.

Although I had to admit Timur was nothing like those unremarkable boys. Having known him most of my life, I'd seen his respect for women firsthand. And although he was as much a warrior as any other man of his rank, his education equaled or surpassed my own. In fact, we shared many interests: poetry and music, art and history, politics and literature, riding and falconry. In that sense, he was my ideal mate.

While I lost myself in this revelation, my sister grabbed Timur by the arm and dragged him off to meet her children. Tempted to follow them, I stopped. I refused to spend the evening mooning over my brother-in-law's son, ideal husband or not; it was unseemly and undignified. So I stayed in the deserted sewing room and pondered what to do next.

I could return to the study and my writing, but for once that seemed like the safe, boring choice. Fulfilling Maria's earlier request to supervise the servants would set a bad precedent as well as taking myself out of the arena where things were happening. Visiting Anna made no sense before Alexei returned and I could find out what business at court required the formal approval of boyars, church hierarchs, and even the ruling khan of Kasimov, Timur's great-uncle Shah-Ali.

So instead I went to my own chamber. There, despite my best intentions, I sat in the window seat and stared dreamily at the yard below. The frost that edged the panes fractured what usually appeared as a single scene into a series of pictures, like miniatures in a book. Wrapped tightly in a fur throw, I gazed at one frozen scene after another, as if floating in a mystical realm where the cold air couldn't touch me.

The church bells rang twice before Alexei rode into the courtyard on Ajdar, his beautiful dark bay gelding. I half-expected to see him trailed by a massive litter bearing the khan of Kasimov—who had, so far as I knew, no other family members in Moscow—but only Nikita and the small group of bodyguards who accompanied Alexei whenever he left the estate followed him in. From the speed with which my brother-in-law leaped off his horse and vanished into the covered staircase, leaving Ajdar in the hands of the nearest servant, I deduced that Shah-Ali had told Alexei of his son's arrival.

Time to pull myself together. I went downstairs.

Chapter 2

"He must have known that a dragon lurked nearby"

The jabber of excited voices led me to Maria's sitting room once more. I took my seat beside my sister, who had resumed her stitching, and watched Alexei, his arm slung around his son's shoulders as the two of them engaged in a rapid-fire exchange in Tatar.

"What are they saying?" Maria asked, keeping her voice low. "Can you follow it?"

"I'm out of practice," I admitted. "Give me a moment." When Timur lived in the house, the two of us spoke Tatar to each other most of the time. I insisted on it, because I wanted to learn the language, and he obliged me—amused, I think, by my determination. But after years of only occasional speaking or listening, my ears felt rusty.

After a while, though, the words stopped sounding like a collection of meaningless syllables and arranged themselves into combinations I recognized. "They're talking about Shah-Ali's decision to camp with his men on the far side of the river rather than move in here. And about Timur's plans," I told Maria. "Whether he can stay in Moscow for a while. Whether he wants to—he does, if his great-uncle can spare him." My cheeks warmed, and I stumbled on, irritated by my renewed discomfort but unable to control it. "Whether he's ready to marry and start a family, now that he's nineteen."

"Hmm." Maria assessed me, an expression in her eyes that I could not read. "And why does that last bring color to your face, I wonder?"

I wondered, too. Timur hadn't had this effect on me before. Although I *had* pretended during our games, at six or seven or even eight, that we were husband and wife, an idea he was kind enough to put up with, playing along even as he laughed at me. That was before I fully understood that the world saw us as brother and sister, despite us being no such thing.

I could have shared my confusion, at least, with Maria, but I didn't want to risk Timur or Alexei overhearing me. "No reason," I said. "Except that it's hot in here."

I should have guessed such a weak attempt to mislead her wouldn't work. "Do you think I'm blind?" she asked. Her brown eyes glittered with anger.

I bristled at the edge to her voice, but she cut off any protest before I could form the words. "It's easy to understand. He's a personable young man, and you're of an age to notice. It won't do, though. I know you're related only through marriage, but a father and son may not marry two sisters. Even if you could talk Papa round, and there is no hope of persuading him to consider any other husband before the grand prince selects his bride, the Church would not authorize the match."

"I know," I said, to pacify her—although the dictates of the Church meant nothing to Timur, a Muslim who had every reason to resist conversion, which would prevent him from someday leading any Tatar city or horde. "I have weddings on the brain, that's all, with the bride show looming. Let's interrupt them. Don't you want to find out what took Alexei to the Kremlin?"

She gazed at me with a frown that suggested she didn't believe me, but I widened my eyes and stared back at her as if I couldn't imagine what other explanation there could be.

After a long pause, she turned toward the men. "Alexei, Timur, I hate to interrupt your reunion, but can you not speak in Russian? And tell us what happened during the meeting with Grand Prince Ivan?" Before they could answer, she looked at me. "Lyuba, ask Tanya to fetch refreshments. And let her know that dinner may be delayed."

I obeyed, moving as fast as possible. Luck favored me, because I found Tanya in the first room I checked, which happened to be the dining hall, and delivered my orders. I was back at the sitting-room door by the time Alexei had the chance (or so I assumed) to complete whatever he'd been discussing with his son and respond to Maria's request.

"Grand Prince Ivan," he said as I returned to my seat. "Well, that's the first piece of news. After discussion with Metropolitan Macarius, the grand prince has decided—and the boyars have agreed—on the details of his coronation. As of January 16, 1547, he will no longer be grand prince but tsar."

"Tsar," Maria repeated. I heard my own amazement echoed in her voice—not so much at the nobles' and the grand prince's decision but at the news that the head of the Russian Church had thrown his weight behind the idea. "A proclamation of his equality with the emperors of Constantinople and the khans of the Horde," my sister added. "They're making a statement, then."

"Yes." Alexei crossed the room and settled himself on the bench that adjoined ours, then beckoned to Timur, who took the seat next to me. I felt acutely, physically conscious of him, although I kept my eyes focused on Alexei, who was still talking. "The move is long overdue. Ivan's father and grandfather played with the title; the coronation makes it official."

"The Poles will hate it." I concentrated on the political question to steady myself. "So will the Holy Roman Emperor. It's a direct challenge to him."

"Good girl," Alexei said. "I knew you'd pick that up. The foreign powers probably won't acknowledge the change right away; they'll see it as over-reaching. But it's a good idea, in my view. The Russian lands are growing stronger, and we deserve respect."

I wondered about that. Suppose the foreign powers went to war to rein in our over-reaching tsar? That would endanger us all. But before I could voice my concerns, Timur spoke.

"It's a direct challenge to the khans, too," he said. "Crimea and Kazan, especially. They may see it as aggression and respond accordingly."

"They may," Alexei agreed. "That conflict's already brewing, though. I doubt a declaration of an equality everyone already recognizes will make much difference."

What Timur might have replied to that went unsaid, because Maria interjected, changing the subject. "We can talk politics later," she announced in firm tones. "You mentioned other news. What is it?"

Servants arrived with steaming jugs and a platter of glistening turnovers that emitted the aroma of apples and spices. Alexei waited for them to distribute the food and leave before he answered. When he did, he looked straight at me. "Ivan expressed his intent to marry. He has Macarius's blessing, and thus the support of the entire Church, to seek a Russian wife. That means there will be a bride show, with candidates from towns throughout the various principalities as well as the great Moscow families. The call will go out by the end of the week, but during the meeting several of the boyars put their eligible virgins on the list. Your father was one of them, and Igor Bezzubtsev another."

My gut clenched at the news. So it had happened. I'd known it would, yet I felt far from ready. In fact, I felt less prepared than before, because of Timur's extraordinary effect on me. Fighting a sensation perilously close to panic, I glanced his way. He'd compressed his lips into a thin line and stared straight ahead. Hoping that meant he liked this announcement no better than I did, I forced my eyes toward Alexei and Maria. "I suppose I shouldn't be surprised," I said. "Papa's predicted this for months. Of course, he would jump at the opportunity." Although I strove to sound calm, I could tell from the tremor in my voice that I wasn't likely to fool anyone. "How does it work, this bride show? What does it mean that Papa put my name on the list?"

"The details are still under discussion." Alexei gave me a sympathetic smile. He'd heard the tremor, then. "Having your name on the list means the government knows you exist, but not much more than that. Because of your rank, I assume you'll be summoned to the Kremlin, but the state secretaries must check the records for the last bride show before they decide exactly how the presentations will take place. Even then, the boyars' wives will examine the candidates before selecting a dozen or so to meet with the tsar. I should have more information soon."

None of which told me much. "I don't want to marry Grand Prince Ivan," I said, knowing my words would have little effect. Papa didn't care about my preferences, and Alexei, who did, could hardly defy the entire government because one headstrong girl had no desire to become the sovereign's wife. Still, if I didn't defend myself, who would?

"Are you sure?" Alexei raised one elegant eyebrow. "Most girls your age dream of becoming queen. And our tsar is young. Quite good-looking, too."

"That life wouldn't suit me." I silenced the mental voice that whispered Timur's name in my thoughts. Marriage to him might someday make me a queen as well, and that prospect appealed to me far more. "I'd hate being cooped up in the Terem Palace except for the half-dozen times a year I'm allowed out to worship at some monastery, never mind spending every spare minute pregnant—and with a bad-tempered husband ordering me around, to boot."

Timur muttered something under his breath that sounded like, "Who wouldn't?" His father frowned at the interruption, then returned his attention to me. "Don't say such things outside this house," he warned. "Not even to your father." He paused, then added, "Especially not to your father."

"I won't," I said, hurt by his lack of faith. I'd learned long ago never to confide in Papa, no matter what. "I understand I can't refuse. I don't want to get you in trouble. I don't mind marrying, either. I'd like to have a family one day. But I would rather live with a man who values learning and has a sense of humor, someone who sees his wife as more than a brood mare." I forced myself *not* to glance at Timur as I finished, but I felt his eyes on me, and the sensation again raised the temperature in my cheeks. Maria emitted a long sigh, which only added to my distress.

"I understand," Alexei said. "If the choice were mine, I would search for such a husband for you. Alas, your father has preempted that option."

And that was the problem in a nutshell, wasn't it? I gripped my hands together, fending off an onslaught of despair. "Is there anything we can do?"

"Of course," Alexei said. "Being on the list is not the same as being chosen. There will be many other candidates, each with her own version of your father desperate to succeed. In the end, the selection will depend on which Moscow clan negotiates with the others most successfully. That's where we need to focus our efforts." He grinned at my sister. "We're back to politics, I'm afraid."

Maria nodded, a rueful smile on her lips. "You're right, though. The real game will be played outside the bride show. Your options for influencing the outcome are limited; you're one pawn among many, and like the others, you must appear pretty and demure and willing. Anything else risks causing offense and will ruin your chances of ever making an acceptable match. But the crucial factor is who selects the chosen few, and there Alexei and I may be able to tip the scales away from you. For the moment, the Glinsky clan is riding high. That gives their candidates an advantage."

One small light in a dark forest. "They won't favor Papa," I said. I remembered hearing that Papa had had more than one run-in with Grand Princess Elena Glinskaya, the soon-to-be tsar's mother. From the way he groaned at any mention of her name, I suspected he still hadn't forgiven her—and that her family members might not have forgotten whatever sins they believed he had committed.

"Absolutely not," Maria confirmed. "But they are not the only voices, however powerful at the moment. We can predict that the Shuisky princes plan to use the bride show to restore their eminence. And if the Shuiskys decide to fight *for* something, the Belsky princes will contest them. The other families will jockey for position, trying to figure out which of those three clans will come out ahead."

"And Papa sees me as his way of supporting the Shuiskys' cause," I said gloomily.

"Excuse me?" Timur asked, reminding the rest of us that he'd spent years away from Moscow.

"Papa is a client of the Shuisky clan," I explained. "He has been for years." Another reason why the Glinsky family detested him. "If the grand prince—sorry, tsar—chooses me, it would be good for Papa but also for his patrons. It shows how important they are." I wrinkled my nose. I hated having so little control over my own fate. "There's nothing I can do, then?" I said. "Except cause a scandal, and that would reflect badly on you."

"You could let them see you reading books," Timur suggested. His mischievous tone revived memories of our once-close partnership, which I acknowledged with a conspiratorial glance. "Or worse, writing your stories." He looked at his father. "Suppose we drop a few hints about her scholarship? It's not morally reprehensible, only unusual. And even I know that the Shuisky clan has lots of affiliates. Surely they'll nominate more than one girl to maximize their chances of winning. So raising questions about her suitability may be enough to convince them to support a different candidate."

Alexei's solemn face crinkled into laughter. "It's worth a try," he said. "Few of these noble Russian boors know how to appreciate an intelligent wife." He directed a teasing glance at Maria, whose lips curved in response.

Something about their silent exchange caught my attention, reminding me of the days right after their marriage, when he and his stepmother insisted that my sister learn to read and write, to ride a horse, and to collect information about the ins and outs of the court so she could become her husband's most intimate adviser.

Timur had lived with us then. I turned my head his way, wondering if he also recalled those days, whether he'd seen enough yet to grasp how far my sister had retreated from the wider world in the years since he left this house. Instead, I found him gazing at me. Uncertain, I looked away. I couldn't help believing that he might be as taken with me as I was with him. The tingling in my midriff intensified at the thought.

"I will sponsor you," Maria announced, startling me. Perhaps Alexei's teasing remark had revived her memories of her mother-in-law's lectures as it had mine. "I've stayed away from the court since Grand Princess Elena died, but the bride show gives me the perfect opportunity to reassert myself among the boyars' wives. I'll be at your side and can advise you on how to proceed. In fact, tell Anna I will sponsor you both."

"Will Papa allow that?" I asked.

"He has no choice." Maria stared at me as if she didn't believe I'd posed such a silly question. "He can't sponsor you himself. No man can enter the women's quarters of another family, and that's where much of the contest will take place. Whom else would he ask?"

"I don't know," I admitted. "No one else would equal you in rank, anyway." As the daughter-in-law of a khan—a tsarevna—Maria stood right below the royal family in the court hierarchy. "I meant would he fuss about you sponsoring Anna as well, but I suppose he has no say in that either."

"None at all." The corners of her mouth turned upward in a wicked smile. "It will unsettle him, which is all to the good where Papa is concerned. He plans for the long term; it's when he has to respond fast to shifting circumstances that he's most likely to make mistakes. We want to keep him on the defensive as much as possible. He has enemies as well as allies, even among the Shuisky faction, and we can use that to our advantage. He would get a big boost from becoming the new tsar's father-in-law, and those enemies will want to keep him in his place."

Watching her, I felt as if I had waved a magic wand and brought the sister I dimly remembered from a decade ago back to brilliant, sparkling life. The thought of having her at my side as I traversed the treacherous forest ahead heartened me as nothing else could have done.

Well, almost nothing: the revival of my friendship with Timur shone equally bright. Like Papa, he could not follow me into the women's quarters, but his support still warmed my soul.

Alexei regarded his wife as if he, too, barely remembered this vibrant woman who so instinctively grasped the ins and outs of court politics. As if he rejoiced as much as I did, seeing her old self restored. I couldn't help it; I yearned to see Timur look at me that way one day.

Maria laughed, her face alight with mischief. "And in addition to your love of books and your ambitious parent, I will drop hints about your disinclination to stitch and your insistence on thinking for yourself. Those four things together may be enough to convince the boyars that you'll cause too much trouble as tsaritsa. Wasn't that what made them dislike Elena Glinskaya—her foreign upbringing and her desire to rule? Alas for Anna, she embroiders like a born seamstress and has the temperament of an angel."

"Thank you for agreeing to sponsor us." Belatedly, I realized I hadn't acknowledged the gift she'd offered. I reached for her hand. "I couldn't bear to go through this without you at my side. And you're right about Anna. She's the perfect candidate, poor thing."

I grimaced, remembering the events of last summer. If there was one young woman in Russia who hated the idea of marrying the soon-to-be Tsar Ivan more than I did, Anna was that person, and with good reason. "I'd better visit her, don't you think?" I asked. "She'll have heard the news by now, and she must be devastated. She hasn't recovered from losing Yuri, and she hates Ivan for robbing her of the man she loves." I added the last for Timur's benefit, since the others knew how Ivan had forced Anna's contracted husband to take monastic vows—on a whim, with no justification, less than six months ago. Yuri had narrowly escaped execution, despite having committed no crime.

Timur rose from the bench. "I'll escort you to your friend's house, Lyuba, if you permit."

"Don't," Alexei warned. "Now that her father has listed her as one of the tsar's potential brides, she can't be seen in the company of a young, unmarried man, even her brother-in-law's son. Nikita Andreevich will escort her—he's Anna's uncle, so no one will suspect him of impropriety—and Anna's stepfather will bring Lyuba home."

I bit my lip but didn't protest, because I knew he was right.

"Damnation," Timur said. I couldn't agree more.

As it turned out, Niki had no need to cut short his workday. I hadn't had time to call for my outdoor clothes before Tanya opened the sitting-room door and my best friend dashed in. Confronted by four people, two of them male, in a place usually reserved for my sister and me, Anna skidded to a stop. Tanya grabbed the opportunity to divest my friend of her hooded cloak, then left the room. Anna, under normal circumstances a perfect model of decorum, stood panting near the doorway.

After a while, she composed herself enough to move to the center of the room and bow. "Greetings, Tsarevich Alexei," she said in an unsteady voice. "Tsarevna Maria, Lyuba, … and?"

I hugged her. "I was about to come and visit you. Have you already heard about the bride show? Is that what's put you in such a state?"

"Yes, I heard." She returned the hug. "Anfim sent Mama a message, letting her know he'll be late for supper as a result." Anfim Fadeyev was her stepfather and a high-ranking member of the government. "He and the other state secretaries have orders to plan the bride show and draft the wedding ceremonial. There are travel assignments, too—pairs of associate boyars and officials leaving for the towns on Friday to search for candidates. He's allowed to skip that journey, since he already traveled twice on state business this year. But Cousin Igor will be heading back to Kolomna and other points south, as the associate boyar in charge."

"Poor candidates." I grimaced. Anna's cousin Igor, in my mind, teetered between a menace and a joke. Since last summer, he'd taken a hard lurch toward the "menace" side, precipitating the exile of her Yuri. "Poor state secretary, stuck spending a couple of weeks with Igor—especially on business that, if successful, will interfere with your cousin's plans to make *you* the next royal bride."

"And will get them both in trouble if it fails. Yes, my thoughts precisely. Poor state secretary. I'm glad Anfim will escape the snare this time." Anna tipped her head toward Timur. "But I still don't know whom to address."

"Forgive me. You did ask, and I forgot to answer." I stepped back and extended my hand, palm up, toward Alexei's son. "Let me reintroduce you to Timur Alexeevich. You met him several times when we were younger, but he hasn't visited us for years. He arrived in Moscow this morning with Shah-Ali Khan of Kasimov. Timur, this is Anna Semyonovna Kolycheva."

While I spoke, Anna's breath had slowed, enabling her to produce a more graceful bow, which he returned. "Prince Timur," she said. "It's a pleasure to see you again."

Something in her tone caused me to look sharply at her. Unlike me, Anna was the epitome of Russian beauty: blonde and blue-eyed and graceful as a doe. Once I'd have considered her too quiet and self-contained to attract a man from Alexei's family, which was filled to the brim with passionate, outspoken women who rarely doubted their own talents or tolerated condescension from their husbands or brothers. But over the last six months, my friend had revealed an inner strength that impressed me—and no one could regard *her* as Timur's sister.

Again I bit my tongue. Was I jealous of my best friend, who still pined for her exiled monk, because of a man I couldn't have? That made no sense!

"If you will excuse us," I said to my family, "I'll take Anna upstairs and we can talk there."

"Of course," Maria said. "I'll send a maid to fetch you when dinner starts. Anna, you're welcome to join us."

"Thank you." My friend, restored to her usual calm and polite state, at least on the surface, bowed once more. "I can't stay today, though. I promised Mama that I would help Lara and Tolya with their lessons. Seryozha's nursemaid fell ill yesterday, and Mama wants to keep an eye on him. After losing three boys in a row, she's beside herself, especially with Anfim stuck at the office, and I don't know how to reassure her except by providing the help she asks for."

"Yes, that's difficult," Maria said. "Two-month-old infants do succumb without warning to this malady or that, as your mother well knows."

"Precisely." Anna twisted her hands together, a gesture I interpreted as evidence of frustration. Then she added, "Could you ask Niki to see me home before your meal begins?"

"I'll ask him." Alexei stood and beckoned to his son. "Come with me, Timur, and I'll introduce you to Nikita. Let me also reacquaint you with my warriors—or present you to those who joined my force after you went south. You can tell me about your grandparents on the way. They were both well when you left Kasimov, I hope." He turned to Maria. "I'll make him repeat the whole for you, *kaderle*, when we meet for dinner."

Kaderle. The Tatar word meant "sweetheart" or "darling." Again, as if pulled by a string, my eyes sought Timur's, but he was watching his father. Just as well, I thought as I turned my gaze back to Anna, although my rebellious heart disagreed.

Timur bowed to Anna and me, placing his right hand on his chest in the Tatar way. Then he turned to my sister. "As always, you welcome me with an open heart, Auntie Maria. I'm most grateful—and sorry I haven't seen you in so long."

"And I you," she said with a gracious nod. "Stay with us for a while. We've missed you."

"He will," Alexei told her. "I spoke to my uncle, who has given him leave until the spring. We can see then whether we should extend it. That's what we were talking about earlier."

Maria glanced at me, and I suppressed a smile. We both knew they'd discussed more than Timur's leave.

"That's good news," I said. If they chose to believe that I hadn't understood them, I saw no reason to disillusion them. They would find out the truth soon enough. Besides, I wanted to get away and compare notes with Anna, who had as much to lose as I did if we couldn't avoid the snare set by the heads of our clans—her cousin Igor and my father.

"We'll be in my chamber if you need us," I told my sister. When she dipped her head in acknowledgment, I took Anna's elbow and we walked side-by-side to the door.

I'm sure it was only in my imagination that Timur's eyes followed us as we left. Even so, an infuriatingly stubborn part of my soul insisted on asking which of us had his attention and whether, if he wanted, he could convince Anna to abandon her Yuri.

I really did not like myself at that moment.

Chapter 3

"And that a fair maiden's happiness was at stake"

Tanya brought us warm cider, served us, and left. Anna sipped from the cup as I talked. "Maria's promised to sponsor us," I said once we found seats near the flue of the stove that warmed most of the rooms in the women's quarters, including mine. "For the bride show, I mean."

"Really?" Anna looked amazed. "That's good of her. What does a sponsor do, exactly?"

"I don't know," I admitted. "She seemed excited by the idea, though. You should have heard her going over what would appeal to the boyars and what wouldn't." I stopped to breathe, and a memory surfaced. "She sounded like Papa. A nicer version of Papa, of course, intent on helping us and not herself. Still, it shocked me. Only a couple of hours before, I'd have sworn she couldn't think of anything but laundry."

Anna continued to sip cider, but the way she played with the fringe on a cushion with her free hand told me her mind was elsewhere. "I'm glad she wants to help us," she said after a moment. "Mama knows everyone who has a say in selecting a royal bride, especially the women, but I can't see her going to court right now —maybe ever. She says the other highborn ladies will snub her for marrying below her station."

"She can talk to Maria, though. Can't you imagine the pair of them plotting strategy? Papa and your cousin won't stand a chance!" I giggled at the thought, my tension ebbing for the first time that day.

Anna put down her cup and wrung her hands. "But Lyuba, suppose they fail? I will *not* marry the grand prince. I don't care what Cousin Igor says. I'm betrothed to Yuri!"

"Who's a monk," I reminded her. A voice in my head chided me for my recent flashes of jealousy. Clearly, she still thought only of her beloved. "I know you hate it that the grand prince ordered Yuri to take the tonsure, but the moment he did, the contract became null and void. He can't wed you now, although I'm sure he wants to."

And why was I pushing her to see that? I couldn't have said, except that she was my friend, and I cared about her. I wanted her to be happy.

Just not with Timur. I sighed. When had I become such a mess?

Anna plaited the fringe between her fingers, as if the force of her gaze could turn it into a magic carpet that would transport her beloved into her arms. "Yuri told me to be strong," she said in a firm voice. "He said he loves me, that all is not lost. He *will* come back, one way or another. I feel it in my bones."

"I remember what he said," I told her. "But that was three months ago. Has he sent another message?"

"Not yet." She reached for the cup and sipped. "I wrote back to him in September, right after I got the letter. Anfim sent it north by courier. But the courier planned to stop by the monastery on his way to Kolmogory and the islands in the White Sea. It's no surprise that he hasn't returned yet. I'm sure he'll bring an answer when he does."

I bit back the urge to argue. Who knew what might have happened to Yuri since he wrote his letter? I'd heard his advice to Anna a hundred times, and I was sure he meant what he said. He was a dear man—good-looking, highborn, kind-hearted, and a skilled warrior—the perfect husband for Anna. He said he loved her, and I knew she loved him, and it was a terrible tragedy that the grand prince (no, we had to start calling him tsar) had stripped Yuri of his property before dispatching him to the monastery at Ferapontovo in July. But even if Yuri had somehow managed to delay his tonsure for a few weeks, the chances that he could resist for months or years were basically nil. And he was smart enough to realize that giving Anna false hope would do more damage in the long run than cutting his ties with her altogether. At the same time, it wasn't hard to imagine him failing to send the letter that would crush her dreams forever, especially when they were his dreams, too. His dithering, in a sense, let them both nurture their illusions for a while longer.

I kept those thoughts to myself. I'd learned the hard way that, despite Anna's docile exterior, pushing her only caused her to dig her heels in deeper. And it wasn't as though I *knew* Yuri had given in to the pressure imposed on him. "We'll find a solution," I said instead. "Maria promised to help, and I trust her."

"I hope she will," Anna said. "You and I can't hope to navigate that snake pit—that's what Mama calls it—on our own."

"No." I sipped my cider and realized it was getting cold. "Who listens to girls our age? But the boyars' wives can't ignore a tsarevna, and Maria and your mother have maps of the entire elite in their heads. They'll know what to say to whom, starting with the tsar's grandmother. Do you think it's a good omen that her name is Anna, too, or a bad one?"

"Ugh," Anna said. "Don't I have enough on my mind without having to worry about whether our ruler wants a bride with the same name as his grandmother? I wish the whole bride show would go poof and disappear, like the demon in a puppet show!"

"Me too." Laughing, I waved my arm, wielding an imaginary magic wand. "Bride show, begone!"

Anna rose to her feet, giggling, and twirled with both hands in the air while I chanted every silly spell I could think of to banish first the bride show and its unwanted groom, then Papa and Anna's cousin as well.

After a while, we settled back onto our bench, panting for breath. "It's too late to hope for that now," I said. "And Maria told me this morning that Papa intends to marry me off this year anyway, so even if I don't get stuck with the tsar, I'm likely to end up with some doddering ancient or ambitious blockhead. At least Anfim and Solomonida plan to wave that marriage contract in your cousin's face for as long as they can."

Anna regarded me with a mischievous smile. "Maybe Maria can persuade your papa to choose that handsome prince who greeted me when I arrived. Timur Alexeevich, like a name from one of your fairy tales, and he couldn't take his eyes off you."

So even she had noticed the way he looked at me. My insides tingled at the thought, and my cheeks heated to the point where my only choice was to set the cup of cider on a nearby table and cover my face with both hands. I must have turned scarlet. "Oh my, how you blush!" Anna said, confirming my fears. "You like him!"

"Of course I do, silly." I tried to ignore my body's betrayal. "Who wouldn't? But he might as well be my brother."

"Now who's being silly?" Anna, devil take her, was giggling. "If you thought of him as a brother, you wouldn't look like a midsummer beet at the mere mention of his name. You seem to get along with him well enough, too. When did you see him last?"

"Four years ago," I said, counting back. "He lived on the steppe with his uncle Ogodai from the time he turned twelve, and Alexei visited him there, but Maria and I didn't because at the time the Crimeans were raiding along the Oka River and it wasn't safe. Then Timur went straight to his great-uncle in Kasimov when he turned fifteen. We all saw him then, but that was the last time." I interrogated those hazy memories. "He looked like a gangly bean-pole, and we barely exchanged two words, but now he's a man, and I'm the one who's blushing and can't talk."

"Well, of course," Anna said. "He's the best-looking man I've ever seen, and a charmer to boot. Mother of God, why are you protesting? As the grandson of a khan, he must be high-ranking enough to impress even your father."

Did she truly not remember? Had she ever known? "He's the son of my sister's husband," I said. "She already told me the Church would forbid any match between us." I gulped. "Besides, he's Muslim, and I'm not." *Which is why he won't care what the Church says*, muttered the treacherous voice in my head.

Anna shrugged one elegant shoulder. "Alexei converted. So could you. I think I might, if Timur looked at me like that. If I weren't already in love with Yuri, of course." She giggled once more. "If the tsar doesn't choose you, you can persuade Prince Timur to run off with you!"

It was as if she'd read my mind. And the picture she painted was too alluring for words. "Hah," I said, in a last-ditch attempt to hold on to my common sense. "I'm sure he has girls chasing him in droves."

She laughed harder. "Listen to you. Tell me you wouldn't prefer him as a husband over one of your papa's cronies. Or are you holding out for Prince Pavel Shuisky? He was so eager to impress you at my betrothal party in March!"

At that absurdity, I too burst out laughing. "When he wasn't making cow eyes at you! If he could have picked Yuri up by the collar and tossed him through the window without causing a scandal, he would have. And what an idiot—going on about how a girl like me wouldn't know the location of Smolensk. He even announced that I must be so busy doing needlework that I couldn't possibly understand the allure of riding a horse. The man hasn't a thing to recommend him except that he's about the right age. And not bad-looking, I suppose."

"Nowhere near as handsome as Timur, though," she said.

"Not even close," I agreed. "And Timur would never patronize me like that. He wouldn't dare."

In my mind, I heard a woman's voice saying, *I know you don't get to choose for yourself, but ask your brother-in-law and your sister to pick a man who will love you for the person you are, not the person* he *wants you to be.*

Who said that, and when? I recalled the words clearly, but not the circumstances. Yet the advice got to the heart of what troubled me about the bride show. Would the tsar love me for the person I was? Hardly. He wanted someone to bear him an army of sons, one after another until her body gave out. That had happened to my mother; I didn't want to abandon my children as death had forced her to abandon me. Papa's cronies would be the same, but older—or if young, then intolerably dull and pompous, like Prince Pavel. I didn't worry that Papa would pick Pavel *himself* as my husband, because Maria had once told me that Pavel's father was responsible for most of the things that went wrong in Papa's life. He'd want a different alliance, but it wouldn't necessarily be a better one, from my point of view.

Timur, though—he had a sense of who I was, developed over years, not days. When I'd run into him in the study, he pronounced himself engrossed in my stories, not knowing who had written them. He called me accomplished and a beauty, despite my red hair and green eyes. My unfeminine education and interests, my hatred of needlework, my love of riding and hawking—these things increased my value, in his view. And according to Anna, he had eyes for no one else.

Again, the thought fluttered before my eyes like a lure. *Could* I wed Timur one day, if Tsar Ivan didn't pick me for his bride? I'd had no reason to consider conversion until now, but perhaps I should ...

While I pondered, Anna continued to laugh. "And the way he scowled when you put him in his place," she said, still referring to Prince Pavel.

Preoccupied with visions of Timur, I didn't answer. Prince Pavel was a straw man as far as I was concerned; if he posed a threat to anyone, that person was Anna, whose Cousin Igor considered Pavel a lesser but still suitable alternative to the young tsar. I refused to waste another instant on Pavel Shuisky.

Anna asked what had me looking so pensive, and I told her about the remembered words. We turned over possibilities for a while without any result; then she announced she had to go home. I walked her downstairs to the study, where her uncle stood deep in conversation with Alexei and Timur, and left her there while I headed for the dining room, still pondering the meaning of those out-of-context sentences. Like a prophecy in a tale, they clung to me, but I saw no way to turn them into reality or even to uncover their source.

An hour or so later, the prospect of marrying a man who cared for me rather than the status and sons I represented retreated even farther into the shadows. A short time after we finished our mid-day dinner, my father showed up unannounced. (I should mention, in the spirit of fairness, that Papa *had* to show up unannounced, since his inability to get along with my brother-in-law meant that Papa was, as a general rule, barred from the house. It took a sneak attack for him to gain entry, and even that succeeded only if Alexei happened to be in a forgiving mood.)

Alas for me, Alexei, mellowed by the return of his son, chose to accept Papa's declaration that he wanted a cozy chat with his daughters. I sent Maria a pleading glance as my brother-in-law produced an infinitesimal bow and ushered Timur from the sitting room without reintroducing him. Timur must have seen my expression, because he raised an eyebrow, then smiled encouragingly before he left.

I glowered at his back. Of course, I didn't expect him to disobey his own father to stay and support me, but why should he escape when I did not? Whatever Papa said, I didn't need to be a prophetess to predict that he hadn't come to chat, cozily or in any other way. He'd come to ensure that I would do my part in the bride show. And if I knew Papa at all, he would not only dangle a carrot—Mama's jewels? a brand-new wardrobe?—but would also wave the stick of alternative husbands. Aged sixty or corpulent, ugly or cruel or dull as a log—the man wouldn't matter so long as the options convinced me to cooperate with Papa's plans.

I studied him as he approached us. It had been months since he last wangled his way into the house, but I saw few changes in him. At forty-six, he looked sleek and comfortably well-to-do, his hair graying at the temples, his face mostly free of wrinkles, and his air of confidence unshaken. His medium height and slender frame—but most of all the sense he conveyed of meriting everyone's attention—left him with a distinct resemblance to a coursing hound. He'd exhausted my mother, betrayed his ruler, alienated Maria and her husband, and driven his second wife away through betrayal and neglect, but none of it touched him. He remained ever-ready to grasp the next opportunity for advancement. If anything, he seemed even more pleased with life than the last time we'd met.

As he bent to kiss first Maria's cheeks, then mine, I remembered who had spoken the phrases that haunted me. The advice came from that abandoned second wife, now Juliana Ossolinska, and she had offered it the day she obtained her divorce. I'd seen her only once since then, because she lived in Poland with her new husband, Lord Felix Ossolinski. I didn't think of her often, which explained, no doubt, why I had let her words slip from my mind. And although I knew her to be often manipulative and unkind, on that particular occasion she had sounded completely sincere, even concerned about my welfare. So I was sure she'd been trying to help.

While I mulled over my recollections, Papa settled onto the bench opposite me. We exchanged rounds of meaningless pleasantries for a while until Maria asked, "Have you eaten?"

"I have," Papa admitted, "although I wouldn't mind a goblet of wine."

We were well into mid-afternoon, but it was still early for wine. Nonetheless, Maria rose to summon a servant and sent him in search of a flask and goblets. "And bring some of those butter cookies the cook made earlier today," she added before turning to our father once more.

"Now tell us, Papa," she commanded. "What brings you here?"

Papa looked hurt. He was good at that. "Why should I not want to visit my darling daughters?"

She regarded him with a steady gaze, as though deciding whether he was friend or foe. "Papa, please. Do you take us for fools? Alexei told us about the bride show a few hours ago, including that you put Lyuba's name on the list of candidates. She can't withdraw now, whether we like it or not, so what need have you to visit us?"

The servant returned with wine and cups on a tray, as well as the promised cookies. Maria dismissed him, then poured the wine herself. She held out a goblet to our father and, when he took it, resumed her seat. "Well?" she said. "What do you want from us?"

"To drink to my youngest daughter's good fortune." He extended the solid brass goblet, decorated with vine-like engravings, toward me. "But how can I lead a toast when you do not partake, Maria?"

Again I expected her to argue with him, but instead she poured a small amount of wine into a second goblet. An even smaller amount went into a third, which she diluted with boiled water from another flask before handing me the cup and a pair of cookies on a folded linen cloth. I gazed into the crimson depths, swirling gently from the movement of Maria's hand, and took an experimental sip. No one had offered me wine before, and I was curious to learn why others prized it.

It had a fruity aroma and a smooth taste, slightly tart —pleasant but not memorable. I set the goblet aside, satisfied that I could describe the drink next time it came up in a story, and nibbled on a cookie. The treat was delicious, buttery and crumbly, but tension about what would happen next constricted my throat, and after the first bite I returned it to its napkin bed.

"You can toast now," my sister said, her voice more acidic than the wine.

"To my lovely daughter Lyuba." Papa waved his goblet with a flourish. "Who will make her father happy and secure the family's fortune by winning the favor of the new tsar." He swallowed a large gulp, and Maria responded with considerably less enthusiasm. I bowed my head to hide the rebellious urge that ran through me.

Papa took another long drink and set the cup aside. "And, I confess, I came to offer a short homily on the desirability of that end and advice on how to achieve it."

Rather than attract his attention by groaning, I took another sip of wine and prepared to listen to his suggestions. That way, I would know which tactics to avoid at all costs. With a certain resentment, I noted he hadn't even offered the expected bribe, instead moving straight to exhortation, as if he took my obedience for granted. You'd think he, not Maria and Alexei, had raised me for the last decade.

Maria stepped into the breach before he could begin his speech, thwarting my efforts to find out more. "No need to worry, Papa," she told him in a voice sweet as dew dripping from a honeycomb. "I intend to sponsor Lyuba and will guide her every step of the way. But if you have information about how the selection will take place, do share it with us. We want to be fully prepared."

Papa narrowed his eyes. "I do not. The plans are still being made."

"Then how can you advise us?" Maria asked. "Perhaps you should return when you know more. Your time is precious, after all."

He scowled, no doubt guessing that his chances of slipping past the guards twice were slim. Although I'd urge her to let him in: the more information we had, the better prepared we would be, and milking Papa for what he could gather at court was one way to obtain it.

"Will that bastard you married admit me?" he growled, confirming my supposition.

"That depends on you," she said with regal serenity. "If my *husband*"—her emphasis conveyed a subtle reproach—"believes you have Lyuba's best interests at heart, I'm sure he will greet you with open arms."

That silenced Papa for a moment, but he soon snapped his head toward me. "And what of you? Are you committed to winning the tsar's ring? Or must I remind you of the husbands I can find for you if you undermine my plans?"

His willingness to threaten me before I'd so much as hinted at resistance raised my hackles. I straightened my shoulders, looked him in the eye, and said, "I promise you, Papa, I will follow Maria's guidance to the letter. And when you find out more, I would like to hear it."

Papa frowned, as if weighing my response for sincerity, but before he could say anything else, Alexei and Timur returned. "Did your daughters reassure you of their continued well-being?" my brother-in-law inquired in the bland tone he reserved for days when Papa had given no particular offense.

"I believe we're finished here," Maria said in the same level voice. "I promised Papa to help Lyuba with the bride show, and she swore to follow my advice."

"Good." Alexei turned to Papa. "It's been a pleasure. Sorry you can't stay."

My father muttered something under his breath, but he must have recognized the futility of arguing, because he rose and stalked off rather than respond.

Watching the door close behind him, I shivered. I knew from the tales circulating among my nearest and dearest that Papa made a dangerous enemy. I could only hope he wouldn't decide that he had one in me.

Chapter 4

"As if a menacing dragon were not enough"

"Are you ready, Lyuba?" It was the next morning, and Maria stood at the door to my room. The fox fur that lined her coat of tanned leather spilled over the collar and rimmed the attached hood. The muff she carried in one hand matched the coat, a combination of restraint and luxury. But the clothes were mere trappings: her queenly bearing proclaimed her a tsarevna, whatever she wore.

"Where are we going?" I looked up from the piece of paper on which I had been diligently scratching the first few pages of Tolya's promised tale. Inspired by the events of yesterday—Timur's unexpected return, the looming bride show, my selfish and uncaring parent—words flowed from my pen like a summer storm. A dragon threatened a peasant village, and the villagers, desperate to save their crops from fiery destruction, had met in the leader's house to debate their options. Of course, every reader would know that the peasants must swallow their pride and find a knight to defend them, but a good story requires that the proper steps be followed, and Tolya would fuss if I defied his expectations.

"Are you writing up here?" Maria asked, rather than answer my question. I heard a note of exasperation in her voice, which only grew as she added, "Yes, you must be. You have a smear of ink on your nose and a blot on your thumb. A good thing we're only visiting Solomonida. But do wash off the marks as best you can, and get your outdoor clothes on. Why are you writing in your room anyway? Did Alexei ban you from the study?"

"No." I stood, more than a little grumpy. Why did people who lived without stories buzzing in their heads believe that a writer was not doing anything useful and could be interrupted without so much as an apology? My sister would never make the same assumption about a clerk. "But he and Timur are using it. I brought my paper and ink here after supper yesterday so I could avoid being distracted by their endless conversations about troop formations and battles."

I went to wash my face and hands as directed, moving more slowly than usual to express my annoyance. When I finished, I discovered my sister perusing my first three pages. "Instead, you're writing about knights and dragons," she said. "Is that any different?"

"Yes." I donned my hooded coat, a shade darker than Maria's, with sleeves that widened at the wrists. "There will be a beautiful maiden for my knight to rescue, as well as a sorcerer for him to defeat. And although he must fight the dragon, he and the maiden will talk of things other than war. So altogether different. But why are we visiting Solomonida? I thought there was sickness at her house."

"She sent a message this morning," Maria said. "The nursemaid's illness isn't serious, and Anna told her about my offer to sponsor you both at court. Solomonida invited us to stop by."

I closed the last button on my coat. "See, I'm ready."

"Not quite." Maria picked up a comb and used it to subdue flyaway strands of hair before pulling the hood over my head. "There, now you are. Let's go."

She turned and led the way down to the second floor, then to the staircase that connected the main entrance to the courtyard below. I'd listened for the servants' chatter as we entered the corridor;

C. P. LESLEY

an inner stairway allowed them to enter through the storerooms at ground level and move around as needed within the house. But as we reached the courtyard, I heard only the stamping of hooves from the waiting sleigh and the driver muttering reassurances to the restive horses. On a warmer day, I'd expect to see maids running to and fro between storerooms and kitchen while clouds of steam, scented with meat and herbs, billowed behind them. Menservants would be engaged in crafts, caring for animals, or performing chores. Yet glances in every direction revealed no more than the occasional shivering carpenter or seamstress dashing from one building to the next, even though the household supported more than a hundred souls, not counting Alexei's warriors.

The moment I stepped off the wooden platform at the base of the stairs, I understood why the yard hosted no one but the driver and his team. A frosty wind sent whirls of snow into the air, and by the time I jumped into the sleigh and pulled the sable blanket up to my chin, my cloak looked like something Grandfather Frost might wear.

"It's brutal out here," I told Maria as she collapsed onto the seat next to me, then signaled to the coachman to start. A snap of the reins, and the sleigh moved swiftly across the snow-covered ground. "It wasn't half as cold yesterday."

"Horrible," she agreed. "I fear for the poor beasts in this weather. But we can't afford to wait for a warmer day: Alexei has heard rumors that the men traveling to the towns to look for bridal candidates will move out as early as Friday. He and his uncle are summoned to another council session at the Kremlin the same day, so the plans are moving fast."

I winced. The tighter the schedule, the less prepared I felt to handle it.

Maria didn't notice my reaction. "The driver can stable the horses at Anfim's house until we're ready to leave," she went on.

"Meanwhile, we'll be discussing how best to proceed. We need to decide which old acquaintances to tap for news."

"Don't forget Papa," I said, grinning at the thought of squeezing my twisty father for information. "He'll be back to bother us as soon as the plans are set."

She laughed. "Yes. I may even let him in if he promises to stop insulting my husband. Alexei will find out how many candidates they anticipate, which steps you'll go through, how long they expect the process to last, and so on. So it's not essential that we talk to Papa, but if I think he has something useful to tell us, I will."

"Has Alexei said nothing so far?" That seemed unlikely. He and Maria seemed to have no secrets from each other. "He must know how many towns they are visiting, at least."

"They assigned twelve pairs," she said, "but some of them will go to more than one town. It sounded like twenty or twenty-five locations altogether."

"So there could be hundreds of girls." Awe filled me at the thought of such a crowd—and relief, too. "Anna and I would never stand out among so many."

"I doubt it," she said with a shake of her head. "It would make life easier, and you'd think the fathers would want their daughters to become the first tsaritsa, but it didn't work that way the last time. Most of the provincial families worry about something going wrong if they send their daughters to Moscow. It's a long way, and if a girl isn't chosen, the local boys may decide there's something wrong with her. Then she will die unwed."

I made a face at the snow outside. "Let's hope you're wrong, then. If I have to go through this, making lots of new friends would at least be fun. I could find out what life is like in other places as well. For my stories, you know." I imagined the icy flakes that swirled around the sleigh as beautiful girls dressed in satin and velvet, arms raised high in a dance as handkerchiefs dangled from clasped fingers and thumbs.

Maria patted my hand in a reassuring manner but didn't speak. "How long is the list from Moscow?" I asked after a while.

"Don't know," Maria said. "That's one thing I plan to ask Solomonida. She's a few years older than I am, so I'm hoping she will remember the size of the group from which Grand Prince Vasily chose Elena Glinskaya. And how the selection process worked. It's Elena's mother, after all, who will have the greatest say in this contest, because the bridegroom is Elena's son. I'd expect her to apply the same principles that favored her daughter."

"Princess Anna Glinskaya," I murmured, to show that I knew whom she had in mind. "What's she like?"

"A bit of a battle-ax, I'm afraid."

I groaned. "Oh, great. Something else to worry about." But a new thought slipped into my head, and my mood lightened. "Maybe she'll take a dislike to me."

Maria patted my hand. "It's quite likely she already favors someone else. She's no supporter of Papa's."

Reassured, I braced my arm against the side of the swiftly moving sleigh and mumbled a response, hoping she would keep talking. Instead she gazed off to her right, clearly lost in thought, beating a gentle rhythm against the railing with her muff.

Outside, the snowflakes whirled ever thicker, transforming the dancing maidens into monsters caught in a maelstrom powerful enough to swallow Jonah's whale.

A short while later, we pulled into the courtyard of the estate where Anfim Fadeyev, Solomonida, and—since our return from the country in August—Anna lived. One of many government-owned buildings assigned to officials, the house resembled ours on the outside: a three-story structure surrounded by a series of one-room storehouses, a kitchen, workrooms, and a stable, all enclosed by a wooden fence.

Inside, though, the decor looked nothing like the Tatar-inspired design to which I'd become accustomed. Here mica window panes glowed pale yellow instead of our pure Crimean glass, and swirling patterns of painted birds and flowers displayed against backgrounds of cream and gold decorated the walls instead of carpets and tapestry of Oriental design. Even the furniture looked strange to my eyes each time I saw it: the tables too solid and rectangular, the cushions on the window seats too small, the rooms with their squat pillars cluttered and airless, the dark corners where the icons clustered more fearsome than uplifting.

Solomonida greeted us as we bowed to those intimidating icons. Instead of her usual elaborate robes, she wore a wrinkled homespun dress, and wisps of blonde hair had escaped her kerchief. She looked like a tired, older Anna—a lot older, I realized, seeing her so bedraggled.

"Are you sure you want to entertain us?" Maria asked. She walked forward to hug Solomonida. "You're exhausted, poor thing. Tell me quickly: how is Seryozha?"

"He's fine." Solomonida returned the hug, then moved to me. She smelled of milk and sweat. "I look terrible because I spent the night fussing over him, for no good reason except that I lost every one of his half-brothers without warning." Which seemed like a good reason to me, but I said nothing, because Solomonida was still talking. "He slept—not through the night, because he's not old enough, but for three hours at a stretch. I stayed in the nursery with him, worrying myself into a frenzy. Anna's with him now. But I'm glad you're here. I invited you, remember?"

"And what of Anfim?" Maria asked.

"He's well. He returned after dark and left early this morning, but he stopped by the nursery long enough to tell me that once the council session ends on Friday, he can spend more time at home. Having him nearby will calm my nerves." She stopped and ran a hand across her brow. "Listen to me, I'm babbling. Go upstairs, and I'll change my dress and join you as soon as I can. Anna and Lara will be happy to see you, and I look forward to chatting with you. I haven't seen a soul from outside my own household in days."

We climbed the inner stairs to the nursery, where we found Anna rocking her baby brother in his cradle, singing a lullaby. Lara, her ten-year-old stepsister, sat nearby with a pen and a single piece of paper. From the way she scrunched up her nose and bent over her work, I guessed she was preparing for tomorrow's lessons.

"Sums or history?" I asked her. Father Job, who once taught me, had been educating Lara and her younger brother Tolya—the same Tolya who received my tales with such joy—several days a week for the last three years.

"Sums." She looked up just long enough to answer my question. "Father Job is due this afternoon. I want to finish these before he gets here. Besides, I'd much rather do sums than history."

"I know," I told her. "And your brother is the opposite. I started a new story for him, but it's a long way from done." I glanced around the room. "I don't see him, though. Where is he?"

"Playing with the dog. Auntie Darya and Uncle Niki decided Laika should live here from now on, because Tolya spends much more time with her than they do. She arrived yesterday." Lara peered at her paper, touching the numbers one by one as if adding them in her head.

I didn't want to be the reason she failed to complete her schoolwork on time, so I turned my attention to Anna, seated next to the cradle on the side of the room as far from the window as possible. I didn't feel the slightest draft, but I could imagine

Solomonida, in her anxiety, wanting to keep the baby in the room's warmest spot.

"Sweet darling baby," my friend crooned. "Don't lie near the edge of the bed, or a gray wolf will grab you ..."

Despite the pretty tune, I cringed. I'd never understood why mothers singing a child to sleep warned of wolves prowling in the night eager to drag infants off to the woods and devour them. Seryozha was too young for nightmares or even to understand the verses, but still, why not sing of fragrant gardens filled with fountains and fruit trees? I hummed the tune, thinking of some of the Persian poetry I loved and wondering if the words would fit. My stepmother, Juliana, made up her own songs, but she had a beautiful voice and a talent for the lute. I could lay claim to neither. I could translate verses for others to sing, though.

Anna looked up and smiled before gesturing with her free hand at the bench near the stove, inviting us to sit. I removed my coat and took my place there. My sister, too, stripped off her outerwear and hung it near the stove to dry, then sat in the room's one armchair.

When we both looked at Anna expectantly, she ended her song, although she continued to rock the cradle with her foot. "Does Mama know you're here?" she asked, keeping her voice low.

"We ran into her on the second floor," Maria said. "She seemed a bit ... distracted. Is your brother all right?"

Anna beckoned, and Maria moved to stand over the cradle. With a soft sigh, my sister bent and pressed her palm gently against the baby's cheek and forehead. "Yes, he's sleeping normally, with no signs of fever," she said, and I heard relief in her voice. "And the nursemaid?"

"One of those winter ailments." Anna stilled the cradle. "She felt miserable for a few days, but she's back on her feet now and will return to work tomorrow. None of the other maids have fallen ill, so I think Agasha must have caught the sickness elsewhere. You're here in response to Mama's invitation?"

"Yes," I said. "And to find out what you've learned from Anfim about the bride show, since he's involved in the planning."

"He hasn't said much yet." Anna resumed her gentle rocking with one foot. "They're checking the old records to see how it was done last time, but so far they've only found the plans for the wedding ceremony itself."

"The grannies will remember," Maria said. "It must have been the high point of their lives." She grinned at us. "Some people are more excited at the thought of marrying a ruler than you two are."

Before Anna or I could come up with a reply, Solomonida arrived, her dress and hair restored to their usual neatness. Only the strain on her face spoke of her restless night. She poured cups of sweet, spiced cider, warm and fragrant, and passed around a basket containing golden-brown cakes, light as puffed air. Maria offered her the central chair, but Solomonida refused; after a quick examination of the sleeping baby, she took a seat near the window.

A brief exchange of pleasantries followed, then a summary of yesterday's visit from Papa. That led Solomonida to say, "Anna told me about your offer to act as sponsor, Maria. Of course, I'm happy to accept. It will be a big help to have someone as highly connected as you at Anna's side."

"My pleasure," Maria said. "I've stayed away from the court for too long. It's time I got back in the game—not just for Anna but on Alexei's and Lyuba's behalf as well. This is the perfect opportunity. But fill me in. What have you heard from your friends?"

Solomonida traced an intricate pattern against the frosted mica pane, as if doing so focused her thoughts. "That the person we most need to worry about is the tsar's grandmother. Have you much acquaintance with her? Anfim says that she and her sons have strengthened their influence over young Ivan in the last few months."

Maria sipped from her cup, then placed it on the floor beside her chair. "I don't. When I last visited her daughter, Princess Anna was not welcome at court. But Alexei says the same: that the tsar has made his peace with his relatives over the last six months, especially his grandmother."

"My husband believes the tsar will soon appoint his uncle Mikhail master of horse," Solomonida added. "The idea is to raise the status of the Glinsky clan in advance of the coronation by proclaiming royal support for them."

"Have the Glinskys already won, then?" I asked, remembering yesterday's conversation. "Alexei and Maria thought the main battle would be fought between the Shuisky princes and the Glinskys, with the other clans watching for a chance to benefit from their rivals' conflict."

"They haven't won, but it strengthens their side," Maria said. "Which is good news for you, since it makes the Shuiskys' task harder—and perhaps for Anna as well, because the tsar's grandmother still considers Semyon Kolychev a villain of the worst sort."

Solomonida wrinkled her nose in a moue of disgust at the mention of her long-dead and unlamented first husband. "Semyon *was* a villain of the worst sort—and a traitor as well. I'm astonished that Cousin Igor even dared put our Anna's name on the list."

I glanced at Anna, wondering at her silence. This was, after all, her father being discussed. She stared at her baby brother, whose cradle she still rocked gently with her foot. I hoped she wasn't brooding about her absent Yuri, but there wasn't much I could do about it if she was.

"I'd guess Igor knows nothing about that," Maria said. "It was hushed up at the time, remember? But it may come back to haunt both him and Papa, because the tsar's grandmother and uncles won't have forgotten what Semyon did—or the rumors that he acted at my father's behest."

This last comment caught Anna's attention, and mine too. "Did he?" I gasped. "Solomonida didn't tell us *that* bit last summer."

"He did," Maria said. "I'll share the whole story when we get home. But it's true that Semyon took his orders from Papa. That's not the only reason the Glinskys hate our family, but it's the main reason."

Shocked by the news that my father might have masterminded a scheme to kidnap the grand prince, then three years old, and his even younger brother—and that my beloved sister had kept Papa's secret for more than a decade!—I lost track of the conversation for a while. I had long since accepted that my father cared only for his own well-being, but convincing himself that committing a crime against the crown could advance his interests? That bordered on insanity.

Anna, perhaps less affected by the news because she had already come to terms with her own father's villainy, rallied first. "Who else will be involved in the selection?" she asked, pulling me out of my mental fog. "Besides Anna Glinskaya, that is."

"Princess Anastasia Petrovna," Solomonida said. "She's Tsar Ivan's first cousin, so she will play a role in selecting his bride. Nadezhda Shuiskaya is close to Anastasia. The pair of them will be promoting candidates favored by the Shuisky clan, including Lyuba."

I gritted my teeth at that news. "The Shuiskys have more than one candidate, then?" I asked. Timur had suggested they might, but Solomonida sounded as if she had specific information.

"Two others, at least," she said. "Fetinya Blednaya and Ustinya Paletskaya."

Both princesses. I brightened. Although … "Ivan would never pick Fetinya. She looks like a stick with large teeth, and acts like one too." That was mean but true. "But Ustinya's a beauty, and when she wants something, she usually doesn't rest until she gets it."

"She *is* lovely," Anna said. "Although she can be cruel."

"Only with other girls, though," I pointed out. "The boyars' wives will never see that side of her."

"Assuming she wants to wed the tsar." Anna stopped rocking the cradle and picked up her embroidery, sliding her blue-threaded needle through the cloth with an ease I couldn't help but envy.

"I believe she does," Solomonida said. "Nadezhda thinks so, in any case, and she's Ustinya's sponsor."

"Is she? How odd." Maria paused, frowning, then finished, "I thought her husband died a few months ago. It seems rather soon for her to sponsor anyone."

Solomonida rose to check on her sleeping son, speaking over her shoulder as she bent over the cradle. "She doesn't mourn that dreadful man, and she's spent enough time pretending to grieve to satisfy the gossips. Nor is this her first foray back into society. Gavriil Vorontsov told me before he retreated to his country estate two months ago that he'd run into her at her nephew's wedding—chatting with your father, of all people."

"Papa?" Maria and I said at the same time.

"Why would she chat with Papa?" Maria added.

"No idea," Solomonida said. "It was news to me that they'd ever spoken, especially since her husband had much to do with your father's disgrace. But from what Gavriil told me, they seemed quite friendly."

I suppressed another groan. Just my luck to have my fate hang on the actions of a woman desperate enough to flirt with Papa!

My sister frowned. "That's not good. He'll have filled her ears with how much he wants a royal marriage for his darling Lyuba. I'll have to approach her carefully, in that case."

"She'll still put Ustinya first." Solomonida paused for a moment, then spoke again. "Why not ask Nadezhda to introduce Lyuba and Anna to Anastasia Petrovna? If you can convince Anastasia that our girls are not well suited to the position of royal wife, you may get them eliminated as candidates before the bride show even begins. Your father will complain, no doubt, but Nadezhda won't. It will make her life easier if she can focus her attention on Ustinya."

"Good idea," Maria said. "I'll try to arrange that."

Solomonida refilled our cups before returning to her seat at the window. "Who else can we call on?" she asked as she resumed her seat.

"Katya Vorontsova," Maria said. Katya was the wife of Anna's detested cousin Igor. "She hasn't forgiven her husband for taking part in her family's disgrace. Her Aunt Liza would be an excellent ally, higher-ranking as well as more forceful and straightforward. She's kept her distance from the court since Demid's death, though. I can hardly blame her for that. They'd been married thirty years ..."

She let the sentence trail off, but I filled in the missing words. Liza was the aunt of Anna's Yuri, and her husband had been beheaded during the same incident that led to Yuri's banishment and forced tonsure. It was a miracle that Yuri hadn't suffered the same fate as his uncle.

Anna winced at this reminder of her sorrow and jabbed at her hapless embroidery as if the linen could fight back. I reached out a hand to console her, but I sat too far away for the gesture to have a real impact.

"Liza might appreciate the distraction," Solomonida said, breaking the awkward silence. "And she has plans to sponsor the two Morozov girls—those nieces of hers who look like twins. But her influence at court doesn't extend to the Glinsky faction. They've benefited from her husband's death."

Maria nodded. "True. Let's stick with Anastasia Petrovna and Nadezhda Shuiskaya for now—and Katya Vorontsova, of course, since she's a friend."

"I'll approach Katya, shall I?" Solomonida gestured at the cradle as she spoke. "I'll take Seryozha with me. Even Cousin Igor can't complain about two new mothers sharing baby stories."

"I'll send a message to Nadezhda Shuiskaya." Maria shifted her attention to me and Anna. "While I wait for her to respond, I'll train you two in court protocol. You'll need new clothes as well. I remember the fuss my mother-in-law made about even my best robes not being suitable for royalty. I was fuming by the time she left." She laughed at the memory and held up her right hand, thumb and forefinger separated by a hair's breadth. "She made me feel about this big, but when I walked into the Terem Palace, I realized she was right."

"Anfim knows the silk merchants." Solomonida rubbed the cuff of her sleeve between her fingers, as if in illustration. "There's a lovely Italian who comes up from Caffa every year. And we still have bales of cloth from Bukhara and Samarkand—"

Just as she reached that point, her steward appeared at the door, most apologetic, to announce the arrival of none other than Cousin Igor.

Leaving Lara in charge of the sleeping baby, the rest of us went downstairs to the sitting room on the main floor. I assumed that Anna's cousin wanted to see her and her mother, not Maria and me—in Igor's mind, I was a rival candidate set on undermining his plans. But Solomonida asked us to accompany her and Anna, so Maria accepted. I had nothing to do but tag along, although I looked forward to seeing Igor squirm when we walked in.

And squirm he did. In fact, he shied like a startled horse when we followed Solomonida through the door, then cast a dismayed glance at his leather riding trousers and plain caftan. The outfit was far below his usual standards—probably a misguided attempt to put Solomonida in her place by showing he had no desire to impress her with his clothing—although his brimmed hat, which he removed and set to one side as we arrived, sported a wide band of sky-blue brocade adorned with exotic birds flitting amid wispy clouds and a long feather dyed to match. I imagined him preening before the mirror, congratulating himself on having chosen a color that complemented his chestnut hair and blue eyes. A few fingers' width above medium height, Igor had a well-proportioned body and a face that would please anyone who failed to notice how often his expression tended toward petulant or supercilious.

At this moment, however, he appeared mostly embarrassed, like a boy caught with his hand in the sweets. In this guise, he bore little resemblance to the man who (with Papa's help) had committed outright fraud in an attempt to steal his cousin's estate, then spent the last year threatening, extorting, and manipulating them to surrender it voluntarily. Watching him, I could only wonder what new scheme lay fermenting in his fertile brain.

"Tsarevna Maria," he said with an audible gulp. "I didn't expect to encounter you here." After a brief pause, he added, "Nor Lyubov Fyodorovna, of course." He bowed first to my sister, then to me.

"Igor Grigorevich Bezzubtsev," Solomonida proclaimed before Maria had a chance to reply. "What an unexpected pleasure." Her sarcastic tone undercut any hint of welcome, although she returned his bow with one every bit as sketchy. He scowled, a reaction she ignored. "You haven't deigned to visit me since I married. What brings you here?"

His cheeks flushed, and he didn't reply at first. Then he said, "I came to speak with you and your daughter about the bride show. Perhaps I should return at another time."

"I am here." Anna took two steps forward, clasped her hands together, and dipped her head—to remind him of his manners, I assumed, since he could have acknowledged her at any time since we entered the room. "But I see no reason for a private discussion. Lyuba's father has entered her in the bride show as well. You can speak in front of her and her sister."

Igor looked as if he'd like to protest, but Maria forestalled him by crossing the room and taking a seat near the window. I followed her, and as one we turned to face Solomonida, Anna, and their visitor. Now he had to choose between saying his piece before company; offending Maria, who outranked him; or leaving and gambling that Solomonida would admit him if he tried to return. I watched, fascinated and taking mental notes for a future story, while he wrestled with his various options. If I was right about his character, he would choose to go on rather than take the chance of insulting Maria, even obliquely, or putting himself in a position where he would risk facing rejection from someone he saw as beneath him.

It didn't take him long to decide. With a swirl of his caftan, he settled himself near the stove. *Good.* I had accurately predicted his behavior. Solomonida and Anna found places on a high-backed bench placed at an angle that allowed them to easily engage with all their guests. The four of us women gazed expectantly at Igor, and after some awkward shuffling of his feet, he said, "I have received an offer for Anna's hand from Prince Pavel Ilich Shuisky."

A shocked murmur ran around the room. This was the last thing I had anticipated, and I had to assume the others felt the same way. It wasn't Pavel Shuisky's proposal that surprised me: the bumptious fool had shown an interest in my friend since the moment they met. But why had Igor decided to start his conversation about the bride show with that?

"And did you accept?" Solomonida asked, her voice even tarter than before. "You seem to have lost all sense of direction. First you entered Anna in the bride show, even though you knew she was already contracted. You did that without consulting her stepfather and me, which was at best improper. You obviously have not considered how the senior members of the royal family will react when they learn you have concealed the truth of her betrothal from them. And now you are entertaining an offer from Prince Pavel?"

"That contract won't stand." Igor flicked his fingers across the cuff of his tunic, as if brushing the unwanted document aside. "And I haven't accepted Prince Pavel's offer *yet*. We will all benefit if Anna succeeds in obtaining the tsar's favor." He leaned toward Maria with what could be construed as an apologetic expression. "Forgive me, Tsarevna. We need that boon more than your sister, now that Solomonida has chosen to marry beneath her station."

Maria's lips twitched, and a gurgle escaped her throat. I could guess why. Forget the fact that neither Anna nor I wanted that "boon." Did Igor honestly believe that our father would step aside in response to a plea from the competition? Papa had been planning for this moment since the year I turned two!

After a quick glance at my sister, I stared straight ahead, because otherwise we would both burst out laughing. Igor, however, had already returned his gaze to Anna and her mother. "I wanted to assure Anna that I have her best interests at heart," he said glibly. "Should she fail to attract the tsar, I have another eager bridegroom waiting for my consent."

Anna pressed her lips together in a stubborn line and didn't speak.

Her self-control impressed me, I had to admit. I knew Pavel Shuisky repelled her as much as he did me.

"How farsighted of you, cousin," Solomonida said. Again, her tone contradicted her words. "Anfim and I will discuss Prince Pavel's offer." How to circumvent it, more like. I'd heard her express her opinion of the prince more than once—and never favorably. "But you cannot dismiss her existing betrothal so cursorily. Gavriil Vorontsov has refused to abrogate the contract you both signed. The tsar has yet to make his selection. In fairness to Prince Pavel, you should have refused his offer—or, better yet, referred him to us."

Igor waved a careless hand. "Such objections are meaningless. I have already stated my intention to await the outcome of the bride show. As for the prior agreement, Yuri Gavriilovich's enforced tonsure means that he cannot fulfill its terms, as his father must acknowledge someday. And you and your ingrate of a husband cannot oppose your daughter's union with a prince from the most powerful clan in the Russian lands, then claim you have her best interests at heart. No one will believe you."

My hands clenched with the yearning to throttle him, even though he was not my cousin or threatening to wed *me* to a titled nincompoop.

I could only imagine Anna's fury. Her self-control held, though. She glared at him yet somehow maintained her silence.

While I fumed, Solomonida responded in the same chilly voice. "We'll see about that. In the meantime, have you any advice on how Anna might succeed on this quest you have devised for her? To attract the tsar, I mean."

Igor rose from his seat, unruffled by her challenge. "Why, no. I leave the details to you, cousin. Now that you understand the options available, I feel certain you will make the right choice. I'd prefer an alliance with the tsar, but Prince Pavel will suit me as well. So think carefully before you decide where to focus your efforts." He strode from the room, leaving Solomonida sputtering, Anna doing a better imitation of a thundercloud than I'd ever seen from her, Maria shaking her head, and myself subject to a certain unwilling admiration.

Papa had tried to rein me in with a similar threat, but his had been less specific and therefore less effective. The prospect of a life-time with either the soon-to-be Tsar Ivan or Prince Pavel Shuisky was enough to give a girl nightmares.

Chapter 5

"A beautiful sorceress appeared"

Three days after our visit to Solomonida and Anna, I joined Maria in her sitting room. She had almost completed work on her daughter's robe, and I was deep into my tale about the village attacked by a dragon. The peasant elders had already decided that only an epic knight could meet this challenge, and the fairest maiden in the community had volunteered to seek out a suitable hero and bend him to her will. The sorcerer had yet to make his appearance, but I had strewn hints in the form of unwise deeds committed by the villagers. They had taken over a sacred wood and felled some of its trees for lumber. Sorcerers are busy creatures, after all; they don't have time to waste attacking sober citizens. Their victims must first draw attention to themselves by flouting natural law or, at a minimum, showing disrespect for the sorcerer's feelings and power.

I was congratulating myself on having most of the pieces in place and looking forward to introducing knight and maiden when the sound of sleigh bells and horses in the courtyard brought me to my feet. Only a quick grab kept my quill from scattering ink droplets across the paper. I ran to the window, silently thanking my brother-in-law once again for the inspired decision to replace the original translucent panes with glass. Unlike in my father's house or Solomonida's, here a person could actually see through the windows.

"Who is it?" Maria asked.

"I can't tell." The window didn't open, so I pressed my face as close as I dared to the glass. "I see a large sleigh pulled by four horses, and two smaller sleds behind it. One carries baggage, I think; it's completely covered by a cloth. The other must hold people, but it's not so fancy as the big one—servants, perhaps?"

"But you don't know who's in the main sleigh? We'd best go downstairs then." Maria set her sewing aside and headed for the door.

"You weren't expecting visitors, were you?" I stood on tiptoe, but that changed nothing. The sleigh had stopped next to the outside staircase, and the roof blocked the passengers from view. "I wonder who it can be."

My sister didn't answer, and when I glanced over my shoulder, I discovered she had left the room. I rushed after her, racing down the steps and colliding with Timur as I reached the bottom.

He steadied me, laughing. "Whoa. Where are you off to in such a hurry?"

Over the last few days, I'd become accustomed to the sight of him, but moments like this, when he stood right next to me—indeed, his hand touched my waist—still brought the heat to my cheeks. "We have guests," I said, breathless from my dash down the stairs—or his proximity. "Maria's gone to greet them, but we don't yet know who they are."

"A fancy couple in Polish dress." He released his hold on my waist and stepped back, and I quashed a ripple of regret. "I don't recognize the man," he added. "But the woman looks like that hussy who ran off with my father, then married yours." I heard distaste in his voice, an emotion I'd once shared.

"Juliana and Felix!" Without a second thought, I grabbed his hand and pulled. "Come on, we must go and greet them. I can't imagine what brings them here, but I'm glad they came."

He dug in his heels. "You're glad to see your stepmother? I thought you detested her. And her name is Roxelana."

"I did, and it was," I said, unable to contain my impatience. "But then she converted to Catholicism and divorced Papa. She goes by Juliana now. Didn't your father tell you?"

"Not a word. And you say they divorced? I thought 'till death do you part' was the rule for Christians." His eyes sparkled with wicked amusement, as they always did when he caught others in an act of hypocrisy.

I didn't want to explain right then. "It's a long story," I said, "and I promise I'll share the whole thing with you later. For now, let's go. We don't want to keep Maria waiting."

"Really? What's so urgent that you can't spare half an hour?"

"I'll happily give you as long as it takes." I tugged at him again. "After we're done here."

I braced myself for more resistance. He was clearly set on being difficult, although I couldn't imagine why. There was a long pause in which he studied me with an unreadable expression. Then he shrugged and tightened his grip on my hand. "Lead the way, Lady Love," he said in Tatar.

I stared at him, speechless. My name—Lyuba, short for Lyubov—means "love" in Russian, as he well knew. But he hadn't used my name or the Russian for "lady." Instead, he'd translated the whole phrase—*soyarké khatun*—as if he were flirting with me.

Or needling me. He'd done that often enough when we were children—calling me "Goose," for example, even though he knew it irritated me.

I sighed. Yes, needling was much more likely.

"You do still understand Tatar?" he asked, switching back to Russian. I remembered the mischievous look in his eyes all too well.

As I opened my mouth to retort "of course," I thought better of it. Letting him know that his jabs got under my skin would only encourage him to continue. "Well enough," I said in Tatar. "Now stop stalling, or we'll miss half the conversation."

Without waiting for a reply, I set off with a determined stride. He kept pace with me without effort, and after the first few steps I slowed down. I noticed he didn't release my hand.

Only when we reached the sitting-room door did Timur let go. He straightened the upright collar of his robe and gazed down at me. "You got your wish, *soyarké*. We're here. Now what?"

"We go in, of course." I waved at the door, but he merely produced an elaborate flourish with his arm, like a Polish courtier.

"Ladies first," he said, grinning at me in a way that made me want to poke him in the ribs, just to see him squirm. But I wasn't nine years old anymore, so I raised my chin in the queenly manner my sister carried off with such perfection and opened the door.

"Not bad, *soyarké*. We may make a khan's wife of you yet." The whispered comment, delivered in Tatar, ruffled my composure anew, but I gritted my teeth, ignored his teasing, and preceded him into the room.

"There you are," Maria said as I entered. "And you brought Timur. Good. I was about to send Tanya to fetch you both. Look who just arrived from Cracow!"

The room contained four people besides Timur and myself: my sister and Alexei, Juliana and Felix. I don't know what I'd expected, but our guests looked the same as they had on their visit three years ago. They were sumptuously dressed in the Polish style, and Tanya had already borne away their hats and cloaks. Juliana, who must have reached her early thirties, was as stunning as ever

—slender and graceful, her dark hair coiled at the nape of her neck, her brown eyes gleaming, and the scars from her bout with smallpox barely visible. Lord Felix, gray eyes alight in his mobile, clever face, leaned on his cane, a detail that suggested my conversation with Timur had taken much less time than I'd thought. Our guests had not been in the room long enough for Felix to sit. I went to each of them in turn and embraced them, then retreated far enough that I could observe both our guests and my sister and brother-in-law.

Timur had followed me in and stopped at my right shoulder. I heard him draw in his breath as he caught sight of Juliana. "Lady Juliana Ossolinska," I told him, "and her husband, Lord Felix Ossolinski." I turned my attention to Juliana and Felix. "Congratulations on your marriage. It took place last year, did it not?"

"Thank you," Juliana said. "Yes, last year, not long before Advent. And who is your companion?"

"Timur." I extended my right hand toward him as I spoke his name. "Alexei's son. He was in Kasimov when you visited us before, but you will remember him, Juliana, from boyhood."

She regarded him with her head tipped to one side. "Alexei's son, but not Maria's? Yes, that must be so. I've seen Maria's son, and he's eight or nine …"

That thought must have tripped her memory, because she smacked her closed fan against her palm. "Oh, of course! You're Guzel's boy. Your uncle brought you to Moscow for your father's wedding, and after that you lived here for a while. Such a handsome lad, the spitting image of Alexei! I should have recognized you right away."

She glanced at my brother-in-law then, and although I sensed nothing lascivious in her manner, the familiarity with which she regarded him revealed how long and intimately they'd known each other.

Turning my head toward Timur, I marked the tight corners of his mouth and the set to his shoulders. His mother blamed Juliana for taking Alexei away from his family, and with good reason. There was another story I must put in writing one day.

I touched Timur's wrist to convey sympathy, and he glanced at me. His rather grim expression dissolved into a smile, but when he returned his attention to the group, he still radiated hostility. Lord Felix regarded us with a thoughtful, steady gaze, and I wondered what he made of the connection, such as it was, between his wife and Alexei.

"Yes," Timur said to the silent room. "Guzel's boy. I still remember the day you left the camp with *Ata*, riding a white horse." I heard the edge to his voice and saw Juliana wince. Maybe Timur noticed as well, because he continued in a more even tone. "But that was a long time ago, and much has changed since."

"Well said." Lord Felix leaned rather more heavily on his cane, making it possible for him to manage a cursory bow. "A pleasure to meet you, Prince Timur. And to see you again, Lyubov Fyodorovna. You've become a young lady since we last visited the Russian lands."

"Call me Lyuba, Lord Felix," I said. "You always did before."

"If you drop the 'lord,' I will," he promised. A flicker of pain crossed his face, hastily suppressed, and I thought of the long hours he had spent stuck in a carriage and the number of steps he'd climbed to reach this floor. Both must have strained his injured leg.

I was searching for a way to invite him to sit without usurping my sister's role as hostess when Maria took over. She pointed to the sofas that lined the room, their vermilion cushions mirroring the carpet and wall hangings. "Please, make yourselves comfortable. There's no need for us to stand around as if we were attending a royal audience. Tanya is supervising the preparation of a room for you; then she will return with bread and salt to welcome you to our home and refreshments to help you recover from your journey. Did you stop even once after Smolensk?"

"In Vyazma, overnight." Juliana slipped a hand under Felix's elbow and, with an unobtrusive skill I could only admire, lowered him to the nearest cushion, then sat next to him on the sofa. "That still meant four full days in the sleigh, with only a few hours' rest at the posting station. And the beds were execrable, lumpy and thin, even for our ambassadorial party. Neither damp nor flea-ridden, though, so I suppose we must be grateful for small mercies."

While Maria murmured empathetic phrases, Timur ushered me to the farthest corner, leaving the section opposite our guests for my sister and Alexei. Our portion of the sofa was just wide enough for two, and I could easily participate in the conversation. "I would love to visit you someday," I said when Maria finished. "What a journey that must be! And I've heard that Cracow is lovely. But what made you leave Poland for Moscow?"

Tanya came in then, cutting off any answer they might have made. Of medium height, with a stocky frame, blue eyes, and blonde hair fading to gray, she no longer bore much resemblance to the beauty who had once adorned the harem of Alexei's father, but her competence as a housekeeper was unparalleled. She carried a large platter holding a ring of bread, formed in such a way that a bowl of salt could be arranged at its center. Behind her came servants bearing platters of smoked salmon and white sturgeon, a bowl of black caviar, and an array of jugs—some emitting herbal-scented steam, and others glistening with condensation from the icehouse. The men laid out their offerings on the sideboard closest to the door while maids arrived with linen napkins and brightly painted cups, then waited as Tanya bowed in front of Lord Felix.

Maria joined them, and Alexei stood beside her. "Welcome to our home," he said.

"Your presence brings us joy," Maria added, and they both bowed as she reached the last word.

Felix dipped his head in response. Having visited Moscow before, he knew to rip off a portion of the loaf, dip it in the salt, and eat it. "Your hospitality honors me," he said once the bread had slid down his throat. My sister and brother-in-law then repeated the ritual with Juliana, who not only echoed her husband's words but rose to her feet and curtseyed.

Watching her graceful performance of a gesture never attempted in Russia except by foreigners—and female visitors from abroad were rare indeed—I sighed. Whatever happened between me and Timur, I could never equal Juliana in the arts of seduction. I wouldn't know where to start.

A thought occurred to me, and I perked up. *Why not make the sorcerer in my tale a sorceress? Who better to ensnare the hero with her wiles?*

And with that, I relaxed against the cushions, observing Juliana with great interest and taking mental notes all the while.

By the time Tanya and the servants left, having seen us well supplied with food and drink, I'd remembered that, as the youngest person present, I should keep quiet while my sister and brother-in-law directed the conversation. And direct it they did, covering many of the major developments of the last three years.

Some of it was interesting. For example, I found it curious and rather touching that Juliana, who had earlier demonstrated her lack of interest in children by struggling to recall Timur, admitted to informally adopting a niece of Felix's. The seven-year-old, named Klara, had lost her mother in childbirth.

That was the high point. Contrast it with a long, meandering discussion about life on the Ossolinski estates and the relative merits of wheat versus rye, which left me yearning for news of a wicked scandal among the servants or, failing that, a pair of tiny sticks to prop open my eyes. Only the occasional sideways glance at Timur, whose fixed stare suggested I was not alone in my boredom, kept me in my seat.

I was pondering excuses that would justify a quick exit when Maria at last revived the topic I'd raised eons ago. "But we never got an answer to Lyuba's question," she said as the wheat/rye comparison limped to its pitiful close. "What lured you away from your rural paradise and caused you to undertake this arduous journey to Moscow?"

"I see we've given you the wrong impression," Juliana replied in that smooth way of hers. "We do still travel. We wintered in Bari last year and brought Queen Bona Sforza news of her homeland on our return. And we left the countryside for Cracow in October—without Klara, since the court is no fun for a child. It could be six months or more before we get back to the estates. I hate to leave her with her other aunt and uncle for so long, but my first duty is to Felix."

A very neat avoidance of the question. I sent Juliana a silent tip of the hat—her deviousness, as ever, both amused and repelled me—and bit back the urge to demand more information.

Alexei, who harbored even fewer illusions about Juliana than the rest of us, stepped into the breach. "That leaves it up to you, Felix. Do you not trust us to keep a secret?"

Put like that, it was a difficult request to refuse. Felix could offend his host or provide an answer. I sent Timur another sideways glance, inviting him to share my appreciation of his father's straightforward approach, and felt my insides warm as I realized he'd been watching me. The corners of his mouth tipped up, and I returned his smile without a second thought. I knew from the heat in my cheeks that I must be blushing yet again. That tingle in my stomach had strengthened as well. I could only hope no one would notice.

"It's not a secret," Felix said. "King Sigismund and Queen Bona asked us to accompany the envoys. News of the bride show didn't reach us until we got to Vyazma, but rumors that it would take place have circulated in Cracow for months. I'm sure it won't surprise you to hear that Russia's neighbors are eager to find out which clan will come out on top. It could make the difference between peace and war."

"I suspected as much." Alexei's lips curved—in gratitude for the honest response, I assumed. "There's little I can tell you at present, however. I mean that literally, not in the sense of government restrictions on what I can say. The battle lines have not yet been drawn, although Fyodor Koshkin has ensured that Lyuba's name appears on the list of potential brides."

Juliana scrunched her beautiful face into an expression of dislike. "That goes without saying. He's been plotting paths to the position of royal father-in-law from the moment we met."

"Oh, much longer than that," Maria said. "He tried to marry me off to the current ruler's uncle when I was seventeen, in the belief that he could bring about a change of rule. And what trouble that caused!"

"Now there's a story I'd like to hear," Juliana said.

I understood her reaction. It was a great tale, one I'd heard myself only a day ago—the reason for his long-ago plot with Anna's father, which had alienated the Glinsky family and might yet save me from marriage to the tsar. It would definitely form the heart of my family saga someday.

Juliana was still talking, though, so I didn't interrupt her. "He never mentioned his plans for you, but he did talk about a wedding between Lyuba and Grand Prince Ivan and how fortunate it was that they were so close in age. I suppose Koshkin has support from the Shuisky clan? He's been their toady for the last decade."

"Tsar," Alexei corrected her. "Ivan will be crowned tsar next month."

She nodded. "I'll try to remember, at least while I'm here. I doubt our king and queen will accept Ivan's new title. It sounds too much like a grab for power. But what of the Shuiskys? Will they back Koshkin? That might guarantee Lyuba's selection."

Quaking at the thought, I pressed my palms against the sofa, secure in the knowledge that they lay hidden beneath my skirt. Timur slid his hand under the silk and clasped my fingers. Eager not to draw attention to myself, I kept my eyes fixed on the company, but his gesture comforted me.

"As I said, it's hard to tell who supports whom at this point." Alexei shrugged. From watching past conversations like this one, I could predict that he would not reveal privileged information, however amenable he appeared. Juliana must know that, too. "Only a few candidates from the center have been named. The provinces have yet to report. The Shuiskys *may* back Koshkin, but they are a large and powerful clan. They already have other clients' daughters in the contest. Your ex-husband may not be the man they choose to advance."

"And the Shuiskys have enemies, including some in the royal family, who will want to stop them from securing the ultimate prize of a marital alliance with the ruler," Felix said. "Isn't that how the game is played?"

Maria laughed. "You think the bride show has rules?" she asked. "If so, they must change on a whim. Which is, you must admit, exactly the kind of game my father loves to play."

"And what of Lyuba?" Juliana looked my way, and I hastily pressed my lips, which I only then realized I'd parted in fascination, together. "Is that what *you* want, Lyuba—to become the first tsaritsa of Russia?"

"Not in the least." I tried to keep my tone as level as Alexei's, although Timur undermined that effort by tightening his grip on my hand. I prayed that the rest of the company would attribute my blazing cheeks to discomfort at being caught off-guard by Juliana's question. "But Papa has announced his intention to marry me off this year no matter what, so I fear I may escape a wedding to the tsar only to end up with someone even worse than that Prince Pavel who's offered for my friend Anna Kolycheva. You met her during your last visit."

Juliana frowned, as if struggling to recall my friend. "I did," she said after a short pause. "The blonde girl who lived in the Sheremetev house. By Our Lady, she's even younger than you: what's the rush? And who's Prince Pavel?"

"Ilya Shuisky's older son." I didn't correct her about Anna's age. Although we were only five months apart, Anna always *seemed* younger, because she was so quiet and deferential.

"That rapist," Juliana hissed. "The things he did to me while I was under arrest at his house. If Tsaritsa Sumbeka hadn't intervened …"

She left the sentence unfinished. I stared at her, nonplussed. How could Prince Pavel have raped anyone? He was a boy when Juliana left Russia.

Alexei regarded her with a slight frown. "You're being obscure, Juliana. By 'that rapist,' I assume you mean Ilya, not Pavel."

"Yes, of course," Juliana snapped. "But imagine what such a father would teach his son. I wouldn't let Pavel near Anna, if she were my daughter." Felix reached for her hand, a sympathetic expression on his face.

I was still absorbing this new information when Juliana spoke again, looking straight at my sister. "We must intervene, Maria, don't you think?"

"Without a doubt," my sister said. "Solomonida and her new husband are already looking for a solution. Meanwhile, Anna's cousin Igor has nominated her for the bride show as well, and he will force Prince Pavel to wait for a decision. She's also betrothed to Gavriil Vorontsov's youngest son, although that may not come to pass—another long story. Let's discuss it later."

At that moment, Tanya returned to announce that the visitors' chambers were ready, and Timur and I took the opportunity to slip away.

We went no farther than Alexei's study. There I headed for a distant corner of the room, behind a freestanding bookshelf, where we could sit in the window seat and achieve a measure of privacy without appearing secretive. Timur had released my hand when I rose from the sofa in the living room, and I'd kept my arms crossed at my waist during the walk to avoid even the semblance of impropriety, but as I settled onto the cushioned bench I let my palm rest on the sill. He sat next to me and did the same. Our fingertips touched. He raised an eyebrow at me—inviting me to explain why I'd brought us here, I assumed.

"You wanted to know when my feelings changed toward my stepmother," I reminded him.

"I do," he confirmed. "But forgive me, she doesn't seem much different—except when she dropped that shocking revelation about Prince Ilya. And the bit about adopting a daughter, I suppose, although I notice she left the child in Poland."

I studied him. I had no reason to believe he felt anything but dislike for the woman he'd known as Roxelana. Yet I hadn't forgotten how seductive she could be. So, feeling somewhat foolish, I asked, "She doesn't appeal to you, then? Most men fall at her feet and worship her because of her beauty."

69

"Oh, please!" He leaned against the wall, openly laughing at me. "She was my father's mistress, back when I was six. Why would I fall for an old woman that *Ata* rejected when I can look at beautiful girls like you and Anna? Tell me why you've changed your mind about her, and how she came to divorce your father. Then we need never talk about her again."

His laughter told me he meant what he said, and the glow lit my heart once more. Indeed, I rather wished I'd never brought up the idea that Juliana had hidden depths.

But I had, so I should fulfill the promise I'd made. "I was eleven when they divorced, so I don't know the details. You'd already been living with your uncle Ogodai for two years the first time she came to Moscow with Felix. They weren't married then, although even at eleven I understood that he cared for her, and she for him. She looked different: she'd recovered from smallpox not long before, and the scars were still visible. Maria told me Juliana traveled as a man—"

"A *man*? Now that I can't envision." He leaned forward again, elbows on his knees, as if caught up in my tale.

"Yes, although she wasn't dressed in men's clothes when I saw her. We took turns reading from *The Conference of Birds*, and I realized she was far more intelligent and cultured than I'd believed when she was swanning round our house, taking jabs at everyone who crossed her path. It was the first time she treated me like a person instead of a nuisance. But Papa found out she was in Moscow. He tried to make her go back to him. I saw that myself; he stormed into the reception room—the same one where we were just now—and scared me witless, shouting and threatening her. Alexei threw him out—I'd never imagined your father had such a temper—and Juliana burst into tears. Maria sent me upstairs, and I don't know what happened after that. But the next morning, Juliana and Felix came in together ..." I let the sentence trail off as memory burst into full flower. That's when she told me I should ask Alexei and Maria to find me a husband who would love me for myself. Because …

"Go on," Timur said. "They came in together and?"

I heard concern in his voice. "I'm trying to recall her exact words," I told him. "She apologized for frightening me. I asked her if Papa had scared her—because he'd scared me—and she said Papa was a good man but incapable of separating what was right for others from what he wanted for himself. You have to admit that's insightful. And kind—if she really thought he was a good man, she wouldn't have asked for a divorce. So she must have wanted to spare my feelings."

He nodded. "I don't know your father well, but that fits what I've heard about him. What then?"

"She told me not to accept my father's choice but to ask Alexei and Maria to find a husband who would truly care for me. Shortly after that, Alexei arrived with the letter of divorce. He'd wangled it out of Papa somehow. I could hear Juliana singing, laughing, clapping her hands. She sounded happy—genuinely happy, like another person altogether. That's when I realized there was more to her than I'd believed."

He listened without interrupting, and that struck me too—not because it was atypical, like Juliana's behavior on the day of her divorce, but because it was what I'd come to expect from him. He'd learned the behavior from his father, probably; Alexei had the same gift of attentive silence. But amid the teasing and the competitiveness and the older brother know-it-all quality, which so often hid other elements of Timur's personality from view, I had always admired his capacity for stillness.

No, more than admired. I'd missed it. I'd missed *him*: the closeness we'd developed over those three magical years; the knowledge that one person in the house was my equal and my friend, ready to participate in any childhood adventure.

"And that was it?" he asked after a while.

"More or less," I said. "She left Moscow with Felix not long afterward. She was dressed as a man then, so I suppose Maria was right. They came back a year later, and from what I heard, she drove Anna's cousin Igor almost insane by flirting with him non-stop—quite deliberately, to get him to answer the same kind of questions she was asking today."

"So she hasn't changed *that* much." Timur grinned at me, as if challenging me to disprove it.

"No," I admitted. "Only now I know that her brittleness and manipulation are on the surface. She can act differently when she wants, and she feels more than she lets others see. And in her own way, she will help people she cares about."

"Let's hope she decides to help you, then. I don't like the situation you're facing." He stared at me for a moment, and I strove not to read too much into his last statement. While I searched for the right response, he patted my hand and rose. "I'd better find *Ata*, before he walks in and decides I'm courting you in defiance of his orders. Have a pleasant afternoon, *soyarké khatun*."

Hearing an odd note in his voice, I asked, "Why would your father decide you're courting me?"

He laughed. "Because it's true?"

Even if I could have framed a response, I had no time to form the words before he bent and kissed my cheek, then left the room. Frozen in shock, I sat on the window seat for a long time, watching him emerge from the bottom of the stairs and cross the court-yard.

He wants me, just as I want him. Dare I hope that he loves me and would like to wed me, whatever the Church decrees?

I couldn't be sure. But only a cad would court a noble maiden *without* intending to offer marriage. Timur was not a cad, which raised an enticing but scary possibility. Scary because I still had to navigate my way out of the bride show and evade Papa's threats of another husband, not because I nurtured doubts about Timur. The dragon still stood between me and my goal.

I don't know how long it took me to corral my unruly emotions, but only when I had reestablished some sort of self-control did I seek out my sister and Juliana.

Chapter 6

"Or did the true danger lie elsewhere?"

O ver the course of the next five days, Maria drove me half-mad with endless dress fittings. I love beautiful clothes as much as the next person, but how many fittings can a robe require when it falls more or less straight from the shoulders and includes false sleeves with loose slits the length of one's upper arm? An initial measurement and another to check the length should suffice!

But Maria did not agree, so I stood motionless for what felt like hours while maids pinned and tucked, basted and stitched, then pinned and tucked some more. I knew better than to complain. I wasn't even sure I wanted to complain, since no one asked me to sew and the fabrics and gowns were exquisite. Yet in the deepest realms of my heart, I would rather have skipped the entire process of preparing to attend court to work on my book of tales. I mulled over plot and characters while avoiding the prick of carelessly thrust pins, but without access to quill and paper I didn't dare imagine dialogue that might escape the bounds of memory before I had a chance to write down the words.

As a result, I teetered at the edge of irritable when my sister danced into the room early in the morning on the twenty-third of December, a robe the pale yellow of April sunshine draped over one arm and a pearl-rimmed, pointed headdress dangling from her other wrist. "Tasha," she said to the maid in charge of that day's torture, "put that robe away for now and help Lady Lyuba get into this one. We have an appointment."

My ears perked like a cat's. An appointment had to be better than avoiding loose pins. "With whom?" I asked.

"One moment." Maria transferred the robe and headdress to the back of a chair and approached close enough to rub the fabric of my ivory tunic between her fingers. "Silk," she said in a satisfied tone. "This will do nicely." She released my sleeve and eased the emerald satin of the half-sewn robe off my right shoulder while Tasha did the same with the left. Once I was free, Tasha carried the dress off for another set of maids to work on, and my sister dropped the finished gown over my head.

Tanya, the housekeeper, came in, holding a pair of freshly polished leather boots. I buttoned the fastenings on the new robe as quickly as I could before slipping my feet into the boots. "Comb and rebraid her hair, Tanya," Maria ordered. "Then I can tie this *kokoshnik*." She meant the headdress, shaped rather like a tent, with a high point in the middle.

I let Tanya push me onto the cushioned seat beside my dressing table, although I twisted to face my sister. "Where are we going?"

"To visit Princess Anastasia Petrovna," she said. "The tsar's cousin. She's one of the women inspecting candidates for the bride show, so it gives us a chance to sway her. We want to convince her that someone else would be a better choice."

"And what of Anna?" I asked. "Would it be wrong to bring her with us? And are we taking Juliana?"

"Not Juliana," Maria replied. "She went off with Felix this morning, and they don't plan to return until suppertime. But Anna will come with us. Princess Nadezhda Shuiskaya set up the meeting as planned, and I asked her to invite Anna as well. I already sent Solomonida a message to expect our carriage before the church bells ring again."

That was good news. If I had to face a pair of haughty noble-women who probably did not have my best interests at heart, at least I could count on support from my closest friend as well as my sister. "Thank you," I said.

As we spoke, Tanya had been tending to my hair. Now she draped a long string of pearls atop the crown of my head and wound the jewels among the three strands of my plait. As she reached the end, near my waist, she tied a slender silk ribbon around the braid and stepped back. Maria positioned the head-dress and tied its strings at the back of my head. She reached for a small jar I hadn't seen her bring in and dabbed powder on my nose and forehead, laughing when I sneezed. A brush across my cheeks from another jar, followed by a pair of dangling gold earrings thrust into my lobes, and she pronounced me ready.

Tanya handed me a brass mirror, and I stared at the polished surface. The image wavered before my eyes, flickering like candle-light. But I saw enough to impart a sense of awe. I didn't look like my usual rumpled and ink-stained self. Anyone walking by would take me for a court lady, which I supposed was the point.

And Timur? What will he think if he sees me dressed like this?

The thought lingered at the back of my mind as I followed my sister downstairs, accepted a cloak lined with silky red-brown fur, and climbed into the sleigh. Alas, I caught no glimpse of Timur.

We stopped first at Anfim's house to collect Anna. Solomonida greeted us in the hallway. I noticed then that Maria looked even more beautiful than usual in a robe of copper silk, cleverly chosen to complement my primrose yellow without drawing attention away from me.

"How grand you are," Solomonida said. "I love those robes." Before we had a chance to respond, Anna came running down the stairs from the third floor. Her dress, the color of violets adorned with silver thread, darkened the blue in her eyes and emphasized the pink in her often pale cheeks.

"Look at Anna," Maria said. "That color suits her perfectly."

My friend slid to a stop before us, releasing the skirt she'd clutched in one hand. "I don't know whether to feel excited or terrified. What is Princess Anastasia like?"

"How to characterize her?" Maria seemed to choose each word with care. "She's an interesting combination of Tatar and Russian, a person of status without genuine power, valued for her bloodline but not for her sharpness of intellect or her education—like so many women."

"Does she *have* an education?" I asked. I'd anticipated an afternoon of gossip intermixed with needlework, but this news inspired hope of conversations that might hold my interest.

"She does," Solomonida said. "I don't know how much of one—probably not as extensive as yours—but better than most Russian noblewomen. Her father was a Tatar tsarevich; he believed women of standing should provide political support for their husbands, just as Alexei does. And her mother died at twenty, so her father's views prevailed."

"It's shocking, when you think of it," Maria put in. "Even a royal princess shouldn't be married off at thirteen. How could such a young girl bear children? It's no wonder four years passed before she gave birth. And a couple of years later, she was dead."

"A tragedy," Solomonida agreed. "Tsarevich Peter never did get the son he wanted. But that's ancient history by now. The point is that Anastasia lost her mother when little more than a babe, Lyuba. You have that in common, as well as the ability to read."

I felt a tug of comradeship toward the princess. "I see Mama in my dreams sometimes." And I did: a sad and wispy person, ephemeral as fog, hovered in the twilight as I fell asleep, but the image evaporated as soon as dawn broke.

I didn't miss her, though. Sometimes I felt bad about that. A daughter *should* miss her mother. Yet a hapless ghost dimly remembered from early childhood couldn't compete with the everyday presence of passionate, capable Maria, with her sharp mind and quick temper, who had taken our real mother's place. I couldn't mourn someone I had never known.

"The princess lost her father, too, when she was quite young," Anna said, surprising me—not for the first time—with her grasp of the tangled threads that linked members of the court. "Then her uncle married Anastasia off as he had her mother."

"And when her first husband died, she wed Vasily Shuisky. Sixty, if he was a day." I scrunched up my nose as I remembered *that* story. "At least the old brute did her a favor and expired within the year." I did a quick sum in my head, concluding that Anastasia had been in her mid-twenties when she became a widow for the second time. "He was as bad as Papa," I finished. "Marrying to make himself more powerful."

"He was Papa's patron," Maria pointed out. "They were two of a kind."

"And that's enough gossip for the moment." Solomonida gave her daughter a small push. "Let's get you on your way."

"Wait!" I fought off a flash of panic. I felt unprepared for the meeting to come. "What do we say to Princess Anastasia? If she has an education, how can I convince her not to recommend me? We planned to present me as too scholarly for a tsaritsa, remember?"

"Hmm." Maria put a finger under her chin, giving her an uncanny resemblance to Father Job presented with a problematic assignment from a student. "You're right. I think we should stick with that strategy for now, though. As Solomonida said, Anastasia's education is less extensive than yours. So it may still work, and if it doesn't, it may help Anna."

Anna brightened at that comment, while I fought the urge to wring my hands like one of my fairy-tale princesses facing the dragon. I didn't protest, though. By most people's standards, Anna *was* in more danger of being selected than I was, because she met every criterion of an exemplary tsaritsa. Even her criminal father might not be sufficient to get her declared unsuitable, since he had died more than a decade ago, whereas mine was still around, causing trouble.

"And that would be good." Solomonida put my thoughts into words. "Then we can concentrate our efforts on convincing some of the other court ladies that Lyuba's too learned and independent to perform the role expected of her." She gave Anna a little push. "Off with you, or you'll be late."

I gave a small moan of protest, which went unheard amid the noise of Solomonida bustling us into the sleigh. Who cared if we were late? Princess Anastasia might take offense and cross us both off her list on the spot.

But Maria was already inside the carriage and beckoning. "Stop dawdling, Lyuba," she ordered.

Solomonida shoved me in the back, not hard but with enough force to make me move. "I look forward to hearing the whole tale when you get home," she said firmly. Seeing no alternative, I climbed into the sleigh, and we were off.

Few nobles still ranked high enough to live within the Kremlin walls, but thanks to her royal heritage, Princess Anastasia belonged in that select category. I watched with interest as we passed through the Frolov Gate, the main entrance to the Kremlin fortress—a journey I'd heard my sister describe but had never taken myself. The brick walls of the Ascension Convent rose to one side, but the gilded cupolas of Cathedral Square still lay ahead when the carriage took a sharp turn to the right, passing through a set of wooden doors that protected our destination from unwanted entry.

Our vehicle pulled to a stop, and the coachman opened the door. Maria got out first, with Anna and me close behind. Ahead of us stood a house much like Alexei's, except this one was made of stone and sported the usual dull windows. A stairway covered with a planked roof, its edges decorated with lively carvings of forest creatures peeking out from a riot of greenery, pointed the way to the visitors' entrance. As I drew closer, I realized that the stone façade didn't extend to the third floor. I remarked on this to my sister as we approached the top step, but she didn't even glance up before answering.

"Stone withstands fire," she said, "but wood holds the heat. The family quarters are always made of wood."

I bit my lip, not wanting to admit that her comment made me feel very young. Although I saw little point in building a house of stone if the central living space could still go up in flames, it shocked me that I'd never considered the benefits of a stone house until then, despite having lived within three streets of the Kremlin my entire life. Surely a writer should know more than I did!

The door ahead of us opened, and a woman who reminded me of Tanya in age, general appearance, and dress bowed in greeting. "Tsarevna Maria," she said to my sister. "These must be your sister and her friend. Come in, all of you. Princess Anastasia and her niece, Princess Nadezhda, are ready to receive you."

Her niece? At that moment, something clicked in my brain, and I at last put the pieces together. The ancient Shuisky prince who had become Princess Anastasia's second husband was also the uncle of the abominable Prince Ilya Shuisky—Nadezhda's spouse, happily deceased—who was in turn the father of Prince Pavel, the self-satisfied fool who yearned to make my friend Anna his bride. Hence two women who were at most two or three years apart in age could be described as aunt and niece.

Next to such twisty genealogical connections, the ins and outs of my story worlds displayed the simplicity of a child's drawings. Wasn't that in part why writing appealed to me? Unlike real life, the complicated plots I constructed always made sense in the end.

We followed the housekeeper down a short corridor, then through a series of linked chambers until we reached a large and sunny sitting room. The two women who awaited us had dark hair, but there the resemblance between them ended. The one with gray eyes and narrow shoulders matched my sister's description of Princess Nadezhda. Princess Anastasia's flashing black gaze and lively air hinted at a vibrant personality, and I experienced an immediate sense of kinship with her. As the two women rose to greet us, I saw that Princess Anastasia, although shorter than her niece and relatively slender, had the ability to command attention. Juliana had the same gift, although she manipulated it with greater deliberation. In comparison, Nadezhda appeared attractive but bland. Perhaps marriage to Prince Pavel's father had worn her down.

Maria embraced each woman in turn before introducing first me, then Anna. I bent my head, but Princess Anastasia clasped me by the shoulders and kissed me on both cheeks. She moved on to Anna, and Nadezhda copied the gesture with both of us. You'd have thought we were family.

Their warmth should have reassured me but didn't, because it suggested they might be predisposed to consider Anna and me as desirable candidates. Without knowing which qualities they valued in a royal bride, how could we convince them to eliminate either of us, never mind both?

These thoughts raced through my head like lightning. Nadezhda released Anna, and Anastasia spoke. "Welcome, my dears. We have not met before, but my nephew Pavel has shared his impressions with me." She gestured at a wooden settle in the center of the room. "Sit, and let us become acquainted, so that we may decide if either of you has the qualities required of Russia's first tsaritsa."

Pavel. Well, that was a plus. Pavel would praise Anna, not me. Reassured, I took a seat and hoped for the best.

The conversation started off well. The three women chattered amiably about children and other family members, requiring no more from Anna and me than an attentive demeanor. By her first husband, Princess Anastasia had a sixteen-year-old son as well as the daughter from her second marriage, a year younger than Maria's Alexander. Princess Nadezhda was the mother not only of the self-centered Prince Pavel but another boy I'd seen at the occasional wedding but never spoken to. I had a vague impression of brown hair darker than Pavel's, a lot of energy, and a less obnoxious personality. He couldn't be more than thirteen, but I thought I might like him better than his older brother. I could hardly like him less.

I listened more carefully when the women moved to discussing the Glinsky family and its grip on power. I didn't learn much, unfortunately, and the intensity of my concentration left me unprepared when Anastasia Petrovna, out of the blue, plucked a book from the table next to her. She turned back the cover and handed the book to me. "Read the first page," she said in a tone so authoritative that, without thinking, I did exactly what she said.

"'Once upon a time from all the circles seven / between the steadfast earth and rolling heaven' ... why, it's *The Conference of Birds*!" I looked up to find the two princesses regarding me with the kind of stunned curiosity I might direct toward a strange animal that strolled across my path. A small smile played about my sister's lips, reassuring me that I hadn't committed some dreadful offense, but what had shocked the others? Anastasia had asked me to read, so she must have assumed I knew how.

I flicked through the pages, looking for an answer. Only then did I realize that the words were written in Persian. I had read them aloud—and in Russian!—without even noticing. My stomach seized up, and I fought off a sense of having been tricked.

Wasn't revealing myself as a scholar what I was supposed to do, though? If only Anastasia didn't look so ... *approving*.

The silence lengthened as I debated how to respond. After a while, I raised my chin, stared at Anastasia, and said in a voice that shook, "Should I continue, Princess?"

"That won't be necessary." She held out her hand, and I gave her the book. "Although you have a beautiful voice, and the facility with which you translated the words into Russian is quite impressive. I haven't heard those lines spoken since my father died." She stared wistfully at the small but richly decorated cover, and again I felt that odd sense of connection with her.

"But this was a test?" I asked, since I could think of no other reason for her actions.

"I had heard you were learned." She waved a careless hand, indicating the answer was obvious. "I see that rumor, for once, did not exaggerate."

I had no time to form a reply—or even to decide what that reply should be—before she held the book out to Anna.

My friend blushed and clasped her hands above her heart. "I can read a bible, Princess, but not works in other languages."

"Very appropriate." Nadezhda joined the conversation. "And what do *you* do with your time?"

A flicker of fear crossed Anna's face in response to the princess's praise, but she answered the question, speaking rather too fast. "I help my mother with the household, watch my sister and brothers, and embroider."

The two princesses nodded in quiet approbation. "And what are you embroidering?" Anastasia asked.

Anna—her words spilling out like water, her shoulders tense—described her latest project. I appeared to listen, but my thoughts tumbled in every direction, undisciplined as kittens, as I wrestled with the question of whether I had or had not made myself a less appealing candidate.

I must have. Maria's smile suggested as much, and the encouragement the princesses bestowed on Anna showed that my ability to read Persian weighed far less than my friend's gift with a needle. We still had to find a way to protect her, but we could devote our full attention to that problem now that I'd put myself out of the running. The anxiety that had gripped me since the moment Maria announced this visit seeped away as the princesses continued to grill Anna and ignore me. I had my response ready by the time Nadezhda turned to me once more. "Do you embroider, Lyuba? Do you help your sister manage the household?"

"I have become quite accustomed to supervising the servants," I said before landing what I hoped would be the decisive blow. "But my embroidery is terrible, I'm afraid." I held up the index finger of my right hand, revealing the ink blot that even the pumice stone could not completely erase. "I much prefer to write stories."

"Stories?" Nadezhda asked in astonished tones. "Do you mean biblical stories? Saints' lives? That's a task for churchmen!"

I gave her my most impish smile. "No, tales of love and adventure, mostly. Right now, I'm working on one where a village threatened by a dragon and a sorceress calls in a noble warrior to defend it. And to rescue the innocent maidens before the dragon eats them, of course."

Nadezhda visibly started. "How ... extraordinary," she managed after a moment. "Have you written a lot of these stories?"

"Yes, many," I said, as if this were the most natural thing in the world instead of the most outrageous. "Would you like to see one?"

Maria groaned, although I suspected that was for effect because her eyes were dancing. Anna stared at me with a kind of awe—as if, despite our planning, she couldn't believe I would have the nerve to admit that I'd rather write than stitch.

Princess Anastasia, however, regarded me with a steady gaze that made me uneasy. "Such an interesting young woman," she said after a short pause. "I do believe you might be exactly what my cousin Ivan needs in a bride."

I gripped my hands together so hard the knuckles turned white and bit my tongue to keep any rash words inside. I hadn't put myself out of the running at all. Instead I'd played right into her hands.

Chapter 7

"Yet love blossomed against all odds"

H ow to respond? I couldn't say what I felt. A noble maiden should experience nothing but joy at the thought that her tsar might select her as his companion for life. And speaking the truth might anger this woman who far outranked me, thus placing not only myself but my family at risk. Still less could I scream my frustration to the skies: behaving like a madwoman might lead to confinement in a convent, ending any hope that I might someday be united with Timur.

In fact, since I have vowed to be completely honest in this account of mine, even those possibilities did not occur to me at first. With no more than an instant to run potential replies through my head, the only one I could imagine was to bow my head and murmur my thanks. After that, I sat, shocked as a baby bird surprised in its nest, while the conversation wound to its inevitable close. Even when Maria, Anna, and I at last made our way down the stairs and into the waiting sleigh, I listened to the two of them comparing notes while resisting their efforts to draw me in. While they chattered and speculated, I stared at the passing streets—or what I could see of them through the translucent carriage windows. The wintry scene, stripped of its details, acquired a certain unearthly purity.

"I don't understand what happened," I told Maria when she pressed me. We had left Anna at her house by then, and I needed my sister's advice. I felt more comfortable speaking freely, too, if it didn't mean scaring my friend. "Princess Nadezhda preferred Anna, I'm sure. They should *both* have preferred Anna. Helping her mother, looking after children, loving embroidery, reading just enough to satisfy her spiritual obligations—is that not the description of most people's perfect woman? And Anna does those things naturally. I'd already started to think of what we might do to rescue her after they declared *her* the ideal bride. What possessed Princess Anastasia to settle on me as a possible tsaritsa?"

Maria gazed at me with amusement. "You do yourself a disservice. You're young and beautiful and well connected. You have a mother who bore four sons who lived to adulthood, so they may hope you will do the same. And if young Ivan likes women of spirit, you are certainly the better choice."

"But I don't want to be the better choice!"

"I know," Maria said in reassuring tones. "But I'm impressed by Anastasia. Perhaps she has taken her father's lessons to heart and realizes that a ruler can benefit from a wife who grasps how the wider world works."

"Perhaps," I said, still fighting despair. "I suppose next time I'll have to go on endlessly about storing mushrooms and pretend to have forgotten everything I've learned. To think my dreadful needlework may be the only thing that saves me!" Maria laughed, and after a moment's pause I joined in.

By the time we reached our own courtyard, though, I was ready to burst with anxiety. I leaped out of the sleigh, leaving my sister gathering her skirts, and tore into the house, narrowly avoiding a second collision with Timur as I crossed the threshold.

He grabbed my arm. "Don't you ever look where you're going?" he asked, sounding more amused than annoyed. "I'll need to wear armor around the house if you keep running into me."

"Sorry," I said, too overwrought for genuine remorse. "I'm about to jump out of my skin. I've been on my best behavior for hours, I got terrible news, and if I don't *move*, I may explode."

"Terrible news? Don't tell me someone died!"

"Not that kind of news. Anastasia Petrovna announced that I might be the perfect wife for the tsar. I hope she was joking, but with my luck she'll tell the other women, and before long Papa will be marching me to the altar even if he has to gag me first."

I expected a protest—or laughter. Instead he gestured at the door behind me. "Come riding with me. It's a beautiful day, quite mild for December. Let's take the falcons and an escort, and we'll leave the city behind for the afternoon. You can tell me the whole on the way."

Impulsively, I hugged him. "Yes, yes! I haven't gone hawking in ages. I would love to!"

He gripped my waist, then stepped back. "Change your clothes then, and I'll meet you at the stable. Do you have a favorite horse? I can order the grooms to saddle her."

"I'll take Kumai." I named my sister's mare. "Maria still rides, but she's been busy lately, and Kumai needs exercise. I'll join you soon."

He nodded, and I dashed up the stairs, my fears forgotten in the lure of the chase.

We headed south, along the Ordynka—meaning the road that led to the Horde, and therefore the steppe. It was the same route the Nogai used to drive their horse herds to the city every August, a sight that never failed to delight me. At first, the crowded streets kept our twenty bodyguards occupied, leaving Timur, as their leader, with scant leisure for conversation. But once we crossed the narrow wooden bridge that spanned the Moscow River, the countryside opened up before us. These fields were where the warriors from Kasimov had camped, and off to one side I saw numerous round felt tents surrounding a single massive central one. There a banner of nine white horse tails blew in the light breeze, indicating that Timur's Uncle Shah-Ali was in residence. Beyond that, a golden cupola suggested the presence of Russians, although the tents blocked any wooden huts from view.

Most likely, there weren't many. Peasants and artisans—even merchants—tended to cluster on the northern and eastern sides of the city. Few people wanted to build along the main invasion route from the south, even if most of the "invaders" these days were riderless mares and geldings. Slave raids from Crimea, even all-out attacks, still took place with disturbing regularity every five to ten years.

While I waited for Timur to join me, I murmured reassurances to the beautiful, hooded merlin who gripped my leather-clad wrist. Her name was Tizilek, which meant "speed," and Alexei had given her to me to mark my sixteenth name day. Timur carried his father's peregrine, known as Ferz, a magnificent bird that I exercised close to home but found rather heavy to manage on a trip like today's.

"Hush, Tizilek," I said as the bird shifted her claws against my glove. "You will be flying soon." She responded by spreading her wings wide, but the jesses kept her attached to my arm. "Patience," I told her. "As soon as Timur and Ferz get here, I'll release you."

The warriors spread out, forming a circle around me and my hawk. Timur remained in conversation with the captain. To conceal my impatience, I surveyed the surrounding terrain. It was a beautiful sight. Forest banded the snow-covered fields, marked only by the occasional tracks of predators and prey. The noonday sun cast its winter glow over the land, giving it a fairy-tale sheen. The visit to Princess Anastasia had taken less time than I'd thought. And we had the road almost to ourselves. I saw people moving among the tents, smelled the smoke that rose in wisps from the domed centers, heard the whinnying of horses. Otherwise, the area appeared deserted.

For a moment, I wondered if the absence of people meant that the weather would soon turn on us, but the ice-blue sky revealed no looming clouds or signs of incipient blizzard, only the glistening orb of the sun. Having lived in Moscow my entire life, I could detect the signs of wintry weather with ease, and I saw no indications of trouble to come. As Timur had said, it was exceptionally fine for the twenty-third of December.

When I rode out with Maria and Alexei, we most often headed for the New Maidens' Convent, one loop of the river to the west, but Timur had chosen the most direct route out of the city. A few hours ahead of us lay the original St. Daniil's Monastery, abandoned since my grandfather's day. Almost a decade ago, another Daniil, the husband of Alexei's sister, had been imprisoned there. He would have died in captivity if his wife had not launched a raid on the compound and rescued him. And Maria had dressed as a boy to help with the reconnaissance! Theirs was another of the many tales I planned to write down one day.

Were we heading to the monastery, then? I frowned. We would have clear ground to release the birds, but such a trip would bring us home well after dark. My sister would worry if I returned so late.

At last Timur separated from the pack and rode toward me, guiding his horse one-handed with effortless grace and balancing Ferz—a bird twice as long and at least three times as heavy as Tizilek—on his right wrist. When he came close enough, I asked if he planned to ride far.

"No," he said. "We'll release the birds close to those trees." An expansive wave of his arm indicated the looming woods beyond the fields where in August and September the horse herds would graze. "Plenty of space for them to hunt."

I fell into place beside him, and we resumed our journey. "You have your lure?" he asked as we closed the short distance that separated us from the forest.

In answer, I raised the string and showed him the attached slice of meat. Tizilek sniffed the air, her beak raised. Again she shifted her talons against my glove. She fluffed her light brown feathers, each with a darker line at its center. I could almost believe she understood what we were saying, that she would soon return to her natural element—the sky.

"Ready?" Timur gazed at me, challenge in his eyes.

I waited no longer, slipping the knot that kept the hood bound over Tizilek's eyes and releasing her jesses. She spread her wings wide, and I propelled her upward with a flick of my wrist. Timur released Ferz at the same moment, and the two birds shot into the heavens, Tizilek at first outpacing her larger companion. But I knew that in the stoop their positions would be reversed, for no other bird could match a peregrine when it dove.

I stood in my stirrups, gazing at the retreating specks, and laughed out loud at the joy of their flight. If only I could be so untrammeled by convention and the loving demands of family! Among the trees to my right, I heard the rustling of rodents and similar animals seeking shelter. I doubted the falcons would catch anything today; most of the smaller birds that they preferred to hunt had flown south in the fall and would not return for months. That pleased me, because I didn't like to watch the kill. What I loved were the exhilaration of the release, the speed with which the birds took off, and most of all, the drama of the stoop—feathered cannonballs plummeting earthward, faster than an arrow and more accurate than any bullet, with the ability to reverse course and soar once more into the ether and their effortless glide. We fed Ferz and Tizilek every day, so they could live without hunting, but they needed to fly high amid the clouds.

"Come on." Timur grasped my reins. When I dropped back onto the saddle and turned my head toward him, he released his hold and signaled to his men. "We'll freeze if we sit here like logs. The birds will find us. We're not going far. I'll race you to that big oak."

He was riding his father's stallion, Ajdar. My beautiful mare had little chance against him, but I loved a challenge. "If I win," I told him, "you owe me a description of your life on the steppe. I need it for a story I'm crafting."

"Agreed," he said, laughing. "And if you lose, beautiful maiden?"

"That's for you to decide." I pressed my heels against Kumai's flanks as I finished the sentence and whispered encouragement in her ear, directing her toward the oak.

Timur cursed. I leaned low over the horse's neck, not acknowledging his words with so much as a glance. Already I heard the pounding hooves behind me, and I knew he would catch me if I allowed myself even a moment of distraction. I urged Kumai to run faster, promising her carrots and apples and a warm blanket when we returned to the house. Above me, Tizilek trilled her approval. Wings fluttered over my bent head, but that, too, I let pass without a flick of my eyes to see whether my own hawk or Ferz had chosen to join the game.

I almost made it. The oak Timur had selected lay just beyond the reach of my outstretched arm when Ajdar swept past us. I straightened in my saddle and suppressed a curse of my own at the sight of the horse-shaped barrier between me and my goal. That Timur looked as serene as a man taking a midsummer stroll in a rural meadow, not to mention disgustingly proud of himself, did nothing to improve my temper. I patted Kumai's mane and murmured encouraging words. Her flanks heaved beneath my heels, and I dismounted to give her time to recover.

Timur swung off his father's horse, positioning the two animals to form a rough triangle with the oak as its third side. Glancing back the way we'd come, I saw that the warriors hadn't followed us. Instead, they clustered in small groups, walking their horses in circles as they chatted and waited for us and our birds to return.

I returned my attention to Timur. "Congratulations," I said in a voice that I hoped sounded more gracious than grudging. He had the better mount, but he'd beaten me fair and square despite the head start I'd grabbed for myself.

In truth, watching him ride was a thing of beauty. Like all children raised on the steppe, he'd sat his first horse before he could walk, held in his father's arms. These days, he controlled his mount as if it were an extension of himself. I had no doubt he deserved to win. My only regret was that I'd spent most of the race bent over Kumai's neck, missing an opportunity to appreciate his skill. "And what is my forfeit?" I added, raising my chin to show him I retained my dignity. I would not be a sore loser.

In answer, he wrapped an arm around my waist. "You need to ask?" He was smiling at me, and a wicked gleam lit his dark eyes. "My father must have told you about the steppe game, 'Kiss the Girl.' You select the man you want, you race—even with a head start—and if you win, you get to smack him with your riding crop. But if *he* wins …" He left the phrase unfinished, sweeping me against his chest and kissing me soundly.

I should have pushed him away, but I didn't. Warmth flooded my body as I yielded to his touch, and the sensations of his mouth against mine, his grip on my waist, his strong torso pressing me against the oak tree were the sweetest I had ever experienced. Heedless, I wrapped my arms around his neck, closed my eyes, and returned the kiss in full measure.

I'd never experienced anything like it. Russians brushed lips across cheeks a dozen times a day, but no one had ever kissed me like this. I wanted it to go on and on, rich and rewarding and deeply passionate, as if Timur's embrace opened a magical door to a fairyland of my own invention. If this was what my princesses felt in the arms of their heroes, no wonder they moved mountains and faced down dragons to overcome whatever barriers lay in their path.

At last, Timur raised his head. I came back to earth to find him staring at me, his eyes hazy and his expression soft in a way I rarely saw. "Well, well," he said, his words halting, as if he could breathe no more easily than I, struggling to slow my racing heart. "You never fail to surprise me, Lady Love, but I don't think you've ever surprised me more than today."

I wriggled free, thrown off-balance by this odd statement. "What's that supposed to mean?"

He continued to gaze at me with that addled look in his eyes, as if he couldn't quite believe what he'd seen—or what he'd done?

This was ridiculous. Frustrated passion gave way to anger and confusion. I placed a foot on Kumai's stirrup and swung myself into the saddle without asking for a hand up, then glared at him from my lofty seat. "Never mind." I risked a glance at the sky, where two distant flecks stood out against the still-brilliant sun, already noticeably lower in the sky, before dropping my chin again to survey my stunned and uncooperative companion. "If you don't want to answer, then don't. We should summon the birds and start back. Maria will have a fit if we miss supper."

He mounted Ajdar with his usual unconscious grace—so much a part of him that it often escaped my notice. His eyes met mine, their expression serious now. "I meant no insult, Lyuba. I've dreamed of finding a woman like you. But I didn't expect it to happen today."

My lips tingled from his kiss, my body burned with a wicked desire I couldn't name and had no idea how to handle, and the combination of delight and disappointment had me fighting tears I was determined not to let him see. What did that mean—he'd dreamed of finding a woman like me but hadn't expected it to happen today? It could be read two ways—that he hadn't expected me to be the one, or he hadn't expected to kiss me this afternoon. My tight throat and still-pounding heart made it impossible to speak. He might read my silence as understanding or as ... I didn't know what.

Unable to finish the sentence, I turned the mare's head back the way we had come. The clop of Ajdar's hooves reassured me that I did not ride alone.

Once we had achieved a certain distance from the trees and my pulse slowed to a normal rate, I pulled the lure from my glove and whirled it in the air, summoning Tizilek. It took longer than usual to get the birds' attention, even with Timur calling as well, probably because our race and the kiss had taken less time in reality than in my perceptions of a world shifting beneath my feet.

At last my merlin came into view, the peregrine's darker plumage creating a shadow behind her. I held my arm out straight, and Tizilek grabbed the meat from the lure as she swept by, then settled onto my wrist. While she shredded the food with her sharp beak, I tied the jesses, then hooded her once more, pulling the string taut with my teeth. I noticed blood on her talons, so perhaps she had surprised a squirrel in a tree.

By the time I had her secured, Timur was hooding Ferz. I rode toward the warriors without waiting for him. As I approached, they broke away from their clusters and reconstituted their enclosing circle. Nothing about their stance or behavior suggested they had seen me kiss their leader. That was some comfort, I supposed.

Timur soon joined us. Our return to Moscow was swift, but this time he and I rode together, surrounded by guards. My anguish slowly dissipated, and after a while Timur and I fell into easy conversation. I took the opportunity to explain what had upset me about the meeting at Princess Anastasia's house. His reaction to the kiss still puzzled me, but when I finished, he said, "But that's dreadful. How are we to dissuade her?"

The concern in his voice reassured me. "I have no idea," I told him. "She'll never believe now that I'm an untutored ninny. And if I act differently with the other ladies"—I'd realized this on the ride out—"they will think I'm far too suitable, even though I can't do more with a needle than pitch it in the fire."

"Maybe you can remind them of your father's insalubrious past," he suggested.

I wrinkled my nose in distaste, but I had no better idea to offer. "Perhaps. They must know, and I'd have to be careful not to implicate Maria or Alexei, but I can think about ways to make that work."

We settled into idle chatter, memories of the kiss blazoned in my mind like a banner. The skies darkened steadily during our hour or so on the road, but sufficient light remained when we entered the gates for us to stable the horses and transfer the falcons to their perches without difficulty. As we strolled toward the house —hand in hand, not speaking—we saw servants hanging lanterns at intervals around the enclosing fence, and the dim glow of the candles helped offset the encroaching twilight.

The lingering day also revealed Alexei standing at the top of the stairs. His crossed arms, narrowed eyes, and tight lips left no doubt as to his fury. Recalling too late how he'd ordered Timur not to escort me on another occasion, I tried to tug my hand away, but Timur tightened his clasp. "Don't worry," he muttered. "We weren't alone. We didn't do anything wrong."

I didn't dare take my eyes off Alexei. "I don't think your father agrees."

"He will," Timur said.

But I didn't believe him. I wasn't sure he believed himself.

With a punctilious politeness more threatening than any shout of rage, Alexei ushered Timur and me into his study and waited, without speaking, until the two of us settled onto the sofa he pointed out to us. Only then did he take a seat behind his desk. Words jostled for space against my tongue as I battled the urge to protest, explain, excuse—without even knowing the accusation, just to break the silence. But the burning, delightful memory of Timur's embrace kept me silent. Whatever drove Alexei's fury, having him find out about the kiss would only make matters worse.

After studying us throughout an uncomfortable pause that could not possibly have lasted as long as I believed, Alexei addressed us in biting tones, "And what, precisely, did the two of you think you were doing, riding out alone?"

I opened my mouth, but despite the words whirling in my head, no acceptable answer presented itself. Timur responded first. "We did not ride alone," he said. "Twenty warriors accompanied us, and we were never out of their sight."

Except when you pressed me against an oak tree and kissed me into a state of ecstasy.

I suppressed the words, but the memory brought a heat to my cheeks I would have preferred to avoid.

After an even more uncomfortable pause, Alexei responded. "I told you not to escort her even so far as her friend's house," he reminded Timur in the same chilly tone. "And I explained why. How could you imagine that riding out with her for hours was not covered by that prohibition?"

"She was upset," Timur said. "I sought to distract her. To comfort her, if possible. What harm could I do, surrounded by guards? And what harm do you imagine I would wish to do? I love her, too." With less experience than his father in controlling his anger, he let a note of irritation creep into his voice. A mistake, I thought, but I knew better than to point that out. The tension in the room was already high.

Timur's declaration that he loved me, whatever he meant by that, pushed me into speech. It wasn't like me to sit mute while people talked about me as if I were deaf. "It's true." I tried to sound firm, although the quiver in my voice gave me away. "We went to exercise the horses and the falcons, nothing more." Not when we set out, in any event.

Alexei's expression went from frigid to thunderous in the blink of an eye. "That's enough out of you, Lyuba," he snapped. "As of today, you are confined to the house unless your sister or I give you permission to leave. That lasts until the bride show ends. If you are not chosen, *then* we can discuss your future. Do I make myself clear?"

I recoiled. The lump in my throat robbed me of speech, and the tears I'd fought off earlier massed in droves behind my eyes. I could only nod.

"Then go. Maria is waiting for you," he said.

Making no attempt to argue, I obeyed. With luck, my knees wouldn't fail me before I left the room.

As I moved to close the door, I heard him address Timur. "Let me explain something to you, son." The blistering anger he'd directed at me had already mellowed into man-to-man camaraderie, and the unfairness of it made me want to pound my fists against the wall. Timur had suggested the ride, not I, although I leaped at the chance. Timur had kissed *me*, not the reverse (but Alexei did not, thank the Mother of God, know about the kiss). Why should I be rebuked and dismissed like an unruly child while Timur suffered nothing worse than benign if heavy-handed instruction?

"Lyuba." My sister's voice interrupted my tumultuous thoughts. "Come up here this instant. I have something to say to you." I climbed the stairs as slowly as I dared, eager to postpone a discussion I could not hope to avoid.

Indeed, the next half-hour was every bit as unpleasant as I'd feared. Not even the sympathetic glances Juliana sent my way from time to time could raise spirits crushed by Maria's declared loss of faith in me.

But when I at last escaped to my room, it was the memory of Timur's kiss that stayed with me.

Chapter 8

"Boulders obstructed the path leading to the dragon's lair"

I cornered Timur in the library the next morning after ensuring that his father had left the house. The last thing I wanted was another run-in with Alexei. I had yet to recover from yesterday's encounter.

"What did he say to you after I left?" I grabbed Timur's arm and pulled him with me to the far corner of the room. I assumed he knew I was asking about his father.

"Calm yourself, *kaderle.*" He stroked my cheek, but I pulled away. His use of the endearment soothed my ragged nerves, but I didn't want any man—even this one—condescending to me.

"*Ata's* upset with us," he said in reassuring tones. "It's not the end of the world."

"Don't humor me," I snapped. "I'm not some silly maiden from a book. Alexei sent me away so he could—what?—lay down the law in a way only a *man* is supposed to understand?"

"Something like that." He grinned sheepishly. "Don't rip up at me, Lady Love. It's not my fault your fiend of a father entered you in this wretched bride show or even that this crazy world of yours insists on treating us as if we were brother and sister when we're nothing of the sort. I'd sweep you onto my horse and ride off with you like one of your fairy-tale knights without a second thought, but *Ata* has threatened to disown me if I damage your reputation. Even being seen with me in the open fields is enough, it seems, to cast doubt on your purity—despite the twenty guards." He touched his forehead, then his heart, ending with an elaborate flourish of his arm. "Say the word, though, *soyarké*, and we'll flee for the steppe." This time, his caressing finger passed across my lips.

The memory of his kiss filled my head, sweeping my irritation away. I yearned to say yes. But as I parted my lips to agree, a new vision replaced the beauty of the kiss: Timur disowned as his father had been at the age of sixteen, abandoned by his family, dependent on the kindness of strangers. Even to save myself, I couldn't do that to this man who meant so much to me.

"Not at the cost of your father's love," I said, making no effort to hide my reluctance. I took a step back and returned to my original question. "That was it, then? Alexei warned you off?"

He raised both eyebrows, as if he could tell how much I wanted to jump at the chance to escape. "More or less. He'd prefer that I marry a Tatar princess, one whose father could make me a khan one day. He's fond of you, but he doesn't think I have anything to gain from our match, because he already has an unsatisfactory alliance with your papa." His lips twitched. "He did suggest you might make the perfect second wife."

I gasped. Shocked and horrified and furious, all at the same time, I couldn't stop myself. I'd flirted with the idea of conversion, but a *second* wife? Never! "And what did you tell him?" I said when I could speak.

His incipient smile broadened into a full-fledged grin. "What do you think, *kaderle*? That he could stuff that idea in his saddle bags, of course." His face turned serious. "Don't misunderstand me, sweetheart. I know he loves Maria, and so do I, but I saw what it did to my mother when he ran off with Juliana, then married your sister. I wouldn't do that to you, and I don't want a political marriage for myself. He'll have to accept that."

"I hope he will, then," I said, and his words did comfort me—although I knew how determined my brother-in-law could be. Timur and I had been reunited for little more than a week, and I would soon be sent off, perhaps never to return. Alexei had every reason to bide his time. "Did he tell you anything about the bride show?"

"The idea behind it, what it entails, the costs of not participating after having been named—not just to you but to your entire clan." Timur counted points on his fingers. "Sometime after Epiphany, you depart for a house in the Kremlin, where you remain until you are chosen or disqualified, whichever comes first. I agreed to wait and see, but I can't say I'm happy about it."

"You know more than I do then." Driven by a sense of looming disaster, I prowled the small area behind the freestanding shelves. It was Christmas Eve, so Epiphany lay less than two weeks away. The bride show loomed ever closer, like a dense fog separating me from Timur. "Maria just hammered into my head that I can't please myself. She says I needn't encourage the tsar, but she expects me to act as though becoming tsaritsa is my deepest desire. Otherwise, I will cause offense, and we will all suffer the consequences." I smacked a shelf in frustration. "Including you, or so she insists. Sometimes I wish I'd never been born."

He'd followed my restless promenade. When I stopped, he reached out and flicked my cheek. "Don't despair, Lady Love. We'll find a way." A rustle—the kind made by silk skirts—sounded from outside the room, and he tilted his head, listening. When he turned back to face me, his smile had vanished. "For now, I'd better take my leave. I don't want to cause more trouble for you."

He caught my chin in his right hand, bent his head, and kissed me hard on the mouth, then left before I found words to beg him to remain. From my corner, I heard him greeting my sister. Then the door shut softly, and I pressed both hands over my trembling lips as if by doing so I could preserve our love from harm. For the first time in years, I had no idea how my story would end. I only knew, with quiet desperation, what I wanted the ending to be—and marriage to the ruler of all Russia was not it.

From what Timur had said about the bride show, I anticipated two more weeks of relative tranquillity before my life careened onto a road flanked by the twin ditches of pleasing and offending the young tsar and his relatives. I left the library and returned to my own chamber with plans to complete my story about the princess and the dragon, including a passionate embrace bestowed on said princess by the hero. Since I couldn't get Timur's kisses out of my head, I might as well turn them into a spectacular scene.

An hour later, I had sketched out the sorceress and set her at odds with my heroine. I was considering where to take them next when my sister again interrupted my work, Juliana at her side. A sparkling amusement lit both women's eyes.

I set aside my quill. "What's happened?"

"Papa is hosting a Christmas party!" Maria waved the piece of paper clasped in her forefinger and thumb like a puppeteer manipulating Petrushka. "Midday tomorrow. We're invited—meaning you and me, Alexei and Timur, and Juliana and Felix. As well as every aristocrat in Moscow, male and female, from what Papa writes."

"But why?" I blinked at the window, where dust motes swirled against the panes. A party sounded like fun, especially since "every aristocrat in Moscow" must include at least a few of my friends.

Spend Christmas watching my father scheme, though? I wasn't so sure I looked forward to that. "Papa never throws parties. And Christmas Day isn't the time for such things."

"It is in Poland," Juliana remarked. "We like to commemorate every one of the twelve days with food and drink and merry company." She made it sound as if any civilized country would do the same, but her casual tone didn't fool me. Her marriage to my father hadn't lasted a year, even if the divorce had taken her five times as long to attain, but for that short span she had acted as his hostess. She knew very well that my father did nothing without an ulterior motive, and in the case of parties, that usually meant all-male gatherings of powerful patrons or, more often, cozy one-on-one suppers aimed at concluding secret deals.

I pointed that out, and she laughed. "Or weddings," she said. "Your father loves a good wedding, one where he is the center of attention."

"Yes," I admitted. "But he's had six of those, and he can't arrange mine until the bride show ends. Although I'm sure he dreams of draping the veil over my head and handing me off to the tsar while the court sighs with envy. Of him, not me."

Juliana laughed harder, and Maria waved the invitation again to get our attention. "Let me explain. Papa has asked me to act as hostess for the women's portion of the dinner, and I've agreed on condition that he invite Anna, Anfim, and Solomonida as well. He hopes to influence the men and women who will select which girls to present to the tsar, so he has invited the leading candidates and their sponsors. We can guess that he expects Lyuba to shine and will do everything he can to ensure that she does. But we should attend for our own reasons. It gives us a perfect opportunity to assess the competition. Juliana, you and Felix will accompany us, will you not?"

Juliana pulled a face that made her look about eight years old, and I was hard put not to giggle. She made no secret of how little use she had for Papa; the thought of accepting his hospitality must have stuck in her craw.

After a brief pause, though, she appeared to have second thoughts. "Certainly Felix and I will attend," she said. "What better opportunity to touch the pulse of the court? Given your archaic custom of separating the sexes, I need not worry about enduring an evening with my despicable former husband. And I will do what I can for Lyuba, of course. From what I've heard, she deserves better than your autocrat-to-be." She regarded me with those enigmatic dark eyes. "A handsome Tatar prince, perhaps."

"Enough of that." Annoyance sparked an amber gleam in Maria's eyes, and she crumpled the letter in her hand. "She can't have Timur, and he can't have her, and that's the end of it. Let's not waste the few hours we have to plan our strategy for the party. First, we need to decide on clothes …"

By the time I reached my father's estate around noon the next day, the yard was already so crammed with sleighs that our coachman stopped outside the gates, waited for us to alight, then returned to our own stable. The whole performance had an aura of unreality: we could easily have walked the short distance from our estate to Papa's, which lay a few short streets away. But convention must be observed, and the sleigh served to announce our status, not to satisfy any need for transport. On the contrary, a white sun stood out against clear wintry skies, and the temperature had risen high enough that I would have enjoyed a brisk walk, especially with Timur at my side.

Maria had left our house two hours before to supervise advance preparations for the party, leaving me to travel with Juliana, Felix, Alexei, and Timur. As the youngest female, I had entered the sleigh last, which meant that I emerged first, setting my green leather boot on the swept planks that formed a path to the house and waiting for the others to alight. Juliana came next, then Timur took his place beside me, an encouraging hand on my elbow that he removed in response to a glare from his father. When Alexei turned to help Felix, Timur bent to whisper in my ear, "Good luck, Lady Love," before moving off to offer his arm to Juliana. She took it with a seductive smile, although the wink she sent my way reinforced the idea that I had *one* ally in my quest to spend my life with Timur rather than the tsar.

I shook out my robe of blue-green velvet, admiring the gold embroidery that rimmed the cream-colored tunic beneath and the intermixed sapphires and pearls that formed panels down both sides of the opening and rimmed the high collar. Once satisfied that I looked my best, I let my cloak fall back into place and followed Timur and Juliana toward the house. As we drew closer to the staircase, the crowd slowed our progress, forcing us to dodge clumping boots and carelessly flung arms. By the time we attained the lowest step, I was fighting the temptation to clutch Juliana's skirt like a child. My father might not host parties often, but he certainly knew how to attract a crowd.

I worried about Felix, forced to maneuver the packed stairway with his cane, but when the three of us at last got through the door at the top, he was waiting for us, Alexei at his side. Only then did I realize that, while I focused on the mob ahead of us, my brother-in-law must have taken Felix through the storeroom on the ground floor and helped him mount the servants' stairs.

Alexei's anger might be legendary, but so was his charm. His dark eyes twinkled as he smiled at me, and I responded in kind, relieved to have the confrontation of two days ago behind us. In many ways, he was my real father, and I hated to think I'd disappointed him.

That brief exchange gave me the confidence I needed to face the man who had sired but not raised me. Papa stood near the entrance to the main dining room, at the end of a hallway awash in richly dressed and effusive nobles. Awaiting my turn to issue a formal greeting, I regarded him with awe. For the occasion, he had donned a cloth-of-gold robe with embroidered scarlet cuffs and a sleeveless overcoat trimmed with sable. His skullcap matched the cuffs, as did the boots I glimpsed beneath his long gown. Although small, sleek, and relatively slender compared to the mammoth boyars who surrounded him, Papa exuded the casual self-assurance of a prince.

As we drew closer, my sense of fun came to the fore. I had never seen a play, although Juliana had told me about the productions put on for the court in Cracow. But this whole scene had an aura of unreality that reminded me of the stories I wrote. The scribe who lived at the back of my mind, ever alert for an opportunity for drama, awoke from her nap and jotted down notes for a future tale. A tsar in search of a bride, a roomful of notables, a hero in disguise, a group of lovely maidens, and …

Oh, of course, I must not forget the competitive mamas ready to defend their darlings while eliminating rival candidates from consideration. My spirits rose with each new and outrageous element that came to me, and every one of these was both real and present—except for the tsar, of course. My fingers itched for pen and paper, and I clasped my hands together to still them as the crowd ahead of us passed into the room beyond and those behind pushed us ever closer to my father, in his element as the focus of everyone's attention.

At last, Juliana stopped and curtseyed, her head set at a challenging angle. She did not kiss Papa on both cheeks, according to Russian custom, but released Timur and held out her right hand. After fixing her with an astonished stare, my father took her fingers in his and brushed his lips across her knuckles. When he released her, she stepped aside, and he greeted Timur. Then it was my turn.

"Papa," I said. His cheek felt smooth against mine; he had never favored the luxurious beards so many men cultivated. A faint aroma of something woodsy rose from his well-tended skin. I imagined myself possessing Maria's aplomb as I completed my greeting. "Thank you so much for inviting us today. How did you manage to put together such a large party in so short a time?"

He preened, as I had predicted he would. "I've spent years weaving a web of connections, kitten. And now I intend to use them to advance your cause. Watch, and learn from my example."

An incipient giggle formed in my throat, dispelling any further attempts to imitate my sister. As a small child, I'd idolized my handsome, cunning father, always wishing he would spare me a moment of his time. Then I went to live with Alexei and Maria and learned the difference between loving parents and my self-centered sire. On one memorable occasion, Papa even used me to engineer his own escape from captivity, leaving me to bear the blame while he fled the premises. The incident had taught me to regard my father's protestations of caring with a jaundiced eye. These days I found him sometimes infuriating, sometimes insufferable, but most often ridiculous. Seeing him in full flood, so to speak, I suspected I'd go through all three states before the party ended.

"Of course, Papa." I avoided glancing at Timur or Juliana, both bad influences on the rare occasions when I sought to present myself as accommodating and demure. "Your concern for my future touches me deeply." And with that, I slipped away and left Alexei to dash my father's pretensions with his usual flair. With luck, Papa would never notice that I commended his concern for my future, not for me.

Upstairs, the scene was more appealing, despite the number of guests. Almost right away, I ran into Solomonida, beautiful as ever in silk the color of twilight's first blush, and a radiant Anna clad in a shimmering satin that changed its hue from pink to violet to a soft leafy green as she moved. "From Anfim's silk merchant friend," she said when I commended her on the gown and its stitched silver cuffs—her own work, I felt certain, and for a heart-beat envy at her mastery threatened to undermine my lifetime re-fusal to waste my time on needlework.

"The Italian," she added, in case I had forgotten. "He's our age and very handsome, and he has the most gorgeous fabrics I've ever seen. Some from Hindustan, even Cathay, but this one came from Constantinople, he said." A flush stained her cheeks, making me wonder if the absent, tonsured Yuri was at last loosening his grip on my friend's heart.

I didn't ask. It would be cruel to remind her of her loss. Better to let the young, very handsome Italian silk merchant cast his spell without interference. Her cousin Igor would have a fit if he heard—no one less than a nobleman of high standing would do for him—but Anna and I had already agreed that any spouse of Igor's choosing would make a terrible husband, and an Italian silk merchant was an excellent match for the stepdaughter of a state secretary with connections in trade.

Assuming we could keep Tsar Ivan away from her, of course.

"Walk with me." I took her elbow. "Maria's expecting me to stand next to her and greet the guests as they come in. When did you and your mother arrive?"

"Not long ago." Anna dipped her head toward Solomonida, who was scanning the company for friends, and murmured that she could find us with Maria if necessary.

Solomonida waved us away. "Go. Have fun. I'll fetch you if I need you. And if you're looking for me, you'll find me with Katya

Vorontsova over there or any one of the other friends I last saw a year ago, if then. I feel like a hermit emerging from her cell." She departed without another word, leaving Anna and me chuckling.

I pointed my friend in the right direction. "My sister's over there. I can see the tip of her headdress. Tell me who's already arrived. I thought Maria was exaggerating, but I swear she's right. Papa seems to have invited the entire nobility of Moscow."

"And beyond." Anna pushed past an elderly dowager whom I recognized as Princess Bronislava Blednaya, mother of a reedy prince and a daughter on the bride-show list—the one who looked like a stick with teeth. "I met a girl named Avdotya Gundorova. She came in with her mother from Vyazma, so she's the first contestant from the provinces."

"Interesting," I said, remembering Juliana talking about the posting station in Vyazma and the wretched beds there. "What do you know about her?"

"Not much. She's young, as in barely twelve. But she has curly black hair and a bright smile. A little shy, but she'll respond if you talk to her. And she's a cousin of the Godunov family, so she has relatives in Moscow. Maybe that explains why her father allowed her to travel."

"Maybe." The concerns of Avdotya's father didn't interest me much. He was probably as ambitious as Papa. I shifted to a related topic. "I wonder if your cousin Igor will find any girls."

"What makes you think he will look?" A quick swish of Anna's skirt rescued it from the careless heel of a rotund noblewoman, this one in conversation with Nadezhda Shuiskaya, who tipped her head in greeting as we passed. Next to Nadezhda stood Princess Ustinya Paletskaya, looking pettish and bored. I sent her a sympathetic smile, and she took three steps toward us before Nadezhda jerked her back into place. We bowed and kept walking, while I silently added a grumbling Ustinya as a character in my developing story. At least Maria expected me to stand by her side only long enough to greet the guests.

I turned to share my observations with Anna, but she was still talking about her cousin. "I wish Igor *would* take his commission seriously, because another candidate or two would mean more people to compete with you and me. But it's more likely he'll pretend to look around, announce he can't find anyone, then return as fast as he can, lest I exhibit a spark of independence when his back is turned."

"He and Papa are two of a kind," I grumbled.

"Oh, no," Anna said. "Not at all. Your father is far more dangerous than Igor. Igor responds to the changing wind; sometimes it blows his way, sometimes it doesn't. But your father plans ahead, and he thinks in terms of decades. He has his blind spots—he doesn't understand how much other people hate being treated like chess pieces, for one—and as a result, he doesn't always succeed. But he plots a course and sticks with it, no matter what. Next to him, Igor has the tenacity of a toddler."

I stopped dead in the middle of the room. Two unhappy grandmas cursed me, but I ignored them, struck by my friend's insight. "You're right," I said. "Maria told me Papa had been planning this since *she* was my age. That's very different from your cousin." I murmured apologies to the grandmothers and pulled Anna through the mob until we stood beside my sister, who welcomed us before inviting first Anna, then me, to greet Vera Yureva and her daughter Tasya.

I complied, silently studying Tasya as I did. With every year that passed, she resembled her mother more, and while I grew taller each time we met, she did not. Although we had both almost achieved our adult height, the crown of her head barely reached my shoulder. Small as she was, many people accounted her a beauty because of her dark brown hair and flashing eyes, her symmetrical features, and her pleasing figure. Yet despite a certain liveliness of speech, she hid any hints of willfulness beneath a demure manner.

Watching Tasya, I wondered how much of the general admiration for her derived from her disinterest in challenging society's rules. Next to Maria's vivid coloring and strong personality, instinctive grasp of politics, and willingness to use it to bend the mighty nobles to her will, Tasya's prettiness seemed bland. Whenever I conversed with her, I wished for a hint of spice or a flash of temper to set her apart from the crowd, but she remained utterly conventional. I liked her—there was nothing there to dislike—but if she vanished from the earth one day, years might pass before I noticed her absence.

Her gifts were, of course, the very qualities required of a tsaritsa. In my assigned role as junior hostess for my father, I kissed her cheeks and showered her and her mother with assurances of welcome, asked how she did, and listened with one ear to her reply. And as I dipped my head in pretended agreement with whatever she'd said, I prayed silently that *this* perfect bud of womanhood would be the one to attract the attention of our soon-to-be Tsar Ivan.

Tasya and her mother blended into the crowd, leaving Maria and me to tend to the next guest, then the one after that. After a while, the maidservants stopped bustling about with trays of drinks and platters of appetizers and withdrew to collect the first course. Maria released me from my duties, and I left the doorway, determined to enjoy the rest of my afternoon. Anna had slipped away while I chatted with Tasya and her mother, so I set off in search of my friend. I found her in conversation with Ustinya Paletskaya.

"Congratulations," I said to Ustinya. "How did you manage to escape Princess Nadezhda?"

Her face crinkled with laughter, demonstrating the free spirit that Tasya so conspicuously lacked, the vivacity that drew me to Ustinya despite her capacity for malice. "She got tired of me standing there glumping, as she put it, and told me to go off and not come back until I could reinforce her efforts on my behalf instead of undermining them at every turn."

"*Are* you undermining them?" I asked. Maybe Ustinya didn't want to marry the tsar any more than I did.

"Of course not." The shake of Ustinya's head turned her gold earrings into a spray of gilded light. "I just don't believe that listening to grannies complain about their chilblains will advance my cause. I'm desperate to succeed. Aren't you?"

The sinking feeling that had attacked my midriff when I thought her an unwilling candidate disappeared without a trace. Tempted to say "Not in the least," I remembered my sister's injunctions to keep such thoughts to myself. "May the best candidate win," I said instead.

Ustinya had yet to respond when Maria raised her hand and called for silence. "Ladies," she announced in ringing tones. "We thank you for adding your exalted presence to our celebration. We plan to serve the meal at any moment, but my father has requested that the maidens nominated for the bride show be presented to the noblemen downstairs. Ekaterina Ivanovna and Darya Petrovna have agreed to assist me. I ask Princess Nadezhda to join us while the mothers, sisters, and aunts remain upstairs. We will return as soon as my father permits."

Ustinya headed for the door without so much as a "see you soon." I grabbed Anna's arm before my friend could follow. "Your Aunt Darya's here? I didn't see her while I was on the receiving line—or when we first arrived."

"She's over there." Anna pointed at the door, where, indeed, her aunt stood chatting with Igor's wife, Katya—whom my sister had just addressed by her full name, Ekaterina Ivanovna. "She sent Mama a note to say she'd be late. Andrusha had a tantrum when she went to kiss him goodbye. You know what two-year-olds are like."

"I do." I had a mental image of my nephew and niece, red-faced with impotent fury. It hadn't been fun at the time, but fortunately, those days were past. "Alexander and Dosia threw fits every time they didn't get their way. Poor Darya."

"Anyway, she's here now." Anna waved at her aunt, elegant in turquoise brocade. Darya beckoned to us, indicating we should join the group of brides at the entryway. Still collecting tales for my family saga, I studied Darya as we sauntered toward her. On the surface, she betrayed no more strength of character than Tasya Yureva, but I had seen Darya in action. She might appear to be an observer rather than a director of events, but she had a sharp eye for hidden motives and a stubborn streak I could only admire. Her light brown eyes flashed with intelligence as she pressed her lightly powdered cheek against mine, then Anna's.

Could it be that Tasya, too, concealed a hidden strength of character? That would make her a more interesting character, a potential heroine rather than a pretty face. But I'd drawn no conclusion before I reached the doorway and had to set the possibility aside for later contemplation.

"How lovely to see you," I told Darya in greeting. "Although I hear Andrusha did not approve."

She laughed. "He objected quite vociferously, but a pastry from the kitchen diverted him, and I was able to slip out. I'm sure he'll have forgotten the whole thing by the time I return."

"Probably." I gestured toward the group near the doorway, still beyond hearing distance. "What do you make of the competition?"

"They're a handsome lot," Darya said.

She exaggerated. Tasya and Ustinya were beauties by any standard, and Avdotya from Vyazma would soon equal them. But all three easily eclipsed stick-like Fetinya Blednaya and Serafima Khabarova, an equally plain affiliate of the Belsky clan who stood next to her. On Tasya's other side I saw the two Morozov cousins Solomonida had mentioned, the almost-twins who were the nieces of Katya and Liza Vorontsova.

The cousins, nicknamed Grunya and Dunya by their friends, were alike as two carrots from the same patch, with hair even redder than mine, complexions like skimmed milk, and eyes the blue of a summer sky not long after dawn. They were not beautiful, exactly, but they were striking, especially when viewed side by side. Although downright silly at times, they were seldom boring, so I liked them. I felt myself drawn to Avdotya, too; she had wide dark eyes and a serious face. I still couldn't imagine why her father wanted to marry her off so young, but the more serious competition the better, from my perspective.

Katya stood nearby, ready to escort her nieces downstairs. Tall and stately, Katya often displayed a wit as biting as Juliana's and an even more scathing tongue. Neither of them ever missed a political ploy or a preening ego in need of a set-down. They also loved to hone their knives on each other, not least because Katya's husband thought that roses sprouted in the grass as Juliana passed by. The fact that she adored her husband had no impact on Igor. I saw both women as fun to be around, so long as I stayed on their good side.

Maria interrupted my survey. "The men are waiting," she said. "Let's go." I hung back to let the guests, led by Tasya Yureva, precede me, then fell into place beside Anna as Grunya and Dunya made their tittering way through the door. They were mischief-makers, poking Fetinya in the ribs and prodding

Serafima, then putting both hands behind their backs and looking innocent when their victims turned to scowl. I cast them as naughty house spirits in my unfolding story.

Downstairs, we entered a room transformed for the occasion. Papa had outdone himself: every surface gleamed with polish, crisp white damask covered the tables, gold plate glimmered in the light of a hundred candles, and the sheer weight of the massive platters of food laid out on the sideboard would have buckled any piece of furniture made of less than solid oak. More than one manservant would stagger, groaning and holding his back, from the room tonight.

As was the custom during such ceremonies, we girls lined up —Tasya at the far end, since she'd gone first, and myself next to the door. Glancing from one female face to the next, I wondered if this was how the presentations of bridal candidates to the tsar would take place, or whether we would instead parade past him one at a time.

Papa met us as we came in, stopped to question Maria, and murmured something in Princess Nadezhda's ear that caused her to giggle like one of us girls. Remembering what Solomonida had said about them doing the same at a previous party, I stretched my neck in an attempt to hear what they said, but he had already moved on to greet Darya. She apologized for her late arrival.

"Think nothing of it," he told her. "Your husband explained the circumstances."

Her cheeks pink, she thanked him. Across the room, I saw Nikita, her husband, seated near Alexei. The two of them chatted amiably with a pair of men I couldn't identify, paying little attention to Papa.

As the married women positioned themselves behind our line of girls, I surveyed the other guests. There were too many to count, although I estimated fifty or even seventy-five, twice as many as the women upstairs. I recognized no more than a dozen, most of them relatives, but that was not surprising. I had few chances to meet men outside my family circle.

A number of the guests sprawled on benches near the dining tables. Their disheveled hair and blank stares suggested they had already raised many toasts. Groups of three or four gesticulated and chattered—some loud, some soft. As they became aware of our presence, the din abated. Most gazed at us stolidly, arms lolling at their sides as if they couldn't decide what to make of this feminine invasion. Anna's stepfather, Anfim, raised a goblet in welcome from his place among a quartet of what I assumed were fellow government officials.

In a far corner, Timur stood with a group of youths his own age. I recognized two of them as princes who had often visited our house before Timur left to join his uncle on the steppe: Fyodor Ovchinin, the son of Grand Princess Elena's rumored lover, and his cousin Ivan Poroshin. Their lively expressions and vivid gestures indicated they were comparing notes on the last few years. At first, they didn't notice us, but the lull that fell over the room as the older men abandoned their conversations eventually affected everyone.

Timur performed the same elaborate salute he had given me the day before, touching the center of his forehead and the region over his heart before extending his palm out at waist height. A smile tugged at the corners of his mouth, and he looked straight at me. A sigh rippled through the line of girls, and I wondered if each of them saw the gesture as directed at herself.

But I knew he meant it for me. And I couldn't help smiling back.

Chapter 9

"And the hags of the village fought among themselves"

The rest of the ritual proceeded apace. Papa introduced us, then named Maria, Nadezhda, Katya, and Darya. The solemn groups came to life, treating us to a long examination as if we were animals in the royal menagerie or treats set out on a table for them to sample. Whispers of "most attractive" and "I wish I had the young tsar's choices" and "what about those twins in the middle?"—meaning Grunya and Dunya, I assumed, although they were not twins—assailed my ears, but I managed to keep a straight face. The whole situation seemed absurd. You'd think they'd never seen young women before!

The laughter in Timur's eyes stressed my self-control to the breaking point, and I would have given anything to race to the stable, leap on my horse's back, and ride into the meadows with him at my side.

No chance of that. I breathed deeply and avoided looking directly at any of the others until they stopped muttering.

Papa bowed, signaling that he planned to move to the next stage in the ceremony. Fear gripped my stomach as I realized we might be standing there for hours as one man after another lumbered to his feet and tried to kiss us before we left.

But Papa, too, must have recognized how impractical that would be, because he fended off most of his guests with an outstretched arm while selecting ten of the most illustrious non-relatives, which was more than enough for me. Even as they approached, I knew that none of their damp and flabby lips would have anything like the effect on me that Timur could produce with a single enigmatic glance.

My love, however, was not among the chosen ten. Worse, Prince Pavel Shuisky was. He moved slowly down the line, embracing one maiden after another until he reached Anna. While he gripped her around the waist and bent her half-backward as he kissed her full on the mouth, my friend clenched her fists at her sides, her entire body rigid.

My feet twitched with the urge to kick him in the shins. As I moved to intervene, though, Anna dug her heel into his instep. He released her with a yelp and turned to me, but I fixed him with such a glare that he stopped in his tracks, mouth hanging open, then retreated as if faced with the sorceress from Tolya's tale.

"Beast," I muttered when he was safely out of earshot. "Good work with that heel!"

"I hope I didn't hurt him." She sounded worried, and I gazed at her in disbelief. She was my dearest friend, yet sometimes I despaired of her. She was too virtuous for her own good.

"*I* hope you crippled him for life," I said. "He deserves it, the cad. Staking his claim to you like that—and in public!" Her expression of concern dissolved into a grin.

Before long, we received permission to leave. As we mounted the stairs, I let the stress of the kissing ceremony disperse. I still would have preferred to ride into the sunset with Timur, but since that was out of the question, I decided to spend the next few hours collecting as much information as I could about my fellow candidates in the bride show.

Trouble started as soon as we reached our destination. In our absence, Dimka, Papa's elderly steward, had taken over the third-floor dining area. When we entered the room, he stood at its center, bowing ladies to their assigned places at the tables and fending off Princess Bronislava, who had raised her palms to the skies and was calling the wrath of Heaven down on Dimka's uncaring head. From this bizarre behavior I deduced she had manufactured a crisis that Dimka had no power to resolve.

Sure enough, he sent Maria pleading glances as she swept into the fray. His shoulders slumped with relief when my sister muttered a command and pushed him toward the door, and he tottered off to do her bidding with an audible sigh.

Intrigued, I moved closer, eager to find out more. The other girls followed; I felt their presence at my back as if they were pushing me forward. And who could blame them? A good quarrel was as much fun as a good story, and this one had already distinguished itself: even at sixteen, I'd witnessed enough squabbles to know that women's arguments generally played themselves out through veiled insults and snippy remarks rather than ostentatious prayers to the Almighty. But what was the argument about?

I received my answer as soon as I came within hearing distance. "You cannot expect me to sit below Liza Vorontsova," Bronislava announced in ringing tones. "I am a *princess*, and I have a daughter who may become our first tsaritsa. Liza shouldn't even be here, in mourning as she is." The edge in her voice convinced me she had stated these points more than once, deluging the unfortunate steward with her demands.

"You *are* a princess," Maria replied in soothing tones. She patted Princess Bronislava's arm with the same gesture she might use to calm a restless child. "But Liza Vorontsova agreed to join us at my father's invitation; her family comes from the old Moscow nobility; and her husband was, for much of his career, a favorite of the young tsar. She also has two nieces in the bride show. We are not court recorders, and there is no need to list this seating assignment in any official record. I feel certain that a lady as benevolent as you can honor Elizaveta Vadimovna's grief by yielding one place at the table. My husband would look favorably on a young man whose mother exhibited such generosity of spirit."

I had to bite back a giggle. I could almost hear Alexei swearing, which he would certainly do when he learned how his beloved wife had used his standing at court and the promise of patronage to get her out of an awkward situation. But Maria's subterfuge worked, and the princess, still grumbling, took her assigned seat.

Looking at the women near the head of the table, I realized that my father's plan had succeeded. These were not simply sponsors of bridal candidates but representatives of the highest noble clans. Together with Anastasia Petrovna, whom we'd visited last week, and Princess Anna Glinskaya—both of them too closely related to royalty to attend a party at a subject's house—the Shuisky and Belsky princesses would have a significant voice in selecting the short list of girls to be presented to the tsar. For a moment, I stared at Maria in awe, watching the ease she displayed in handling these often haughty women and wondering if I could ever equal her.

A loud harrumph drew my gaze in the other direction, where my Aunt Theodosia sailed into position opposite Solomonida and glared at the remaining guests, daring them to challenge her for that seat. Not that any of them would do anything so foolish.

Auntie glanced my way before settling onto the bench, and I saw a gleam in her eyes that sent tremors rippling down my spine. My already paltry efforts to remain a detached spectator suffered a serious blow. Aunt Theodosia was deaf as a post, and her voice correspondingly loud. She had strong opinions, which she was eager to share, and anything she said would reach every ear in the room.

I shimmied my shoulders, reassuring myself that if I kept my wits, I could dodge any attempts by Auntie to embarrass me. I was one among many, and the other sponsors were also present and armed for the fight. I needed to keep quiet, watch and listen, and speak only when spoken to—except with my friends, of course.

For a while, all went well. The rest of our relatives, under strict orders from Papa to behave themselves, took their seats at the lower half of the table without a word of protest. A wave of my sister's hand sent us girls to our places opposite the ranked ladies. I ended up right in the middle of the candidates, which suited me admirably. Ustinya Paletskaya sat closest to Maria, with bland Serafima and stiff-spined Fetinya next in line. Then came Anna, be-, cause although her stepfather lacked noble rank, her cousin Igor was on the royal council. My father was *not* on the royal council; he had served there once upon a time, before his troubles started, but he had recovered his position sufficiently to justify my placement on Anna's left, directly opposite Juliana. That left giggling Grunya and Dunya, Tasya Yureva, and Avdotya from Vyazma—who, poor thing, had ended up in Aunt Theodosia's direct line of fire. She'd do all right, though, because the other women at her end of the table would step in to protect her, if need be. Solomonida was charming and good-natured, Vera Yureva as quiet and conventional as her daughter, Darya far too kind to stand by while our aunt bullied a young girl. Tasya, Grunya, and Dunya might help without meaning to, by drawing Auntie's attention to themselves. In fact, the more I thought about it, the less likely it seemed that Auntie would waste her ammunition on a twelve-year-old from the provinces when she had so many better targets to hand.

Anna and I were not as well positioned, but we could reasonably hope to escape notice. Katya and Juliana wouldn't bother us. Princess Bronislava posed the biggest threat, although the battle she'd just lost might constrain her. Liza Vorontsova approved of

Anna and would leave my friend alone, although I could only hope that my status as the host's daughter would spare me the flick of her occasionally viperous tongue. With luck, any conflict would play itself out at the top of the table, where the Shuisky and Belsky princesses sat. Those two clans seldom let slip an opportunity to test each other's mettle.

The food arrived, and for a while, I ate in peace, watching my predictions play out with an uncanny accuracy that made me feel even more like a writer creating a real-life story with a flick of her magic wand. While the rest of us said as little as possible, the highborn ladies spent a lot of time quizzing the girls closest to them about things like embroidery skills (admirable), physical activity (questionable), and domestic management (expected). It felt like a dry run for the bride show to come, and predictably, some candidates did better than others. Ustinya Paletskaya chatted amiably, her vivid face and hand gestures weaving a kind of spell over her audience, whereas plain Serafima mumbled and blushed. Fetinya the Stick managed one moment of defiance, declaring, "I love plants. I have an entire garden of my own." Then, pinned by her mother's gimlet gaze, she turned from pale to ashen and stuttered into silence. Anna's gentle demeanor and musical voice carried her through the inquisition unscathed.

Then my turn came. "And what of you, Lyubov Fyodorovna?" Princess Sophia Belskaya shot a glance at Nadezhda Shuiskaya, then went straight for the jugular. "Word has reached us that you do not choose to spend your time on embroidery. Can you explain that?"

Faced with such a direct confrontation, I panicked. The answers I'd practiced with Maria fled from my brain, leaving only the horror I'd felt when Anastasia Petrovna declared that I might be suitable precisely because of my unfeminine interest in the written word.

After an awkward pause, I recalled one potential response and uttered it before my nerve failed me altogether. "I lack my sister's skill with the needle. And despite years of practice, I have not improved, so I choose to spare the world from my stitched abominations."

A titter of laughter ran around the table at that, although some of the more conventional aunts and cousins frowned. Princess Sophia also furrowed her brows, and I allowed myself a moment of hope that the questions would end.

They didn't. "How, then, do you occupy yourself?" she asked, and I heard astonishment in her voice.

Again I hesitated, afraid of unleashing a tempest by saying the wrong thing. "I write," although true, would provoke a swirl of controversy. "I attend religious services" would paint a false picture of my piety and offset any bad impression left by my failures as a needlewoman. "I supervise the servants" could only further undermine my quest to be considered too eccentric for a royal bride. I could count on "I ride and exercise my brother-in-law's falcons" having the opposite effect—unless Princess Anastasia Petrovna turned out to adore hawks, hounds, and horses. In that case, I'd have sealed my own fate.

I looked wildly around the table for support. My sister sent me an encouraging nod, but inspiration continued to lurk in the shadows.

In the end, I gave the simplest answer possible, despite the potential danger posed by my love of learning. "I read books."

"What kind of books?" Princess Bronislava entered the conversation like a general taking command of his troops. The horror in her voice suggested that she expected my next confession to involve tormenting small animals.

Juliana reached across the table and patted my hand, giving me the courage to reply. "The usual kind," I said. "Saints' lives, old sagas about heroes, that sort of thing." I didn't mention the histories or the books in foreign languages. Nadezhda Shuiskaya could regale them with those details if she chose. She probably already had.

"How very peculiar," Princess Sophia drawled, as if I were a freak encountered at a county fair.

Peculiar is good, I assured myself. They wouldn't want a freak as tsaritsa.

"And the servants?" she added, when I made no attempt to respond. "You have reached marriageable age." Her eyes flicked to the end of the table, where twelve-year-old Avdotya sat. "Or more," she continued, returning her gaze to me. "You must know how to run a household by now."

"My sister takes care of that," I said, as demurely as I could, determined not to give her any reason to change her mind about me.

Aunt Theodosia couldn't let that statement pass unchallenged. I'd have sworn I'd spoken too low for her to hear me, but I was mistaken. She announced at top volume, "Don't be ridiculous, girl. Of course, you can manage a noble household. What have we been teaching you all these years?"

Several of the ladies laughed. I bit my lip and stared at the trencher before me as if I were too embarrassed to respond, and the moment passed. When I looked up again, Princess Sophia had moved on to quizzing Grunya, who squirmed under the lash of the princess's tongue just as I had. I allowed myself a quiet sigh of relief and prayed that my moment in the sun had ended.

To ensure that I stayed in the shadows, I returned my attention to the meal in front of me. I broke fresh-smelling bread into pieces and dipped it in luscious, tender beef gravy. The small bowl of noodles dripping with butter and flecked with parsley delighted me with memories of childhood feasts. Cherry juice brought straight from the icehouse cut the grease with its sweet/tart edge. Anyone who didn't know might mistake it for red wine, which the older guests sipped with abandon. I didn't object to being banned from the wine jugs; the taste hadn't impressed me the one time I tried it. But I liked the sense of sophistication associated with that rich crimson hue.

Servants arrived with the next course, a honey-sweetened fruit aspic called kissel. It was a light and refreshing way to end the heavy meal. As I dipped my spoon into the luscious confection, scraps of conversation drifted past me, more savory than sweet.

"*My* daughter has the patience of a saint."

"Ah yes, but mine embroiders like an angel."

"As if that matters. When did your line last have sons? Mine raises three or more to adulthood in each generation."

"And how will an ugly girl get sons? Beauties like my nieces aren't found under every bush, you know."

Unbidden, an image of Timur's salute, his laughing eyes, hovered like a vision before me. That in turn sparked memories of our ride and the kiss that followed. My cheek tingled with the phantom touch of his fingers. He'd admitted he was courting me. He'd offered to run off with me. If only I could!

I glanced across the table, where I found Juliana watching me with the intent, focused attention she displayed at times. When I returned her gaze, she treated me to her mysterious smile, then started a discussion about music with Darya and Katya. At times, her perspicacity disturbed me. I wondered if she'd guessed my thoughts and, if so, what gave me away. A dreamy expression in my eyes, a flush to my cheeks?

Taking care not to draw attention to myself, I joined Anna's discussion with Fetinya of what we'd witnessed downstairs. As I listened to them, I found myself pondering what I'd learned so far. Except for Anastasia Petrovna, the women agreed on the criteria that favored a royal bride: housekeeping, embroidery, beauty, health, and a demure and obedient character. My sister had been right about that. Yet I'd also discovered that the candidates' sponsors had talons sharper than my falcon's and no more compunction about using them on their prey.

But would their competitiveness aid me or destroy me? That I still didn't know.

Chapter 10

"The dragon bared his teeth, spouting flames and destruction"

"You won't believe what's going on outside." Timur stood at the entrance to Alexei's study, where I'd reclaimed my writing space and sat hunched over my fully drafted story, pondering what needed to change to increase the dramatic impact of my tale. Arms crossed over his chest, he leaned against the door jamb, but I'd barely had a chance to register his presence before he abandoned his position and strode past me, stopping only when he reached the window.

Unlike most of the panes in the house, those in the study had metal clasps. Timur threw this one open. Sunshine poured into the room, chased by a freezing wind that wrung an involuntary yelp out of me. I leaped to my feet, slapped the ink pot onto papers already lifting in the breeze, and ran to see what had caught his attention. It was the third of January, little more than a week after my father's party, and the unseasonable warmth had retreated long before December left the scene.

The courtyard stood empty, as it had the day we drove to consult with Solomonida—and for the same reason. It was bitterly cold, and anyone with a reason to stay indoors had done so. In the distance, I heard roars—whether of approval or shock I couldn't tell—punctuated by piercing screams that set my stomach churning.

"What's happening?" I asked.

Timur shut the window and turned. Only then did I notice that he was dressed for riding. Snow frosted his shoulders and melted in his hair. He must have seen something on his way home, since nothing visible from this room explained the screams. Instead of answering me, he tore off his hat and flung it across the room, where it landed atop an enamel-tiled table and drooped like the headgear of a woodland troll. Under other circumstances, it would have been comic, but there was nothing humorous about Timur's taut stance and clenched fists.

Shocked and scared, I waited. His grim expression told me I wouldn't like whatever he had to say.

His silence lasted so long that I reached out and laid my hand on his arm, offering comfort in the only way I knew how. His muscles lay rigid under my touch, but after a short pause he exhaled a long *whoosh* of air and said, in a tone so wooden that he sounded like someone else altogether, "The Glinskys, Mikhail and his mother, ordered Fyodor Ovchinin impaled on a stake driven into the ice of the Moscow River. They've also had his cousin Poroshin beheaded."

I blinked. I couldn't have heard that correctly. The uncle and grandmother of our soon-to-be-crowned tsar had ordered the brutal execution of two men under the age of twenty? "Why?" I said. A phantom giant gripped my throat, and I could manage no more than the one word. Tears clouded my vision, and filtered through them I saw again the presentation at Papa's party—Timur in the far corner, laughing and joking with his friends, one already murdered and the other subjected to a slow, excruciating torture that must have him longing for death.

"Because of who they are." Timur gripped my hand, which still rested on his arm. "Or were. Not because of anything they've done."

I heard the anguish in his voice and understood its source. These were his friends. I didn't want to make things worse for him by forcing him to explain, so I tried to figure out for myself what he had in mind. What did that mean—because of who they were?

Ovchinin was the only legitimate son of Ivan Telepnev, assumed by most people to have been Grand Princess Elena's lover. Her husband had not produced an heir in more than twenty years of marriage, despite scandalously divorcing his first wife and marrying Elena. Because he then miraculously sired a pair of boys in quick succession, many also regarded Telepnev as the true father of our soon-to-be tsar and his younger brother. If true, that would make Ovchinin an older, unacknowledged half-brother of the tsar. It was a stretch to regard Ovchinin as a threat, since no one had ever suggested he should rule. Still, I could see why the Glinskys might want to get rid of him to prevent any such ideas from surfacing—although nothing could justify the brutality of the punishment. And even that didn't explain the decision to execute his cousin. Poroshin posed no danger to the crown or anyone associated with it.

"Clan politics," Timur said, still sounding as if it pained him to speak. "The tsar just appointed his uncle as master of horse."

I stared at him. Memory tugged at my brain, yet comprehension hovered just out of reach. "Solomonida told us he would," I said. "To enhance the status of his relatives before the coronation."

"Remember what happened last July?"

Wheels spun in my head. Last July? Last July the not-yet-tsar had ordered the execution of Demid Vorontsov and another prince. He had banished Anna's Yuri, and …

Light dawned. "The grand prince stripped Ivan Fyodorov of his position as master of horse—the same position Telepnev once held." Excitement at solving the puzzle tinged my voice, but mindful of Timur's grief, I suppressed it. "And Ivan Fyodorov is your friend Poroshin's stepfather. Is *that* what this is all about: attacking Telepnev's heirs so no one is left to challenge Mikhail

Glinsky's right to serve as master of horse?" That made even less sense than preventing a potential uprising!

"I think so." Timur's eyes were bleak, his mouth set in a grim line. "I can't be sure, but it's the one thing Fyodorov, Poroshin, and Ovchinin have in common—they're descendants of, or married into, the Cheliadnin line."

The screams outside rose and fell—haunting, harrowing, heart-rending. Imaginary ants crawled across my skin, and spectral tears traced lines along my cheeks. I shuddered, unable to imagine the agony poor Ovchinin must be suffering. My sorrow and Timur's seemed trivial by comparison.

"And the cruelty?" I asked. "There are more humane ways to kill." I hated what this was doing to the man I loved, but if I could understand its cause, we need never talk about it again.

He gave a slight, helpless shrug. "To prove the Glinskys' power, I assume. To inspire fear and head off any challenges as they tighten their grip with the bride show."

The bride show. "Oh, Mother of God," I blurted out. "I have to go into the Kremlin and pretend I want to marry the tsar, knowing that he and his relatives are capable of such atrocities? I can't do it. No one can expect it of me."

But even as the words left my mouth, I knew I had no choice. Defy the tsar, and Alexei might be the next man impaled on a stake—or Timur. A family determined to destroy two young men just to prove that it could was not likely to care about the preferences of one obstinate young woman.

I pulled my hand free and wrapped both arms around Timur's waist. He pulled me close, murmuring endearments into my hair. But whether I sought comfort or offered it, I could not have said.

The general gloom caused by the dual execution still hung over the household three days later. In my case, the approaching bride show—had not Alexei told Timur that we would be summoned to the Kremlin as soon as the Christmas season ended?—intensified my woes. Anna was beside herself, announcing that, come what may, she would not wed the tsar. I listened and murmured agreement, never once mentioning that her stepfather Anfim's status of state secretary left him even more vulnerable to royal punishment than Alexei or Timur. I shared her feelings, after all.

Rank brings responsibility, though, so on January 6, 1547, our entire household attended the Blessing of the Waters ceremony on the banks of the Moscow River—everyone except Felix, whose injured leg made standing for hours in freezing temperatures intolerable. Although it was not Timur's ritual or even his religion, he chose to come along, saying he wanted to spend time with me while he still had the opportunity.

His decision raised my spirits. I'd seen little of him the last three days; he'd spent most of his time outdoors—as if hard work could distract him from thoughts of what had happened to his childhood friends. I'd caught him the day before in Alexei's study, staring out the window as he had when he delivered the news, and when I went to stand beside him in silent camaraderie, he pulled me into an embrace, resting his chin atop my head. "Wouldn't you love to leave Moscow behind?" he asked. "The steppe has enemies too, but at least there it's a clean fight." I folded my arms over his and told him I understood, but I knew he wouldn't leave. In fact, I hoped he wouldn't go until the bride show was done. If I had the chance then, I'd gladly ride south with him.

So I was happy when he agreed to attend the Blessing of the Waters. Epiphany was special, after all. The ceremony required Alexei to march with the rest of the high nobility and the prelates of the Church in the royal procession from the Kremlin to the

Moscow River. While Maria was preoccupied with her children, Timur and I lost ourselves among the throng of happy citizens celebrating the arrival of the Magi and the banishment of demonic spirits from the water. There, out of our relatives' line of sight, we shared treats from the market stalls and ignored the biting winds. The bitter cold continued, and I reveled in the strength of my love's arm around my waist, the softness of his fur coat against my cheek, and the heat his nearness always provoked in me. We even managed to sneak a kiss or two behind the stalls.

Hearing the ceremony approach its ending, we reluctantly yielded to the demands of common sense and returned before Maria could send out a search party. On the way back, we ran into Anna and Solomonida, walking with Anfim and his two children. "Tolya, your book of tales is almost ready," I said. He let out a yell that would draw a sleeping dragon from its lair.

I introduced Timur to Anfim, Solomonida, and the children before inviting the five of them to accompany us. My motives were not driven purely by the demands of friendship. With luck, my sister wouldn't realize that Timur and I had spent a good hour alone and unsupervised. The twinkle in my love's eyes assured me he had guessed the direction of my thoughts.

It took a while to push through the dispersing crowds, and by the time we found Maria and Juliana, Alexei had joined them. His frown suggested that he suspected Timur and me of disobeying his orders to stay apart, but by then we were walking on opposite sides of the group looking as innocent as we could manage, so he didn't comment. Instead he greeted Solomonida, Anna, and Anfim with courtesy. Lara and Tolya regarded him with awe, behaving like model children whenever his eye rested on them. I understood the impulse.

"Why don't you come with us?" Solomonida said after a while. "Katya's house is around the corner, and I promised to visit her."

"Not I," Alexei said. "Timur, we should go home. Igor Grigorevich is still away, and it would not be proper for us to call on his wife when he is absent. Besides, Felix has been left to his own devices long enough."

Timur nodded. I smiled but made no attempt to detain him. I had lovely memories of our time alone to sustain me, and those would suffice for a while.

Maria laughed openly at her husband, saying, "As if you would agree if Igor were there. I wasn't born yesterday, you know." When Alexei acknowledged her point with the sheepish expression of a boy caught in the midst of some childish crime, she tucked one hand in the curve of my arm and the other in Juliana's. "We should go, though," she added. "I haven't seen Katya since the party, and I'm sure there's much to discuss."

Anfim excused himself as well, taking Lara and Tolya with him. And so we went, Solomonida and Anna in the lead and the rest of us following, since the wooden planking that lined the streets—swept free of snow that very morning—was too narrow for five.

It was not a long walk. Nothing in that section of the city, its boundaries determined by three streets radiating out from the moat surrounding the central fortress like so many spokes of a wheel, could be considered a long walk. Cross-streets connected the main thoroughfares at irregular intervals, permitting access to the areas between. In this case, we had a stroll of no more than two blocks. The estate assigned to Igor and Katya faced directly onto Varvarka Street, with the house where Solomonida had grown up next to it. We could easily reach our destination before the wintry weather turned our cheeks to reddened ice, although Alexei called after us that he would send the sleigh to collect us before dusk. I sent him grateful thoughts for his consideration.

The fences surrounding noble estates hemmed us in on both sides, creating a tunnel through which a chilly breeze blew. A gray veil covered the sky, dull and ominous as lead. I anticipated snow before nightfall.

But when we reached the gates, we saw that Alexei was mistaken: Cousin Igor had returned. At least, that seemed the most likely explanation for the flurry of activity in the courtyard, since Igor himself was not visible when we arrived. Servants bustled back and forth carrying mountains of luggage, raised voices from the kitchen and storerooms begged for joints of beef and flagons of beer, and three bewildered noblewomen huddled shivering in the scant shelter offered by an overhanging eave. As we stopped, caught off-guard by the scene before us, Katya ran down the stairs.

She looked as if she'd grabbed the first robe that lay to hand and flung a fur-lined cape over it. Her manner was frazzled, and her hair fell in two fat braids down her back, with curly wisps escaping here and there. I stared, unable to believe my eyes. I'd never seen her with her head uncovered, and I wondered if she'd been napping when the sounds of her visitors' arrival woke her. Even that seemed unlike her—and who could sleep in the middle of the afternoon, amid a festival attended by the entire city?—but then I realized that a mid-afternoon nap was not so hard to understand. Her son was not yet six months old. Although she didn't nurse him as Solomonida did Seryozha, I knew enough about babies to imagine other ways in which they might keep their mothers awake at night.

Katya came to us first, pressing her cheek against each of ours. "No, not at all," she said when Maria asked if we should postpone our visit. "I'll be glad of your company." Her gaze swept the courtyard before returning to us. "It's too cold to stand about in this wind. Go upstairs while I find out who these visitors are and what my husband expects of me, and I'll join you in the women's quarters." My sister nodded, and one after another, we climbed the steps. Anna and I went last, and the way the two of us craned our necks to catch a glimpse of what was happening below, it was a wonder we didn't tumble to our deaths over the railing. When we reached Katya's sitting room, the five of us stripped off our outer garments and huddled round the stove.

My desire for heat soon gave way to curiosity, however. I moved to the window, eager for another sight of the visitors we'd left below. Katya didn't know who they were, so she couldn't have had advance warning of their arrival. She hadn't expected Igor this soon, either, or she would have been better prepared. But he was here, with two young women and an older one. All that suggested he'd exceeded our predictions and found a *pair* of potential royal brides, whom he'd brought to Moscow even though doing so made it less likely that Anna would win him the prize he craved. But why? Could he imagine that he would benefit from having any girl he'd nominated chosen as the next tsaritsa? From the little Maria had told me, that seemed unlikely, but it would explain his behavior.

Twist and turn as I might, I caught no glimpse of my quarry. Katya arrived while I was still cursing (under my breath, fortunately, so she didn't hear me) the stubborn opacity of the mica window panes, which blocked an otherwise clear view of the courtyard. I noticed she'd taken time to spruce herself up a bit. She was alone—another surprise, but one she explained as soon as she crossed the threshold. "Igor asks us to join him in the main sitting room. He wants to introduce us to the women he brought from Kolomna. To meet the competition, as he put it." So I'd guessed right about the younger newcomers being potential brides.

Katya beckoned from the doorway, inviting us to head downstairs. This was my chance to find out more about the visitors— and Igor's reasons for bringing them to Moscow. A thrill, almost like the thrill of the chase, ran through me. I wanted to meet the competition. Indeed, I hoped they could put Anna and me in the shade, although the glimpse of them I'd received in the court-yard hadn't offered much hope of that.

Maria, Solomonida, and Juliana passed through the doorway. Katya jerked her chin toward the stairs and left the room. I grabbed Anna's elbow and whispered, "Let's go." We followed, arm in arm, united against Cousin Igor, his visitors, and his plans.

Chapter 11

"To appease the dragon, the villagers gathered maidens from afar"

I gor greeted us with cries of delight as we entered the sitting room. He bowed to Maria with a flourish, embraced Anna and me until we squirmed away, and bestowed a curt nod on Solomonida. Juliana's unexpected appearance sent him over the moon. He kissed her hand with fervor and mumbled compliments that embarrassed *me*. I could only imagine how Katya felt, but the stony glare she fixed on them said louder than words why she and Juliana had trouble getting along.

To Juliana's credit, she tried to discourage him, withdrawing her hand and curtseying. "Lord Felix," she said, emphasizing the name, "—we've married, you know, since you last saw us in Moscow—apologizes for not accompanying me. Urgent business kept him at home today." Although I knew the "urgent business" was a desire to avoid having his injured leg seize up, I admired the way she slid over his disability and forestalled any impression of weakness that Igor might have harbored if she'd told the truth.

The effect, however, was probably not what she intended. Igor launched into another flood of compliments on her marriage, her looks, and his abject distress that he had kept her waiting for so much as a moment before extending his hand in greeting. He even muttered a few phrases about looking forward to hosting Lord Felix in his home in the near future, but with such patent insincerity that even someone as inexperienced as I couldn't take his words at face value.

Waiting for the deluge to end, I surveyed the room, starting with our host. To my critical eye, Igor appeared less resplendent than usual, although better dressed than on the day of his surprise visit to Solomonida. He'd removed the coat he must have worn against the chill of the journey and replaced whatever headgear he'd sported on the road with a simple skull cap made of emerald silk. A whiff of leather and sweat defied the perfume he'd splashed on—recently, I guessed, from the intensity of the musky aroma. Moisture stained his boots and the trousers tucked into them, undercutting the elegance of a velvet robe the color of a midnight sky. Most telling was the absence of jewelry, which Igor generally piled on like a Tatar khan at his coronation. I concluded that he'd thrown the robe over his riding gear rather than forcing his guests to wait while he changed, a long process at the best of times.

I turned my attention to the more important and interesting question of the three visitors. Divested of their outerwear, they observed Igor's performance silently, casting inquiring glances our way from time to time. Even in the courtyard, I'd noticed that their party consisted of two girls close in years to Anna and me, accompanied by a short, stout woman of middle age, her pleasant face round and wrinkled as a winter apple. Whatever position she occupied—mother, aunt, guardian?—she stood in the center, flanked by her charges. Now that they were out of the cold wind, I could tell that the girl on her right, tall and slim with a light brown braid draped over her shoulder, could have been pretty, but the sharp line of her cheekbones, the tightness of her lips, and her pale complexion undercut any impression of beauty. My scrutiny caused her to narrow her eyes in a sly expression, and I decided right then that I neither liked nor trusted her. Yet she exuded confidence, subjecting first Anna, then me, to an examination every bit as searching as ours of her. I placed her age at nineteen or twenty.

The second girl had the stocky body and puppy fat of someone still making the transition from childhood to adulthood. She seemed so young, even compared to Avdotya, that I doubted she'd reached the marriageable age of twelve. Igor might regard her as competition, but I couldn't see her holding her own against the likes of Ustinya Paletskaya or Tasya Yureva. She gaped at us open-mouthed, as if stunned by our finery, then plucked at her own clothes and stared at her companions with dismay. When Igor introduced my sister as Tsarevna Maria, I expected the child to throw herself to the floor in obeisance, but the girls' companion restrained her with a tight grip on her arm and a hissed comment that I didn't catch. The child responded by tugging at her sandy braid until the woman slapped her hand away.

"The boyars' daughters Anna Semyonovna Kolycheva and Lyubov Fyodorovna Koshkina," Igor announced, indicating Anna and me with a sweep of his arm. "Lady Juliana Ossolinska." He sent Juliana another yearning glance, and I heard her snort. Igor, intent on his performance, appeared not to notice. "And Solomonida, wife of State Secretary Anfim Fadeyev," he added in a grudging tone.

"Who is also a boyar's daughter," Katya interjected smoothly. Igor glared at her, but she ignored him. "This is Fevronia Ignatyeva and her nieces Dina and Melita," she said, completing the introductions. "Their father belongs to the provincial gentry, but they are distant relatives of the Shein clan, who added their names to the list and summoned them to take part in the bride show." So that explained how Igor managed to persuade their father to hand over the two girls. Their family had set it up in advance.

"A pleasure to meet you." Fevronia Ignatyeva put her palms together and bowed. "Very prolific relatives, let me add. They have six brothers and four times as many male cousins. We breed sons in each generation, but God granted my brother these two girls, and we rejoice at the opportunity to present them to the tsar."

It was an odd way to introduce oneself. "How fortunate for you," Juliana said. From the amusement in her voice, I guessed that she, too, found Fevronia's comment strange.

Glancing around the room, I saw Katya and Solomonida suppressing smiles. "Congratulations to your family," my sister said in that cool, aristocratic way she had when dealing with people she didn't much like. "And welcome to Moscow. Have you visited the royal city before?"

Fevronia answered in the affirmative, although the two girls shook their heads. Katya gestured at the settles lining the walls. "Let me call for refreshments. You must be weary after such a long journey. Please sit and make yourselves comfortable. I will fetch bread and salt to welcome you properly into our home."

Maria, Juliana, Solomonida—even Anna moved to obey. The visitors waited for us to seat ourselves before accepting places on the other settle. In response to a tug of Anna's hand on my sleeve, I followed her to the place my sister had chosen for us, but I couldn't keep my eyes off Igor. He looked like a fox caught heading out of the henhouse with a mouth full of feathers.

Which made me wonder what he was up to now.

While waiting for Katya to return with bread and salt, I kept expecting Igor to make his bows and depart, but in blatant defiance of society's rule that men should not associate with women unrelated to them, he stayed. Perhaps the fact that he had escorted the newcomers from Kolomna made them as good as family in his eyes. More likely, he wanted a chance to crow about his cleverness. Or maybe he'd grabbed the chance to flirt with Juliana, even if doing so angered Katya. Had he forgotten he had a wife and Juliana a husband?

If he had, I felt pretty certain Juliana hadn't. Her initial reticence had vanished, and even I could see she was playing with him. The wicked gleam in her eyes reminded me of a predator—not a falcon, swift and deadly like Tizilek dispatching her prey in mid-flight, but a cat toying with a mouse before the kill. Igor leaned forward, unable to take his eyes off her, as fascinated as that silly mouse venturing out of the wainscoting in search of cheese. "Tell me more about King Sigismund the Old and Queen Bona," he begged. "They say your monarch entered his eighth decade this past week. How is it that he still rules? Meanwhile, rumor has it that his son in Vilnius is causing a scandal by demanding to wed his beautiful mistress."

"Igor Grigorevich!" She reared back, sounding astonished, although the sparkle in her eyes gave her away. "You expect me to speak of such salacious topics before innocent girls?"

Every head in the room instantly turned toward her, unable to resist the opportunity for gossip—the more salacious, the better. Alas, Katya walked in right at that moment, balancing a large platter of bread and salt on her forearms. "What salacious topics are those?" she asked. "Igor, are you embarrassing our guests?"

"Not at all," he said in a sulky tone. He straightened his spine, reducing his resemblance to a lovesick swain, and Juliana bit her lip as if trying not to laugh. "I was asking Lady Juliana about the situation at the Polish court. Nothing salacious about it."

Katya sent the two of them a suspicious glance, but she soon pulled herself together and performed the hospitality ritual with Fevronia and her nieces, just as Maria and Alexei had done while welcoming Juliana and Felix to our house. The rest of us sat and waited patiently for her to finish. I spent the time wondering whether Juliana would deign to answer the questions Igor had asked about King Sigismund and his family, especially the son's bizarre infatuation with his mistress.

I should rephrase that. The infatuation was not bizarre. Why would a man take a mistress unless he desired her? But I knew from my history books that kings weren't supposed to *marry* their mistresses. The job of monarchs was to make politically advantageous matches and produce legitimate heirs with their spouses, whether they loved someone else or not. It sounded grim, but it was the price of rulership.

And it was what Alexei expected of Timur. My brother-in-law, whom I loved and thought of as a second father, would consign me to the position of that royal mistress if he had his way. I wondered if I could ever forgive him for slighting me. Of course, he hadn't expected Timur to tell me, but it still hurt.

Maybe that was why our tsar preferred the bride show. At least it gave him a say in selecting the woman he must bed. And he could hope for a healthy and pretty wife, not a sickly princess like the one imposed on the young Polish king. I imagined weaving him and his mistress into a future tale. I could make sure *he* ended up with the person he loved, even if I did not.

"King Sigismund is now old in fact as well as in name," Juliana said, answering Igor's question at last. "That he reached eighty at all is a miracle. I still remember the party they held when he turned seventy-five." She flinched for reasons I didn't understand, but a quick calculation in my head revealed that she had been recovering from smallpox then. No doubt the memories were painful.

She went on. "Alas, the poor man was too ill to attend any celebration. He has little role in governance these days, but Queen Bona does an admirable job of filling his shoes." Another short pause, and she added, "It is common knowledge that she and her son have fallen out over the younger Sigismund's insistence on wedding his Lithuanian noblewoman. That makes it … difficult for Sigismund Augustus to exercise the power that is his by right of birth and election."

She didn't say that the joint Polish-Lithuanian state faced a perilous transition, but it sounded like that to me. I studied the faces of the others in the room, wondering what they had heard. Maria nodded without speaking, as if she too had grasped Juliana's hidden meaning. Solomonida and Katya also had an intent look in their eyes that suggested comprehension. The rest— not just Dina and Melita but their aunt and Anna and, most startling, Igor—looked blank. Yet this news affected us all: for as long as I could remember, Russia had been riven by dynastic strife, and here, as we emerged from the shadows, Poland faced a similar fate. That must strengthen our position and weaken theirs, must it not? No wonder Juliana and Felix were here gathering information.

In that moment, I also understood why Anastasia Petrovna, at least, might view me as the best wife for her cousin, who would have to navigate the treacherous shoals of his own country's politics as well as those of the surrounding lands. It didn't change my feelings about becoming the tsar's bride; I disliked the idea as much as ever. But Timur, too, must one day sail those dangerous international waters, and he would need a politically astute wife at his side. If I could avoid being selected by Tsar Ivan, that argument, plus Timur's determination to wed me and no other, might convince Alexei to accept me as his daughter-in-law.

Servants arrived with jugs and bowls and platters. Igor rose to his feet, snatched a tankard of ale from the closest tray, and swept his arm in an expansive gesture that included his wife and guests but nearly upended the unlucky maid attempting to serve Fevronia and her nieces. She scuttled to a safe corner while her master, beaming, raised his tankard in a toast. "To our bridal candidates from Kolomna and here in Moscow, to the relatives who have cared for them, and to those who, recognizing their virtue and their suitability to become our next tsaritsa, will conduct them to the house set aside for them in the Kremlin for the next stage of the competition!" He took a long swig of his ale, burped, and finished with, "No other boyar has managed to secure two potential brides for the tsar. This is a great day, a very great day."

Juliana emitted a gurgle of laughter and quickly turned it into a cough. Katya, standing behind her jubilant husband, stared at him as if she couldn't believe his foolishness. Maria and Solomonida developed a heretofore unsuspected interest in the cushions beneath them, although I saw the way they covered their mouths with their hands. Anna looked appalled—an emotion I shared, although I hoped it didn't show as clearly on my face as it did on hers. The three visitors from Kolomna stared at Igor without emotion, and I wondered what they made of his performance.

Their reaction, though, was unimportant compared to the reminder Igor had delivered through his toast. Any day now, Anna and I, with Maria in attendance, could expect a summons to appear in the Kremlin, where the bride show would begin in earnest.

Igor took himself off after a while, leaving us and the visitors to regard one another with a certain wary acceptance. While Maria, Solomonida, and Katya engaged Fevronia in conversation, Anna and I set out to find out more about Dina and Melita. In particular, we wanted to establish as soon as possible whether we should regard them as friends, enemies, or neither—at least, I did. I hadn't had a chance to talk privately with Anna, so I could only guess what she sought.

She went first, asking Dina and Melita what it was like to grow up with so many boys. "Are they older than you, or younger?"

"Two are older than me," Dina said. "I'm nineteen. I should have married by now, but when Papa heard there might be a bride show, he delayed calling in the matchmakers. He remembered that last time they searched the provinces for girls." She waved a hand at Melita. "She's the youngest. Eleven and a half, but she will turn twelve soon enough. As for what it's like, don't you have brothers?"

"I do," I admitted. "Four, as well as another sister who lives in Murom." I smiled at Melita, still gaping at us as if she couldn't muster a single word. "I'm the youngest, too, but I went to live with Maria and her husband when I was six. By then, only David and Timofei were still at home, and they didn't spend much time with us girls. So I don't know my brothers well."

"And I was an only child," Anna said, "for most of my life. I have a stepsister and a stepbrother who've lived with us since 1543, but Tolya is still only seven. And I have an infant half-brother. I'm more like a second mother to both boys than a sister."

I watched Dina figure that out. "Your mother is the one who married the state secretary?" she asked after a pause. Her sly face expressed a disdain that made my foot twitch. It was all I could do not to kick her ankle. How dare she look down on Solomonida?

"Three years ago?" she went on. "The stepchildren are his, I assume."

"Yes. Anfim is his name," Anna said. "Lara and Tolya are his, but he didn't marry Mama until this past spring. His children stayed with us while he went on a journey down the Volga. He comes from a merchant family. They went to explore and to trade." She touched the exquisite brocade of her sleeve. "This is some of the fabric they brought back."

Dina nodded, her thin lips tightening as if a merchant family lay far beneath her notice. Melita, though, reached out a tentative finger and reverently brushed it across Anna's sleeve. "It's lovely," she said—the first words she'd spoken so far. "And the embroidery—those rose-pink swirls are amazing. Did you do that?"

"I did," Anna said. "Do you like to sew?" It was the encouraging tone she used with Lara, and I could see that it set Melita at ease.

Melita nodded with enthusiasm, her head bobbing like a straw puppet's, but Dina cut off any response her sister might have made. "How does a boyar's daughter have a merchant stepfather? I thought that wasn't allowed."

Her voice carried. I flicked my head in Solomonida's direction and saw her flinch, but she continued to watch Fevronia, who gave no sign that she'd heard Dina's tart response. I switched my gaze to Anna, unsure what to expect from her. My friend had not at first welcomed her mother's marriage to Anfim, even though Anna liked the man himself.

Anna didn't hesitate, however. "My father was from a boyar clan, as is my mother," she said in a cool tone, with a hint of distaste that implicitly condemned Dina's blunt question. "And Mama lived as a widow for many years before she accepted Anfim's proposal. She had no male relative to oppose her decision—except Cousin Igor, who has still not quite forgiven her, as you've seen—and it has worked out well. They're very fond of each other, and I love him too. He's a wonderful stepfather."

Dina sniffed, and my dislike for her intensified. Melita emitted a groan of distaste at the sound of Igor's name. "Do you want to marry the tsar?" I asked her, as much to turn the focus away from Anna's family as out of real curiosity. "Eleven seems too young to become anyone's wife."

"You don't think Tsar Ivan will pick her over me, do you?" Dina interjected, her face puckered like someone who'd bitten into a raw quince. "Look at her, great lump that she is. Papa sent us both with Aunt Fevronia to get her out of the way. Mama is set to produce her seventh son any day."

"You're such a beast, Dina!" Melita wailed.

"Girls, girls," Fevronia said from the women's circle.

"It's nothing, Auntie," Dina called. "Just Melita making a fuss."

My dislike flared into anger, and I said, "Most likely, the tsar won't pick any of us. There are several beautiful and accomplished girls on the list—princesses, even. Best that you enjoy your trip to Moscow while you can, so you'll have plenty of tales to tell your friends when you return to Kolomna next month." I knew I sounded snippy, but I didn't care.

Anna sent me a mischievous glance, confirming that she shared my reaction to Dina. "Princess Ustinya is the prettiest," my friend said in honeyed tones. "And she has the backing of the highest clan in the land. The Yureva daughter has charm as well as looks, and there's a striking pair of redheaded cousins representing the old Moscow nobility. Lyuba and I would swoon in shock if either of us won." And wasn't *that* the truth, if not in quite the way Anna made it sound?

Dina glared at us but didn't speak. Melita stopped gaping and looked thoughtful, as if she heard not only our unspoken support for her but the hint that Anna and I might not welcome success in this endeavor our fathers had forced on us all.

After a brief, chilly pause, Dina rallied. "Thank you for the warning," she said in a facile tone that told me she meant nothing of the sort. "I must confess, I would like to become the first tsar-itsa. The clothes, the jewels, the riches! Who would not want to stand above every other woman in the land?"

The tip of my tongue trembled with the desire to point out that the wealth and glory she sought would come at the cost of marriage to an undisciplined, hot-tempered boy almost three years younger than herself. But to say such things about the tsar was unwise, and I had no intention of sharing dangerous thoughts with a girl I distrusted. So I raised the cup I still held and said, "May the prize go to the one who wants it most!"

Although if that person turned out to be Dina, I would have yet another reason to flee for the steppe with Timur. I could never accept such a nasty girl as my ruler.

The remaining pairs of boyars and state secretaries straggled in from the provinces about a week before the new tsar's coronation, set for January 16. Altogether, almost sixty girls, including those already resident in Moscow, gathered in the capital for the tsar's perusal. Assigned to one of five groups, we were told to prepare ourselves for a stay in the Kremlin that might last up to a week.

Although Igor no longer had reason to crow about having trounced everyone else in the procurement of potential brides, that detail seemed to pass him by. On the afternoon when the news of our imminent move to the Kremlin reached us, he invited my sister and me—with Juliana, Anna, and Solomonida—to visit his house. There he sang his own praises while parading before us one more newcomer, Zoya Gerasimova, and her unremarkable mother. The seven of us sipped cider and munched appetizers when not pretending to applaud Igor's remarkable success.

Zoya herself seemed pleasant enough. Fair-haired and slender, she resembled a washed-out, more bashful version of Anna. The spitting image of her mother, who had accompanied her from Uglich to act as sponsor, Zoya exuded a sense of wanting to fade into the woodwork. How her father thought she would survive the cut-throat politics of the bride show defied belief. But she was additional competition, and I wished her well.

Zoya's arrival completed our group of twelve: she, Dina, Melita, and Avdotya Gundorova from the provinces; Princesses Ustinya Paletskaya and Fetinya Blednaya; boyars' daughters Serafima Khabarova, Grunya and Dunya, Tasya Yureva, Anna, and myself. According to what Maria had learned from her husband, the tsar's female relatives would winnow us and the other groups into a select group of choices so wholly acceptable that Tsar Ivan could pick any one of us without upsetting the Moscow nobles' political hierarchy.

Anna and I just had to figure out how to get eliminated before the final round.

Chapter 12

"The dragon lured them into his cave"

Over the next five days, I spent as much time as I could with Timur, dodging my sister and brother-in-law to fend off any potential opposition. I'd have loved to go riding and hawking again, but that would have raised too many eyebrows, in particular Alexei's. I had no desire for another confrontation, not least because I was still angry with him for urging Timur to pick a different bride.

Instead, I visited the study whenever Alexei was elsewhere—finishing my collection of tales for Tolya, selecting books to take with me, and awaiting those precious moments when my love could join me. I looked forward to the coronation, which would not only provide me with yet another store of wonderful details for my stories but required my brother-in-law to leave the house early in the morning to attend the young tsar. Felix and Juliana were invited to join the Polish delegation for the day, and Maria had plans to call on Ivan's grandmother. With Timur too young to be regarded as a visiting dignitary and barred from entering the cathedral because of his Muslim faith, I had hopes that we might spend hours together, so long as we avoided the scrutiny of anyone who might report us to my sister and her husband.

Unfortunately, none of that happened. On January 14, two days before the solemn ritual that would transform our young grand prince into the equivalent of an emperor, a courier arrived with the expected orders for Anna and me to report the next morning to a house in the Kremlin, not far from Anastasia Petrovna's residence. There we would remain until the final selection took place. Maria's visit to the tsar's grandmother was canceled.

The message set off a flurry of last-minute planning. As a subject of the king of Poland, Juliana could not accompany Maria into the Kremlin without an invitation. At the same time, she was staying in my sister and brother-in-law's house, so abandoning her violated the rules of hospitality. After much discussion, all agreed that Juliana could spend her days with Darya. Meanwhile, Maria would return home each evening, then leave the next morning to supervise Anna and me in the Kremlin.

"With luck," my sister said as she informed me of this plan, "the whole thing will be over in a few days, and life can return to normal." Without waiting for a reply, she went off to supervise the packing.

She expected me to go with her, but I slipped away in search of Timur, whom I'd seen heading in the direction of the stable while my sister spoke. If I moved fast, I'd catch him before he saddled his horse. So I pulled my hooded cloak from its hook and wrapped it around me as I dashed down the stairs. I couldn't let him go without grabbing what might be my one chance to say goodbye in private.

I found him overseeing the boy tasked with adjusting the length of the stirrups to his satisfaction. He turned his head as I approached, and even in the dim light of the stable, I saw his eyebrows rise. "Have the dragons released you to ride with me, Lady Love?"

The question made me blush. "I wish they would," I told Timur, ignoring the grinning stable boy. "But no. Can you spare a moment?"

A lump formed in my throat. I'd never sought him out in front of the staff. Suppose he refused? I couldn't count on seeing him in private later, yet I didn't want to spill out my feelings before a servant.

My turmoil must have shown on my face, because Timur stepped forward and took my elbow. "Of course." He looked over his shoulder at the stable boy. "Finish up here, then walk the horse to keep him warm. I'll be back soon." He didn't wait for an acknowledgment before leading me to another stall three doors down.

There, observed only by the mare who nuzzled my shoulder in greeting, he wrapped his arm around my waist. "What's the trouble, Lady Love? Has the dreaded summons come?"

I took a deep breath, fighting the urge to drop my head against his chest and sob. "Just now," I managed after a while. "We leave tomorrow. Maria's already supervising the packing. If things don't go according to plan—and that assumes I have a plan, which I don't—I may never see you again. Not like this, in any case. Royal brides don't leave the Terem Palace except on ceremonial occasions. But oh, Timur, I don't want to *be* a royal bride!" At that point, I lost the little control I had and wept.

He pulled me closer and patted my back. "I don't want you to be a royal bride either, *soyarké*," he said in an unsteady voice. "What do you say? Shall we make a run for Kasimov?"

I hesitated, sorely tempted. But I hadn't forgotten Alexei's threat to disown him—or the horrible punishments inflicted on his friends. "I can't," I said when I could speak. "Not after seeing what the Glinskys are capable of."

He flinched at the reminder but continued, undeterred. "I'd find a way. Kasimov is the gateway to the steppe. We can go beyond Moscow's reach." He rubbed my tears away with his thumb. "You know I love you. I'm not the kind of man to stand by and let a foreign prince steal the wife I want."

He loves me!

I pressed my cheek against his fingers. "I love you, too. It's my dearest hope to wed you."

"You'll come with me, then? We can leave tonight."

Again, temptation waved its lure. "Yes" trembled on my tongue, but a small voice in my head urged me to wait. "I want to," I said after a while, letting the murky, hidden thoughts flow into words. "But it's too soon. I may not be chosen, and in that case, I'll find a way for us to marry even if it means defying my father and yours. I won't run the risk of you being disgraced or executed, though. And what of Alexei and Maria? They will pay a price as well if I don't report as ordered. I can't forget the many things they've done for me, however upset I am with them at the moment. If our decision leads to their pain or their deaths, that would taint our love forever."

He didn't like that, I could tell. He didn't release me, but he stopped caressing my cheek and straightened. After a moment's silence—long enough to make me wonder if I'd thrown away my one chance at happiness—I saw the wry twist to his mouth and relaxed. He wasn't angry, as I'd feared. "You're right, Lady Love. *Ata* drives me crazy at times, but he's very dear to me, and your sister, too. What next, then?"

"I find a solution." I brushed his ear with my fingers. "I haven't figured one out yet, but I will. Once I'm past the bride show, we can run off if we have to."

"It's a deal, *soyarké*, and I'll hold you to it." He kissed me then, his lips warm and soft. His tongue probed my mouth. One arm, strong against my back, kept me upright, while his other hand reached under the cloak and roamed over my body. I gave myself over to pleasure, memorizing every sensation to comfort me in the long hours and days to come—a lifetime, if I misplayed my pawns and became the queen. Despite what I'd said to console him, I might still mess this up. But I would worry about that another day.

How long the kiss lasted I neither knew nor cared. I would have stood there for an eternity and never noticed the passage of time. But the jingling of horse tack and the tromp of boot heels crashed into my consciousness like an unwelcome storm. The stable boy returning, a warrior, Alexei himself?

Timur pulled back at the same instant I did. I stared at him, my breath rapid as artillery fire. He wasn't much better off, although he recovered faster. He touched a finger to my lips and peered around the edge of the almost shut stall door.

"A few moments, Vanka," he said in a good approximation of normal speech. He ducked back inside and kissed me once more, a fleeting thing.

"I must go," he said softly. "So must you. Next time it *will* be my father, having a fit if he catches us together. He threatened to send me back to Kasimov if I disobey him again. I can't let that happen when you need me here. Not unless you come with me."

"He said that? The day he told you he wants you to marry a princess?" I was shocked, although given the other threats, I really shouldn't have been.

"No, not then. It was after the Blessing of the Waters, when we slipped away. Remember?"

"Of course, I remember." I frowned. "I didn't think he knew about that."

"He didn't," Timur said. He must have seen how that confused me, because he explained. "He didn't *know* we slipped away. He wasn't there. But Maria said something about losing sight of us, so he warned me off, just in case."

I nodded my understanding. "Why didn't you tell me?"

"You were upset enough," he said with a shrug. "And I don't intend to let it happen. I'll defy him one day, if that's what it takes to wed you—no matter what they say on the steppe about a father's power being absolute. But not when it means leaving you to deal with this bride-show nonsense alone. Stand firm, my love, and don't let the Russians get you down. I'll wait and watch and make plans for your release."

I doubted there was much he could do against the power of the entire government, but I loved knowing he would fight for me. "I will," I said. Another thought crossed my mind, and I added, "Will you exercise my falcon while I'm gone? I can look out from my Kremlin prison, see the birds in flight, and think of you."

That made him laugh. "I don't think they have a dungeon planned for you, *kaderle*. But yes, I'll exercise your Tizilek. It's the least I can do for you, but it won't be the last, I promise."

And with that he kissed me once more and stood aside while I dashed from the stable, wishing with every step I took that I could run the other way, back into his arms.

Supper began as a quiet affair, although I alternated between humming with joy whenever I remembered Timur's expressions of love—especially the kisses!—and fighting off fears of a permanent separation. No matter how I tried to reassure myself that Alexei and Maria, even Timur, could continue to visit me even if I somehow failed utterly to prevent my own selection during the bride show, nightmare visions of never seeing any of them again plagued me whenever I let down my guard. Peeking at Timur from time to time, I concluded he was not much better off.

Alas, two of the others at the table knew us as well as we knew each other. Whenever I looked at my sister, I found her studying us. Alexei's brow creased in a way that suggested he, too, noticed the secret smiles and longing glances that passed between his son and me. But neither of them challenged us. In my melancholy, I decided they believed we were doomed, which just depressed me further.

Juliana, sitting opposite me between Alexei and Timur, at first acted as if she didn't notice the tension in the room. "Where did your travels take you today, Felix? For a while I wondered if you would return in time for the meal."

He *had* reached the house not long before supper, so late that Maria's steward had been about to clear his place when Felix at last appeared on the doorstep. I looked to my left—he sat next to me —and saw an amused expression on his face. "I strolled about the streets for a while, to hear what people were saying about the coronation—and the bride show, now that the summons has gone out." He dipped his head toward Alexei. "Apologies for my tardiness. I again underestimated how long it would take me to climb your stairs."

Alexei accepted the apology with a tip of his chin. "What did you hear, Felix? Are people in the town interested in such matters?"

"Some of them." Felix accepted the basket of bread Maria held out to him, removed a slice, and passed it on to me. "I heard comments from only a few, and those mostly pleased that their ruler had reached an age to wed. Favorable impressions of the coronation. A certain bellicosity, perhaps provoked by my western clothes: the tsar would have sons and show the Poles which land held the power, and so on. Others speculated on why the tsar had to send repeated messages to the provinces ordering the gentry there to submit their girls for inspection. 'What's wrong with the nobles? I'd send my girl if I thought he'd take her.' That kind of thing. No discussion of the candidates and their families."

"No, I wouldn't expect that." Alexei signaled to a servant, who placed bowls of mutton stew, fragrant with herbs grown under

Maria's supervision, before each place. I dipped my bread in the gravy and spooned the meat into my mouth. Although in general not restricted from participating in any conversation within a family setting, I had little to contribute here and much to learn. So I kept quiet and listened, gazing at Timur and fighting the sensation of tiny, flitting birds beneath my ribs, then pretending to concentrate on my food whenever Maria glanced my way.

"The boyars don't proclaim their conflicts and negotiations to the world," Alexei went on. "Ordinary people have no way of knowing how those decisions are reached. I doubt they have any idea of whose names are on the list."

"Understood." Felix's voice still carried an undertone of amusement. "But they do speak of what concerns them and what they know—or believe they know—whereas the nobles are as tight-lipped as a barrel of oysters."

Was that a reproach? Searching Alexei's face for a clue, I saw his lips quirk, as if in an acknowledgment of the hit. "Fair enough," he said. "But I couldn't reveal state secrets if I had them, any more than you can, and in this case, I don't. My concern here is to protect Lyuba from the effects of her father's schemes, but even for that, I lack sufficient information to predict which way the dice will fall."

"But you know more than we do." Juliana abandoned her pretense of disinterest and leaned forward. Her intent gaze—and even more, her dress, which unlike the one she'd worn to befuddle Igor covered her all the way to her chin, ending in a small ruff—told me that she was, for once, serious. "Rank the candidates for us, if you please. And I don't mean their political alliances but their chances of success. Does Lyuba have cause for concern? Who might win, if not she? Can we tip the scales in the direction of those other girls?"

Maria had stayed out of the conversation until then, but these questions brought her into it. "From what I've seen so far, Lyuba is a strong candidate. Papa lost his rank as associate boyar twelve years ago; he has four sons but no living brothers; and he has long enjoyed the patronage of the Shuisky clan. Those three factors mean that he can be moved up within the existing hierarchy without displacing too many people. And selecting his daughter is not a direct endorsement of the Shuisky, Belsky, or Glinsky clans, although it does give an indirect nod to the Shuiskys."

Listening to my "assets" laid out in that forthright but unemotional way, I shuddered and cast a desperate glance at Timur. Did I have any chance of attaining the future I wanted for myself?

"Anna has a similar history," I said, tamping down my fear. "And even fewer male relatives. Only Niki, really, since her father's clan is scattered and Anfim doesn't come from a noble family."

"Yes, Anna is a strong candidate as well." Alexei handed his empty bowl to a hovering servant before continuing. "Stronger in some ways, because everyone likes Nikita, whose lack of ambition and service to me keep him from impinging on anyone else's interests. In the absence of her father's clan, though, there's no one to push her forward except Igor Bezzubtsev. At the moment, he enjoys the tsar's favor, but I wouldn't wager on his odds of retaining that."

"And Papa?" I asked. The tremor in my voice mirrored the shaking of my insides. "He doesn't enjoy the tsar's favor, does he?"

Alexei rested his chin on his fingers, considering. "No, and both he and Anna's father have a history of treasonous acts, although they committed their worst offenses far enough in the past that most people have forgotten. Your best weapon is to remind people that he hopes to become the tsar's closest adviser; his enemies—and he has quite a few in high places—will do whatever it takes to prevent that."

I was wondering what else I should ask when Juliana stepped in once more. "And the girls from the provinces?"

"No real contenders among the ones I've seen. Three of them are very young, and most of them don't have the right kind of connections." Maria ticked off factors disqualifying the candidates on her fingers. "Igor's two come with an army of male relatives. Even their link to the highly respected Shein clan won't compensate for the havoc introducing so many new members would wreak on the current balance of power. The pretty little girl from Vyazma is best positioned in that regard; the Godunovs came over from the Tatars not long ago, so their numbers are relatively small and many of them already placed. But it will be three or four years before she reaches womanhood and another before they can expect an heir. I doubt the clans want to wait so long. The other twelve-year-olds pose the same problem." She didn't add what we all knew: that with the tsar's brother disabled, only one cousin stood between stability and calamity should anything happen to the soon-to-be crowned tsar. To mention a ruler's potential death was treasonous.

"And the girl brought in from ... Uglich, was it?" Felix asked, smoothing over the awkward silence that followed.

"I met her," Juliana said. "Not a shred of personality. She hasn't a hope of attracting a young man with blood in his veins. Especially when there were real beauties at my ex-husband's Christmas party." She nodded at me as if including me in that category, which was nice of her. Off to her right, I saw Timur gazing at me as if he agreed. I wanted to blow him a kiss, but I didn't dare.

"Even if what's her name—Zoya?—gets to the final round," Juliana finished with a dismissive wave of her hand, "the others will defeat her without trying."

Remembering that she had a vast acquaintance with what appealed to young men, I realized that here was an opportunity to learn something useful.

"What would you recommend, Juliana?" I kept my voice light, despite the thumping of my heart. "How do I get myself ranked lower among the candidates or, if that fails, make myself less appealing to the tsar? Let me add that reading to Anastasia Petrovna, even when it involved translating from Persian by accident, didn't put her off in the least. Quite the opposite, in fact."

Timur emitted a muffled cough that sounded suspiciously like suppressed laughter, and I glared at him for a moment before returning my attention to Juliana. Easy for him to laugh, when as a man he had more say in whom he married than I ever would.

Juliana, too, looked amused. I sighed and gave up. I couldn't remain angry at my friends when enemies would surround me within hours. "I know," I said, aiming the words at Timur more than anyone. "It's absurd that Russian noblewomen are *so* deprived of learning, but I did hope that my interest in history and literature and the like would make me appear unwomanly. Just my luck that the first person I encountered had a Tatar education. Some of the women at the Christmas party were suitably appalled when I mentioned preferring to spend time with my nose in a book, but I'm still terrified whenever I mention reading that it will work against me instead of for me."

"Poor Lyuba," Timur said, still laughing. "But all those hours of study will make you the perfect wife for a more enlightened man."

I blushed. I couldn't help it, although I'd have given anything to conceal my reaction. Memories of his kisses and the certainty of which enlightened man he had in mind left me temporarily speechless.

Alexei sent his son a thunderous look, dashing any hopes that he'd missed the exchange. Juliana, struggling even harder to conceal her delight, broke the hostile (or, in my case, embarrassed) silence with her usual aplomb. "Lyuba asks an interesting question. Her lineage and looks are fixed, her father has his enemies and his allies, each contender has her female champion, but ultimately this contest comes down to a young man and a maiden. Or in this case, a selection of maidens. And although we can only speculate on what attracts and repels this particular young man, one thing I know for certain is that young men seldom want what older women want *for* them. Even older men often forget how the hot blood of youth drives decisions."

She sent Alexei an impish glance that made me clench my jaw to keep my mouth from dropping open. Did she guess what had gone on between myself and Timur this afternoon, or the day we exercised the falcons? It seemed impossible; it must be a stab in the dark on her part, if not an attempt to solicit information she didn't have.

I flicked my eyes in Timur's direction, then at my sister, and saw no evidence either of them had noticed anything. Felix watched with his usual quiet attention, and Alexei raised his eyebrows at her, as if daring her to continue. I would get no answer if I asked her to elaborate, and I'd head into dangerous territory at the same time, so I addressed her main point instead.

"What *does* the tsar want, then?" I said. "Do you have any tricks guaranteed to convince him to look the other way?"

Maria chuckled at that, while Juliana treated me to her feline smile. "Let's see. Your dress and appearance must be flawless, or you will reflect badly on your sister. An autocratic young man might object to a forthright gaze, which you do well. I would watch and see how he reacts to the others, who will be schooled in demure passivity, before you decide whether to look him in the eye. Another tactic is to make use of subtle cues: an off-kilter scent to evoke unpleasant sensations; a shade of fabric that drains your skin or makes you appear sallow—violet might have that effect on you, or scarlet." Her smile widened to a full-out grin. "Then there's the question of manner. Melodramatic often terrifies young men. Bright and brainless repels some, but you couldn't manage that in a lifetime, and a certain kind of bridegroom might like it. Could you work on listless and melancholy?"

"Maybe." I saw Timur in the throes of laughter again, but struggling to recall a time when I had experienced melancholy for more than half an hour, except in connection with the bride show, I didn't have time to deal with his foolishness. "What would that look like?"

Maria smacked Timur on the arm, not hard. "You're no help," she told him.

He straightened in his seat and tried to control his expression, with a lamentable lack of success. "Come on, Auntie Maria," he said when he could speak. "Lyuba, melancholic and listless? She wouldn't know where to start. You'll have to dose her with saltpeter or something to make her melancholic, and if you're going to do that, why not just give her an emetic and be done with it? I'm sure the tsar won't want a wife who throws up all over his feet."

"I'll be melancholic enough if I have to marry him," I pointed out with some asperity. "But by then it will be too late." I turned to Juliana. "Thank you. Those are good ideas. Even if *some* people" —I glared at Timur, who had collapsed once more into something perilously close to a guffaw—"don't appreciate them."

"Hopeless," Maria said, shaking her head at my overwhelmed love. "Anyone would think you *wanted* her to spend her life as the next tsaritsa."

That sobered him up. He stopped laughing at once and stared into my eyes. "Now that is a slander if I ever heard one. Seeing Lyuba as the next tsaritsa is the *last* thing I want."

I nodded. "Thank you." I hadn't doubted him, despite his annoying behavior. I knew how he felt about me.

Alexei cleared his throat, and I turned my head toward him. What I saw on his face caused my jaw to drop. In contrast to the anger he'd shown earlier, he looked calm, even resigned, but the tight corners of his mouth indicated concern. Felix and Juliana radiated nothing but polite interest, but my sister, when I glanced at her, had the same fixed expression as her husband.

They could see that Timur and I loved each other, and it worried them. Because of the bride show, of course; the religious prohibition, perhaps. And of course, there was that political marriage that Alexei had in mind for his son. But if we found a way to address their concerns, could we convince them to support us?

Even the possibility strengthened my determination to succeed.

Chapter 13

"Leaving the prince in the wilderness"

T he next morning, I had one foot raised to join Maria in the carriage when a call sounded from the main gate. I turned my head toward the noise and saw my father waving wildly near the entrance to our estate—not within the gate, which two stalwart guards barred with crossed lances, but on the far side. I lifted a hand in greeting, then bent to speak to my sister through the open door. "Papa's here," I said. "Should I tell the guards to let him in?"

She climbed out, grumbling. "What does *he* want?" Hands on her hips, she surveyed the scene at the gate. "A few more moments, and we'd have been on our way."

I didn't respond. I had no more desire to talk to Papa than she did, because I could guess that he'd come only to exhort me once more to excel at the bride show or face the consequences of failure. Even knowing that dealing with him would delay the moment of departure couldn't make up for that. "Shall I get in the carriage, then? It's a bit late to pretend I didn't see him."

"No, tell the guards to admit him. We'll talk out here, and I'll get rid of him as soon as possible." She glanced around, as if searching for reinforcements, but the courtyard was empty except for ourselves and the driver. Timur had passed by not long ago, heading for the stable and surrounded by warriors. He'd saluted me, hand over heart, and I blew him a kiss behind my sister's back.

I'd have liked to throw myself at him and beg him to run off with me after all, but that was no more possible this morning than it had been yesterday. An escape that left those we loved to suffer the consequences would haunt us both.

At least I had Maria at my side. With a sigh, I gave up and walked to the gate.

"Let him in," I told the guards, who straightened their lances to an upright position. To my father I added, "We're leaving for the Kremlin, Papa. You can't stay long."

"Don't be impertinent." He caught my elbow and half-dragged me toward the carriage where Maria stood, tapping an impatient foot. "What a pair," he said as he reached her. "No respect for your poor old father who devotes every minute to advancing your interests."

"Enough of that," Maria retorted. "What brings you to our house today? And make it brief: we don't want to keep the tsar's grandmother waiting."

He muttered something about ungrateful daughters that I didn't attempt to decipher. But when neither of us responded, he abandoned the guise of wounded innocent and spoke at a normal level. "I came to say that I have done my best to influence the outcome in Lyuba's favor. It is crucial, daughter"—he looked at me as he said this—"that you not trust any of the other candidates, including your friend Anna. Or their sponsors. Your sister has your best interests at heart, and Princess Nadezhda Shuiskaya has promised to support you to the fullest extent possible. The rest will do whatever they can to tear you down. Do you understand?"

This blanket condemnation of the potential brides and their sponsors struck me as extreme. I opened my mouth to tell him he was exaggerating, or even to remind him that Princess Nadezhda had another candidate in her care, then realized that arguing with him would not change his mind. "I understand perfectly, Papa," I said instead. "May we get started now?"

He glared at me. "You remember what will happen if you fail? Gavriil Vorontsov is still in need of a wife, I believe. And there are many like him."

"Stop your silliness." Maria had lost patience with Papa long ago; as a married woman, she occupied a much stronger position than I did and didn't hesitate to put him in his place. "Gavriil Vorontsov's in his fifties—no proper husband for a sixteen-year-old, whatever his virtues. You must have been drinking if you think Alexei would agree to him or any of his fellows marrying Lyuba."

"It won't be Alexei's choice." Papa squared his shoulders and put both hands on his hips, giving him a pugnacious air. "She's mine to dispose of, and your bastard of a husband has no right to oppose me."

Maria looked at him as if he were dirt under her shoe. I bit my lip to keep from laughing, because as horrible as my father's threats were, his insistence that Alexei couldn't browbeat him into submission was ludicrous. I had personally witnessed half a dozen such incidents and heard of many more. Alexei's opposition bothered me ten times as much as anything Papa might try.

"We're leaving now," my sister said in icy tones. "Lyuba, get in the carriage."

"Goodbye, Papa," I said, then ducked through the opening. I heard Maria summoning the guards to escort our father out, and in no time she slid onto the seat beside me and shut the door behind her. The carriage immediately rocked into motion, and we were on our way to collect Anna.

"Is Papa gone?" I asked once we cleared the gate. She nodded, and I went on. "I didn't understand what he meant about trusting no one but you and Princess Nadezhda. Isn't she sponsoring

Ustinya? I'm rather counting on her *not* giving me or Anna any support."

"Yes, that's strange," Maria agreed. "What has he cooked up with her, I wonder? May the devil take him and his scheming."

"What should I do? I don't want her spying on me. She could tell him all kinds of lies." And truths, which would be even more devastating if she realized that I was doing everything I could to avoid getting picked.

"Pay no attention to Papa," Maria said, brushing our absent father away with a wave of her hand. "You'll go mad if you get caught up in his bizarre plots. We'll watch out for Princess Nadezhda. One way or another, we'll see you through this, and then we'll find you a decent husband. It won't be Alexei's choice, says Papa. Well, he's in for a surprise. Sometimes I think our father has lost his mind!"

I joined in her laughter, but a small voice of doubt whispered in my head. A match proposed by Maria and Alexei would be more suitable than one of Papa's cronies, but that would only make their choice harder to resist. Suppose I was wrong about my sister and her husband coming around to the idea of my marrying Timur? I'd be in the same place I was now.

Even running off to Kasimov wouldn't solve *that* problem.

The wintry sun hovered halfway between the horizon and over-head by the time the carriage bearing the three of us drove through the Kremlin gates. Our baggage, designed to keep Anna and me clothed and comfortable for up to ten days, had preceded us. I watched with mixed curiosity and anxiety as we lurched along the wooden pathway, dodging a cloister to our right or a noble estate to our left before pulling up in front of an oddly misshapen house. Tall and thin, with an upper story cantilevered over the three floors below, it resembled an elongated version of Baba Yaga's hut, missing only the chicken feet at the bottom. Ideas for a new story flooded my head as I emerged from the carriage, and I was glad I had finished my tale of the princess, the knight, and the dragon in time to hand it off to Tolya this morning. Lucky, too, that I had packed an ample supply of paper and quills.

"What an astonishing place," I said to Anna as we followed my sister up the stairs. Beyond the house, I could see Anastasia Petrovna's estate off to the right and, when we reached the landing, the royal palaces and cathedrals straight ahead. From the top floor, we might even be able to peer over the walls, as I had promised when asking Timur to exercise my falcon. "Have you ever seen a house that looked so much like a squared-off kulich?" Add the letters XB on the top, and it would indeed look like an Easter sweet bread produced for a giant.

"Trust you to come up with that," Anna said. "I'm so nervous my skin is crawling. I can't think of anything but what lies ahead."

I patted her arm. "I'm just as anxious as you. The only difference is that I distract myself by looking at everything else. And wondering what's going to happen next—where we'll sleep, what tests they'll do on us, how we're going to fail them without dishonoring ourselves and Maria—"

"Please stop." Anna sounded frantic. "You're making it worse. I don't want to worry about any of those things until I have to."

"All right, all right, I will." And I did … stop talking, that is. Thoughts flew through my brain like bats disturbed in an attic, and I couldn't understand why my friend insisted on ignoring the obvious. It would take planning and skill to avoid the snare my father had laid out for me, and the greater the number of alternatives I could consider, the better my chances of escape.

I wished for a person to confide in—Timur, for preference, with his quick mind, ready smile, and confidence that he need only take a stand and everything would come out well in the end. But I hated to add to Anna's troubles, since I loved her, too. So I kept the circling thought-bats at bay by focusing on the immediate future. Where in this rickety pile would we sleep?

That answer, at least, came quickly. Maria led the way through the door at the top of the stairs, and a woman in servants' clothes met us on the other side. She carried a piece of paper and a stick of charcoal, which she used to mark off the sheet when Maria pointed out our names. "I am Dobrinya, the housekeeper," she said, then bowed to each of us in turn. "Tsarevna Maria, Lyubov Fyodorovna, Anna Semyonovna, welcome. Permit me to show you to your rooms."

We followed Dobrinya along a short hallway, flanked on either side by open doors. Through one I saw what must be a sitting room, filled with girls and women—the bridal candidates and their sponsors. I'd wondered if all sixty of us would be staying in the same place, but I saw only the girls from our group of twelve.

Thanks to the delay caused by Papa's unannounced visit, we were the last to arrive. On the other side of the corridor, I saw a dining hall, tables already laid out for the midday meal, although that must still be an hour or two away. The decor ranged from sumptuous to garish, with brightly painted walls covered in swirling patterns, opulent cushions, gold plate, even elaborately embroidered cloths atop solid wood tables flanked by engraved and polished benches with animal claws for feet.

We climbed one indoor staircase, then another, emerging on what I assumed must be the cantilevered fourth floor. "We have set aside six bedrooms for the girls." Dobrinya gestured at the closed doors as we passed them. "Anna Semyonovna and Lyubov Fyodorovna will share a room. Each chaperone is assigned an anteroom near her charges' sleeping quarters. Here is yours, Tsarevna." She flung open the last door on the left and ushered us into a small chamber containing a bed, a large chest on the floor, and a waist-high table holding a jug and basin of water. A chamber pot sat in a corner, and pegs on the wall would hold clothes. At the far side, a second opening indicated the location of another room, most likely the one where Anna and I would sleep.

"I will not be staying overnight," Maria told the housekeeper. "I have guests in my home who require my attention. So I will leave at dusk and return in the early morning, but I am glad to have the use of this space for the hours I am present."

Dobrinya looked alarmed. "But, Tsarevna, who will watch over your girls throughout the night?"

Maria glanced at me, then Anna, and I saw the amusement in her eyes. "I don't think they can get themselves into trouble from the fourth floor of a locked and guarded house," she said. "They are marriageable young women, not children set on causing mischief because they cannot imagine the consequences."

My sister's rank left the housekeeper with no choice but to bow, but the grim expression on her face revealed her true feelings about what she must see as an unconventional arrangement. She walked to the open door on the far side and beckoned to Anna and me. We followed her into a pretty room decorated in shades of pink and cream—roses, mostly, against an off-white background. A large bed stood in the center, already made up with lace-trimmed linen pillow cases and sheets, heavy coverlets, and a fur wrap laid across the end. Four posters held up a canopy, and tied-back curtains, once released from their bindings, would challenge even the slightest draft to break through and disturb the sleepers. The rest of the furnishings much resembled the layout in the antechamber, but I was delighted to see—next to a vanity and stool, where we could comb our hair with the help of a hand mirror—a small desk and chair, perfect for recording the ideas buzzing in my head. A pile of belongings that I recognized as ours sat in a corner.

"We have maids assigned to wait on each pair of young ladies," Dobrinya said. "Yours is Galya. Shall I send her up to you?"

"Get her started on the unpacking." Maria pointed to the pile in the corner. "I will see my sister and her friend divested of their outer garments, then escort them downstairs to join the other candidates. Later, I will be able to tell you what else we need."

Dobrinya bowed once more and left. I had already shed my cloak, so I hung it on a peg and laid my muff on the desk. Then I walked to the window and pushed the shutters aside. My sister and Anna yelped in protest as the cold breeze blew past me, but I ignored them.

To my astonished delight, I had a clear view of the snow -covered meadows where Timur and I had ridden that magical day when he first kissed me. The Moscow River curved around its lower edge like a snake, and the walls blocked much of its path. But beyond that, the vista opened up. A group of armored riders who could be Alexei's warriors circled on a swath swept free of drifts by the unrelenting wind. I craned my neck to identify the man in the lead, but I was too far away to name Timur with any certainty.

A pair of brown dots in the sky caught my eye.

Can it be ... the falcons?

I blinked my eyes, waiting for the dots to disappear. Then one plummeted, like a stone pitched from a great height. An instant later, the second bird dove, a little slower in the stoop—Tizilek, following Alexei's Ferz. My heart soared. I might be stuck in this witch's house, but my bird flew free. And the man I loved was out there, as he'd promised, waiting for me.

"For love of the Virgin Mother, Lyuba, close the window. Do you want us to freeze to death?"

"Forgive me, Maria. It's so beautiful out there." With leaden fingers I drew the shutters closed, shutting out the brilliant sunshine, the galloping horsemen, and the sight of my falcon gliding with her companion on the wintry winds. I felt more confined than ever, yet at the same time my soul, like Tizilek, spread her wings and rejoiced.

Somehow, I must find my way home.

In the sitting room downstairs, Anna and I huddled near the stove and surveyed the company. The Moscow maidens clustered in family groups with their sponsors, separated by invisible lines delineating the factions at court. I saw a Shuisky contingent— Princesses Nadezhda and Ustinya, chatting with Bronislava Blednaya and her unfortunate daughter. Liza Vorontsova and her nieces, Grunya and Dunya, sat in one corner with Vera Yureva and Tasya, a rare display of cross-clan camaraderie that probably reflected the relative independence of their fathers and brothers. On a settle near the door, Princess Sophia Belskaya formed a two-person group with Serafima Khabarova, both of them behaving as if they could render the rest of us invisible by acting as if we did not exist.

The women from the provinces, in contrast, seemed to have fallen into easy conversation. The same could not be said of their charges, who sat within hearing range of Anna and me. Dina exchanged stiff, even biting, remarks with the hapless Zoya; Melita and Avdotya stared at each other, hands clasped in their laps as if neither could decide where to start.

"*Bozhe moi*, what a stuffy bunch," Maria murmured. "They might as well be waiting for the Second Coming. Let's stir things up, shall we?"

"Stir things up?" I echoed. "How?"

Anna, who sat between my sister and me, widened her eyes in a way that reminded me of a startled rabbit and did not speak. Maria gave me a mischievous smile. "You want to know what's going to happen next," she said, keeping her voice low. "You won't find out from me. Go and tackle the Shuisky group, and I'll take the Belsky pair. Anna can apply her experience with Lara to get those two little girls talking. They won't know much; nor will their mothers and aunt. But you won't be sitting here on your own, Anna, and helping them feel comfortable will relieve your own fears."

She nodded and rose to obey. I resisted, although I appreciated what my sister was trying to do. "What about Liza Vorontsova? She's more likely to share what she knows."

"Yes, but for that reason we can talk with her later. Sophia Belskaya's a more difficult case. She won't confide in you, because you're young and a potential threat to her plans. But she may talk to me. Unlike Papa, Alexei has always maintained good relations with her menfolk, as he has with the Shuisky and Glinsky princes. I'll sound her out while you take advantage of whatever arrangement Papa has made with Nadezhda Shuiskaya. You've met her twice, so start by reminding her of the Christmas party. The others were there, too."

"Very well." I left to do her bidding. It made no real difference to me which group I infiltrated. And since the only way out of Papa's snare was by successfully navigating the bride show, I might as well find out as much as I could.

"May I join you?" I asked a few moments later. With a strategic bow, I directed my request to Nadezhda Shuiskaya, the highest-ranking of the four women, before extending my salutation toward

Ustinya Paletskaya, then the two Blednaya princesses. "You remember me from Papa's Christmas dinner, I hope." That was for the two women; the girls both knew me well. "My father asked me to convey his greetings."

"Did he now?" Princess Nadezhda tipped her head to one side and surveyed me as a wolf might survey a tasty lamb. "And what else did he tell you, I wonder?"

I hadn't expected a challenge. How did she expect me to respond? "That I might count on your friendship," I said after a pause.

"Which you may, of course. Please be seated, and welcome." She indicated an empty place on her left, and I settled between her and Ustinya.

"You know everyone from that party of your father's," Nadezhda went on. "A most pleasant occasion."

"I do, and from before that afternoon as well." I greeted the other three one by one before turning back to Nadezhda. "I'm glad you enjoyed the party. I will tell Papa when I see him again, but that won't be until after the tsar makes his choice."

"Oh, your father knows," she said with a languid lift of her hand. "I thanked him myself upon leaving."

I let the topic die, having nothing to add, and was framing a question about what to expect tomorrow when Nadezhda continued. "Your sister has decided to woo the Belsky faction, I see. Surely your father will not be happy about that."

Well, *that* was an opening of sorts, if a rather aggressive one. "She's not wooing anyone." I feigned calm rather than add to the tension. "Maria's husband refuses to ally himself with any court faction. But since we are forced together for the duration of the bride show, she suggested that it would benefit us to talk to as many people as possible, rather than sit in a corner and brood."

"Very sensible," Princess Bronislava said with magisterial calm. "You're a quick-witted chit, aren't you? Too bad you waste your time reading books and associating with that Polish slut. None of that will help you get a husband, especially a royal one. Virtue, deportment, household management, needlework—those are the skills that distinguish a bride. And lineage—you do have that, thanks to your parents and your sister's marriage."

I bit my tongue, since an honest response to her attack on me could only cause offense. At the same time, I wasn't in the mood to tolerate her abuse of Juliana. "Lady Ossolinska is the wife of a Polish magnate and a favorite of Queen Bona Sforza. She speaks five languages and has an extensive knowledge of poetry, literature, art, and music. I hardly think she merits being dismissed in such a way."

Bronislava snorted. "Just the kind of nonsense I'd expect from a girl who reads books. I don't know what your father was thinking, proposing you as our next tsaritsa. And why is your sister sponsoring the Kolychev girl as well as yourself? That can only further diminish your chances."

I clenched my fists against the edge of my seat, hoping no one would notice how this old hag was getting to me. "Anna is a close friend of my family," I said in the most measured tone I could muster. "Her mother has a new baby who needs her care, so Maria offered, in the spirit of Christian charity, to sponsor Anna as well."

Another grunt from the harpy. "Her mother can't show her face at court since she married beneath her. You see what I mean about the fatal consequences of reading?"

Nadezhda murmured a protest, and for a moment I stared, perplexed—not by Bronislava's hostility, which obviously reflected her belief that I might outshine her daughter, but by the complete illogic of her train of thought. She couldn't honestly believe that Solomonida had married Anfim as the result of reading books!

An image of how Timur would laugh when I relayed this conversation filled my head. Would I ever see him again—as an unmarried girl with the right to love him, that is?

I remembered the soaring falcons and my determination to stand firm. Bronislava had handed me a chance to convey my unsuitability for the position of royal bride, and I should take it. "Women who read can also practice virtue and deportment," I said in what I hoped was a serene, respectful voice. "I learn many important things from books, including the details of household management. And although it is true that I don't like to stitch, I have other skills. I ride well, for example." I deliberately did not mention my knowledge of the world, which had so impressed Anastasia Petrovna, since I had no wish to remind anyone present that I also had abilities that might make me a useful counselor, especially for a ruler.

Princess Bronislava sniffed. "Just what I would expect from a young woman raised by a tsarevich. A tsaritsa has no need to ride. Carriages will take you to pilgrimage sites. No other journeys are necessary."

In her words, I heard a prejudice against Tatars that appalled me. Whatever anger I still nurtured against Alexei for opposing my marriage to his son, he was *family*. I could not let such sentiments pass unchallenged. Words leaped to my tongue, overwhelming my efforts to remain calm and reasonable. "Is that so, Princess? My brother-in-law is renowned for his courtesy, his loyalty, and his competence. I have heard nothing to his discredit. And I recall you wanting his patronage for your son. Yet now you insult him?"

Princess Bronislava blanched, her mouth tight and her eyes furious. "Do you challenge me, Miss Impertinence? Your own courtesy leaves much to be desired!"

Fetinya, whose presence I'd almost forgotten, snickered, provoking a glare from her enraged parent. Ustinya patted my hand in an encouraging way, but she didn't speak up on my behalf. Hoping my defense of Alexei hadn't done more harm than good, I raised my chin and stared at the furious princess, neither replying nor yielding. A telling pause ensued, through which I heard Maria's cheerful chatter with Sophia and Serafima, Anna in happy exchange with the two youngest brides. Their mothers, in contrast, had stopped their conversation to observe us, their faces a mix of curiosity and concern.

"Come, ladies," Princess Nadezhda said smoothly as the silence stretched to the point of discomfort. "We're shut up here, so let's not make life unpleasant by arguing with one another. Shall we find another topic of discussion? Our plans for the rest of your time here, perhaps?"

At last, the information that Maria had sent me here to collect. I nodded vigorously, as did Ustinya. Even Fetinya managed a murmur of agreement, although her mother's stance did not relax in the slightest. I shifted sideways in my seat, facing Nadezhda and avoiding Bronislava's irate gaze.

"Over the next day or two, you and your sponsors will meet with the royal princesses, Anna Glinskaya and Anastasia Petrovna," Nadezhda said with impressive authority. "They will question you about your upbringing and your character, your relatives and their health. The government scribes have undertaken extensive study of your lineages, both maternal and paternal, and you should be prepared to answer any questions they raise. These include illnesses, failed pregnancies, and other health problems that could affect your ability to fulfill your obligations as tsaritsa."

She looked meaningfully at me as she reached the midpoint of this speech, and I felt my heart leap—whether from fear or joy, I couldn't tell for certain. Mama, although she had produced seven living children, had buried as many more, and her health had deteriorated as a result. And Papa's career, as reflected in the records, might raise many questions that would require careful handling if they were to get me out of the bride show without catapulting the entire family into disgrace.

"And then?" I asked in a voice less steady than I would have liked.

Nadezhda shrugged an elegant shoulder. "After that come the medical and virginity examinations—one girl at a time, with her sponsor as chaperone. Once we have those results, the princesses and boyars' wives will confer, and most of the candidates will be dismissed. Those who remain will live under observation in this house for up to a week. At the end of that time, they will be presented to the tsar, one after another, and he will make his choice. There is a specific protocol for that, in which we will instruct those selected for presentation."

I felt as a soldier must while waiting for the battle to commence. My heart pounded, and I chastised myself for an attack of nerves I seemed incapable of controlling. So many pitfalls to avoid, and such a narrow path to traverse between a dishonorable but welcome dismissal and a dreaded but prestigious acceptance. Papa would be furious if I failed, and Timur and myself devastated if I succeeded. Not for the first time, I wished myself elsewhere.

At the same time, a small flame of excitement flickered into life inside my chest at the challenge to come. It wasn't like me to sit quietly by the hearthside while others took charge of events. I liked to be in the thick of things.

As I sat between Nadezhda and Ustinya, listening with one ear and doing my best to look interested, a new story took shape in my head: a heroine under siege, desperate for reunion with the hero she loved but surrounded by obstacles of every description, including a wicked hag (take that, Princess Bronislava!) and a shape-shifting demon (surely no one would connect him with the young tsar). With the hero barred from the heroine's palace, only she could free herself from the demon's power, with a little assistance from a well-intentioned sprite or two.

What should I call my main character? Svetlana, I decided, derived from *svet*—light. I would give her hair the color of wheat and eyes like the sky on a cloudy day. And my hero would be Ruslan, a name more Tatar than Russian—dark-haired, a bruising rider and a warrior for the ages, with laughing eyes and a falcon perched on his wrist.

Dobrinya the housekeeper called us into dinner not long after I reached that point. Seated next to Anna once more, I ate with indecent speed, barely participating in the conversation. Even so, it seemed like hours before I could dash upstairs and pen the first lines of my tale.

Chapter 14

*"The dragon spied on the maidens, searching for one
that appealed to him"*

The next morning brought the tsar's coronation. Although
not allowed to attend, we took turns watching the panoply
and splendor from the outside staircase, admiring the gorgeous
robes of the nobility and the young ruler's bejeweled cloth-of-
gold. I had an opportunity to wave at Alexei as he passed by, near
the front of the procession. I even caught a glimpse of Timur
among his uncle's entourage, and he too lifted a hand in greeting.
For one bright moment, life seemed normal.

The day after that—dressed in our second-best court robes
because only our formal presentation to the tsar would be more
consequential than this meeting—Anna and I accompanied
Maria to a room set aside on the second floor. Anastasia
Petrovna greeted us, then announced that she saw no reason to
interview us again. I squelched a moan of protest—a foolish
moan, since Princess Anastasia was the only person so far to
think me a suitable bride for her royal cousin, but a moan
nonetheless. I liked her, and under normal circumstances I would
love to know her better. The sight of her stately companion, in
contrast, made my heart pound with anxiety. This was the
woman who, according to rumor, had ordered the brutal
execution of Timur's friends. It wouldn't take much for things to
go very, very wrong.

"Princess Anna," Anastasia said, addressing the older woman while extending her hand toward us. "I believe you know Tsarevna Maria. The girls are her sister Lyubov Fyodorovna Koshkina and their friend Anna Semyonovna Kolycheva. Anna's mother has a three-month-old infant, so she has consigned her daughter to Maria's care." With the introductions concluded, Anastasia dipped her head and left. We made our bows to Princess Anna Glinskaya, the young tsar's grandmother.

To the extent possible without appearing rude, I searched her face for clues to her interests and personality. I realized right away that she was an absolute ancient, but one in extraordinarily good health. She must have entered her sixth decade, if not her seventh, because her youngest child—Grand Princess Elena, the mother of Tsar Ivan—had married more than twenty years ago, at the age of eighteen or thereabouts. Elena had been accounted a great beauty, and I saw evidence of that heritage in her mother's high cheekbones and large blue eyes, despite the damage wrought by wrinkles and overeating. Princess Anna's manner, too, communicated the kind of innate confidence that someone accustomed to being the object of admiration would feel. A Serbian princess who had married a Lithuanian prince of Tatar descent, Princess Anna moved with a certain exotic flair that I could adapt for the demon in my new story. It was no wonder that the populace dubbed her a witch. She looked like a sorceress with a sultry foreign allure, conveyed through the flash of gems on her ring-bedecked hands and the eagle-like hauteur of her gaze.

As the thought crossed my mind, she proved its worth. Frowning at Anna, Glinskaya said, "Semyon Kolychev. A criminal and a traitor. Who proposed his daughter as a suitable mate for the tsar?"

Anna took a sobbing breath, then rallied. "My cousin Igor Bezzubtsev, Princess."

"*That* fool. It stands to reason he would not consider your past, only the potential advantage to himself." Glinskaya's scowl deepened as she spoke.

It sounded if she planned to dismiss Anna on the spot. And if she did, would she not dismiss me too? My spirits rose at the thought.

I waited for Maria's response. "Anna's father was everything you say." She clasped her hands together and bowed. "A despicable man, mourned by no one. If you wish us to withdraw her candidacy, we will gladly obey."

The princess responded to this expression of compliance by narrowing her eyes at my sister and me. "And you are Fyodor Koshkin's daughters. Should I not consider your lineage, too? Your father stands high in the esteem of the Shuisky clan now, but that was not always the case."

By then I didn't know what to think. Should I hope for release or fear some dreadful retribution against my family? I stood, arms wrapped tight around my waist, incapable of speech.

"As I know too well," Maria said smoothly. "My father did not ask for my advice before proposing my sister as a potential bride for your grandson. If he had, I would have urged him to take his own mistakes into account and let this opportunity pass. Igor Grigorevich, too, failed to consult with Anna or her mother before adding her name to the list. I doubt he even knows the extent of Semyon Kolychev's crimes. As I said, I am prepared to take the girls home and inform the men of your displeasure. I ask you only to keep in mind that my husband has always been loyal. I would hate to see *his* reputation—or those of Anna and her mother—tarnished as a result of our relatives' misdeeds."

Again, for a blissful moment I believed my sister's offer might do the trick and free us both. I held my breath almost to the point of collapsing. Next to me Anna stood equally still, and I could guess she felt the same way.

Princess Anna's frown vanished in a smile. A rather wolfish smile, of the sort I would definitely assign to my demon, but a genuine curve of the lips that extended to her eyes. "A good answer, Maria Fyodorovna," she said. "You are a wise daughter and a faithful wife. I hope that husband of yours appreciates you. The girls will stay. For now."

Silently cursing, I released that held breath and dipped my head. *So close!* But protests would not help. We would only undo Maria's good work.

Anna copied my gesture of obedience, and at a signal from Princess Anna, the three of us arrayed ourselves around the room. Maria listened while we answered one question after another about our mothers, our upbringing, our interests, and our uninformed views of how a royal wife should behave. The whole interview matched with uncanny exactness our questioning by Anastasia Petrovna, and by the time we staggered from the room what felt like hours later, I understood why Princess Anastasia had no desire to waste more time on us: she would have to sit through many, many such interviews with other, as yet unexamined brides.

Recalling that previous interview and Anastasia's reaction to me, I had gone out of my way to say nothing to the tsar's grandmother that would distinguish me from any other candidate. Leave it to Princess Bronislava to comment on my unmaidenly interest in reading and politics and history, my failures as a needlewoman, my love of horses, and anything else that might disqualify me in this contest. I did *not* want to stand out as particularly astute or even interesting, if I could help it.

But by the time Princess Anna dismissed us, I still didn't know whether I'd succeeded.

The rest of the day passed much like the afternoon before, in the sitting room with candidates separated by factions. As before, Maria sent Anna and me to different corners of the room. Anna went to sit with bland Zoya, deep in conversation with Fetinya Blednaya—discussing the relative virtues of hawthorn and sloe, from what I overheard. I suppressed a yawn and looked around for more interesting company. About to join the redheaded Morozov "twins," I stopped when I saw their Aunt Liza give them a shove and point at the far window, where the youngest girls were attempting to lure Anna to their side. Actually, the only attempts came from Avdotya; Melita—clutching the bench with both hands—looked as though she'd rather be back in her bedchamber, fast asleep. The redheads took one look and escaped, capturing the chairs next to Tasya Yureva before their aunt could intervene.

No one but me seemed to have noticed Melita's distress. I set out to investigate, but a hand on my arm stopped me: my sister, suggesting I join Dina and Serafima Khabarova—again sitting apart with Princess Sophia. With a suppressed groan, I agreed. Sophia gladly exchanged her seat for one closer to Tasya Yureva's mother, and I took the chair she had vacated. Maria found a place among the Shuisky princesses.

With the women occupied elsewhere, Dina, Serafima, and I fell into what began as a stilted conversation but improved as we compared notes on the day's ordeal. At first, I cast the occasional glance at Melita, wondering what ailed her, but when I questioned Dina, she brushed off my concern. After that, I focused on finding out as much as I could about what my companions had gone through. By the time the conversation ended, I had found out only that Princesses Anna and Anastasia had grilled everyone with equal intensity, pulling old scandals and real or imagined injuries from the recesses of history and demanding explanations for decisions made by male relatives when we girls were in leading strings. At least the absurdity of the whole thing gave me an excuse to laugh, and that in itself made me feel better. Serafima revealed previously unsuspected talents as a mimic; her imitation of Princess Anna's lofty manner had Dina and me holding our sides.

There was one odd moment, although I didn't grasp the significance of it until later. We had moved on from the interviews by then, and I was listening to Dina talk about her brothers' antics and the tricks they loved to play on her. Halfway through one detailed description, a chuckle from behind me caused me to look over my shoulder, and I felt my jaw drop. Painted flowers covered the wall, and at the center of one a small peephole had appeared. A bright blue eye was clearly visible. While I watched openmouthed, the eye winked at me, then disappeared. The peephole closed, leaving the center of its flower indistinguishable from those around it.

Someone was observing us without making his presence known. The tsar, most likely, or someone acting on behalf of the tsar—because no one else had so much riding on the outcome of the bride show. I couldn't blame him for wanting to see the candidates for himself. I would do the same in his shoes.

But how long had he been there before I discovered him? And was this the first time he'd spied on us? He might have heard my squabble the other day with Princess Bronislava or our mockery of his grandmother just now, and if so, I could only guess what he would make of either.

What I did know was that I'd identified yet another hurdle between me and my goal. With his secret peephole, the observer— let's say the tsar, for simplicity's sake—had the ability to judge for himself the girls vying to become his bride. Once he decided which of us best suited him, I couldn't imagine him standing back and letting his grandmother persuade him to accept someone else.

And what should I make of that wink? Was it just an acknowledgment that I'd caught the observer redhanded, or an expression of camaraderie I had no desire to encourage?

I was still puzzling over what I'd seen—as well as my earlier encounter with the tsar's grandmother—when the housekeeper arrived to announce dinner. As I followed the clicking heels of more than twenty women and girls to the dining hall, I noticed that Melita looked even more tired and wan. I caught Dina's arm, since she was right ahead of me, and she stopped her conversation with Serafima long enough to treat me to an impatient frown.

"Are you *sure* your sister is well?" I indicated Melita with one upturned palm. "Look how pale she is. She can barely walk."

Dina snapped her head around, then returned her attention to me almost as fast. "I'm sure she's fine. She's probably faking illness in the hopes of attracting attention."

I didn't believe her for a moment. Rather than waste time arguing with her, I glanced around the room, assessing my options.

A small crowd stood between me and Melita's aunt, so I could alert her only by shoving aside almost a dozen princesses and noblewomen—not a good idea. Melita herself could answer questions, and might appreciate a sympathetic inquiry, but as I watched, she staggered, then pushed her way between two burly matrons and vanished. Even from where I stood, I heard them curse her as she passed.

That left Maria, who had already entered the dining hall. Deciding that asking her advice was my best course, I sidestepped

Dina and Serafima and walked as rapidly as I could without running into anyone.

Once there, I realized that confiding in Maria must wait. As the only tsarevna, she stood near the top of the table, surrounded by princesses eager to solicit her opinion on every topic imaginable. At last, a tart command from Princess Anastasia sent the other women scurrying to their places, and I settled onto my assigned bench, shared with Maria and Anna. Then came announcements about what we should expect on the following day, to which I half-listened while searching the room for Melita.

I located her at the very end of the table, next to her sister and aunt. If she had looked pale before, by then her skin appeared waxen, and I saw her touch a hand to her brow and scrunch up her eyes as if in pain.

More concerned than ever, I turned to ask Maria what she thought. The words never left my mouth. A crash, followed by a trio of screams, drew all eyes to the far side of the room. As one, the three of us leaped to our feet, upending the bench. Everyone else in the room did the same. But in that brief moment before swirls of multicolored silk and angled bodies again blocked my view, I saw a pair of feet clad in red leather waving in the air. Without seeing her face, I could guess from the placement of those feet that they belonged to Melita.

With the efficiency of a general deploying his troops, Princess Anastasia cleared the room, ordering most of the bridal candidates and their sponsors back to the sitting room and summoning servants to deliver platters of bread, cheese, and cold meat to them there. As the highest-ranking woman present other than Anastasia herself, my sister shooed the others out, but when Anna and I turned to follow them, Maria grabbed our arms. "Stay here," she said. "You two have at least a limited acquaintance with Melita and her family. Anna, see what you can find out from Dina while Lyuba and I help Fevronia tend to Melita." Anna set off across the room, and I sent her silent good wishes that Dina would prove more cooperative with her than with me.

Maria beckoned to me. I tugged her sleeve as we walked toward whatever awaited us at the end of the table. "Whatever happened to Melita probably started a while ago," I whispered. "When we first entered the sitting room, I noticed how pale she was, and I saw her stagger as we lined up to come here. Dina insisted her sister was malingering, but it didn't seem that way to me."

Maria squeezed my hand in acknowledgment, but we had already reached the cluster of women surrounding the red boots, so she didn't speak. I released her arm, and she pushed Dina aside. "Let me see."

Her voice snapped like a whip. Dina skidded sideways, and Anna grabbed the chance to pull her away. I heard without comprehending my friend's rapid speech, but my whole attention was on the scene before me.

Melita lay curled in a ball on her right side, her knees pulled up to her chest. Foam circled her lips, and she jerked convulsively. The sour smell of vomit overwhelmed the meaty herbal aromas of the dishes that the servants had yet to clear.

"What's wrong with her?" I asked.

"Isn't it obvious?" the girl's aunt snapped. "She's been poisoned!"

The Kremlin was perhaps the only place in Russia where one could find a Western doctor. After the shock of Fevronia's announcement abated, Princess Anastasia sent for him. While we waited, the women tried to make Melita as comfortable as possible, feeling her forehead and plying her with sips of water that led only to more frothing and vomiting. Maria's questions went unanswered, and I stood helplessly to one side until a barked command sent me to wait for the doctor and usher him toward the dining area.

In fact, I saw him as soon as I went through the door. A wispy man of around forty, he wore a dark robe that fell in folds to his feet, with wide, puffed sleeves in the Polish style and a flat cap of black velvet atop his graying hair. He assessed me with serious blue eyes, then bowed and said, "I am Nikolaus Baer. I understand one of the young ladies requires my services. And you are?" Although he spoke Russian fluently, his strong accent distorted the sounds. But I understood enough to answer him.

"Lyubov Fyodorovna," I said. "Your patient is in the room behind us. Please come with me." He nodded but did not follow, instead peppering me with questions. In response, I told him what I had observed and when, little as that was. More than anything, I wanted reassurance that Melita would recover and, which seemed even more childish, that no one would really be wicked enough to poison a twelve-year-old. But since he couldn't tell me those things before seeing his patient, I refrained from asking.

When his interrogation subsided, I led him to the dining room and indicated the cluster of women. I pointed out my sister and Princess Anastasia, then followed the doctor as he strode toward the group. They parted at his approach, and through the space thus created, I watched him kneel and touch Melita's chin. She hadn't moved since I left the room, and although she looked no better than before, she also appeared no worse. He placed a hand against her throat, parted her closed lids with the other thumb and forefinger, and spouted a series of questions in a rapid staccato, first to Melita's aunt and then to her sister. Only then did he stand and offer his opinion.

"Indeed, the child has been poisoned—most likely, with an excess of tansy." He glared at Fevronia, who looked worried, and Dina, whose expression might better be characterized as smug.

I frowned. Dina wouldn't have poisoned her own sister, would she? Tansy tea was a common enough remedy, given for everything from worms to abortions, but finding the correct dose demanded knowledge and a careful eye. I wouldn't dare administer it myself.

The doctor shifted his attention to Princess Anastasia and Maria. "With God's grace and the right care, she will recover. The only cure is to flush it out of her with water. Give her as much as she can hold, and let her sleep it off."

"But where did she get tansy?" Maria asked Fevronia. "Did one of you dose her? She didn't appear to be sick yesterday."

"Of course not," Fevronia said. "I had no need. She's perfectly well." Dina didn't speak.

"Well, someone did." Maria gazed into one face after another, ending with the doctor. When he shrugged, she returned her attention to Anastasia. "We must find out who."

"Tansy is quite distinctive," the doctor said. "Bright yellow flowers, even when dried. Although your poisoner may have used tansy oil, which is harder to trace."

"We'll check the rooms." Anastasia beckoned to the closest servant. "Tell the housekeeper to begin right now, starting with the victim's chamber." She turned to Nikolaus Baer. "Thank you, Doctor. You may depart. Please return tomorrow to check on the girl."

The doctor bowed and left, and the princess ordered the maids to make Melita comfortable until she could be carried to her room. Then she addressed Fevronia. "You heard what the doctor said. We will follow his instructions, and we will investigate. Whoever administered that potion will be punished. Such behavior is not tolerated here."

Dina's smugness vanished, replaced by a scowl. Maria bowed to the princess but spoke to Anna and me, "Well, girls, shall we join the others? You must be hungry."

I echoed my sister's farewells and followed her from the room, but in fact hunger was the last thing on my mind. The whole incident had shaken me to the core. Bad enough if Dina's smugness, as I half-suspected, meant that she had dosed her younger sister as a wicked prank. But if someone else had administered the poison, what would *that* mean for Anna and me?

I didn't want to become tsaritsa, but I also had no desire to die at sixteen. The stakes in this game had risen in a way I couldn't have predicted.

Maria stayed until the housekeeper announced that we could return to our rooms. The servants had failed to find any poisons, although a stoppered clay vial on Dina's dressing table raised eyebrows. It was empty, and she insisted it had contained a lotion for pimples, so Princess Anastasia ordered no action be taken. The vial only heightened my suspicions of a girl I had never much liked.

With the search complete, my sister warned us to watch what we ate and drank, then left for home as she had the day before. I sent my regards to Juliana and Felix, Alexei and Timur, Alexander and Dosya—carefully slipping my love into the middle of the list so as not to draw attention to him. Anna asked that news of the day be delivered to her own family, and Maria swore she would see to it. Once she had gone, I shut the door to the room set aside for her and placed a wooden chair under the knob to alert us if anyone tried to enter. It was early enough in the evening that the other girls and their sponsors were still roaming around or gathered in the sitting area, but I had too much on my mind to tolerate their endless conversations.

Anna lifted her brows at the barrier I'd created, then headed without speaking for the chamber we shared. I checked the walls for peepholes and didn't find any, but that didn't mean much. I'd never have suspected there was one in the sitting room if I hadn't seen it in operation. Still on edge, I went to join my friend.

I found her sitting on the bed, a piece of paper in her hand. She glanced my way as I entered and immediately folded the paper into quarters. "What's that?" I asked.

She blushed, so obviously discomfited by the question that for a moment I expected a refusal to answer—or, worse, a lie. "You can tell me," I said. "I'm your best friend. Is it Yuri's letter?" I couldn't imagine what else she might treat with such reverence, for lack of a better word. And here I'd believed she might be forgetting him in favor of an Italian silk merchant. "It may not have been a good idea to bring it here. People snoop, you know."

Again she hesitated. I was losing patience—not unusual at the best of times, and I'd had a stressful day—when she said, "I had to. It came just as we left the house. I had no chance to read it before you and your sister arrived with the carriage."

"A *new* letter?" That did surprise me. I'd been certain Yuri sought to spare Anna the news that he'd given in to the pressure to take his vows. "What does he say?"

Wordlessly she held out the message. I unfolded it and moved to the window, then turned to let the light fall on the paper.

Your missive warms my heart, Yuri had written. *With each day that passes, I yearn for you more. I can't go on like this, with no hope that we will ever be together. You are the sun that lights my way, the lodestar that draws me forward. And whatever your wretched cousin believes, the contract between us stands.*

Yet I hear that plans are afoot to wrest you from me. Stay strong, my darling. Don't yield to Igor's ambitious schemes. Wait, and I will come for you.

I kiss you a thousand times,
Your soon-to-be husband, Yuri

I fought for breath. My teeth gripped my lip, and it was all I could do not to throw the letter at Anna. Of course, I wanted to see my dear friend happily settled with the man she loved. But if the wrong person found this message …

"We should burn it," I said, ignoring her yelp of dismay. Remembering the eye in the room below, I sat next to her and kept my voice low. "Suppose someone discovered it when they searched our room just now?"

"I didn't leave it out. I hid it among those papers of yours." She pointed to the desk, piled high with notes and discarded first drafts of my Svetlana story.

I wanted to shake her. So she'd involved me in this madness and hadn't even told me? "Do you have any idea how much trouble this letter could cause—for you and for Yuri? We have to burn it right away. Then, even if someone reported it, there will be no proof." My words came out harsher than intended.

"Could *you* burn it, if Timur sent it to you?"

Thinking of my beloved's kisses and their effect on me, the light in his eyes when he laughed or even smiled, the eagerness with which I searched for him in the meadows beyond the Kremlin walls, I admitted to myself I could not. I was still too annoyed by her carelessness, though, to tell her the truth. "I'd have to," I said. "For his sake."

Her mouth compressed in a stubborn line. I shifted tactics. "Then promise me you'll give it to Maria to take with her when she leaves tomorrow. It's only for a few days, but it could save Yuri's life. Especially if he's avoided taking vows as ordered—which he must have, if he thinks the contract between you stands." I shared my story about the peephole in the room below. She glanced nervously at the walls, and I knew she'd understood.

"Do you really think the tsar would peek at us in our bedchambers?" she asked. "We're supposed to be innocent virgins!"

I hadn't known a whispered exclamation was possible, but Anna managed it. "I don't," I admitted. "But it never occurred to me that he'd sneak a look at us anywhere, and once the peephole closed, I couldn't see where it had been. If there is one here or in Maria's room, we might never discover it. Think, Anna! Yuri narrowly escaped execution once, and now he's defied a direct order from the tsar. He sent the message to your home; he trusts you to keep it safe, and if you love him, you must. You don't want him to be the next man impaled on the ice!"

That was even harsher, but it got through. I saw her blanch. "Very well. I'll give it to Maria tomorrow, I promise." She took the letter from me, refolded it, and tucked it into a cunning little pouch sewn into her robe. "Until then, I'll keep it here, on my person. I don't want to endanger Yuri—or you. I'm sorry. I didn't think what it would mean if anyone found it, but I also didn't think they would search."

Only then did I permit myself a sigh of relief. "Neither did I," I said. "It's been a horrible day, hasn't it? I hope Melita took the poison by accident—or even that Dina did it, to be mean. The alternative is terrifying."

She exhaled a gasping breath and agreed. Needing a distraction and not knowing what else to do, I sat at the desk, intending to work on my new story, but I kept being distracted by a nagging fear. Suppose a servant *had* already discovered Yuri's letter? I couldn't see much evidence of their search, just the odd item not quite as we left it in a chest or at the dressing table where we arranged our hair.

I glanced at the surface of the desk, covered with sheets of paper filled with yesterday's scribbles. So many years had passed since I first learned to read that I found it difficult to imagine how those papers might appear to an illiterate. One would look much like another, would it not?

Perhaps we were safe, after all. Maybe the searchers had not bothered to check the individual sheets of paper. But in case I was wrong, I intended to make sure Anna kept her promise to send Yuri's note home with my sister.

I pushed thoughts of the letter aside and settled in to create a word picture of my heroine Svetlana. *Don't borrow trouble*, Maria always said. We had enough to worry about with the medical examinations tomorrow.

Could we do something to have one or both of us ruled unfit?

Chapter 15

"A wicked witch tormented the princess"

A nna did in fact slip her letter into Maria's hand when my sister arrived the next morning, whispering a quick explanation that brought a frown to Maria's face. She didn't chastise Anna, though, just tucked the folded paper into her jeweled purse.

"Come with me," she said. "You're both assigned to the first group the doctor will see. Each of you needs a chaperone, however. Princess Nadezhda has agreed to act as Lyuba's, since Ustinya is in the second group. Let's go downstairs."

This time we went all the way to the ground floor, where a pair of storerooms had been converted to a large, open space. Sunlight pouring through the high windows illuminated whitewashed walls, giving the chamber an airy lightness that reminded me of Alexei's house, a welcome relief from the heavy decor that characterized the upper stories. I need not fear hidden peepholes here, because they would stand out against the plain paint, although an elaborately carved wooden screen set in one corner might conceal an observer. I decided on the spot to stay as far away from the screen as possible.

Half a dozen beds surrounded by curtains had been set up around the room, three of them already occupied—or so I assumed from the drawn drapes around them. Nadezhda Shuiskaya met me at the door and ushered me to a fourth bed while Maria led Anna to the one closest to the windows. Fetinya Blednaya and her mother came in just as Nadezhda closed the curtains around me.

"Six girls and only one doctor, so we must wait." Nadezhda pointed to my robes. "Please remove everything but your shift. The doctor will examine you first; one of the royal midwives will assist me in conducting a more intimate probe after he finishes."

If the doctor's visit sounded nasty, thoughts of the "intimate probe" turned my stomach. I tried to keep my face straight, but I knew I hadn't succeeded when Nadezhda sent me a sympathetic glance. "Believe me," she said. "I don't enjoy this either, but it's required, so we both have to put up with it." She pointed to a chamber pot in one corner. "You need to use that, too. The doctor wishes to examine your urine for signs of ill health."

I sighed but complied, first stripping off the robes I'd donned with care less than an hour before, then squatting over the chamber pot. Fortunately, I'd drunk a fair amount of apple juice that morning to wash down the buttered bread that the servants brought to break our fast. The doctor would have ample liquid to peruse.

Once finished, I washed my hands in a nearby bowl before taking a seat on the bed next to Princess Nadezhda, who chatted amiably about my father's Christmas party, the beauty of his house, my qualifications as a candidate and how they compared to Princess Ustinya's (poorly, I was glad to note), as well as many other things that I let slip past in an endless stream of words.

I noticed that she had a keen eye; her grasp of the layout of Papa's estate was extraordinary, and her understanding of his character no less impressive—especially for someone who admitted to only a passing acquaintance. Murmuring the occasional response to keep her going, I listened to her amusing insights with one ear while plotting Svetlana's adventures, separating what I could safely write here from what must wait until after the bride show.

Nadezhda's chatter obscured the passage of time, but eventually the doctor arrived. I recognized him from the day before. He bowed and said, "Lyubov Fyodorovna, I believe. We meet again."

"Good morning, Doctor Baer," I said, dreading what he might do. I studied him as he greeted Nadezhda Shuiskaya, who responded in kind. Then he returned his attention to me, and the inquisition began.

First came questions about the time and place of my birth. "Why do you need to know?" I asked, startled. The priests emphasized that illness or health lay in God's hands, and although I knew several old women skilled in the use of herbs, I'd never encountered one who worried about what day I'd arrived on this earth. Nor had my studies included any medical books.

He must hear the same question often, because he didn't so much as blink in response. "It tells me how the movement of the stars may affect you, the likely balance of your humors, and therefore the kinds of diseases to which you may be prone."

I didn't accept his explanation. I recalled Father Job, in a rare moment of anger, condemning astrology and almanacs as the devil's work. But in the hope that the information might reveal some defect I couldn't imagine that would make me an unsuitable tsaritsa, I decided to tell him. "In Moscow, on the thirtieth day of September, in the year 7038." He looked puzzled at the last, although you'd think he'd spent enough time in Russia to know how we told time. I did a quick sum in my head. "It would be 1530, in German years."

He nodded. "So you are sixteen and a half, more or less, born under the sign of Libra. And at what time of day?"

"Not long after dawn. They were singing Lauds, my sister told me."

The doctor's brow creased as he scribbled in his notebook. "Very well."

"Is that good?" I asked.

He sent me an impatient glance, as if annoyed by my questions. "It is neither good nor bad. It simply is. Not the best match for a Virgo like the tsar"—my spirits drifted upward, only to dive once more as he finished his sentence—"but not terrible either. Hold out your hand. I need to take your pulse."

He set his notebook aside, and I did as he asked, wincing at his clammy touch, provoking yet another frown.

"Calm down," he said. "I won't hurt you. Your heart is pounding so hard I can't get a proper reading."

He was right, but I couldn't make myself care. Having him declare me unwell offered the perfect solution to my dilemma, securing my release without any blame directed at my sister. "I'm scared," I told him. "I've never been examined by a doctor before."

He grunted in response, released my wrist to jot something else in his notebook, then tested my temperature by holding his hand against my forehead. He pressed his thumb against both sides of my neck, ignoring my involuntary wince, then ran his fingers down my arms and inspected my palms before lifting each foot and palpating it with his roughened palms as if I were meat he considered purchasing. It was all I could do not to kick him away. I didn't even try to conceal my distaste.

When he lifted the chemise to reveal my calves, Princess Nadezhda issued a sharp reproof, and he dropped the linen so fast it slapped against my skin. "Ahem," he said. "And where is the urine sample?"

I indicated the chamber pot, and he picked it up, swirling the contents in a way that struck me as dangerous. I risked another question. So what if I angered him? His good opinion could not benefit me. "What will it tell you?"

He stopped rummaging in the bag he'd dumped on a nearby table and stared at me. "Inquisitive, aren't you?"

I shrugged, faking unconcern. "I like to know what's going on. If it affects me, that is."

"It's unseemly in a woman," he announced with a lofty air, "but I will answer you. The state of your urine is the best indicator of overall health. It should be clear and a nice, pale yellow—neither dark nor reddened." While I clenched my hands into fists against the sheet and sent thoughts to the chamber pot, willing the liquid within to discolor or cloud, he pulled a flask from the bag he'd dumped on a nearby table and poured some of the liquid into its wide mouth. Then he returned the chamber pot to its corner and held the flask up to the light.

"Excellent, excellent." Apparently satisfied, he poured the extracted urine back into the chamber pot and wiped his hands on a rag. While I gazed at him, disliking his complacent expression, he scribbled more notes. I craned my neck to see what he had written, but I couldn't decipher the spidery script.

"Well?" Nadezhda asked as he tucked the notebook away and picked up his bag.

"Oh, she's perfectly healthy." He pushed the curtains aside and left. "I'm sure she'll make a fine tsaritsa, if it comes to that."

Nadezhda muttered a disbelieving curse at his back, and I forced myself not to do the same. For once, I agreed with her wholeheartedly.

Despite his clammy hands and irritable manner, the Western doctor was an innocuous sweetheart compared to the terrifyingly efficient Rinka Fedotova, who pushed her way through the curtains as soon as he left. Like the sorceress in the tale I'd constructed for Tolya, Rinka radiated a calm that chilled the bones. I had the sense that a dragon could spew flames over her head, only to have her convert them into icicles and send them crashing to the ground. Add a puff of smoke surrounding her entrance, and the resemblance would be complete.

Or perhaps that was my fear talking. Maria had warned me about the virginity test, and I knew from Anna's experience before her family signed the marriage contract with Yuri Vorontsov just how horrid it would feel for someone to probe around in a place no one else had ever touched. But knowing what to expect didn't lessen my anxiety in the slightest. If I had dreaded the doctor's hands on me, the thought of what Rinka planned left me hovering close to panic, and no amount of focusing on the ceiling and imagining stories could corral my scattered thoughts into something coherent. I told myself that Anna had endured this and survived—passed with flying colors, in fact. I reminded myself I had done nothing that would make the outcome different for me. But none of it helped.

Rinka herself did not *look* scary. In yet another ineffective attempt to stop my trembling, I took stock of her appearance. She was younger than I'd expected, probably no more than thirty-five. Her sense of style was equal to her unflappable manner—another surprise, because most of the midwives I'd seen were rotund peasant women with white hair and faces as wrinkled as their workaday clothes. Rinka, in contrast, wore a simple dark blue robe of light wool. A scarf covered her head, brown curls escaping at the sides, and she had tied it in a way that mimicked a noble headdress, with a starched tip that reached skyward and a knot near her nape holding the contraption together. If we had met under other circumstances, I could imagine liking her.

Nadezhda performed a brief introduction. My throat tightened to the point where I couldn't speak, so I acknowledged them only with a nod.

"Lie back." Nadezhda gave me a slight push. I was still wriggling myself into a comfortable position when Rinka, without a word, launched into her task.

At first, it wasn't too bad. I lay, gritting my teeth and counting petals on the painted ceiling while she patted and poked my body from temples to toes. Eyes, ears, jawline—she even ordered me to open my mouth so she could examine my teeth.

But then she moved her hands farther down, and things got worse. Anger unleashed fear's grip on my throat, but my protests earned me only silence or a slap. Nothing was sacred. She measured my hips with her hands and frowned. She kneaded my breasts as if they were rolls being prepared for the oven. She prodded my stomach and thighs, then squeezed my waist until I emitted an outraged hiss, receiving nothing but a glare in return.

"Your hands are cold," I raged. "And what gives you the right to maul me this way?"

She stopped with her fingers on the hem of my shift and glared at me. "Stop behaving like a brat. You're no better than any other candidate. And if you must blame someone, blame your father—or whoever nominated you for the position of tsar's bride. I'm doing the job they pay me for, and that's that."

I bit my tongue, too upset to come up with a good response. But then she turned back the hem of my chemise and called Nadezhda to her side. Together, they pushed my knees toward the ceiling and held them there while Rinka reached deep inside my most private parts and ran her finger in a circle around the edge.

I couldn't stop myself. I thrashed and kicked out. Nadezhda swore, and Rinka pulled her hand away. I shimmied backward, propping myself on my elbows, then pushing into a sitting position. I glowered at the two women, and they scowled right back at me. I shoved the fabric of my chemise down and pulled up my knees, wrapping both arms around my calves.

Nadezhda's scowl faded fast, giving way to a mixture of disbelief and calculating curiosity that at the time I didn't know how to read. Rinka still looked furious, which I sort of understood, but also contemptuous, which made no sense to me at all. Shocked and scared, I continued to hug my knees to my chest, physically shutting them away from any further access to my private parts. The sensation of Rinka's groping fingers still sent rivulets of disgust down my spine. Again my ability to push words past the lump in my throat deserted me, although I was desperate to hear that everything was fine. But the expressions on their faces suggested that something was not fine, and I had no idea what or why.

Belatedly I wondered whether I shouldn't simply have refused to let Rinka conduct the examination and let the royal women dismiss me. Papa would have been livid, of course, but that bothered me less than the possibility of Maria suffering because of my intransigence. In any case, it was too late now.

Like two puppets pulled by a single string, the women turned toward each other, and as I watched, astonishment robbing me of speech, they engaged in an intense exchange pitched too low for my ears. Without releasing my knees, I scrunched forward to listen, but to no avail. As if alerted to my approach, they pivoted to face me, then back. "Should we reexamine her?" Nadezhda asked.

"Over my dead body," I muttered, staring at the junction where my hands gripped my knees.

I doubted they heard me; certainly they gave no sign. "Do you want me to?" Rinka said, her tone so indifferent I would gladly have smacked her. "I know what I felt, and what I didn't."

At that moment, my discomfort bloomed into pure, unadulterated terror.

What she didn't? Does she think I'm not a virgin? That's impossible!

"Hmm, then you're right; it would only make things worse." Nadezhda raised her shoulders almost to her ears and emitted a huge sigh, as if shaking my troubles off her shoulders. "Well, I promised her father. Say nothing for now. I'll do what needs to be done."

And while I stared in horror, Nadezhda reached into her purse and handed Rinka two gold coins. Rinka gave a quick nod and headed for the curtains, leaving me befuddled. I wanted to ask Nadezhda what had happened, but I didn't dare. Better to save the questions for my sister.

"Get dressed." Nadezhda gestured at the neat pile of clothes. I tried without success to make sense of her behavior as I released the grip on my knees and stood, letting my chemise swirl around my legs. I donned my tunic, then my robe and slippers, glad that I hadn't worn a headdress. It would take time to arrange, and I wanted to get out of that curtained torture chamber as fast as possible.

"Thank you. With your permission, I will leave you now." I bowed to the princess and received a haughty dip of the chin in return. She pulled back the curtains, and I looked around the room for Maria. Not finding either her or Anna, I bowed once more and went upstairs, worried and perplexed. Whatever promises Nadezhda had made to my father, I didn't trust her.

I found Maria and Anna in the second-floor sitting room, surrounded by chattering, relieved-looking candidates and sponsors. The Morozov cousins formed a group in the center, with Zoya and Dina. Seeing no sign of little Melita or her aunt, I wondered in passing whether they were downstairs for the examination or if she was still recovering from yesterday's poison. Then Maria looked my way, and my own troubles surged to the fore. I beckoned to her, rather frantically. She stood, then bent to murmur something in Anna's ear as she passed. "Stay here," I assumed, from the hand Maria placed on my friend's shoulder and Anna's nod of acquiescence.

I grabbed my sister's arm as she reached me and pointed at the ceiling with my free hand. "Something strange happened. I have to tell you right away." I kept my voice low, but not low enough: the girls nearby sent us questioning glances.

"Come." Maria climbed the stairs to the rooms assigned to us without waiting for my assent. I followed close behind, grateful for her quick comprehension and desperate to share my confusion with someone more capable of understanding and handling the situation than myself.

Before long, we shut the door of her chamber behind us, but Maria didn't stop there, pushing a small chest against the door and walking through to the bedroom Anna and I shared. A maid eager to air out the sheets had turned back the covers and left the shutters wide open. But when I went to shut out the wintry breeze, my sister caught my arm. "Better to let it blow," she said.

Because it would make our words harder to intercept. "Understood." I pulled my fur cloak off its peg and handed her Anna's. Maria wrapped the garment around herself. I did the same, then crossed the room and stood once more at the window.

In the meadow I saw the circling horsemen, Timur in the lead, the hovering falcons brown dots in the sky. I wished with every bone in my body that I could take wing like Tizilek and fly over the red brick walls, put this contest behind me, and join them.

And if he doubts my virtue? I could no longer count on his love. Not if Rinka was right.

With that dismal thought pounding in my brain, I turned away from the man I loved, sat next to Maria, and told her every detail of my examination, ending with Rinka's comment and Princess Nadezhda's response.

When I finished, she touched a finger to my lips. "You're not going to like this," she said. Her tone set off a sinking feeling in my chest, but I didn't speak. I wasn't sure I wanted to find out what came next. She didn't spare me, though. "I have to repeat that part of the examination, so I know what they found."

With my sister, I didn't have to suppress my distaste. But without a word of protest, I went to the bed, lay down, and allowed her to duplicate Rinka's probing. I stared at the canopy throughout, hating every moment, but I still couldn't figure out what, exactly, had gone wrong. How could I lose my virginity when I'd never lain with a man?

The humiliation ended at last. "Sit up and rearrange your clothes," Maria said in a grim voice I seldom heard from her—usually in response to some abomination of Papa's. "Then tell me what you and Timur have been doing behind my back. Unless you were silly enough to let yourself be sweet-talked by a servant, but I think I'd have seen evidence of that."

I stared at her, shivering in response to her anger but no less confused than before. "Sweet-talked by a servant?" I'd let Timur kiss me, of course, and that was wrong, given that we weren't married, but I'd never kissed a servant. "I don't understand," I said, feeling like a fool. "Sweet-talked into what? Timur and I haven't done anything we shouldn't."

She glared at me. "Tell me the truth, Lyuba. Alexei was furious when you went hawking with his son. You put your reputation at risk. But did anything happen during the ride?"

I stared at her, uncertain how to respond. So it *was* about the kisses, even though I'd kept that story to myself, not sharing it even with Anna. I was pretty sure Timur hadn't told his father, either. "No, nothing," I said after a pause that probably lasted too long. "And we weren't alone. We rode with an escort of twenty men. What does that have to do with Nadezhda Shuiskaya, anyway?"

"Lyuba, don't play games with me," Maria said, still frowning. "I know you and Timur well enough to guess that two hundred warriors wouldn't stop you if you had your minds set on something. What I'm asking is whether Timur or some other man ..." She paused for a moment before adding, "has ever touched you down there." She pointed at my belly in illustration.

"Touched me down there?" I couldn't keep the incredulity out of my voice. And here I'd worried about a kiss or two! "Of course not," I snapped, hoping the heat in my cheeks, if it showed, would come across as embarrassment rather than guilt. "We were in sight of his warriors the whole time!"

That was not *absolutely* true, of course, since there had been those few moments when he shielded me from view with his body, but I'd realized by then that Maria had more on her mind than kissing.

My indignation seemed to reassure her. She patted my hand, but she still looked concerned. "Sweetheart, has anyone told you how babies are produced?"

Again I stared at her. How much should I admit? My friends and I speculated among ourselves, but we didn't share that with grownups. Young girls were expected to learn such things from their husbands. "Not exactly," I said, again skating the edge of truth. "My friends talk, but none of them are married yet, so they can't *know*."

"Very well." Maria sounded resigned, but at least she didn't press for more details. "We can go over that part later, then. Right now, we have to get you out of this without destroying your future."

It was my turn to frown. "I thought that was our goal from the beginning. Can't you just tell them that I'm a virgin?"

Maria pressed her hand to her head, as if my ignorance caused her physical pain. "Lyuba, your maidenhead is missing. That's what Rinka discovered. That's why I asked about Timur. If you are in fact a virgin—you swear to me that's true?"

"Yes. I am a virgin." I looked her in the eye, and she let her hand drop. "I swear neither Timur nor any other man has touched the places the midwife examined." I made the sign of the cross to show my sincerity.

She continued to scowl at me. "Where *has* Timur touched you, then? Because I know you're hiding something."

I sighed. If I didn't confess the least shameful thing, she would never let up. "He kissed me the day we went hawking. We raced to a tree, and I lost. He said it was a steppe game, and I think that's true, because I remember Alexei's sister mentioning it when I was little."

"And that was it? One kiss in the woods?"

"Yes." I gripped my hands together behind my back. "I won't do it again, I promise."

That hard stare of hers rested on me a little longer, but at last she relented enough to go on. "Then we're in trouble," she said, "because no one here will believe you. The *best* that can happen is for you to be dismissed from the bride show for no specific reason. Even then, finding a good husband for you will be hard, because we can't ever agree to another examination. But that's a minor problem compared to what we face right now. For some reason, Nadezhda Shuiskaya bribed the midwife to hide what they found—"

"She said she promised Papa," I interjected. "He told us we could count on her, remember? But I don't know why she would agree, when she's backing Ustinya."

"Exactly," Maria said. "Ustinya can only benefit from having you knocked out of the contest. And since Nadezhda must know she can't keep your secret forever, I have to assume she intends to discredit you at the worst possible moment. I'll watch her and will intervene if I can, but there are no guarantees that will work." She exhaled like a gust of wind. "I'll talk to Alexei tonight. I'd better stay here until we get through this, even though it means abandoning my guests."

"You don't have to do that. I can watch Nadezhda until I'm sent home." I heard the tremor in my own voice.

Maria's shake of the head sent her earrings into a flashing dance. "It's an emergency. Juliana will understand. I have to go home tonight and explain, but then I'll stay until they dismiss you."

I nodded my thanks. The prospect of a public unmasking terrified me. The test had been uncomfortable, the results of it humiliating, but the thought of standing firm while a roomful of girls and women snickered at my dishonor turned my insides to the consistency of aspic. I forced my next words out, despite the apple-sized lump in my throat. "Nadezhda said she would do what needs to be done. I assume she means if it looks like I might win."

"I think so, too."

I shuddered at the thought, but that wasn't the only part of this situation that bothered me. "How could it happen?" I asked. "Was I born that way?"

Maria's frown returned. "Good question. I've heard that girls can be born without a maidenhead, but of course, we never had a reason to check for yours. Alexei once told me that his people don't subject their girls to the test, because riding can break the ring—and nomad women ride from the moment they're old enough to sit on a horse."

Was it possible, then, that Timur wouldn't blame me for a transgression I'd never committed? A flash of hope ran through me, then my brow crinkled like my sister's as a memory tugged at my brain. "*I've* been riding since I was six," I said slowly, letting the long-ago incident surface at its own pace. "And there was that time when I fell, remember? I wanted Kumai to jump a fence—

which was stupid, because she's not a jumper. I aimed her at it, though, and she balked at the last minute."

"Throwing you over her head," Maria finished for me. "Yes, I do remember. You were ten, and you screamed blue murder."

"Because it hurt like the devil." I pointed at my crotch, sensing an echo of the searing pain that had ripped my insides. "It was right there, too. I slid along the saddle, and it burned as if someone had started a bonfire inside me."

My sister nodded. "Yes, that may have done it. I suppose we'll never know for certain. But in this witches' cauldron even that explanation won't save you if Nadezhda or Rinka decides to share what they found out. I'll defend you, of course, but the disappointed candidates—and their sponsors—will do their best to destroy you, even if it means manufacturing lies. We have to get you away from here before that can happen."

And I will see Timur once more. Mother of God, let him not reject me.

As if pulled by a string, I walked to the window, where the racing riders and soaring birds were still visible. Timur would understand about the riding accident, wouldn't he? He'd grown up with nomadic women. Papa would be livid, but his options for retaliation would be limited. Certainly he could not carry out his threat to wed me to an ugly old nobleman!

Something brushed my right arm, and I turned my head. Maria regarded me with troubled eyes before gesturing at the window. "He's not for you," she reminded me. "Alexei has other plans for him."

"Has he already selected someone?" I tried to keep my voice even, but my heart—so recently restored to pumping at its usual rate—doubled its tempo once more.

"Not yet." The crease between her brows told me she recognized the anxiety I tried to conceal. "But he's considering one of the steppe leaders' daughters. Yusuf Bey is particularly influential; he's already placed one girl in Kazan."

"I see." By keeping my response short, I managed to sound neutral, but not to control my jangled nerves. Matters seemed to be proceeding apace, and not in a direction that suited me.

Maria's expression softened. "It wasn't meant to be, Lyuba. If you did manage to talk Alexei round, the Church would still prohibit any match between you."

So we were back to that. Crestfallen, I shifted my position again to stare out the window. "Don't worry," I said. "I won't do anything foolish."

But as the words left my mouth, I recognized them for the lie they were. Gazing at the distant horsemen, I vowed to win the husband I desired, no matter what. The echo of Timur's urging—*Run away with me to Kasimov*—drowned out the demands of propriety. I'd endured the bride show for the sake of my family. Once my time here was done, I could pursue my own goals. Timur might reject me for this flaw that was no fault of mine, but if he did not, I would go with him. Nothing else mattered.

If only I could convince myself that were true.

And just like that, my spirits headed for the ditch once more.

Chapter 16

"All seemed lost"

With the physical examinations done, the pace of events accelerated. Late that afternoon, before my sister departed for home, the call came for us girls to report to the ground-floor room. There we would find out who could leave and who would stay. I already knew which group I would be in, but that did nothing to alleviate my tension. However much I welcomed the thought of dismissal, I still feared public embarrassment.

Melita had not returned to the group, so I assumed her aunt had withdrawn her name from consideration. Dina marched with the rest of us, oblivious—on the surface, at least—to backbiting comments and suspicious glances. Ustinya Paletskaya led the way, flanked by Tasya Yureva and Fetinya Blednaya. Anna and I fell into place behind the redheaded Morozovs, while the others brought up the rear. I tried to keep my face expressionless despite my roiling emotions as we walked down the stairs. I hoped Anna wouldn't feel betrayed when she found out I'd be leaving her here. But with so many candidates and so few places, perhaps we would both be released and this nightmare would end.

The chamber that awaited us was so changed as to be unrecognizable. The removal of tables and curtains transformed the makeshift doctor's office into an audience hall. Long rows of benches held too many girls to count, most of them unfamiliar. Against the back wall, a single table stood, covered with a cloth and holding folded squares of embroidered silk banded in gold, piled high.

The noise made by the girls was deafening. I could only assume that all sixty candidates had been summoned for this momentous announcement. I gazed at one unfamiliar face after another, not chatting with Anna because we could never make ourselves heard over the din. I yearned for the moment of dismissal, praying that the princesses would not cry my shame to the world. An hour or less, and I could leave this house. I clung to that thought, twisting my hands together and wishing my ordeal would end.

The bang of a gong cut through the hum of voices. Heads turned and necks craned as Princesses Anna Glinskaya, Anastasia Petrovna, and Nadezhda Shuiskaya strode toward the front of the hall. The three of them faced the silenced crowd, and Anastasia raised a hand.

"We have made our decision. These are the candidates whom we will present to the tsar. When we call your name, please rise and move to the back of the hall. The housekeeper will meet you there, and if you have been living in a different house, she will show you to your new accommodations. The rest of you, stay in your seats, and we will bring you up one by one to receive your parting gift of a ceremonial kerchief." She touched the pile of folded cloths.

My heart sped up. Soon I could take my kerchief and go home, where Timur would be waiting for me.

"And now to the candidates," Anastasia said. "Princess Ustinya Paletskaya." Ustinya rose, blushing, and moved to the back of the room.

"Tasya Yureva." Tasya, even more overwhelmed, stood and produced a jerky bow before exiting.

"Anna Kolycheva." Next to me, Anna drew in her breath sharply and clasped my hand. "No, I can't. Yuri!" she whispered into my ear.

I squeezed her fingers, feeling like a complete traitor. She would have to stay here alone while I went home, and I might not even have a chance to explain why I was abandoning her until after her presentation.

"It will be all right," I whispered back, although I didn't believe a word of it. "We'll do what we can. And I'll let Yuri know you received his letter."

Her eyes widened in horror. "You can't write to him from here. Lyuba, you wretch, what have you done?"

"Nothing," I said. Too late, I realized I'd given myself away.

"Anna Semyonovna Kolycheva, are you here?" Anastasia Petrovna called. I heard a distinct edge to her voice, as if she viewed Anna's reluctance as disrespect.

My friend stood. "Yes, Princess. My apologies. I was overwhelmed with joy." Her voice and face contradicted her words. I reached for her, but like a sleepwalker, she slapped my hand away and pushed past the waiting candidates. Reaching the end of the bench, she turned and moved toward the door without so much as a backward glance.

This was worse than I'd imagined. Would she ever forgive me?

An image of Timur filled my head, and I let it expand to soothe my aching heart. I was going home, to the man I loved. Who would not reject me, please, Mother of God. From there I could help my friend, whether she appreciated my efforts or not.

"Lyubov Koshkina," Anastasia said.

What? For a stunned moment I sat, flabbergasted, while every head in the room sought me out. My stomach plummeted like Tizilek in the stoop, and my next exhalation caught in my throat. As I stared dumbstruck at the three princesses, Nadezhda Shuiskaya smiled, her disdain impossible to miss.

Her scorn acted like a tonic to my befuddled brain. Before Anastasia had to repeat my name, too, I lurched to my feet, dipped my head in her direction, and stumbled from the room. Anna met me at the door with a hug, and I followed her out, but as I reached the other side of the door, I cast one last glance over my shoulder.

Nadezhda was still watching me. The conclusion was inescapable: despite the failed virginity test that should have ended my candidacy, she wanted me to be named for presentation to the tsar, and by bribing the midwife, she had made that happen. But she despised me nonetheless, and before the presentation could take place, she would, most likely, denounce me to strengthen the chances of Ustinya Paletskaya.

I was doomed. My infernal father had a lot to answer for.

"You scared me. For a moment, I thought you'd made some kind of deal with the princesses that would let you go home while I stayed here!" Anna dragged me up the stairs toward the sitting room. "Stop being such a slowpoke. Don't you want to tell Maria the news?"

"I don't want the news to be true." I couldn't pull back or I'd fall down the stairs, but I resisted as much as seemed feasible and kept my voice just above audible. "Silly me, I thought you felt the same. Why are you in such a rush? Have you forgotten poor Yuri now that the tsar is a real possibility?"

"Don't be a beast," she said, somehow matching my near-whisper despite the emotion I heard in her voice. "You know better than that. I was so devastated I could barely stand. I want to get as far away from that room as possible. Maria may not be *my* sister, but she's the next best thing."

"I'm sorry." And I *was* sorry for misjudging her. "You can see I'm upset as well. I hoped we'd both be released, and instead neither of us has been. As for Maria, she's going to be as shocked as I am. She's the one who warned me that I shouldn't expect to be picked, for a good reason that I haven't had a chance to tell you yet. We need a plan. There's more at stake here than you know, but I can't explain it until we're alone."

Anna frowned at that, but the sound of footsteps as more candidates left the chamber below cut off further conversation. As fast as we could, the two of us climbed the stairs to the second-floor sitting room. One look at us, and Maria pulled us into a corner. Nowhere in the chamber was completely private, even without the peephole—which I could see at a glance was in use again.

Fortunately, we sat a good distance away from that observant eye. Nevertheless, I murmured a warning to my sister, and she nodded. "We have to stay for the moment," she said in a quiet voice. "We were told to wait until all eight candidates arrived, then join our own girls if they were not chosen." Her brow creased in worry. "You came up quickly. Are you in the final group?"

"Yes, both of us. Princess Nadezhda seemed quite comfortable with that outcome." I sent my sister what I hoped she would interpret as a meaningful look.

I must have gotten my point across, because she said, "Hmm." She turned her head to gaze at Ustinya Paletskaya. "I wonder why."

"A mystery to me," I said. Maria nodded, and I interpreted the unspoken message without difficulty. We would continue the discussion upstairs.

Four more girls entered the room, but I didn't recognize any of them. Though all were attractive, none could compare with Tasya Yureva, Ustinya, or Anna. Meanwhile, the rest of our original group remained downstairs. Maria had mentioned eight chosen candidates, so Zoya, Dina, Serafima, and even the Morozov cousins must have been eliminated. I was glad to escape further interactions with Princess Bronislava and her daughter, although

I would miss some of the others—especially those from the provinces, whom I might never see again.

In that moment, I truly did feel melancholic. Perhaps the watching eye would notice and reject me. Juliana's advice still lingered in my brain, but implementing it without the ability to predict when the tsar might be present to notice lay beyond my powers.

But it turned out that the drama of the day had barely begun. As the last candidate arrived, trailed by the housekeeper, Dobrinya, Fevronia barreled into the room, her niece gripped in one hand and Zoya in the other. Zoya's mother, wringing her hands and expostulating, followed them in.

"Where is Princess Anastasia?" Fevronia demanded. "I must see her at once."

"She is still downstairs," Dobrinya said in a lofty tone. "With the other princesses, distributing kerchiefs to the girls who were not chosen." She frowned. "Which includes these two. Why have you brought them here?"

"Because this one"—Fevronia shook Zoya, who protested—"has committed a grave injustice against my family. As a result, one of my nieces was sickened, and the other"—she dragged Dina forward—"eliminated unfairly from the competition. I seek justice!"

"Justice!" Zoya tugged at her arm, but Fevronia's grip was strong. "Let me go, you old harridan! I've done nothing to you and yours."

"Nothing? Nothing, you say?" Fevronia, almost frothing at the mouth, released Dina and applied both hands to the task of shaking Zoya. The girl's headdress tipped to one side, and her earrings swung like a pendulum. Her mother's complaints rose in volume, but Fevronia paid no heed. "You poisoned my niece with tansy, you wicked girl, and then said nothing, knowing that everyone suspected Dina. She'd have been selected for presentation to the tsar if not for you!"

Zoya was anything but colorless now. Her eyes flashed, and the shaking had reddened her skin. She looked as if she'd spent hours in the sun. "I did no such thing."

"You did! Melita told me the tea came from you." Fevronia sputtered, then focused once more on Dobrinya. "Do you see? I demand to speak to Princess Anastasia at once!"

"She is busy." The housekeeper glanced around the room, as if begging someone to step in. Nadezhda Shuiskaya was still downstairs, Sophia Belskaya nowhere to be seen. That left only my sister, Vera Yureva, and the provincial ladies, two of whom were involved in the conflict.

Maria straightened her shoulders and sailed into the fray with her usual aplomb. "Dobrinya, stand by the door. Fevronia, release the girl and let's get to the bottom of this. You say Melita told you she received tansy tea from Zoya? But why would she drink it?"

With a defiant glare, Fevronia released her prisoner, who promptly burrowed her face in her mother's shoulder. Maria waited, her face implacable. The silence in the room lay thick, like fog.

After a long pause, Fevronia spoke. "That brat left the tansy tea for Dina," she said, her tone reluctant. "Melita didn't realize what it was. She thought it was sweet, because it came with honey, and she likes sweet things. But of course, tansy is bitter, so she didn't finish the drink. She poured out the rest and rinsed the cup. A good thing, or we might have lost her." She pointed at Zoya with a trembling finger. "No thanks to this one that we didn't."

Maria folded her arms across her chest and tapped a toe. The way she narrowed her eyes told me she was not happy with this explanation, and indeed it left much to be desired. I studied the faces across from me, trying to discern what they had not said.

Zoya—drab, silent Zoya!—pulled away from her mother and regarded the rest of of us with a mix of anger and contempt. Dina had a triumphant air, which I understood, but only in part. She'd been cleared from suspicion, but whatever her aunt said, she couldn't believe that the only impediment to her selection was a false accusation, could she? Meanwhile, Zoya's mother—whose name I'd forgotten, because she seemed like even more of a nonentity than her daughter—stood chewing her lip.

"And why would Zoya have tansy?" Maria asked. "I doubt she has worms, and unless she's been fooling around in ways that would disqualify her as a bridal candidate, she can't need something to bring on her courses."

I squirmed in discomfort. One well-known use of tansy was to prevent a pregnancy from starting, and if Zoya had it for that reason, then I must not be the only candidate to fail the virginity exam.

Fortunately, no one seemed to notice my reaction. They were too focused on the confrontation.

But Maria's question tipped the scales. Zoya's mother stepped forward. "The tansy is mine," she said. A gasp ran round the room. "I have more children than I can handle already, and I sought to prevent another conception. I wondered why my supply ran out so fast, but when I asked Zoya, she claimed to know nothing about it. I thought one of the servants must have taken it, but I didn't want to make a fuss." She bowed to Fevronia. "When your niece fell ill, I wondered if *she* had taken it, although I couldn't imagine why she would, young as she is. But once she recovered, I saw no reason to cause further trouble for her."

"You caused trouble for Dina," Maria pointed out in a chilling voice. "And your actions, Zoya, might have killed a child." She turned to the housekeeper, still barring the door. "Send for the guards, Dobrinya. We'll let Princesses Anna Glinskaya and Anastasia Petrovna decide what to do with them."

Dobrinya departed while I was still exchanging amazed glances with Anna. Who would have guessed that Zoya, of all people, could have carried out such a scheme? Belatedly, I recalled her chatting about plants, so it made sense that she might know what tansy did. But I couldn't imagine why she saw Dina as a greater rival than, say, Princess Ustinya. Because they both came from the provinces, perhaps?

I might not have another chance to find out. So at the risk of drawing unwanted attention to myself, I said, "But why attack Dina, in particular?" Mid-sentence, I realized how hurtful and rude it would be to point out that at least half a dozen contestants had a better chance of attracting the tsar, so I stopped there.

Everyone turned to stare at me, but fortunately, Maria intervened before anyone else could speak. "Yes, Lyuba asks a good question. Answer it, Zoya. If you don't, I can assure you the royal investigators will, and they will not accept silence as an answer."

She meant torture, and even the thought made me flinch. Whatever Zoya had sought to gain, she'd unleashed a pack of wolves with her actions, and they would not hesitate to hunt her down.

Her mother emitted a moan of dismay, as if this thought had just occurred to her, and Zoya's complexion blanched to the color of skimmed milk. I watched her weigh the pros and cons of confession, but Maria's steely gaze bored into her until she at last blurted out, "It was a test. I thought no one would care, because she was so nasty—even to her own sister."

Dina gave a shriek of protest, but her aunt shushed her before she could speak. Maria's eyebrows almost disappeared beneath the rim of her veil. "A *test*?" she repeated. "You intended to sicken other candidates as well?"

Zoya pressed her lips together and said no more. Maria studied her with an expression of disbelief, then spoke to Zoya's mother. "Your daughter has committed a grave crime. She's lucky the child did not die—and that she had no opportunity to enact the rest of her wicked scheme. Even so, you and your family will pay a high price for her sins."

"And so they should," Fevronia put in. "What that evil girl did to my niece was an outrage. And to deny Dina her chance of becoming tsaritsa!" She turned to her niece. "Go upstairs, Dina, and check on your sister while I take this news to the princesses. Perhaps they will change their minds about you."

Dina left, and her aunt, still muttering, followed. I doubted her quest would succeed, but we would soon find out. The door had barely closed behind them when two hastily summoned guards arrived and removed Zoya and her mother. The mere thought of what they would endure over the days to come made my blood run cold.

Not long after that, Dobrinya returned. "If your girl is not here," she announced, "please join her below. I have arranged for the belongings of those not chosen to be packed and conveyed to their homes, and the vacated rooms are ready for their new occupants. Those of you already assigned to this house may return to your quarters for now. Princess Anastasia Petrovna will address everyone at supper."

I rose, eager to compare notes with my sister and friend. Anna and Maria stood as well, and we moved as one toward the door. There we had a brief wait as first the housekeeper, then the disappointed sponsors, filed downstairs.

A hand gripped my arm from behind and spun me around. I jerked in an involuntary spasm at the sight of Princess Bronislava's face, purple with fury, mere finger widths away from my own. "You and that friend of yours are the daughters of traitors. What makes you a suitable tsaritsa when my Fetinya is passed over?" She hissed every *s*, like the villain in one of my stories. "Don't think you've seen the last of me, hussy. I'll bring you both down, and that sister of yours with you."

For once in my life, I had no ready response. To tell her what I really thought of the bride show was suicide; to express my true opinion of her and her daughter could only make matters worse. It was risky even to point out, as Maria had done with Princess Anna, that Anna and I bore no responsibility for our fathers' misdeeds. Besides, I didn't owe Bronislava an explanation. So I settled on the simplest reply. "Let go of me."

I tugged against her hold, trying to free my arm. When she instead tightened her grip, I stepped forward and bore down on her foot with my heel. That attracted Maria's attention. "Princess Bronislava," she said in tones of astonishment. "What on earth are you doing?"

With a scowl, the princess released me and stormed off. "What got into her?" my sister asked.

I took her elbow in one hand, Anna's in the other. "Let's go upstairs," I said. "Then I'll tell you the whole."

Chapter 17

"And clouds obscured the sun"

W e again took refuge in the bedchamber assigned to Anna and me. A quick opening and closing of the shutters revealed no circling horsemen or birds gliding amid the clouds. I hid my disappointment and turned my attention to my friend, filling her in on the morning's events. She exclaimed in shock when I told her about the virginity test, and I had to assure her several times that I hadn't, in fact, done anything wrong. I apologized, too, for not having prepared her for the possibility that I might be sent home, although in truth I'd had no opportunity to say a word, as we both knew. Still, her face relaxed as she accepted the apology, so I counted it as unnecessary but worthwhile.

"And that's why I was so surprised when Anastasia Petrovna called my name," I finished.

"Not only you," Anna said. "I was stunned when I realized I'd been chosen. From the way Princess Anna talked, I thought for sure my father's crimes would disqualify me. What a time for them to demonstrate forgiveness!"

"Most unfortunate," Maria agreed. "Although I suspect it had less to do with forgiveness than with staying on the right side of your cousin. He's every bit the fool Princess Anna calls him, but he has squeezed several favors out of the young tsar in the last year, which means it's unwise to cross him. I'm more worried about

Nadezhda Shuiskaya. She had a chance to get rid of you without disgracing you, and she let it slip. That strengthens the possibility that she plans to expose you. And here I thought she was a friend of mine."

"Yes, I agree," I said. "Unless we're being unfair to her, and she really was honoring her promise to Papa."

"Well, that's another thing," Maria grumbled. "When has she spent enough time with Papa for him to extract promises from her?"

I frowned, considering this point. "She seemed very familiar with the layout of his estate. I thought she must have a phenomenal memory, since she did attend the Christmas party. Could there be more to it, do you think?"

Anna wrung her hands together, then stammered, "Outside of m-m-m-marriage?"

I shrugged my ignorance, but the more I thought of it, the more likely it seemed that Nadezhda and my father might have an illicit connection. I recalled them joking together at the party with a flirtatious air that I hadn't recognized at the time.

"It's possible," Maria said. "Juliana divorced Papa five years ago, but a decade has passed since they separated. He's in his mid-forties—not so old as to have lost interest in women. Nadezhda is a beautiful widow at the end of her childbearing years. And whatever Papa's flaws, he looks like a saint next to that husband of hers. I can't guess what brought them together, given how seldom we women leave our homes, but the rest seems quite plausible to me. I could confront her and see what she says."

Her matter-of-fact tone tied my tongue. To think of Papa—practically an ancient!—attracted to the not-much-less elderly Nadezhda Shuiskaya in the same way I felt drawn to handsome, dashing Timur stretched my mind to the snapping point. "Why don't you?" I said after a long pause, not envying her that conversation one bit.

Maria's honey-colored eyes sparkled. "I think I will. I'll try to convince her that she's done enough for Papa; Princess Ustinya deserves her full attention now." The twinkle in her eyes dimmed. "Although it's a bit late for that. Better if they'd dismissed you today, without explanation. To do it later will cause a tremendous scandal, and that will hurt us all." She patted Anna's hand. "I'd have stayed with you, Anna, either way."

Anna muttered her thanks. The distant expression in her eyes convinced me that she was remembering her lost Yuri, whom she might never see again. I knew how she felt.

But I couldn't get my mind off my own troubles. "Nadezhda's loyalties are split," I said. "Suppose she plans to tell Papa she tried to help him, only to turn on me now that the other candidates have left? If she waits until the presentation, they won't look for an alternate. And if she can smear Anna at the same time, that leaves Tasya Yureva as Ustinya's only rival. I think we can agree that the girls from the provinces don't pose real competition."

Anna murmured a protest along the lines that Nadezhda would never condone such a scheme, but my sister and I, trained since birth by our father to recognize that some people would go to any lengths in pursuit of political power, ignored her.

"Perhaps," Maria said. "It's a risk. Papa would never forgive her for wrecking his plans. If she *is* his mistress, that would end their affair for good. I'll check into it. In the meantime, you should assume that you will be presented to the tsar. Start thinking about how you will act in the royal presence, and keep an eye open not just for young men observing you but also for tricks that some of your rivals may play. From here on, the stakes are at their highest, and I don't want to bury one of you because a jealous sponsor decided you might displace her darling. I've yet to talk with Alexei, so I have to leave now. I'll be back in the morning." And with that, she kissed us both on the cheek and walked out of the room, leaving us gaping.

It seemed like the day would never end. Anna and I hardly had time to exchange a word before a servant summoned us to supper. Still in our fancy robes, we stumbled downstairs and took our places opposite Ustinya, the one remaining princess. Tasya, as the sole other daughter of the Moscow nobility, faced Anna. I saw no sign of Nadezhda Shuiskaya or any of the other sponsors—which puzzled me, since until then they had always accompanied us to meals. Only Anastasia Petrovna occupied an armchair at the head of the table. Her magisterial calm struck me anew. Did nothing unsettle her?

Waiting for her to speak—or would we eat first?—I surveyed the room. The other girls, however beautifully dressed, didn't hold my attention for long. I imagined Maria dismissing them as she had the first quartet of provincial visitors—"no real contenders there." Although pretty, they didn't stand out as individuals. I shivered, remembering Zoya, who had looked just as undistinguished. I wondered what would happen to her and her mother.

A deep murmur caught my wandering thoughts, and I turned my head toward the sound, only to start with surprise. Throughout the days we'd spent in this house, Dobrinya and her servants had served us at meals. But tonight, a small group of men, none older than twenty, stood in the corner closest to the door, next to a sideboard covered with gold trays. In this house, filled with girls who might become the first tsaritsa, "servants" was a misnomer; only nobles tended to the royal family. Yet I suspected that the vision before my eyes meant something else. The man in the center, in particular, caught my attention; his hair, even redder than mine, and piercing blue eyes—as well as his height and imposing shoulders—indicated that the tsar himself had come to investigate the maidens selected for him.

As soon as the thought crossed my mind, I recognized him. Our paths had not often crossed, but I'd seen him from a distance during various celebrations. We were almost the same age—born just a month apart—and as a result, I'd watched him grow from a child to today's young man.

I'd reached this point in my deliberations when he looked straight at me. I should have lowered my eyes, but shock paralyzed me. As I stared, stupid as a doe at the edge of a campfire, the tsar winked at me.

I gripped my lower lip with my teeth to prevent my mouth dropping open. For that one instant, the winking eye looked exactly like the one I'd surprised at the peephole. My suspicions that the tsar had been watching us from the moment we moved into the Kremlin were confirmed.

And who could blame him? No one had more to lose from a poor choice than he and the bride he selected.

Tsar Ivan grinned at me, then shifted his gaze to Anna. His perusal extended along the table until it had encompassed every girl on my side. After a while, he spoke to his companions, and they moved as a group to stand behind me. I didn't dare turn my head, but from the blushes I saw on Ustinya's face, then Tasya's and on down the length of the opposite bench, I assumed the appraisal continued.

The sound of tromping feet alerted me to expect the men's return to my line of vision. They arrived within moments, and after a second hurried and inaudible exchange, each of them picked up a tray. They spread out around the table, placing a gold goblet next to every trencher. A hand brushed my right shoulder, and hot breath caressed my cheek as a throaty voice whispered in my ear, "Spiced mead to sweeten the tongue of the room's only copper-haired beauty." When I gulped, again stunned into silence, he laughed and withdrew. Moving on, he spoke words I couldn't hear to Anna as well. She didn't reply either, but she gripped my hand under the table.

It took every shred of control I could summon not to react, but I forced myself to stare straight ahead, eyes fixed on the juncture of wall and ceiling. Only when I heard the booted feet retreat did I glance to the left, where the tsar was ignoring the provincial girls. As I watched, he circled the table and repeated his performance with Ustinya and Tasya—placing the goblet before them, brushing their shoulders, murmuring in their ears. I saw Ustinya's mouth open, although I couldn't hear her reply. Tasya giggled. Of the four of us, she was the only one to turn her head, meeting the young man's eyes with an adoring gaze. Clearly, she knew this was the tsar and sought to impress him.

I strove to keep my own face expressionless. Juliana had advised me to collect information before deciding whether a forthright gaze or passive compliance would appeal to or repel the tsar. Among the four of us, though, we had exhibited variations on both, and I still couldn't tell which he preferred.

Right then, he looked up and caught me studying him. His broad lips turned up in a smile, and he winked at me once more before grabbing the arm of a dark-haired youth I belatedly recognized as Prince Andrei Kurbsky, the tsar's friend. The two of them sauntered from the room, their comrades trailing them.

It was all I could do not to groan in frustration. My first opportunity to convince the tsar to settle on anyone but me, and I seemed to have done everything wrong. Not waiting for Anastasia Petrovna's order to begin, I sneaked a sip of mead while she observed the retreating courtiers. The drink had a bubbly sweetness that soothed my anxiety, although I knew it contained enough alcohol that I should sample it sparingly.

Anna still clutched my skirts. I patted her hand in a vain attempt to reassure her. Once the door closed behind the men, she did loosen her grip, although her uneven breathing revealed her lingering panic. I wanted to ask her what the tsar had whispered in *her* ear, but that would have to wait for the supper to end. We still had an entire meal to eat and a set of instructions to absorb.

A group of female servants poured into the room once the men had left. Laden with tureens and baskets, they circled the table, distributing bowls filled with a thick stew of whitefish and vegetables and dropping hunks of thick-crusted bread on our empty trenchers. When at last they withdrew, Anastasia Petrovna pushed back her chair and stood. "Eat," she said. "And listen. I have information to share."

For a wild moment, I wondered if she would comment on the invasion of noblemen, but instead she moved straight into compliments on our selection for presentation to the tsar. Thoughts of the tsar himself didn't bother me so much now that I'd had these minor interactions with him, although I still wanted the presentation over and myself back home with Timur. But the failed virginity test loomed like a giant wave on the horizon, waiting to sweep me away.

And if fears of discovery and disgrace were not enough to have me shaking in my embroidered slippers, the tsar's behavior this evening suggested that Maria and I had assessed the situation correctly: he was most interested in the four Moscow maidens. He had winked at me, twice, as well as referring to me as a copper-haired beauty. He had whispered to all four of us while paying no heed to the girls from the provinces. If he picked Ustinya or Tasya, fine, but suppose he did not? I couldn't wait to get out of the dining room and compare notes with Anna.

Instead, I sat quietly and chewed bread dipped in whitefish stew, taking the occasional sip of mead and focusing my entire attention on Anastasia Petrovna. "We have already interviewed each of you at length," she was saying. "We have investigated your lineages, your capacity for childbearing, your health, your purity." I tried not to wince. "We have drawn preliminary conclusions regarding your ability to fulfill the role expected of you. We have reported this information to the state secretaries and scribes, who have condensed it into summaries and transmitted them to the tsar. The final choice is his, and he will make it according to his own criteria for looks and personality. We have given him a range of types from which to choose."

Really? Mentally disputing that statement, I surveyed the table once more. Perhaps experience skewed my perspective. I thought of my sister, the real copper-haired beauty in the family; Anna's mother, a blonde who still turned heads in her mid-thirties; Katya Vorontsova's dark curls contrasted with twin orbs of cornflower blue. That last image awoke dim memories of Alexei's half-sister Nasan, a vision with porcelain skin, glossy hair that fell like an ebony curtain to her waist, and almond-shaped eyes, set off by an exquisite delicacy of face wholly at odds with her fiery personality. *There* was a range of types, if you wanted one. We eight girls—even the four from Moscow, who at least stood out in terms of coloring and style—seemed like variations on a theme by comparison.

But Anastasia Petrovna had not finished. "The day after tomorrow, we will escort all eight of you to the Terem Palace." Anna gave a soft moan at that, and I elbowed her in the ribs to quiet her. "Your sponsors may accompany you, but you will take direction from Princess Nadezhda and me. Once we're settled in the room set aside for the presentations, the boyar council and the tsar will enter and assess you as a group. When they signal their readiness, Nadezhda will prompt you, one by one. Then you will approach the ruler, bow in greeting, answer his questions, and respond to any commands he issues—to speak or turn around, for example. Everyone else must remain silent. Once he has formed an opinion, he will hand you a ceremonial kerchief, your signal to withdraw. Show no emotion, and do not speak—especially, do not protest. Bow once more to indicate submission, retreat without turning your back to the ruler, then pass through the doors where I will be standing. Wait on the other side. If the tsar hands you a ring in addition to the kerchief, he has chosen you. I suggest a deeper obeisance, in that case, to express your gratitude, but otherwise you should behave in exactly the same way as those he has disappointed."

Then, while the eight of us stared at her in shock, she gave a jerk of her chin and left without waiting for questions.

Chapter 18

"But the maiden fought her way free of the dragon's lair"

Anna and I grabbed Maria the moment she walked through the door the next morning and dragged her to the inner chamber. "What's wrong with you two?" she asked as she set down the bag she was carrying and positioned herself on the window seat. Out of habit, I looked past her, only to have my vision blocked by the shutters. I sent Timur mental reassurances that I would soon be home. Wasted effort, of course; I had no great belief in the power of thought. But it relieved my anxiety enough for me to answer my sister's question.

"The presentations are tomorrow," I said. "Anastasia Petrovna laid out the whole procedure at supper yesterday, after you left. You can accompany us to the palace. Did you get a chance to talk with Princess Nadezhda?"

"We have no plan," Anna interjected before Maria could answer. "And the tsar *likes* us. He called Lyuba a copper-haired beauty and me an angel brought down to earth." She twisted her hands together, as if she couldn't contain her anxiety.

"When did he do that?" Maria said, visibly astonished.

"Yesterday." The memory alone made me gloomy. "He and some of his friends—I think, because I recognized Prince Kurbsky—served us drinks before supper. The tsar ignored everyone but the four Moscow girls, touching each of us on the shoulder and murmuring something in our ears. I don't know what he said to Ustinya and Tasya, but it must have been similar, because they blushed and responded. Tasya even giggled, which was more than I could manage. I felt as if I'd been nailed in place. And he winked at me, twice. I'm sure now that he was the one spying on us."

"All right, let's back up." Maria opened the bag she'd carried and pulled out a square of shiny fabric the color of fresh snow. "To answer your question, I have not yet had a chance to approach Princess Nadezhda. I hope to do so now that I'm here."

"I'm worried," I said. "What Nadezhda knows will destroy me if it comes out, and the only way to prevent that is to go through the presentation but not be selected. Can you imagine the scandal if she waits to reveal all until the morning after the wedding?" I'd be forcibly tonsured and sent off in disgrace to a women's monastery, my dreams shattered.

"Yes, we don't want it to get that far." Maria shook out the snow-white cloth and held it up by what I recognized as the shoulders. It was a silk tunic, embroidered in lavender and sky blue around the neck and cuffs. I sent her a questioning glance.

"How pretty," Anna said. I gave myself a quick shake. How preoccupied I'd been! I'd forgotten, for a moment, that Maria and I weren't alone.

"Yes," Maria said. "It would look divine on you, but it's for Lyuba. I sat down with Juliana yesterday, and we decided that our first line of defense should be for the two of you to switch clothing. You have quite different coloring, so shades that suit Lyuba will make you, Anna, look pale and the same in reverse. The robes are beautiful, so no one can complain that we didn't dress you in a way appropriate to your rank and the occasion. Even Papa won't know what went wrong, although he'll gripe about the results."

"The tsar has seen us, though," I pointed out.

"Yes, that's annoying," Maria agreed. "Still, he's not much more than a boy; he'll react to the change without knowing why. And I'll braid your hair extra-tight. You can rub your forehead in pain and swoon if need be. That will raise questions about your health, despite the medical examination."

"And me?" Anna asked. "We can't both come down with headaches."

Maria rummaged in her bag again, retrieving a container about half the size of her palm, which she held out to Anna. "For you I have this. Dab it on your wrists and your throat." She touched her fingers to the pulse points below her ears, demonstrating.

Anna took the container, twisted off the top, and sniffed. "Strong," she said. "What is it?" She held out the container, and I jerked away. It smelled like a patch of mossy earth.

"Juliana calls it patchouli. She persuaded Anfim to procure it from one of the eastern merchants." Maria's eyes crinkled with laughter—at the look on our faces, no doubt. "I wouldn't touch it—or recommend it to you, under normal circumstances—but it's worth a try. If anyone asks, you can say it's rare and precious, so you wore it to honor the tsar." She stood and held out the tunic. "Put this away, Lyuba, and the two of you exchange the robes you brought for the presentation so that, just in case, they come out of the right chests tomorrow morning."

"Too bad Juliana can't join us," I said. "I'm truly grateful for her help."

"Me too." Anna picked up the white silk tunic and folded it carefully.

"I agree," Maria said. "She has such good ideas. I'd love to have her counsel, just in case something goes wrong at the last moment. And can you imagine what Anastasia Petrovna would make of her?"

Thinking of Juliana's past, I had to laugh, no matter how grim the situation appeared. "She'd probably steal Tsar Ivan out from under our noses," I said, reveling in the thought. "Just for the fun of it, to show that she could. Tsaritsa Juliana—wouldn't that be grand?"

"Better than one of us." Anna put the tunic in my chest, swapping out my ivory one with the gold embroidery.

"Much better," I said. "And when she got tired of him, she could go back to Poland with Felix."

"Silly girls." Maria sounded more amused than annoyed. "Switch the rest of those clothes, then we'll go downstairs."

The three of us moved to the sitting room on the second floor. After Tsar Ivan's behavior the night before, Anna and I saw little point in interrogating the visitors from the provinces, so we sat with Ustinya and Tasya.

I looked around for Princess Nadezhda and didn't see her. "Where's your sponsor?" I asked Ustinya. So close to the presentations, it seemed strange that Nadezhda would leave her protégée to her own devices. And knowing what I did, strange behavior from Nadezhda gave me cause for alarm.

"She's with Anastasia Petrovna." Ustinya pointed in the general direction of the Terem Palace. "They're getting ready for tomorrow."

Well, that made sense. I smothered the inner voice that wondered what the two women were discussing as they worked and turned my attention to Tasya. "Did you know that was the tsar serving us yesterday afternoon?"

"I did," she said. "I recognized him from the Blessing of the Waters ceremony. Didn't you?"

"Of course." I glanced at Anna, recalling that day and the visit to Katya's house that followed. It shone with the patina of ancient history, although not even a month had passed. "What did he say to you?"

"He asked whether I was as perfect a noble maiden as I appeared to be," she said with a repetition of yesterday's giggle. "I told him I would try in every way to please my God-given husband—speaking as if I didn't know who was asking me, of course—and he pinched my shoulder and said he appreciated that. Will he pick me, do you think? What did he say to you two?"

"He remarked on my red hair," I told her. It was true, if only a partial truth, and likely to deflect attention.

Anna followed my lead. "That Moscow girls are the prettiest." An even greater stretch of the truth than mine, but a diplomatic choice—and Anna maximized its effect by including Ustinya with the sweep of her hand. "I expect he will pick one of us, since he already singled us out from the rest."

"Won't it be good to get the waiting over?" Ustinya stared at me so hard and so long that I frowned, hearing an unspoken message that I couldn't decipher. Did she already know about my situation?

That possibility bothered me more than anything Nadezhda might do. Nadezhda had to worry about breaking her promise to my father, at least, but her protégée faced no such constraints.

"Of course," I said as lightly as I could manage. "The uncertainty is killing me." I glanced at Maria, who stood near the window chatting with Tasya's mother as if neither of them had a care in the world. Could I invent an excuse to join them or, better yet, escape upstairs, where my fictional Svetlana remained in partially created limbo?

With a sigh, I concluded that neither option was possible. "What happened to the group from Kolomna?" I asked instead. "I don't see Dina, so I assume her aunt's plea to have her selected for presentation didn't work."

"No, it didn't. They left this morning," Tasya said. "Melita seems quite recovered. Wasn't that a scandal?"

We agreed that indeed it had been. "And I hear the guards escorted that wicked girl and her mother back to Uglich." Ustinya flicked the embroidery needle she held as if banishing Zoya and her mother to a distant realm. "They'll both be forced to take monastic vows, I hear. Serves them right, don't you think?"

I supposed it did, although I couldn't help remembering Yuri and how close he'd come to the same fate. What was the point of pushing people into the monastic life if they had no religious vocation? But I could muster little sympathy for Zoya, who would have caused much greater harm if not stopped and might well have suffered a worse punishment. So rather than dwell on her future, I diverted Ustinya with a question about the sewing project in her lap, a lovely combination of curlicues and small birds. While she launched into a long description of couching and satin stitch, I feigned interest and let my thoughts drift to a land of rocky crags and billowing waves, a dragon-prowed boat on the horizon and my heroine blissfully unaware, as she stood on the shore gazing across the ocean, of disaster to come.

The rest of the day passed quietly. At Maria's suggestion, Anna and I retired early, although neither of us found it easy to sleep. We whispered to each other throughout the night—memories of our childhood, our stay this past summer at her mother's country estate, our hopes that Yuri and Timur were not yet lost to us, and more.

At some point I must have nodded off, despite my fears. I awoke from a nightmare of being stripped naked before the tsar to see the rays of the rising sun filtering past the shutters. I pulled on my braid, the end of which had somehow become trapped under Anna's shoulder. I rubbed my aching forehead—Maria wouldn't need to tighten my plait after that near-sleepless night—and pushed myself to a sitting position, which roused Anna.

"What time is it?" she asked in a groggy voice.

"I have no idea." I rolled out of bed and walked to the window. When I shoved open the shutters, Anna yelped in protest, but I hushed her. "It's early," I said. "The sun isn't even visible yet, just its rays."

As soon as the words left my mouth, I realized how little they meant. It was the third week in January, when daylight came late and faded early. Juliana had talked of clocks in the western lands, machines that marked time in the same increments throughout the year, but here in Russia hours shortened and lengthened to match the sun. I'd been insane to imagine Timur on horseback at this hour, even if it might mark my last day of freedom. Did he know that I looked for him at every opportunity? He must remember me asking him to ride in the meadows where I could see him, but that wouldn't bring him out at daybreak.

"We should get up," I told Anna. "Who knows when the presentations will start?"

She nodded, and I closed the shutters once more. From the other side of the door, I heard my sister moving around—another reason to bestir myself. The sooner we got through this ordeal, the better. I poured water into the basin on a stand near the window, then washed my hands and face, my neck and under my arms. I might not seek to attract, but I hated feeling dirty.

That done, I yielded the basin to my friend and pulled the clothes Solomonida had selected to present Anna in the best light from the chest assigned to me. I topped my own linen shift with the pure-white tunic and added Anna's robe, which did impart a sickly hue to my otherwise creamy complexion. Its deep violet complemented the sky-blue and lavender on the tunic cuffs in an artistic fashion that I undercut by choosing a pair of dark orange slippers intended to go with a different outfit altogether. I had unbraided my hair and was brushing it out when my sister entered the room, a vision of splashy poppies against a gold background, topped with a broad collar. The colors suited her admirably, and each one glowed with a soft sheen. A low cap concealed her hair, but escaping wisps brushed her cheeks.

"You'd better be careful," I told her, laughing. "Tsar Ivan might order your divorce and gift *you* with the bridal ring!"

"Never," she said, joining my laughter. "I'm old enough to be his mother, but thank you for the compliment."

"And what of us?" I held out the violet robe, examining Anna from the corner of my eye as I did. The green Maria had originally chosen for me—the color of a ripening pear—turned Anna's roses-and-milk skin sallow, especially with the effects of too little sleep, although nothing could undercut my friend's good looks for long. "An angel come down to earth," as the tsar had called her, captured her beauty perfectly.

"The switch of clothing will help," Maria said, confirming my own impressions. "I doubt that in itself will change the tsar's mind. He did see you properly dressed, after all. But perhaps it will confirm the impression of illness." She took the brush from my hand, divided the hair in three, pulled it tight, and began to braid.

I thought of telling her I already had a headache, then decided not to bother. So close to the moment that would decide my fate, I needed every advantage I could get.

The odor of wet earth assailed my nostrils, and I twisted my head to smile at Anna, only to see her snap the container shut. "Don't you plan to use it?" I asked, watching her return the perfume to the dresser untouched.

"No," she said. "Suppose the tsar finds it appealing? Besides, I had a better idea last night."

"What?" I demanded.

"I'll tell you if I go through with it. I may not."

I was searching for ways to wring the truth out of her when my sister intervened. "Stop wriggling, Lyuba," Maria ordered. "I've nearly lost my grip twice."

"Forgive me." I returned to staring front until she knotted a lavender ribbon at the end of my copper braid. She arranged the pointed headdress, violet trimmed with silver lace, atop my head and tied the strings in the back, looping them around the braid to hold the contraption in place.

"Nice." I slipped Anna's silver earrings into my lobes, then rose and stood aside while my sister turned her attention to my friend. The tight braid intensified my headache, threatening to induce a sickness I would not need to fake. I sat on the window seat, kicking off my slippers and resting my forehead on my knees. Maria's and Anna's voices mingled in a conversation too muted for me to follow. The day had just begun, yet I longed for it to end. To have the presentation behind me, once and forever.

No, not only for that. I yearned for clean, fresh air, the sensation of Kumai underneath me and Tizilek above me, the certainty that Timur rode at my side and always would. I'd had a surfeit of Kremlin opulence and aristocratic politicking, snide remarks and constant observation, prying eyes and poisonous tongues. I wanted to go home to the family that loved me for myself and a man who could not be deceived by false colors and braids tied too tight, a place where my imaginary Svetlana and I could thrive.

Maria touched my arm, and I looked up to see Anna fully adorned and ready. I staggered to my feet, slipped on my shoes, and followed the two of them down the stairs, wondering how long I could go on with my head pounding so hard.

If only I could think clearly …

My befuddlement worsened when I reached the second floor and discovered Princess Bronislava in intense conversation with Anastasia Petrovna.

I stared at them, trying to straighten my wrinkled brow. Memories assailed my brain, matching the rhythm of my thrumming head. Bronislava's daughter had been eliminated from the contest. Bronislava had threatened me as a result. So what brought her here today?

"Good morning," my sister said when neither woman broke off the exchange long enough to acknowledge her. Beyond them, I fuzzily perceived Ustinya, her face sly; a curious Tasya; and Princess Nadezhda, less composed than usual.

Definitely, something untoward was going on.

Bronislava swung around and pointed a finger at me. "There she is, the slut."

I blinked and shook my head in disbelief—another mistake, because the too-tight braid swung, forcing me to grip my temples in agony. By the time I could see once more, Bronislava had turned her ire on my sister.

"How dare you, Tsarevna, attempt to foist an impure girl on our royal sovereign?" she shouted at a pitch that magnified my pain.

Sickness roiled my stomach, and I stumbled to the closest bench, ignoring my tormentor. I searched for a response, but no words came. The next time I gazed at the arguing women, they had acquired fuzzy edges. Seeing no way to defend myself, I stared at Maria, wondering how she would respond. She had doubted my chastity, too, when she first examined me.

She didn't disappoint me, though. Taking full advantage of her greater height, she stared down her elegant nose at the raging princess. "How dare *you*, Bronislava Blednaya, accuse my sister of impropriety? I don't care what gossip you've heard. I've watched over Lyuba since she turned six, and I can assure you she is everything a first-time bride should be."

Hearing my sister stand up for me, I loved her with a fierce devotion. At the same time, guilty thoughts of Timur's kisses sent heat rushing to my cheeks.

"Really?" Princess Bronislava stepped forward, arms akimbo, only to retreat once more in response to Maria's icy glare. "Then why did Nadezhda Shuiskaya bribe the midwife who performed Lyubov Fyodorovna's virginity examination?"

A gasp drew my wandering attention to Tasya, but it was Ustinya's grin, visible over the other girl's shoulder, that shone a light into my malfunctioning brain. Ustinya, who should have been her sponsor's sole concern, had somehow learned of the bribe. She'd realized Nadezhda might have mixed loyalties, and she'd fought back. Clearly, *she* had no doubts about becoming a royal bride.

Maria took another step forward, forcing a further retreat by Bronislava. "You disappoint me, Bronislava." My sister cast a wintry eye on Ustinya before continuing. "I thought you had better sense than to believe anything a jealous chit tells you. But make no mistake: I will not tolerate aspersions against my sister. If you dare spread your lies, I will ensure that you and yours suffer disgrace. As for Princess Nadezhda, I doubt she and her family appreciate your accusations against her."

"Indeed we do not," Nadezhda said in tones almost as glacial as my sister's. Whatever disdain she had shown toward me, she appeared to have transferred to her accuser. Because she had already achieved her aim through Bronislava, or had I been wrong about her from the beginning?

Bronislava's pale cheeks flushed, but she stood her ground, scowling at each of us in turn. Ustinya, in contrast, looked smug.

Maria raised her chin and, when Bronislava at last lowered her eyes, turned to face Anastasia Petrovna. "Although I accept no slurs against Lyubov Fyodorovna's honor"—she glared once more at Princess Bronislava, then at the grinning Ustinya—"I believe it would be in the best interests of the Russian lands and my own lineage not to present my sister to the sovereign. He has other noble maidens from whom to select a bride. It would not do for his blessed tsaritsa to begin her reign under so undeserved a cloud."

My head thrummed as if besieged by an invading horde. The sickness that had plagued me since I entered the room tripled in strength. I rocked in my seat, clutching the back for support. Then, in a flash of inspiration, I saw how best to support my sister's attempt to free me. I closed my eyes and slid to the floor.

Amid a chorus of exclamations, I heard Anastasia Petrovna say, in that magisterial voice of hers, "I applaud your regard for the good of the realm, Tsarevna. That does seem like the best solution. Indeed, your sister seems quite unwell. Perhaps she has an underlying condition that the physician did not find. Shall we summon Doctor Baer?"

"I doubt that will be necessary," Maria said smoothly. "Please call someone to bring her to our chambers, and we shall see."

Many hands grasped at my limbs, but I lay in my pretended swoon, not moving even when a pair of burly arms lifted me from the floor and carried me upstairs.

My eyes opened on the sight of rich green brocade interwoven with curlicues in red and green. From the angle of the draperies and the pattern in the fabric, I concluded that I lay on the mattress where I had tossed and turned throughout the night. My headache lingered, but a mild throbbing had replaced the searing agony of those last moments in the room below. I propped myself on my elbows and looked around. My braid untwined as I moved. Maria must have loosened it.

"Good." My sister spoke from the direction of the window seat. "You're awake. Are you feeling better?"

I pushed myself to a sitting position and accepted the comb she held out to me, shaking the plait entirely free before pulling the ivory teeth through the strands. "A slight headache, but otherwise yes. I didn't really faint; that was a ruse."

"I'm glad," Maria said. "I was worried about you. Let me reassure Dobrinya that we will not require the physician's services." She left the room. During her absence, I looked around, but I was alone.

"Where's Anna?" I asked my sister when she returned a short while later.

"Making her bow to the tsar. She'll be back at any moment." Maria pointed to the tufted seat near the dressing table. "Sit, and I'll rebraid your hair—properly, this time."

I did as she asked. "What happened after I pretended to swoon? I heard Anastasia Petrovna, but I didn't dare crack my eyelids to check on the others."

"Yes, you timed that perfectly. I think they would have accepted my request to eliminate you, but the faint simplified their decision. They didn't have to worry about offending either Bronislava or Nadezhda; instead they could declare you unwell." She took the comb from my hand, then set it aside to rub my aching scalp with long, soothing strokes. I closed my eyes and released the tension of my narrow escape. Whatever unpleasantness lay ahead, I need not fear marriage to the tsar. Rumors of my impropriety would linger. With luck, though, I need never face any of these people again.

But what of Anna?

Maria was still talking. "After Anastasia Petrovna agreed to let you go, Bronislava Blednaya marched out in a huff, and Nadezhda Shuiskaya grabbed that protégée of hers and dragged her off—for a scolding, I assume, although I can't say Ustinya looked chastened. Before we even had a chance to summon the housekeeper, she arrived to announce that the presentations would begin. The girls—including Anna and Ustinya, once Nadezhda released her—went down to the courtyard, where they took a carriage to the Terem Palace. As soon as they left, I came to check on you."

"So Anna went without a sponsor?" I felt my brows wrinkle as I tried to catch up.

"Vera Yureva agreed to look after her. Of those left among the sponsors, she's the one I trust most." She reached out and brushed the loose hair back from my face. "You come first, dearest. I couldn't leave my little sister lying unconscious in her bedchamber, could I?"

"Thank you, Maria. I don't know how I'd have gotten through this without you." I hugged her, hard, and when I pulled away, I saw the moisture brightening her eyes. We were closer than mother and daughter, yet we didn't often express our affection in words.

The situation might have become awkward, but before that could happen, quick steps sounded in the room beyond. The inner door flew open, and Anna ran in. "It worked," she cried. "He chose someone else!" Her body swayed like a dancer's, as if excitement forbade stillness. When the door swung shut behind her, she waved her hands in the air and twirled around.

"He did?" I leaped to my feet and stared at Anna's joyous face. "That's wonderful!"

"Yes." Anna hugged Maria, then me. "I convinced him not to pick me." She sounded as if this were the most natural thing in the world instead of the most preposterous.

"*What?*" I could hardly believe my ears. Quiet, retiring Anna had convinced the ruler of all Russia to select someone else as his bride? I'd known, of course, that my friend had hidden depths, but this outcome defied my wildest expectations.

"What did you say to him?" Maria asked, sounding as amazed as I was.

Anna grinned—at having confounded us, I assumed. "I waited until he asked me to speak, then threw myself at his feet and begged him to release me, because to wed a betrothed woman would dishonor us both. I thought he might fly into a rage and order my execution on the spot, as he did Yuri's, but instead he raised me up and asked me to explain."

"I'm impressed," Maria said. "What did you tell him?"

"That my wicked cousin had signed a contract for my hand, then tried as hard as he could to end it without paying the penalty to break it honestly. Igor was standing right there, in the middle of a group of boyars, and he protested, but the tsar growled at him to hush, to let me talk. So I told him everything except Yuri's name, because I feared the tsar would remember sending him to a monastery, and that would get Yuri in trouble if it became clear he hadn't taken his vows and undermine my objection if it turned out that he had. I wasn't sure what I would do if the tsar demanded the information, but fortunately, he didn't. He flew into a rage with Cousin Igor and ordered him banished from the court. The tsar's brother was there, watching, and he started clapping his hands and guffawing. Igor tried to protest again, calling me a foolish, ungrateful girl. But the tsar announced that he was proud of my courage and thankful that I had saved him from the sin of bigamy, then shooed Igor from the room. When he was gone, the tsar handed me the kerchief with a flourish, said he hoped my young man appreciated his earthbound angel, and dismissed me. I managed to get out of the room without leaping for joy, and after that it was easy. I just had to stand with the other girls who weren't chosen and try to look sad even though my heart was singing."

"I agree with Tsar Ivan," Maria said. "Good for you. That required real bravery. Your mother will be so proud—and relieved—when she hears."

"That's amazing," I said. "You saved yourself—perhaps Yuri, too. And Cousin Igor will have no choice but to leave you alone for a while."

"No choice at all." Anna twirled again, her arms outstretched. "He's been sent to Vologda in disgrace."

"Vologda." I couldn't suppress a giggle. "The hell-pit of the North. That's what Papa called it when he was stuck there. I can't think of a better place for Igor."

"Nor can I," Maria said.

"And who received the ring?" I picked up the comb to finish rebraiding my hair. I couldn't leave this house soon enough.

"Tasya Yureva." Anna's smile widened, and she raised her shoulders high, then dropped them again, as if releasing the tension of recent weeks. "They're moving her into the Terem Palace now, and the wedding is scheduled for February 3. I guess we'll have to get used to calling her Tsaritsa Anastasia from now on."

Tasya, not Ustinya. Well, that was another blessing. I would never forget Ustinya's attempt to destroy me, even if she *had* inadvertently helped me escape the royal presentation. She hadn't known that I sought to avoid being chosen or that her accusation, delivered through Bronislava Blednaya, handed Maria the perfect opportunity to pull me out of the contest. Ustinya had done her best to shame me. At least the new tsaritsa would be someone I could respect.

"Excellent news." Maria rose to her feet. "Gather your things, girls, while I have a quick chat with Natalya Shuiskaya. I think it's time we collected a few facts from that woman. If I see a servant on my way, I'll send her here, but let's be ready to go as soon as we get our release."

Home. Timur. What about those plans Alexei has for him? Can we ever be together? I both wanted and did not want to find out.

But I will not be tsaritsa, no matter what, I reminded myself. *Nor will I have to wed a graybeard or a dolt.*

Of course, Papa would explode like a badly formed artillery shell when he heard the news. Something else I would have to tackle before I could look to the future.

Chapter 19

"The prince proved his worth"

O ur release came within the hour. By then, we'd already readied our things for departure as Maria had ordered, and my sister sent for the coachman and a separate cart to handle the baggage. An impatient wait near the outside door ended with our descent of the staircase. I was almost fizzing with suppressed emotion by the time the carriage lurched away from the Kremlin. "At least that's done," I said to my companions. They nodded in reply, Maria with a frown of concentration, Anna with an effervescence that matched my own.

We didn't talk much during the short ride. Batted back and forth between joy and terror, I strove to keep both at bay by concentrating on Svetlana's story. Would it change now that Anna and I had escaped the fate our male relatives had crafted for us? Could I use parts of our experience to enliven the tale?

We went first to Solomonida and Anfim's house, where Anna got out, promising to visit us soon. The coachman then turned the carriage toward home. Before long, the gates of our estate opened before us, and the vehicle drew to a halt. As I stepped out into my own courtyard, the late January wind bit my cheeks, but bright sunshine offset the chill. I thought of Tasya Yureva, installed in the Terem Palace awaiting marriage to the tsar. From what I'd seen, Tasya welcomed her fate. I knew she would make Tsar Ivan a good wife, and I hoped he would be a good husband for her. But most of all, I looked forward to my reunion with Timur—in the flesh, not dimly glimpsed through a distant window.

If only it turns out well.

The first person I encountered was Juliana. Ensconced in the main sitting room with Felix at her side, she leaped to her feet as Maria and I came through the door and ran to kiss me on both cheeks. She greeted my sister, then tugged us toward the sofa, saying, "Don't keep me in suspense another minute. Tell me everything."

Maria laughed and pulled her hand free. "Where are Alexei and Timur? They will want to hear the news, too."

"Somewhere," Juliana announced with a dismissive wave of her arm in the direction of the door. "Alexei's study, perhaps? They've been terribly secretive, the pair of them, since you left the house."

"Secretive is not the word I would have chosen." Felix pushed himself to standing with his cane and came to greet us. "Preoccupied, more like. You can hardly expect two warriors to spew their anxiety at us. I don't blame them for distracting themselves with military tasks."

He sounded rather wistful, as if he might have preferred conferring with the men himself. Juliana must have realized that, because she tucked her hand around his elbow and kissed his cheek. "Whereas you stayed with me to keep my spirits up. I do appreciate the sacrifice, love. I'd have gone mad with no one to talk to but the walls." She grinned at Maria. "Not that I bear a grudge, you understand. It can't have been much fun for you either."

"May I never live through anything like that again," my sister said in heartfelt tones. "I'll try the study, then. Lyuba, hold on to your story, or you'll have to repeat it when the others arrive."

She left the room, and I engaged in small talk with Juliana and Felix, doing my best to focus my attention on them rather than on the obstinately shut door that stood between me and my love.

The door opened at last. Maria came in first, patting my arm as she passed and taking a seat on Juliana's right. I accepted a warm hug from Alexei and an uncommonly restrained one from Timur, although he whispered a welcome as he settled into place next to me. I was fighting the fear that his feelings toward me had changed when Tanya the housekeeper arrived to announce the arrival of a new and unwelcome visitor. My father didn't wait for her to finish her sentence before barging into the room, an act of effrontery guaranteed to raise Alexei's hackles.

"Excuse me," my brother-in-law said with icy courtesy. "I don't recall giving you permission to enter."

Papa stopped in his tracks, but his clenched fists and glowering eyes indicated he was beyond reason. "I came to discuss recent events with my daughters," he said. "Don't think you can bar the door to an aggrieved parent."

"I'll bar the door to whomever I like," Alexei told him. "It's my house. But we, too, want to know what happened. You may remain."

The lofty tone in which he made this pronouncement further outraged Papa. "You would deny me a few moments alone with my own children?" he asked in disbelieving fury.

Alexei sank onto the sofa next to Maria and gestured at a chair strategically placed in the center and seldom used, because it isolated the person occupying it. Having watched numerous similar maneuvers by my brother-in-law over the years, I suspected he sought to put Papa, quite literally, in his place.

"Yes, I do deny you," Alexei said. "Your wrath tells me that you intend to bully them, which I do not permit. Say what you came to say in front of us, or leave and remain silent. And don't think you can sneak back and browbeat your daughters later. I will order the guard at the gate to keep you out."

Papa grumbled at that, but he did not depart. If I'd been alone with him, I'd have been shaking in my shoes by then, but the presence of so many protectors reassured me.

And I needed reassuring. I had yet to say two meaningful words to Timur, who sat stolidly at my side without so much as glancing my way. Did he regret his declaration of love? Did he see me as unchaste? I quivered at the thought, and that drew his attention. He smiled at me, a one-sided quirk of his lips designed to hide his reaction from the rest of the room, and brushed my fingers with his own.

At that, I relaxed—until the sound of Papa slumping onto the chair sent waves of tension sliding down my spine once more. "Explain to me, Lyuba," he said with barely repressed rage, "how you failed to perform the perfectly simple, clearly stated task I gave you, thus dashing my hopes and the prospects of our entire lineage. You even had the assistance of the admirable Nadezhda Shuiskaya, yet somehow you managed—she tells me—to faint at precisely the wrong moment, resulting in your elimination from the presentation despite the interest demonstrated in you by the young tsar."

Every eye in the room fixed on me. Juliana, Felix, Alexei, Timur—I'd not had the opportunity to share my story with any of them, and they stared at me openmouthed in response to this recitation by my father, which must sound like a twisted fairy tale.

It would be difficult to answer him, too. I had no intention of sharing the full story with my unhappy parent, so I offered him a simple if incomplete truth. "I felt overwhelmed at the prospect of becoming the first tsaritsa, so I couldn't sleep or eat. I didn't expect to swoon. By the time I woke up, it was over."

He made a disgusted noise. "Maria, Mikhail, and now you. What a useless bunch of brats I sired! Not one of you cares a whit for my unceasing exertions on behalf of the lineage. I should wed you to a provincial servitor. It would serve you right."

I bit my tongue to suppress any reply. I knew I should apologize for disappointing him—not because I felt sorry but because even insincere repentance would mollify him—but I couldn't make my tongue form the words. Protests or attempts to justify myself would only fuel his anger. Telling him why no provincial servitor would want me would be worse than useless. Was it possible that Nadezhda had not shared that detail? If so, I owed her a huge debt of gratitude.

Juliana waded in while I was still pondering how to navigate troubled waters. "Don't be ridiculous, Fyodor. You can't blame Lyuba for what happened before the presentation, and your threat of gentry servitors is nothing but spite. Wake up to your surroundings, and you'll see you can do much better for her—by your standards, never mind hers." She treated Timur to her enigmatic smile, and he shifted uncomfortably in his seat, reviving my anxieties.

"Thus speaks the divorcée," Papa sneered. "But in fact, you don't know what you're talking about. My slut of a daughter—"

Uh, oh. Nadezhda did tell him.

He never finished his sentence. Timur leaped to his feet and grabbed Papa by the shoulders. "You will *not* dishonor Lyuba that way," he snarled. "Take it back."

Astonished and delighted, I stared at my love. He was defending me!

Papa thrashed in Timur's hold. "Let go of me, you brute. She's my daughter, and she failed the virginity examination. I'll refer to her however I want."

"You will not." Timur moved his grip to Papa's throat, and I watched my father's cheeks turn the color of cooked beets.

While I grappled for words, Maria spoke. "Let him go, Timur." He turned his head to stare at her. A long pause ensued while their gazes locked, then he shrugged and released his grip, shoving Papa back against the seat.

"Thank you." She shifted her attention to our father. "You're a fine one to talk, Papa. This is more your fault than anyone's. You entered Lyuba in the bride show in the first place, without consulting us. You started an affair with Nadezhda Shuiskaya, ignored her other commitments, and demanded she help you. And on impulse, to please you, Nadezhda *did* pay the midwife to keep quiet. But when she tried to get Lyuba dismissed without giving a specific cause, Anastasia Petrovna refused. Then Ustinya found out somehow and decided her sponsor wasn't trustworthy, so she blabbed the whole to the person most likely to make it public. I confronted Nadezhda after the presentation, and she admitted the truth. After putting us through hell to satisfy your own ambition, the least you can do is support Lyuba instead of condemning her."

"Never," Papa snarled. "I wash my hands of her. No man of noble birth will sign a contract for her now. Even the gentry servitors may balk."

"*I* will," Timur announced. "I'll marry her tomorrow, if she'll have me."

When I gasped, he turned his head in my direction and smiled, that caressing smile that melted my insides.

Alexei rose to his feet. "Timur, we talked about this. Don't listen to her father. I can find Lyuba a husband. She doesn't need rescuing."

Timur stiffened, and I understood then that his restraint expressed respect for Alexei, not a change in his feelings toward me.

"I'm not rescuing her." He shifted to face his father. "I love her. I waited through that damn bride show, wishing the whole time I could ride into the Kremlin, scoop her up, and head for the steppe. I won't stand by while she weds the first man who can be manipulated into taking her. She doesn't want that either. Ask her."

"That's true," I said. I'd sat like a stone long enough. I moved to stand at his side, and he wrapped an arm around my waist. "I love Timur. I *would* have ridden off with him, except that it would have put the rest of you at risk." I glared at Papa, who was shooting daggers at me with his eyes. "Including you," I added.

Alexei's mouth tightened, and my stomach followed suit. But he must have had second thoughts about arguing with his son in front of Papa, because after a moment, he gave a curt nod. "We'll discuss it among ourselves, then." He glanced at my father. "So you see, Fyodor Mikhailovich, you have no cause for concern. I will provide for your youngest daughter. And that concludes our business. You may depart."

Even for Alexei, that took gall. Papa sputtered like a malfunctioning heating pipe, tightening and loosening his fists as if tempted to strike one of us. In the end, though, he bowed to the inevitable.

"You have disappointed me, daughter," he said, reverting to the chilly tone he'd used when he first came in. "Marry as you please. But don't expect me to forget the way you trampled my dreams."

With a supreme exercise of will, I conquered the nagging desire to beg his forgiveness. Timur had stood by me, and somehow we would find a path to our goal. The wife of a future Tatar khan would not yield to threats. I dipped my head and said, "Thank you, Papa, for your consent. Whether you believe me or not, I wish you health and happiness."

He stalked out of the room, followed by Juliana's dulcet tones. "Farewell, Fyodor. It's been *such* a pleasure watching you at work once more." Felix chided her, but she only laughed.

The door slammed shut behind my father. I doubted that was an accident.

When I felt certain of Papa's departure, I released a long, slow breath and surveyed the room. Alexei looked solemn, Timur defiant, Maria troubled, Juliana curious and amused. "Well," Felix said, "are you going to tell us what that was all about?"

So I did. But the whole time I talked, I studied the faces of my family for clues. I understood the sources of their concern—the advantages of a political match; the inevitable disapproval of the Church; even the speed of our decision, although Timur and I had known each other for years. Yet none of that seemed insurmountable to me. My goal hovered within reach. I could not let it slip from my grasp.

And I yearned for time alone with the man I loved.

But of course, it was not that easy. As if in response to some pre-arranged signal, Juliana and Felix rose as soon as my tale reached its close, claiming a sudden need to walk in the courtyard despite the January chill. Left with Timur, my sister, and Alexei, I knew better than to speak. I'd hoped my brother-in-law, having heard the whole, would hold off on or even abandon his promised discussion, but past experience warned me how unlikely that was.

For several uncomfortable moments, the four of us stared silently at one another. I half-expected Alexei to demand that Maria and I leave the room as well, but he didn't. Instead, he addressed Timur as if we were not present. "I understand the urge to defend Lyuba, son," he said. "I'm proud of you—standing up for her like that. You've created expectations you can't fulfill, though. Lyuba is a noblewoman; I won't permit you to take her as your mistress. It's a wedding or nothing. But marriage isn't about love; it's about politics and alliances. And renewing the alliance with Koshkin offers us no clear advantage. At least when I wed Maria, the connection gave me an entrée into the Russian court. You already have that. What you need is backing that will get you a khanate one day."

Timur leaped to his feet and paced the room, something I remembered him doing as a boy whenever something upset him.

After three turns to the window and back, he stopped, hands on his hips, and glared at Alexei. "So you keep saying. But I'm not you. Suppose I *don't* care about becoming a khan? You were lucky; you fell in love with your political wife. I've already found the woman I want. I'm not going to turn my back on her to make you happy."

"You're too young to know whether she's the one, and so is she." Alexei rose to his feet as well, mimicking his son's pose. "The pair of you haven't spent more than a few weeks together since you were children. Love can fade as well as grow."

Timur's black eyes glittered with anger. "Is that why you abandoned my mother? And for a woman who couldn't hold your interest for three months?"

He'd gone too far. Even I wasn't surprised when Alexei roared, "Enough." Maria reached out a hand in protest, but he ignored her. "I am your father, and I say no. And that's the end of it." I quaked in my seat. I'd never seen him so furious, not even the day he thought we'd defied him by riding off into the fields.

But Timur didn't flinch. "Or what? You'll cast me off as your own father did you? Well, I have news for you, *Ata*. I've spent more years without you than with you, and I can take care of myself. But I *will* marry Lyuba. You can count on that."

And he stormed out the door.

I excused myself from the tense silence that followed Timur's departure and left the room at a run. If I moved fast, I should be able to catch up with him.

I couldn't imagine he would go to his father's study after their confrontation, so I grabbed the first cloak I saw in the coatroom and ran down the stairs. The paths outside had been swept free of snow, so I had little trouble reaching the stable despite not yet having rid myself of my court robes. It was imperative I get to my love before he grabbed a horse and galloped off. Dressed as I was, I couldn't easily ride after him.

I entered the stable to find the air pleasantly warm despite the chill outside. Braziers blazing along the central path lit my way, but even before I saw Timur, the jingle of horse tack told me where to look. "Stop," I said as I reached the doorway. I sounded breathless after my run. "You can't leave before I even have a chance to greet you." He whirled and caught my hand, then pulled me close and kissed me. I reveled in the pressure of his mouth, the strength of his grip around my waist, the sensual aroma of sandalwood that clung to his skin.

"I missed you so much," I said when he drew back after a while. His hands still roamed my body, setting off flickers of desire. "Every day I searched for you in the meadow. On good days I saw you, but that last day I didn't. I feared it was a bad omen."

He brushed his lips across my eyelids. "I went every day, but I didn't know when you might be watching. The longer you stayed away, the more I worried that you'd never find your way home. When Maria told us you'd been selected for presentation despite the virginity test, I was ready to storm the Kremlin."

"Does it bother you?" I heard the hesitancy in my own voice. Part of me didn't want to hear his answer, but I needed to ask. "I swear I *am* a virgin, despite the test."

He laughed softly and stroked my cheek. "You think I can't tell? I don't have a lot of experience in that area, I admit, but I can differentiate between a woman and an untried girl. And Maria told me what happened when you were ten. It's a silly test at the best of times, but lucky for me that your tsar and his handlers think differently. You do want to wed me, don't you?"

"More than anything. I always have, but since the day you returned ..." I let the sentence die unfinished and pressed my palms against his chest. "I've never seen your father so angry, though. I don't want him to disown you."

He gave a quick shake of his head. "He won't. He's mad right now because he hates people defying him—especially me. That whole steppe thing about fathers' wishes being absolute, you know. But he suffered from his own *ata*'s intransigence. I don't think he'll follow through, and if he does, we'll take refuge with my uncle until things calm down."

That thought comforted me a bit. "And their fears that the Church will oppose our marriage? I would convert to Islam if it meant being with you for the rest of my days."

He covered my hands with his own, and a flash of emotion I couldn't read crossed his face—wonder, perhaps. "Would you? It's not essential. I can marry a Christian."

"I'd consider it." In truth, I wasn't sure, although the idea had been coalescing, unnoticed, at the back of my mind since Anna first mentioned it. "The Church would wash its hands of me then, just as Papa has done."

"If you do, there's no going back," he said. "Let's first ensure you know what you're agreeing to."

"You'll teach me?"

"With pleasure. And many other things besides." He released my hands, wrapped his arms again about my waist, and kissed me with tenderness, as if I were a precious jewel entrusted to his care.

After a while, he raised his head. By then, I felt as if the sorceress from Tolya's story had woven a spell and transported me to the magical island hidden in the Ocean-Sea. "What do you say we hold the wedding in Kasimov, and the entire family can attend?" he asked. "Once *Ata* agrees, of course. From there we can go west with the horde. I think you'll love the steppe, despite its inconveniences. There's no more beautiful place on earth, and the women there are like you, bundles of fire and energy."

"I would love that." My spirit, earth-bound during the long weeks of the bride show, soared like Tizilek under the warmth of his gaze. "I've always wanted to see it. Let's hope Alexei and Maria agree soon."

"Yes." He dipped his head once more and pulled me closer. "But right now, I'm going to kiss you again."

That seemed like an excellent plan, so I agreed without hesitation.

"Absolutely in Kasimov," Alexei said. After several days of intense discussion, interspersed with chilly silences, he'd come around as Timur had predicted. It had taken an unexpected intervention by Juliana, of all people, to turn the tide, but turn it had. I quizzed her in private over what she'd said to him, but she would admit only to reminding him of the days when *he* had defied his father—and the price he'd paid for it. I thanked her profusely and made a mental note to find out more one day—for the sake of my family saga, of course. But whether I did or not, I would be eternally grateful to her.

At the moment Alexei made his pronouncement, he and I were sitting with Maria, Timur, Juliana, and Felix in the living room, fortified with cups of steaming tea and flaky pastries filled with sweetened farmer's cheese and cherry preserves. When none of us responded, he went on. "And before Ogodai's horde departs for its summer pastures. Right now, they're south of Kazan, within easy reach of Kasimov." I assumed he added that for Felix's benefit, since Juliana and Timur had once lived in the horde and the rest of us knew its migration schedule, more or less.

"Not before the tsar's wedding," Maria said. "You haven't forgotten, I hope, that you and I have assigned parts to play."

"We couldn't reach everyone by then anyway," I pointed out. "It's next week. That's not enough time to receive a reply from Varvara, never mind those farther away."

"Varvara?" Felix asked.

"Our middle sister in Murom," I explained. "Could we ask her to notify our side of the family? Many of them live close to her."

"Yes," Maria said. "I'll send a note to our two brothers here in Moscow. If we hold the ceremony in Kasimov, we can avoid inviting most of our casual acquaintances in town. But if we want any of the Christian relatives to attend, we have to hold it either before Lent or after Easter."

"Before Lent is the Muslim month of Muharram," Juliana put in. "Not an auspicious time for weddings." Alexei and Timur nodded—in appreciation of this point, I assumed.

"After Easter, then," Maria said. "That gives us more time to prepare. It's late this year, but not so late that the horde will have moved west. Ideally it would be after Pentecost, but that takes us into June. Shall we say late April or early May?"

I turned to Juliana. "Will you and Felix join us? It would be a great pleasure to have you, but I know it means a longer time away from your home and your daughter."

She glanced at Felix. "I think we could manage that. I would love to be part of your ceremony. I'll even take care of your henna paintings." While I murmured my thanks, remembering the designs she had inked onto my sister's hands so many years ago, she patted Felix's arm, which rested next to her on the sofa. "You should see Kasimov, my love—a true window on the east, despite its Russian affiliation, and beautiful to boot."

"We've stayed away a long time already. What's another few months, if it means attending Lyuba and Timur's wedding?" He touched his forehead, as if doffing the cap he wasn't wearing indoors. His gray eyes crinkled at the corners, and I felt myself respond in kind.

"Very well," Maria said. "Let's aim for early May. I'll have the messengers on the road today. Alexei, I should write to your parents to ask their blessing on the match. It is proper, and it will also be a tremendous help, because if I know my mother-in-law, she will have that entire side of the family notified and half the wedding planned within days of receiving the news."

"Only half?" he asked with a grin. "You underestimate her."

"If not sooner," Juliana said at the same moment, and the two of them burst out laughing.

"You'll love Sumbeka Khatun, Felix," she added once she'd achieved some self-control. "A whirlwind of organization and efficiency, but a complete charmer at the same time. It will be fun to see her and the others again."

Maria acknowledged these interruptions with a nod but continued without breaking stride. "Lyuba, are you serious about converting? I should mention it to them, if so."

"I am, but I promised to learn more from Timur first," I reminded her. "He says we can sign the contract whether I do or not, and his own people will recognize it whatever our Church says."

"And if you wait until after the signing," Alexei added, "I can act as your guardian. Otherwise I'll ask my brother to act in my stead, because a Muslim woman must have a Muslim guardian. If you are still Christian, though, that rule doesn't apply."

"I'll wait, then." I squeezed his fingers, acknowledging his smile with one of my own. By then I understood that he had our best interests at heart, even if we'd disagreed for a while about what those were. "You're more of a father to me than Papa has ever been. I would love to have you as my guardian."

He laughed again, but I could tell I'd pleased him. "Some standard he sets. Your falcon could do a better job."

At that moment, Anna dashed in, trailed by her mother. Tanya followed with additional cups of tea and plates of food, which she deposited on the nearest sideboard before collecting our visitors' cloaks.

I leaped up and grabbed Anna's arm, pulling her toward the bench where I'd sat with Timur and whispering the news of my impending wedding into her ears. She pulled free long enough to embrace him, then whirled to face Solomonida. "Mama, Lyuba's going to marry Timur!"

That set off an explosion of exclamations and demands for details. Once everyone settled into place, I gave a summary of events, starting with Papa's arrival and ending with a plea. "You'll come to our wedding, won't you? I can't imagine getting married without you and Anna there to support me!"

"We wouldn't miss it for the world." Solomonida glanced at her daughter, who nodded vigorously. I saw sadness in Anna's eyes and wondered if she thought of Yuri, still confined to his monastery. Secure in my own happiness, I wished desperately for hers, but how she might attain it remained a mystery.

"We had a visitor, too," Anna said. "This very morning, in fact. Cousin Igor, raving about how I had wrest the cup of victory from his hands and threatening to wed me to Prince Pavel at the first opportunity. Fortunately, he hadn't gotten farther than that when the tsar's guards arrived to escort him to his punishment post up north. But he's slippery as a snake. I dread what he'll do next."

"You won your freedom from the tsar," I reminded her, leaning forward and clasping her hand. "You will defeat Cousin Igor as well. If nothing else, we can hide you from him if need be. Have you written to Yuri?"

"Right after I reached home." The tension in her face lessened. "Anfim sent a dedicated courier this time, so I should receive an answer in a couple of weeks, not months."

"There, you see," Maria put in. "We will have you settled long before Cousin Igor weasels his way back into royal favor."

Juliana, so far uncharacteristically silent, raised a regal hand. "But this story I don't know. Anna, come over here and tell me the whole. Who is Yuri, and what makes him unacceptable to your cousin?"

Anna glanced at me, then her mother, who shrugged an elegant shoulder. "Go and explain, dearest. If anyone can bring Igor to his senses, Juliana can. Meanwhile, I'll be discussing wedding plans with Lyuba and Maria."

"Our cue to exit." Timur rose and kissed one female cheek after another before assisting Felix to rise. "You may as well retreat to the study with us," he said. "It will be clothes and flowers and henna from here on. Look, *Ata*'s already out the door."

Indeed, Alexei had made his getaway the moment Solomonida mentioned wedding plans.

"Just remember," Timur added as he ushered Felix from the room. "Tatar weddings have their own customs, a little different from yours."

"Off with you." Juliana interrupted her conversation with Anna long enough to make shooing motions with her hands. "As if I don't know what they are."

That was when I remembered, yet again, the years she had spent in the horde now ruled by Timur's uncle. She had every detail of Tatar life at those elegant fingertips.

"See?" I told him. "Juliana will give us the information we need."

But Timur had already closed the door behind himself and Felix. He didn't hear a word.

Chapter 20

"The village rallied around the maiden"

Somehow everything got done despite the competing demands of Tsar Ivan's wedding to Tasya Yureva—with Alexei in charge of the groom's hat and Maria supporting the bride as she waited for the ceremony to start—and the sheer madness of planning a massive ceremony involving two families with enough members to populate a small town. As Maria had predicted, her mother-in-law leaped into action within hours of receiving the notification of our plans, and between her and my sisters' considerable organizational skills, the whole event went from plan to reality in no time.

I could only watch in awe. While I was still wondering whether my wedding to Timur was more than a pleasant dream, I mounted my mare, saw my beloved falcon safely caged, and set off for Murom with my sister and brother-in-law, Juliana and Felix, Anna and her family, and the two brothers of mine who lived in Moscow. The weather was still cold enough to permit overland travel; the snow lay thick on the ground, and the horses moved swiftly over the ice-covered roads. A month later, and we would have had no choice but to take a boat directly to Kasimov while the rest of my family found its own way south.

But as things stood, we stopped in Murom for a week to rest the horses and collect my two remaining brothers, as well as my sister Varvara and their assorted spouses and children. A surprising number of relatives had chosen to attend, and under Varvara's direction, they had gathered in her home city, awaiting our arrival. Surrounded by Alexei's bodyguard, we looked like an army on the move.

Once we reached our destination, we learned that an even larger crowd of wedding guests would join us: Ogodai Khan and his horde; friends and military associates of Timur and Alexei; and, of course, the entire population of Kasimov. I listened as Timur's grandmother Sumbeka reeled off the names and wondered how I'd ever keep track of so many strangers.

Yet somehow, despite my doubts, everything came together. Six weeks after we reached our destination, resplendent in finery that defied even my vivid imagination, I accepted a seat on a dais in the middle of a hall crammed with women. Anna, radiant in sky blue silk, sat on my left side. Lara, made shy by the crowd, clung to her stepmother on the far side of the room, but Tolya had long since vanished into a wandering herd of small boys. Sumbeka Khatun, my soon-to-be grandmother-in-law, had abandoned the dais on the run when her only daughter, Nasan, appeared in the doorway a short time before. The two of them stood, chatting in a corner, while Nasan's four children laughed and squealed as they were passed from one auntie to the next. From my vantage point I studied mother and daughter, noting how the resemblance between them had strengthened with the years. Nasan's fragile beauty was maturing as she approached thirty into a reflection of Sumbeka's stately calm, despite the contrast between Nasan's ebony locks and her mother's gray. Their animated expressions and vivid hand gestures attested to their kinship as well as to their fiery personalities.

"That gown is gorgeous." Juliana settled onto a stool in front of me and began to lay out her brushes and henna on a nearby octagonal table. "Let me guess—a gift from Sumbeka?"

"Yes," I said. "It should be red, for luck, she told me, but with my hair I'd look like a house on fire—her words." I laughed, remembering the way Anna and I had switched clothes for our presentations to the tsar. "So Timur gets red with gold dragons, and I have cloth-of-gold with red phoenixes." I held out an exquisite sleeve in illustration, admiring it anew. I'd never worn anything so elaborate, but Sumbeka had brushed off any muttered objections that it was too fine for the occasion. Lowering the sleeve, I ran a hand down my sides, where the brocade hugged my waist. "This takes some getting used to, though."

"Very different from our loose Russian robes," Anna agreed. "The tight waist suits you, though. And looking around, it seems to be a style for girls and young women."

Glancing around the room, I realized she was right. "It would be hard to carry off while pregnant, I suppose."

Beyond Anna's right shoulder, two more Tatar women and a third whose light brown hair hinted at a Russian heritage pushed their way through the open door and moved toward Sumbeka. I recognized one of the three as Firuza, Nasan's sister-in-law and the wife of Ogodai Khan, who had tutored Timur for so long and had agreed to accept the two of us into his horde. The second newcomer, whom I guessed to be in her early forties, must have been pretty once, but her looks had faded with the years. Although her dark hair remained lustrous, wrinkles creased her face and her shoulders slumped. Yet something about her seemed familiar.

"Who are the two who came in with Firuza?" I asked Juliana.

She turned her head, a small frown creasing her brow, then stood to survey the company. After resuming her seat, she treated me to her feline smile. "That, my dear, is Timur's mother. Her name is Guzel, and she hates my guts because I ran off with Alexei all those years ago. So you can expect a few tense moments once she realizes who's handling your mehndi designs. But now she's here, I can start work—which is good, because at the rate we're going, you'll have seen the contract signed before the henna can set."

Recalling Timur's initial response to Juliana, I could imagine how much more strongly Guzel might react. From my perch on the dais, I studied my mother-in-law-to-be, wondering whether she would welcome me any more warmly than she did Juliana. Guzel must have had views on whom her son might wed, and although Timur and I had written to invite her to the ceremony, we had not received a response. I'd assumed that was because she objected, but surely she wouldn't travel so far just to make a fuss. Would she?

I would find out soon. In the meantime, I decided to follow the path of maximum discretion and leave Juliana's comment unanswered. "And the Russian woman, if she is Russian, who came in with them?" I asked instead.

"Oh, that must be Grusha," Juliana said without turning her head. "The camp shaman. She's the only Russian woman in the horde. I heard she married one of Alexei's men, so he may have brought her with him to honor his lord. She must know Timur, too, from the years when he lived with his uncle." Again over her shoulder, I saw Solomonida greet the Russian woman as if they were old friends, or at least acquaintances. That surprised me even more than having a real, live shaman at my wedding, but I stashed away the question of how Solomonida knew Grusha and forgot about it.

Indeed, I had little opportunity to ask. Sumbeka broke off her conversation with Nasan long enough to embrace first Firuza, then Guzel, before ushering the three of them in my direction, parting the crowd by what appeared to be pure force of will.

I took a deep breath, readying myself for whatever their arrival might bring. Anna, who'd remained quiet for so long I'd almost forgotten her presence, handed me a cup and a ball of deep-fried dough that Juliana called a *chek-chek*. "Eat and drink," my friend said. "You won't be able to use your hands once Juliana starts working on them, and you'll be starving by the time the henna dries enough for us to unwrap the bandages."

I took the cup and savored the tart sweetness of apple juice against my tongue. The *chek-chek* dripped with honey, and my mouth watered at the sight, but I gazed at my cloth-of-gold sleeves with dismay. "I can't eat that," I told Anna. "I'll make a mess of this gorgeous dress."

Her laughter caught the attention of Sumbeka, now approaching the dais. Anna slipped the treat onto a napkin and positioned it right in front of my face. "Here. I'll hold it. Bite and swallow, and you'll do fine."

"I feel like a baby bird," I said after a few bites, but the *chek-chek* disappeared in no time. Then I was bowing to greet the woman who would become my mother-in-law on the morrow, and any amusement at having to nibble my food vanished in nerves.

Guzel proved to be perfectly charming—to everyone except Juliana. At first she regarded me warily, but my bow, accompanied by a greeting in her own language, brought a smile to her face. "You speak Tatar?" she said, audibly surprised.

"Since childhood," I said. "Timur taught me."

She gave an appreciative nod. "That will make your life among us much easier, *kilen*."

I saw her use of the Tatar word for "daughter-in-law" as a good sign and permitted myself a gentle sigh of relief. Then she added, without so much as glancing at Juliana, "I trust it will not bring you misfortune to allow a snake such as this one to decorate your hands."

Juliana hissed, as if giving form to her attacker's words. "She is a remarkable artist," I said mildly. "I was only six when she drew the mehndi for my sister, but I still remember how beautifully they came out." And what a fit Maria had when she saw the dragon on her right hand, declaring it the devil's work, but I didn't mention that. Nor did I point out how mean Juliana had been to me in those days.

"Thank you," Juliana said in a tone that could only be described as snappish. "Sit, please, and let me begin. It won't do for the men to join us and you still unadorned."

I sat, inviting Guzel to take the one vacant chair. "The men will join us?" I asked Juliana. "Where on earth will they stand? There's not a hand's breadth of free space in the room."

"They'll find a place," Guzel said. "We can always clear out some of the less welcome guests." She glared at Juliana, and I sighed, not with relief. The next few hours looked like they might be painful at best.

The cool sweep of a brush against the backs of my fingers drew my attention. To distract Guzel, I asked her about the khan's camp. "Timur has talked about us living there for a while after we marry," I told her. "What can I expect if we do?"

Her eyes lit up with joy, and I felt real warmth for—and from—her then. "Oh, that would be wonderful. He hasn't been back in so long." She launched into a long discussion of life in the horde, the migrations west and east, the hardships and the pleasures, which lasted us until Juliana completed her patterns on my right hand and turned to the left. Sumbeka arrived around that time with Nasan, and Guzel moved off into the crowd. I watched her go, wondering. Timur had told me she'd chosen never to marry, so he was her only child. What was it like for her, with him away for years at a time?

Nasan bent to kiss my cheeks, and I greeted her with pleasure. I'd seen her only occasionally since she went south a few months before my eighth birthday. I had always admired her, though, and I reveled in my family's reports of her exploits—including the time she rescued her husband from imprisonment and almost certain death at St. Daniil's Monastery, the incident I'd remembered the day I went hawking with Timur. Hers were among the best of the tales I was determined to record one day.

I couldn't hug her, with one hand wrapped to protect the henna as it darkened and the other gripped by Juliana, but I could talk. "Do sit and tell me what's new. It seems like ages since we met. Was that *four* children who came in with you?" Anna had long since vacated the chair to my left, so I pointed toward it. Sumbeka took the seat on the right, but she had barely settled into place before the arrival of another newcomer had her bolting to her feet once more. Again she disappeared into the throng.

"Yes, four. Two boys and two girls." Nasan remained standing long enough to gaze around the room. "I see they're playing with their cousins. Good." She touched Juliana's shoulder. "Welcome. I didn't expect to see you here. Maria says you're married now, to a lovely Polish gentleman, and the two of you have adopted a child."

A very different reaction from Guzel's. Interesting. I made a mental check mark in my ongoing study of the family and its complicated relationships, with a vow to ferret out an explanation from my sister when I had a chance. My thoughts drifted as Juliana talked about her Klara and how much longer they'd been away than expected and her hopes that the child hadn't forgotten her. After a while, I again asked Nasan for news about her life these days, but she barely had time to form an answer before Sumbeka returned once more.

"Nasan, you're needed over there." She pointed in the direction of the Russian shaman—now surrounded by a group of fascinated children, including Lara—before dropping onto the seat reserved for her. "You're almost finished, Juliana. How quick you are. What have you drawn?"

Nasan excused herself and left. Juliana set down her brush and wrapped my left arm in a linen towel. Then she undid a single fold from my right hand, revealing a complicated pattern of splashy flowers with what looked like a furled tail in the center. "Oh, lovely," Sumbeka said. "Phoenixes and roses, and how rich the red is! It will bring you great happiness, Lyuba."

"The color will?" I asked, perplexed. I had witnessed just the one mehndi ceremony, for my sister, and as I mentioned, I was only six then. But I'd never heard of good fortune based on the shade of a dye.

Another detail I could weave into a future story, along with the many other surprises of this day.

Juliana basked in Sumbeka's approval. "Yes, the color," she told me. "The darker the red, the greater the good fortune it confers." She patted me on the cheek and stood in a single, fluid motion, not unlike the cat she so often reminded me of. "Leave the hands wrapped for now. It deepens the shade. I'll be back to remove the towels before the men arrive." She bowed to Sumbeka, then signaled to someone in the crowd. "Here is Solomonida to keep you company for a while." Then, with one more nod, Juliana left the dais.

"Tell me about your maiden's bath," Solomonida said once I had finished grilling her about how she knew Grusha (a former servant at her neighbor's house, it turned out—and, improbably, someone Anfim had wanted to marry before he met Solomonida). "Anna said it was a bit like the maidens' gatherings before our Russian weddings."

I burst out laughing. "Anna must have been at a different party! Yes, it was like ours in the sense that all the people present were women, mostly family and close friends, but Russians don't strip you down and bathe you, never mind removing all the hair from your body with sharply honed shells. I've never experienced anything like it." I held up a wrist for her to sniff. "Lovely perfumes, though, and by the time they declared me ready, my skin felt like fresh cream."

"Lilacs," Solomonida said after a quick inhalation. "Light and delicate, perfect for a wedding. I remember how Nasan used to rave about those indoor baths. I love a Russian bathhouse, but pools of warm water and no rushing through the snow to get there do sound good. Are you prepared for tomorrow?"

"I'm not sure I'm prepared for tonight," I said. "Although at times it seems I've waited for this my whole life."

"I wish you every happiness." She rose and kissed my cheek. "I'll send Anna over here when I find her, but I suppose I'd better pay my respects to as many relatives as I can."

"Ask Varvara to join me if you see her," I begged. I wasn't supposed to leave the dais, but the prospect of sitting there for hours without company held no appeal whatsoever. I didn't even have a book to read.

"I will," Solomonida promised, slipping into the crowd. And she must have taken the request seriously, because I hardly had time to stand and survey the room before my middle sister arrived in a swirl of coral silk. She, Anna, and Maria took turns chatting with me until Juliana returned, unwrapped my hands, and revealed the exquisitely detailed crimson patterns in all their glory. I stared in awe at the intricately intertwined vines, the glorious roses that adorned them, and the two central phoenixes—each mirroring the other from the southernmost tail feather at the top of my fingers to the facing heads halfway between wrist and elbow.

"Aren't they gorgeous?" I exclaimed. Juliana smiled and preened, but the noise of many booted feet drowned out anything she might have said in response.

Men poured into the crowded room, escorting Timur on horseback and depositing him at my side, then removing the horse before it could defile its surroundings. My brothers came in behind him and approached the dais en masse, hugging and congratulating me. As they left, I realized that the horde of wandering children had doubled in size, with boys up to the age of twelve escaping the clutching grasp of younger hands. Anfim, Felix, Ogodai Khan, Alexei, and many other male relatives or close friends pushed their way through the throng to pay their respects, then blended back into the surging crowd like an ebbing tide.

As they retreated, Timur kissed me, then admired my henna paintings while fastening a triple string of pearls around my throat. I pinned the brooch I had brought for him into his cap of dark blue, a contrast to the scarlet robe selected by his grandmother, and we sat in comfortable silence amid the hubbub. Sound rose and fell like waves, only occasionally quieting enough that we could compare notes about our days.

I had long since lost track of time when the horde started to disperse. "I can't wait for tomorrow," he murmured in my ear as his uncles and cousins pulled him away. I squeezed his hand in response, but a flash of anxiety tied my tongue. My whole life would change in the morning, and no matter how much I looked forward to that, I wasn't sure I was ready.

By the time I found the right words, he was gone. The female guests who had retreated into corners to make space for the men flowed back into the hall, leaving the room full once more. By then, I teetered on the edge of exhaustion. Sumbeka released me from the dais, and I escaped in search of company. Movement cleared my head for a while, but no one was gladder than I when the mehndi ceremony ended at last. Maria took my arm, and together we retreated to the wing of the palace temporarily designated as the bride's home, where the actual wedding would take place the next day.

Remembering the night before the royal presentation-that-wasn't, I expected to have trouble sleeping in the beautiful chamber set aside for me. But after hours of pent-up emotion, I fell into slumber as soon as my head touched the pillow. I woke to dawn light and bird song and sat up, blinking.

The reality of my wedding day crashed into me. Soon I would leave everything behind—my family, my home in Moscow, customs familiar since birth, including the calendar and my religion. Was I ready? I spoke Tatar fluently, would join a family of people whose comfort in Russian equaled mine, and had studied their literature and history as intensely as my own. In that sense, I had more arrows in my quiver than Nasan, for example, had when she came to Moscow and married Daniil—or Grusha when she headed south with her newborn son. Solomonida had told me that story while she sat with me last night. And I loved Timur. *How* I loved Timur. Even so, I hesitated.

But when Maria came in, the cloth-of-gold gown draped over her arm and Varvara walking behind her carrying a white gauze veil attached to a small round hat in the same pattern as the dress, I kept my qualms to myself. All brides had jitters. I had chosen this path, and I would follow it to the end.

My sister led me to a room on the ground floor, where with a hug and words of encouragement, she left me at the door. I entered to discover a servant I hadn't met before, an elderly man who ushered me—already hidden from view by the veil—behind a curtain. He pointed to the alcove's one seat and retreated. A quick survey established that I would be able to hear but not observe what went on in the room beyond. I saw no breaks in the fabric that could provide a peephole, and peeking around the edge would probably offend those who had set up this space. I grimaced at the thick blue velvet of the drape, but seeing no alternative, I settled into my assigned seat with an ill grace.

The first to arrive was Alexei, chatting amiably in Tatar with a man whose voice I didn't recognize. Then came Timur, whose greeting revealed that the unfamiliar tones must belong to the mullah chosen to observe the contract signing, and a fourth person that I identified only when Timur addressed him as "uncle." Ogodai Khan, then—Maria had explained that because Alexei was representing me, Ogodai had accepted the father's role on behalf of Timur. Confusing, but evidence that this crucial part of the ceremony—the actual wedding, in fact—was underway. I rallied my spirits and took a deep breath. I had but to sit and listen, because my silence was taken as consent.

As things turned out, I hadn't long to wait. The whole ceremony took less time than I would have believed possible. Alexei accepted on my behalf the predetermined payment for my future subsistence (which he was giving on behalf of his son—I said it was confusing) and agreed to the marriage three times in my name. Ogodai did the same for Timur, and the unknown mullah recited excerpts from the Koran. I recognized most of them—even though he spoke in Arabic, of course—which heartened me; Timur's lessons of the last few months had borne fruit.

Then we were done. Overlapping footsteps signaled the men's retreat, and Alexei stuck his head around the curtain. "You can come out now, *kilen*. It's official." He pushed aside the drape and turned back my veil. As I emerged from my hiding place, he regarded me with a quizzical expression. "Are you having regrets? You look ... thoughtful."

I met his eyes, unsure how to answer. "No," I said slowly, letting my inchoate emotions coalesce as I talked. "Not regrets. But the contract signing happened so fast. I wasn't expecting a public crowning, but I didn't even say 'I do.' You said it for me. I'm not sure I feel married yet. What's different from this morning?"

He laughed and gave me a gentle push toward the door. "What's different, my dear, is that you're now my daughter-in-law. Your sister and my stepmother have spent the last three months preparing the celebration of the century, and I guarantee you will feel married by the time we leave you alone with Timur. Let's go and see what they've produced, shall we?"

Seeing no benefit in further argument, I thanked him for representing me, then lifted my skirt in one hand and sailed out of the room. Besides, I suspected he was right. By the time the party ended, I would feel very much a bride.

To reach me, Timur had first to pay his way into our part of the palace. I watched, amused and amazed, as Maria's two children blended seamlessly into a gaggle of cousins they had met less than two days ago, the whole group jumping up and down and demanding a toll for my bridegroom to pass the gate into the courtyard, then another for entry from the yard into the house. In some ways, it echoed the Russian custom by which a husband-to-be had to buy off the young relative occupying his cushion at the beginning of the betrothal rite, but this was more raucous and less structured. Timur, I soon realized, had come prepared with a sack of treats that Grandfather Frost would have envied, and he doled them out to the waiting children with a glee that equaled theirs.

After the third repetition of this child-led ambush, he made it through the door and, flushed with exertion and laughter, took his place at my side. There we regarded with awe a feast twice the size of yesterday's, with an equal number of male and female relatives as well as long tables filled with visiting guests and resident warriors. For the most part, women sat on one side of the room, men on the other.

Nasan brought her husband, good-looking as ever, to greet me. Ogodai Khan and his wife embraced Timur and me and congratulated us before taking seats on my new husband's right. Alexei clapped his hand on Timur's shoulder, then took his place next to me, Maria at his side. From one end of the table, Anfim bowed to me, hand over his heart. Felix stood nearby, balanced on his cane; Solomonida and Juliana kissed my cheeks as they proceeded to the opposite end. Halfway down the length of the hall, I recognized Grusha standing with a Tatar man who was probably the husband Juliana had mentioned, since he gripped the shoulder of a handsome boy who matched Timur's description of Grusha's son. Two other boys, obviously Tatar from their dress, stood nearby. I whispered a question, and Timur stopped chatting with his uncle long enough to identify the other lads as Ogodai's and Nasan's eldest sons. Then Sumbeka claimed my attention, and I forgot about surveying the crowd.

Unlike Russian weddings, there were no toasts with red wine—nothing identified as alcohol, in fact, although a large quantity of fermented mare's milk poured down male throats—and no demands that Timur and I "sweeten the bitterness" of such toasts with kisses. The variety of foods defied belief. Dishes lay in endless procession along the tables, their contrasting colors as bright as the aromas were appetizing. Huge bowls of rice passed from hand to hand, then gave way to platters of meat—including roast geese, the local equivalent of the swan served at Russian weddings to bring good luck to a bridal couple.

Stomach tight, I pecked at my food. At any moment, although I wasn't sure exactly when, the mothers and aunties would signal that it was time for Timur and me to retreat to the room they had prepared so lovingly for us yesterday. We would be alone, and I would embark on the next stage of life's journey.

I wanted to be Timur's wife in every sense, to love him for the rest of my days, to spend my life at his side. I repeated the words over and over in my mind as I listened to Maria and Sumbeka, chatted with Anna and Guzel, compared notes with Nasan and Firuza, enjoyed Juliana's acidic but humorous comments on the company. And I waited, with growing impatience, for that next stage to begin.

At last, Maria, as the senior woman on my side of the family, rose and beckoned to me. Timur stood as well, and the two of us followed my sister and the other female attendants to a beautifully decorated bedchamber as far as one could get from the banquet hall. They stood back and waited for us to enter. My last sight before Timur closed the door was Anna mouthing, "Good luck."

I held up a finger until the horde of footsteps retreated into silence. Then I tumbled into Timur's arms. He pulled me into his embrace, and I thought of nothing except how much I yearned for him.

Chapter 21

"And the prince and princess lived happily ever after"

S ome indeterminate time later, I opened my eyes and found him regarding me with concern. "Are you all right?" He kissed my forehead. "I didn't hurt you, did I?"

He had, a little, but I understood that he'd had no choice. Maria had warned me that, despite my failed virginity test, discomfort might accompany the transition from maiden to wife. "Not enough to matter," I said. "And now we can both be sure that I was pure when I came to you."

"I never doubted that." He kissed me once more. "But it will reassure our mothers—or sister, in your case."

"We are one now." I stroked his chin, the stubble rough under my fingers, the line of his mustache silky. "I would like to keep my promise."

"Are you sure?" he asked, as he had when I first raised the idea. "Once you say the *Shahada*, you're committed for life."

"I'm sure." I took a deep breath and said the words in Arabic, as he had taught me, then repeated them, just for good measure.

"Once is enough," he said, laughing. "You'll be saying it plenty from now on. Five services a day. And as the witness to your reversion, it's my privilege to give you a new name, for your new life in the faith. Let me see, which one shall I pick? Saadet, because you make me happy? Sabahat, because you are beautiful? Dilnaz, because I love you?" He brushed his finger across the base of my throat as he said each name, like a caress. "No, you are more than beautiful," he went on when I didn't reply. "You are beautiful and bright—like fire, like the moon. And whatever I call you, you'll always be my Lady Love. So I choose Nurai, which means 'bright moon.' Do you like that?"

"Nurai. Noor-EYE." I tasted the syllables on my tongue, weighing them as I would a name for a character in one of my stories, relishing the sounds, the emotions the word conveyed. It spoke of silvery light cast on the river in midsummer, the serene beauty exhibited by the guardian of the night sky, waxing and waning. And it told anyone who would listen what I meant to him.

"I like it," I said after a pause that must have lasted longer than he'd expected, judging from the quirk of his eyebrow. "Nurai it shall be."

The sun hung above the city walls by the time a discreet knock on the door signaled the arrival of Sumbeka, Guzel, my sisters, and any other woman who could stake a claim to be considered a member of the immediate family. They gathered around me and swept me behind a screen to wait while the menfolk arrived to escort Timur to the bathing area. I heard only the mingling of male voices, teasing my new husband about his long night and the reasons for his late awakening—an ordeal he handled with grace.

When the men left, the women stripped me of my clothing and washed me from forehead to toes with soft cloths dipped in warm, scented water before arraying me in another set of robes almost as stunning as those I had donned for the wedding itself.

"Timur was kind?" Guzel asked after a while.

I couldn't imagine my husband's mother wanting anything but a positive response to that question, but fortunately I could give a truthful answer. "Of course," I said. A shiver ran through me as I recalled how different my initiation might have been, and Maria sent me a questioning glance.

"A memory of Papa's graybeards," I told her. "A threat that fortunately never came to pass. Timur makes me quiver with joy."

That provoked laughter among the women, which strengthened when I shared my new name. Guzel hugged me, and so did Maria, whispering best wishes for my future into my ear. Sumbeka flipped back the coverings on the bed, revealing a streak of blood I hadn't expected to see, a sight that caused my heart to flip—or so it felt—once more. Another close escape, since that streak meant that I could have married the tsar if chosen without disgracing myself and my family. Sumbeka gestured to a hovering maidservant, who stripped the bed and relaid it, carrying the soiled sheet away.

I looked around for Anna, knowing she would share my relief, but however hard I searched for my friend among the swirling mass of women, I couldn't find her.

"Where's Anna?" I asked Maria when the crowd dissipated enough that I could catch her sleeve without drawing the attention of everyone in the room. Solomonida had not thrust herself into the circle of immediate family—although I considered her closer to me than Nasan and Firuza, whom I hadn't seen in years. But Anna? My friend had stood at my side throughout the ceremony. Why had she not joined me this morning? No one would have barred her from a ritual that, however trivial on the surface, marked my acceptance into the community as a wife.

Maria's beautiful brows drew together in a frown. She surveyed the room from her post next to me, then moved into the throng for a while before returning. "I don't see her," she said as she rejoined me. "I haven't seen her all morning, in fact. Perhaps she slept in."

"Perhaps." I fought to conceal my disappointment, which seemed childish in the extreme. "She's worked harder than most to support me since we announced the wedding, and nonstop since we reached Kasimov. She's earned her rest." But a treacherous voice in my head whispered that Anna resented my happiness when her own love remained in limbo. She had still not received word from Yuri about his release.

Sumbeka took my arm and gestured toward the door, signaling that we should move toward the banquet hall. There, unlike the day before, we women would feast in one room while the men celebrated in another. When I nodded in response, she led the way, Guzel at her side. Maria and I followed with Varvara, and I heard the rest of the women fall into place behind us.

Solomonida would await us in the chamber beyond, I felt certain, and I would find Anna there with her. Tempted to tease my absent friend for sleeping in, I bit my tongue. Better to test the air first. Once I understood what had kept her away, then I would know how best to respond.

I'd been prepared for a room filled with women, because Sumbeka and Guzel had explained Tatar customs while preparing me for the mehndi ceremony. But I hadn't expected them to turn the chamber into an approximation of a huge nomadic tent, with luxuriant fabrics—cloth of gold intermixed with scarlet silk, for the most part—falling in huge swaths from a central ring, forming a circle. Exquisite Turkish carpets covered the floor, their motifs synchronized in flowery swirls that stood out against backgrounds of cream and dark blue. Low tables decked in white linen and covered with dishes both large and small ran down the center and sides of the makeshift tent, and tasseled cushions served as seats.

At the side of the room farthest from the door, I saw a raised platform fronted by a short series of steps, with rails around its other three sides. Sumbeka and Guzel led me to this structure, then waited as I took my seat in the center. They flanked me, with Maria on Sumbeka's right and Varvara finishing out the row on that side. Nasan came forward with Firuza in tow, and they assumed their places at Guzel's left. With the nearest relatives of bride and groom accounted for, other close friends—Solomonida and Juliana among them—occupied what were clearly assigned seats down the two remaining sides of the platform. Yet still I saw no sign of Anna.

I became concerned. One call to prayer had sounded early this morning; Timur and I had scrambled out of bed to purify ourselves and respond to it. The second had come shortly before the women arrived to bathe me. That meant it was already early afternoon. I had never known Anna to sleep so long unless she was ill. Someone should check on her.

But squeezed between Sumbeka and Guzel, I felt hemmed in and uncomfortable about making a fuss. Suppose I were to confide my fears to them and cause a ruckus that disrupted the celebration, only to discover that Anna was perfectly fine or, worse, hiding her misery? She would hate me for forcing her into the center of everyone's attention. Solomonida must have checked on her daughter before coming here. I would wait until I had a chance to talk with her privately before sounding the alarm.

This ceremony too, although held in my honor, did not require me to speak, which made it easier to conceal my anxiety over my friend's absence. After a while, the festive air—the singing and dancing, the delicious bread slathered in butter and honey (to soften and sweeten me, I was told by a laughing Sumbeka), the cheerful good wishes that came from all sides—relieved my concerns. This was a chance to revel in the knowledge that I had beaten the odds and achieved my deepest desire, and I should celebrate that.

When the feast ended, Sumbeka and Guzel, with the other women in attendance, escorted me outside. There my mother-in-law had ordered the raising of a real tent, so that she could introduce me to the spirits of the hearth fire. I heard drumming as we approached, and when we entered the tent, the woman Juliana had identified as Grusha, the camp shaman, awaited us. She wore a long leather robe, decorated with beads, and held a large drum, which she set aside when we came in. The air was heavy with the scent of sage and another substance I didn't recognize but later learned was juniper.

I stopped at the sight of her, wondering why she was there. Did she intend to perform some ritual? Was that even allowed?

Whatever she'd been doing, though, she seemed to have completed it before we arrived. At a nod from Sumbeka, Grusha handed me a ladle and a small bucket of milk. While she murmured instructions, I dipped the ladle into the bucket and walked around the fire, tossing drops in each of the four directions before sprinkling a small amount on the fire itself. From there the whole group of us went to visit the courtyard well, where Sumbeka urged the water spirits to welcome the family's newest member and to bestow good fortune on Timur, me, and our marriage. As we moved back toward the house, I heard the drumming resume.

"You did well, *kilen*," Guzel told me as the celebrants dispersed. "You're free to rest until the next banquet starts."

Her eyes crinkled at the corners, and I turned my groan into a laugh. "So many parties," I said. "I'm grateful, of course, for everyone's good will, but I'm really much more comfortable *not* spending quite so much time at the center of attention."

"So my son told me," she replied. "But now you have several hours to yourself, so enjoy them."

"But I can't." I looked around for Maria and Solomonida. "Anna still hasn't appeared. She's my best friend. If she's in trouble or even unhappy ..." I left the sentence unfinished.

Guzel nodded. "You must find her. I understand. Is that not her mother over there?"

I followed the direction of her pointing finger and found Solomonida, surrounded by women I didn't recognize. It was so like her to befriend everyone she encountered. It would take me half the afternoon to push my way through that crowd.

Fortunately, she was taller than most of those present, so when I caught her glancing my way, I beckoned. She freed herself with remarkable aplomb and headed toward us. "Anna," I said when she came within hearing distance. "Have you seen her today?"

Solomonida frowned. "Actually, no. I thought her exhausted by yesterday, so I decided she should enjoy her sleep while she could, but that was hours ago. I've been so preoccupied I hadn't noticed. I just assumed she was somewhere about. Let's check on her."

And check on her we did, the three of us with Maria in tow. The men's banquet had broken up too, and Anfim joined us as we entered the house. I'd seen little of him since we reached Kasimov, so I welcomed his hug and whispered congratulations, but my nerves remained taut. I chided myself for reading too much into a situation that probably had a simple explanation. I couldn't control my anxiety, though, even after Timur intercepted us while he was heading for our chamber and decided to come along.

When a gentle knock on Anna's door brought no response, Timur rapped louder, then threw open the door. I'd flung out a hand to stop him—would Anna want the six of us surprising her in her night robes?—but stopped at the sight of the undisturbed sheets. The robe Anna had worn yesterday lay flung across the mattress, a jumbled tangle of clothes spilled from an unlidded chest, a cabinet near the bed stood open, and several of the hooks that bordered the walls were empty. A single round container lay discarded on the dresser, and everything about the room pointed to someone who had packed and departed in haste.

"Where is she?" I demanded. But no one replied. Indeed, what could they say? The only certainty was that Anna had gone.

Anfim was the one who found the message, tucked into a corner where the pillow met the bedding. Lifting the scrap of tight-wrapped paper high, he waved it above his head, then, when we crowded around him, unfolded it. He skimmed the note as I stood, trying not to shout at him to reveal its contents. Timur's palm pressed against my spine, indicating his support.

"What does it say?" Solomonida asked, her hands clasped in a death grip that matched my own. "Where is she? What has she done?"

Anfim surveyed us, five anxious listeners, then focused his full attention on his wife. "Brace yourself, dearest," he said with a heartiness I found quite unconvincing. "Anna has run off."

"*Run off?*" Solomonida choked out the words. "Run off where? With whom? Tell me she wasn't so foolish as to take to the streets on her own. How would she even get out of the palace without anyone seeing her?"

"Where she went I don't know," he said. "Nor can I tell you how she managed to escape notice." He handed her the note. "But the whom you can see for yourself. She left with Yuri Gavriilovich Vorontsov."

Epilogue

Astrakhan, 1582

I lay down my pen once more. Memories of that time, that *self* of thirty-five years ago, swirl around me like ghosts in the mist. I'd forgotten the intense passions of youth, the fear that someone would see through my attempts to play the grownup and discover the uncertainty I strove so hard to conceal. So much has happened since: I've borne half a dozen children, grown into my faith and my name, managed an entire horde, completed my family saga, and drafted this latest installment. I have more grandchildren than I have books, although two daughters and a son have yet to reach marriageable age.

Even so, much of what I have recorded seems like yesterday. I recall with such clarity the hours I spent quizzing my relatives for their stories. Sumbeka Khatun proved invaluable; she had the history of the entire clan at her fingertips, and she could fill in details unknown to those in my generation—Alexei's childhood, those incidents from his past that Juliana used to convince him to accept my marriage to Timur, things said behind the scenes at Nasan's wedding, the legends and beliefs of the Tatars. I could never have finished my saga without her; I miss her every day I sit at my desk.

"Are you still writing, Nurai?" Timur stands in the doorway, his face more lined than on the day we said our vows but his hair only lightly dusted with gray and his shoulders as straight as those of the boy I fell in love with so many years ago. My heart swells with joy—and with pride, that of all the women in the world he chose me.

I point to the heap of paper at one side of my desk, then at the quill resting in its inkwell. "Behold the first draft of a new story." I allow my lips to curve. "*Our* story."

"Good for you." His answering smile lights his eyes as he extends his hand. "Then perhaps you'll join me for supper, *soyarké*. I believe our young Bulat has a tale for you."

I rise, take his arm, and stand on tiptoe to kiss him. "Of course, I will join you, lord of my heart. But don't be surprised if I return here tomorrow."

"I'd expect nothing less," he says as he ushers me out the door. "What else would my favorite storyteller do with her time?"

Historical Note

From the perspective of a historical novelist, the information available about the bride shows of sixteenth-century royal princes, grand princes, and tsars is frustratingly scarce. We know they took place for every ruler and many of his close male relatives, starting with Grand Prince Vasily III's first marriage in 1505 and ending only with Peter the Great's first marriage almost two centuries later. Thanks to Russell E. Martin, whose *A Bride for the Tsar: Bride-Shows and Marriage Politics in Early Modern Russia* (2012) was my bible for this novel, we have a sense of the principles used to weigh bridal candidates, the searches initiated in the provinces, the reluctance of local gentry to participate, and the speed with which the process took place, as well as an overview of the steps used to winnow the field and descriptions of the dirty tricks employed to disqualify rival candidates, some of which I have borrowed for my fictional brides. Records of the wedding ceremonies survive, together with the names and genealogies of the girls chosen and some of their competitors.

But there, more or less, is where what we know founders on the sandbar of what we don't. A few foreigners left accounts of a custom that seemed bizarre and exotic to them, but their reliability leaves much to be desired. The details that bring historical fiction to life—the nature of the tests imposed on potential candidates; the positions and personalities of those who administered them; the locations where the girls stayed and the style of their lodgings; the involvement of their family as support or chaperones; the methods used by the tsar to distinguish among the candidates, make his selection, and indicate his choice to the group—are much murkier than I would have liked. Even the timing of Ivan IV's first bride show (he had seven wives, outdoing even Henry VIII in that respect) is disputed. So beyond the date of his coronation, the fact that the bride show took place, and the date of Ivan's wedding to Anastasia Romanovna Yureva—here called by the nickname Tasya to distinguish her from Ivan's first cousin, Anastasia Petrovna Shuiskaya—everything here should be considered my invention. So should the personalities of the few historical figures who appear among my characters. The best documented of these is, of course, Ivan IV himself—not yet "Terrible" but already exhibiting a hot temper and mood swings. Ivan's vagaries support a small industry of historical literature promoting widely varying views; I have kept my interpretations of him to a minimum, but nevertheless, I'm sure other scholars will disagree.

One element of Russian—and European—society in the sixteenth century that does play an important role in this story is the position of women. Noblewomen seldom had a voice in selecting their own husbands, although unlike in the West, they did retain some control of their property after marriage. Widows sometimes had a say, but young aristocratic maidens and wives were secluded within their households and prohibited from contact with men outside their families. This seclusion did give mothers, grandmothers, and aunts an indirect veto power in the selection of brides, in that only they could enter the women's quarters of other noble households and attest to the virtue, viability, beauty, and health of prospective candidates. But the main point of the system seems to have been to prevent unwanted attachments (such as the love that blossoms between Timur and Lyuba) that might interfere with their male relatives' arrangements for them. Wedding contracts in turn defined political alliances, and that connection explains the importance of making the right match. All these factors were multiplied in the negotiations conducted behind the scenes of royal bride shows, where the choice of one maiden over another would determine the pecking order at court until the next marriage took place. It's no wonder that, as the historian Edward L. Keenan once put it, it was "during the process of betrothal of an heir or royal daughter that one heard the thud of limp bodies in the Kremlin." These are the threatening shoals that Lyuba and Anna must navigate if they are to emerge with intact reputations and even their lives.

As noted above, most of the incidents described here are fictional. But the public execution of the two princes on January 3, 1547, did happen more or less as described.

The reasons for the execution are not specified in the laconic chronicle entries, and only one source links the order to Mikhail Glinsky and his mother, Anna Glinskaya. The explanation given here is, therefore, informed speculation. I decided to include this event because, although I've known about the boys' deaths for years, I have only ever seen them mentioned in passing, as the last stage in the aristocratic strife that characterized Ivan the Terrible's early years. But novels require immersion in an experience, and as I considered who these boys were and how their execution must have affected their friends and family, I saw that the timing—less than two weeks before Ivan's coronation, after his intention to wed had been announced—had a direct impact on my story. Timur's friendship with the two victims is fictional, but we can imagine his shock and revulsion being shared by at least some of the girls selected—most often without their consent—to marry into a family that had chosen to advance its claims in such a brutal way.

The irony here is that the Glinskys overstepped their bounds. The royal marriage did not put an end to the clan warfare of the 1530s and 1540s right away. It took several years for the Yurev family, whom we know as the Romanovs, to consolidate the elite around itself for a decade of relative stability. In the meantime, the Glinsky clan again lost power to its Shuisky rivals. But how that happened forms the background to my next Songs of Steppe & Forest novel, which follows Anna Kolycheva on her flight from Kasimov.

Acknowledgments

I would like to express my thanks for the ongoing help from my invaluable writers' group, which continues to enrich and inform my writing, and to the other authors of Five Directions Press for their encouragement and support. In particular, I thank those who read the entire novel before publication: Courtney J. Hall, Gabrielle Mathieu, Andrea Penrose, and Joan Schweighardt. Ariadne Apostolou not only read the full manuscript but gave me the information that became the basis for Lyuba's riding accident, so double thanks go to her. Ann Kleimola, as always, remains a fount of inspiration and suggestions as well as a reader of early drafts and finished books.

To my husband and son—and, of course, the cat, who monitored my progress every day in my office and purred encouragingly while draping herself in front of the monitor—words cannot express my gratitude. After three years without a feline companion, she has acquired two kitten friends, whom she will, I am sure, train to follow in her pawsteps.

The Author

A s a child, C. P. Lesley thought everyone made up stories while falling asleep. It never occurred to her that anyone would pay her for them, and for a long time, she was right—no one would. But after years of producing horrible prose, reading books about novel writing, and pestering hapless fellow-writers and friends to read her drafts, some of the advice stuck, and she finished *The Not Exactly Scarlet Pimpernel*, then *The Golden Lynx* and its sequels: *The Winged Horse*, *The Swan Princess*, *The Vermilion Bird*, and *The Shattered Drum*. Five Directions Press published *Song of the Siren* in 2019, *Song of the Shaman* in 2020, *Song of the Sisters* in 2021, and *Song of the Sinner* in 2022. You can find Juliana's, Grusha's, Darya's, and Solomonida's stories, respectively, in those last four novels.

She is currently working on the sixth in her Songs of Steppe and Forest series, Song of the Steadfast. When not thinking up new ways to torture her characters, Lesley edits other people's manuscripts, reads voraciously, maintains her website, and practices classical ballet—an interest reflected in Desert Flower and Kingdom of the Shades (Tarkei Chronicles 1 and 2). She also hosts New Books in Historical Fiction, a podcast channel on the New Books Network. You can find out more about her at www.cplesley.com.

FORTHCOMING FROM FIVE DIRECTIONS PRESS

Song of the Steadfast

SONGS OF STEPPE & FOREST 6

Kasimov, May 1547

I hated to abandon Lyuba at her wedding. My best friend since we were six, she had invited me to serve as her main attendant, pleading, "Anna, I can't do this without you!" And of course, I agreed, even though a sinful part of myself wanted to scream with frustration, knowing that she would marry the man she loved while I had no assurance that Yuri, *my* beloved, could ever wed me, since Tsar Ivan had ordered Yuri to take monastic vows nine months before.

I stayed at my friend's side during the first day of her ceremony—a magnificent affair hosted by her new husband's grandparents, Bulat Khan and his chief wife, Sumbeka. As Muslim Tatars, they maintained an even stricter separation between men and women than we Russians did, so I saw the khan only in passing, but Sumbeka—a charming, energetic woman whose exquisite bone structure retained its beauty even in her fifties—was omnipresent, mostly ordering us about. Lyuba attracted the lion's share of her grandmother-in-law's attention, but my mother and I also received our portion.

Kasimov itself opened my eyes. Nothing could have prepared me for an entire town filled with round desert tents, pointed minarets decorated with crescent moons in place of our gilt-domed churches, and a white stucco palace surrounding lush gardens dotted with fountains. The squares rang with calls to prayer five times a day. Scents of exotic perfumes and spices filled the air. The place might have circled a distant star, so little did it resemble my home in Moscow, its cheek-by-jowl wooden houses and winding streets. We had our Kremlin and our red brick outer wall, our glistening cathedrals and noble estates, but none of them looked anything like this small fortress perched above the Oka River like a sparrow hawk in its nest.

But enough about Kasimov. Here I was, at Lyuba's wedding, watching my friend set out on the passage to womanhood that I so longed to take and feared I never would. My moods swinging back and forth like a carnival ride, I stayed with her through the feast that followed the formal contract signing, then accompanied those who escorted her to the chamber where she and Timur would consummate their union. Watching them cross that threshold together was the hardest part. I so yearned to trade places with them, Yuri at my side.

Perhaps that yearning explains, in a way, my reaction to what followed. On my way back to the dining hall, as I walked alone to keep my unseemly jealousy secret from those around me, a maidservant I didn't recognize approached me. Something about her manner struck me as furtive, and I frowned. She stopped an arm's length away, dipped her head, and placed one hand over her heart, signifying obedience. "Anna Semyonovna?" she said, her voice barely above a whisper.

What oddity was this? "Yes," I told her, wondering whether I'd do better to flee while I had the chance.

She reached into her sleeve, retrieved a tied scroll no larger than my index finger, and held it out to me. She had positioned herself so that her body blocked anyone in the room beyond from seeing what she did, which further ignited my curiosity. I took the scroll and tucked it into the small purse that dangled from my wrist. "Where did you get this?" I asked.

Her odd manner set my nerves tingling with anticipation. I did, after all, have a contracted husband who, because of his exile and the demand placed on him that he accept the tonsure, could communicate with me only in secret. But how would he know to write to me here, in Kasimov?

"A warrior," she murmured. "He waits in the garden."

A warrior. Yuri. Somehow he found me, and he has come to claim me, as he promised.

Looking back, my own recklessness amazes me. A warrior could have been anyone—a stranger, a villain, a cad. Yet at the time I felt certain that the man who awaited me was Yuri. I was but sixteen, after all, desperately in love and convinced, despite any evidence to the contrary, that life would always play fair and bring me joy.

https://www.fivedirectionspress.com/song-of-the-steadfast

Song of the Siren

SONGS OF STEPPE & FOREST 1

Wawel Castle, Poland, December 1541

"Lady Juliana will live," a male voice said. "Not as she did before, of course. I doubt the young king will have much use for her now, despite her charms. It's too bad about the scarring. She was a beautiful woman." The cool, dispassionate tone contradicted any hint of concern implied by his words.

Was? She *was* a beautiful woman? I lay flat on my back, too weak and dispirited to demand that he explain what he meant. I tried to force my eyelids open, but I hadn't the strength even for that. Trapped in a nightmare world, I huddled, shivering, waiting for the ogre to appear at the door. I pushed and twisted, but my arms weighed heavy as granite on the bed and my feet stuck to the floor.

The doctor's callous verdict echoed in my head. Too bad about the scarring? She *was* a beautiful woman?

Tragedy bared its teeth, sucked me into its vortex. Without my face I was nothing. I had no purpose, no means of survival, no self. I existed to mirror the desires of men, to fulfill their passions while expressing none of my own. My beauty was the only currency I possessed. If I could not use it to draw men to me, I would starve. What point, then, in living?

Tears slid from the corners of my eyes, wetting the linen beneath my head. I lacked the power to wipe them away. "Oh, look," another voice said. My maidservant, Hanna. "She's crying. Do you think she heard you, Doctor?" A soft cloth touched my cheeks.

"Perhaps." The doctor still sounded indifferent, as if discussing my case at some society of physicians. If I had the energy, I would slap him. "I see no sign that she's awake, but I've had other patients report things I said under similar conditions. Smallpox causes extreme exhaustion. She may be able to hear but not respond. Just in case, you should talk to her, reassure her, like this."

Garlic-inflected breath passed my nose, and I guessed he had bent closer to examine me. "You will recover, Lady Juliana," he said, and this time I heard actual kindness in his voice. "The worst is over."

But I knew he was wrong. The worst lurked somewhere down the road of a bleak future, waiting to pounce when I was least prepared to resist.

http://www.fivedirectionspress.com/song-of-the-siren

WHAT READERS SAY

"C. P. Lesley brings an exotic setting to life with richly textured historical details and a wonderful cast of fascinating characters—it's an enchanting tale worthy of her clever storyteller heroine!"

—Andrea Penrose, author of the Wrexford and Sloane Mysteries

"So rich with historical detail that readers will swear they can taste the foods and stroke the fabrics described, *Song of the Sisters* vividly transports readers to sixteenth-century Russia. C. P. Lesley blends fact and fiction seamlessly to create a sweet tale with more than a hint of intrigue."

—Molly Greeley, author of *The Heiress*

"A vividly told tale full of magic and mysticism, passion and betrayal. The story of Grusha will grab you by the heart and throat as you travel through the medieval world of Russia and the steppe."

—Terry Gamble, author of *The Eulogist* and other novels

"C. P. Lesley's *Song of the Siren* whisks us away to Eastern Europe and Russia in this captivating tale of a heroine with a past. Juliana has lost her looks—or so she believes—but not her faith in her own mind, and as she confronts the enemies of her present and the demons of her childhood, she becomes a woman who cannot, and will not, be conquered. This is a wonderful beginning to a new series, and its exotic characters and setting are a welcome addition to historical fiction. Lesley's fans are sure to be delighted, and new readers will quickly become devoted followers."

—Sarah Kennedy, author of *The Altarpiece* and other novels

If you enjoyed this book, please consider leaving a review at your favorite online bookseller and/or on GoodReads.

FIVE DIRECTIONS PRESS

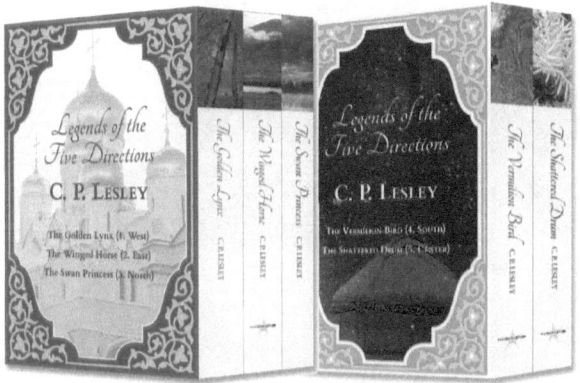

WHO IS THE GOLDEN LYNX?

This question drives the first book in Legends of the Five Directions, a series that will sweep you to the distant world of sixteenth-century Russia, amid the descendants of Genghis Khan and courts that could teach the Borgias a thing or two about political ambition, assassination, and chicanery. Follow Nasan and her kinsfolk as they struggle for power, honor, identity, and love across the steppe and through the vast forests of the Russian North.

"A 'ripping good yarn,' as adventure stories have always been. Enter the exotic, cut-throat world of sixteenth-century Muscovy in the company of a Tatar princess whose skills would have made her equally a heroine on the American frontier. The Kremlin court of the not-yet-Terrible toddler Ivan and his mother-regent Elena Glinskaya, boyar intrigue, arranged political marriages, spirit animals and ancestors pointing the way to restoring balance and order in the universe—what more could a reader want except further adventures, which are heralded by the advent of another animal messenger?"

—Ann M. Kleimola, professor emerita of history

From the glittering Italianate court of King Sigismund the Old of Poland and Queen Bona to the streets of sixteenth-century Moscow and the mobile tents of the steppe nomads, this new series explores themes of espionage, diplomacy, spirituality, love, and war. Follow Juliana, a disfigured courtesan, as she struggles to confront the demons of her past and find a more secure means of supporting herself. Travel to other realms with Grusha, a single mother with shamanic powers. Watch the sisters Darya and Solomonida as they attempt to balance the demands of family expectations and politics in a search for love with overtones of *Pride and Prejudice*. And expand your literary horizons beyond the well-traveled paths of Tudor England and Borgia Italy to discover lands and cultures every bit as dramatic and compelling as those you already know and love.

"C. P. Lesley's *Song of the Siren* takes us to multicultural sixteenth-century Poland-Lithuania and Russia in this part adventure, part love story, part narrative of a woman's self-discovery and empowerment. Readers interested in the European Renaissance will enjoy this beautifully detailed historical novel."

—Charlene Ball, author of *Dark Lady*

http://www.fivedirectionspress.com/historical

FIVE DIRECTIONS PRESS